By James Grippando

Afraid of the Dark*+
Money to Burn+
Intent to Kill
Born to Run*+
Last Call*+
Lying with Strangers
When Darkness Falls*+
Got the Look*+
Hear No Evil*
Last to Die*
Beyond Suspicion*
A King's Ransom
Under Cover of Darkness+
Found Money
The Abduction
The Informant
The Pardon*

Coming Soon in Hardcover
Need You Now+

And for Young Adults
Leapholes

*A Jack Swyteck Novel
+Also featuring FBI agent Andie Henning

JAMES GRIPPANDO

hear no evil

HARPER

An Imprint of HarperCollins*Publishers*

HARPER

An Imprint of HarperCollins*Publishers*
195 Broadway
New York, NY 10007

Copyright © 2004 by James Grippando
Excerpt from *Need You Now* copyright © 2012 by James Grippando
Author photo © Monica Hopkins Photography
ISBN 978-0-06-202456-5

First Harper premium printing: December 2011
First Harper mass market printing: December 2007
First HarperTorch mass market printing: November 2005
First HarperCollins hardcover printing: August 2004

HarperCollins® and Harper® are registered trademarks of Harper-Collins Publishers.

Printed in the United States of America

Visit Harper paperbacks on the World Wide Web at
www.harpercollins.com

HB 08.03.2023

For Tiffany—Happy Tenth!

hear no evil

1
.

"My husband was murdered."

Lindsey Hart spoke in the detached voice of a young widow still grieving. It was as if she still couldn't believe that the words were coming from her mouth, that something so horrible had actually happened. "Shot once in the head."

"I'm very sorry." Jack wished he could say more, but he'd been in this situation before, and he knew there really wasn't anything he could say. It was God's will? Time heals all wounds? None of that would do her any good, certainly not from his lips. People sometimes turned to strangers for that kind of comfort, but rarely when the stranger was a criminal defense lawyer billing by the hour.

Jack Swyteck was among the best Miami's criminal trial bar had to offer, having defended death row inmates for four years before switching sides to become a federal prosecutor. He was in his third year of private practice, steadily building a name for himself, despite the fact that he'd yet to land the kind of high-charged, high-profile jury trial that had vaulted plenty of lesser lawyers into stardom. But he was doing just fine for a guy who'd withstood an indictment for murder, a divorce from a fruitcake, and the unexplained appearance of the naked, dead body of his ex-girlfriend in his bathtub.

"Do the police know who did it?" asked Jack.

"They think they do."

"Who?"

"Me."

The natural follow-up question caught in Jack's throat, and before he could even broach the subject, Lindsey said, "I didn't do it."

"Are there any witnesses who say you did?"

"Not that I know of. Which is to be expected, since I'm innocent."

"Was the murder weapon recovered?"

"Yes. It was on the bedroom floor. Oscar was shot with his own sidearm."

"Where did it happen?"

"In our bedroom. While he was sleeping."

"Were you home?"

"No."

"Then how do you know he was sleeping?"

She hesitated, as if the question had caught her off guard. "The investigators told me he was in bed, no sign of any struggle, so it's only logical that he was either taken completely by surprise or was asleep."

Jack took a moment, not so much to collect his thoughts as to gather his impression of Lindsey Hart. She was a few years younger than he was, he guessed, articulate and composed. Her business suit was charcoal gray, a conservative step beyond the traditional black of mourning, though she allowed herself a little color in the silk blouse and scarf. She was pretty—probably even more attractive than what presently met the eye, as Jack suspected that in her grief she'd lost a little too much weight and paid not enough attention to her appearance.

He said, "I know this is painful for you. But has anyone considered the possibility that your husband's wound was self-inflicted?"

"Oscar didn't commit suicide. He had too much to live for."

"Most people who take their own life do. They just lose perspective."

"His gun was found with the safety on. Not very likely that he shot himself in the head and then put on the safety."

"Can't argue with that. Though it also strikes me as curious that someone would shoot your husband and then take the time to put on the safety."

"There are many curious things about my husband's death. That's why I need you."

"Fair enough. Let's get back to what you were doing the day of his death. What time did you leave the house?"

"Five-thirty. Same as every day. I work at the hospital. My shift begins at six."

"I assume you're having trouble convincing people that he was alive when you left."

"The medical examiner put the time of death sometime before five."

"You've seen the autopsy?" asked Jack.

"Yes, just recently."

"How long ago was your husband killed?"

"Ten weeks yesterday."

"Have you spoken to the police?"

"Of course. I wanted to do everything possible to help catch the killer. Until it started to come clear that I was a suspect. That's when I decided I needed a lawyer."

Jack scratched his head and said, "None of this is ringing a bell for me, and I'm usually something of a newshound when it comes to homicides. Was it City of Miami or Miami-Dade homicide you talked to?"

"Neither. It was NCIS agents. Naval Criminal Investigative Services. This all happened at the naval base."

"Which one?"

"Guantánamo."

"Guantánamo, Cuba?"

"Yes. My husband was career military. We've lived there for almost four years now. Or at least until his death."

"I didn't realize that families even lived there. I thought it was just soldiers keeping an eye on Castro."

"Oh, no. It's a huge living and working community, thousands of people. We have schools, our own newspaper. We even have a McDonald's."

Jack considered it, then said, "I want to be up front about this: I have absolutely no experience in dealing with military matters."

"This isn't strictly military. I'm a civilian, so I would have to be charged as a civilian, even though my husband was a military officer."

"I understand that. But the crime scene is on a naval base, and you've already talked with the NCIS agents on the investigation. Whoever represents you should know how to work his way through military red tape."

"You'll learn." She pulled a file from her purse and laid it on Jack's desk. "This is the NCIS investigative report. I just got it two days ago. Take a look. I think you'll agree that it doesn't pass the smell test."

Jack let it lie, unopened. "I'm not trying to push away the work, but I know several criminal defense lawyers in town with military backgrounds."

"I don't want someone else. I want to hire the lawyer who will fight harder than anyone to prove my innocence. That person is you."

"Thank you. It's nice to know that my reputation extends all the way down to Cuba."

"It has nothing to with your reputation. It's simply a matter of who you are."

"That sounds like a compliment, but I'm not sure I fully understand what you're trying to say."

"Mr. Swyteck, every minute that the investigators spend focusing on me is a wasted minute. If someone doesn't straighten them out, my husband's killer could go unpunished. That would be a terrible tragedy."

"I couldn't agree more."

"Yes, you could. Believe me. This isn't just another case of the authorities chasing after the wrong suspect. If they don't catch the person who killed my husband, it would be a tragedy—*for you*."

"Do I know your husband?"

"No. But that doesn't make it any less personal. My husband . . ." She took a breath, her voice quaking as she tried once more. "My husband was the father of your child."

Jack froze, confused. "Say that again."

"I think you know what I'm saying."

Jack mulled over the possibilities, realizing quickly that there was only *one* explanation. "Your son was adopted?"

She nodded, her expression very serious.

"Are you saying I'm the biological father?"

"The mother was a woman named Jessie Merrill."

Jessie, the last woman he'd dated before falling head over heels for the woman he would marry— and later divorce. Not until his fifth and final year of marriage to Cindy Paige had Jack learned that Jessie was pregnant when they'd split up and that she'd given up their child for adoption.

"I don't know what to say. I don't deny that Jessie had a child and that she said I was the father. I just never followed up on it. Didn't think it was my place to intrude on the adoptive family."

"That was thoughtful of you," she said, her voice still strained by emotion. "But my husband and I realized that someday our son might want to contact his biological parents. We did all the research a few years ago."

"Are you absolutely sure about this?"

"I could show you the paperwork, but I don't think that will be necessary." She dug into her purse again and offered up a snapshot.

"This is Brian," she said.

A moment passed as the photograph seemed to hover before him. Finally, he reached across his desk and took it by the corner, as if his past might burn him if he grasped too much of it. His gaze came to rest on the smiling face of a ten-year-old boy. He'd never seen the child before, but he knew those dark eyes, that Roman nose.

"I'm his father," he said in a distant voice, as if the words were involuntary.

"No," she answered, her tone gentle but firm. "His father's dead. And if you don't help me find the man who killed him, his mother could go to jail for the rest of her life."

Their eyes met, and Jack searched for words that suited a situation no criminal defense lawyer could possibly be prepared to face. "I guess you're right," he said quietly. "This is personal."

$$\frac{2}{\cdot}$$

Jack didn't think of himself as a drinker, but after the head-spinning meeting with the adoptive mother of his biological offspring—"son" seemed way too personal at this point—he found himself in need of a drink. His friend Theo Knight owned a bar called Sparky's near the entrance to the Florida Keys, which was a long way to go for a glassful of solace, but Theo had a way of making it worth the trip.

"Bourbon," Jack told the bartender. He knew the risk of not ordering a premium brand, but just walking through the door at a place like Sparky's was living dangerously, so what the hell?

Sparky's was an old gas station that had been converted into a bar, the term "converted" used loosely. If you looked around, you'd swear the guys from the grease pit had never left, just sidled up to the bar in their grimy coveralls, wondering where the awesome band and drunken bikers had suddenly come from. The joint was a definite moneymaker, often crowded, especially when Theo picked up his sax and blew till dawn. He could have afforded to do a little renovation, but clearly he liked things the way they were. Jack suspected that it was all about ego, that Theo smiled to himself every time some tight ass and his Gucci-clad girlfriend visited a dive they wouldn't ordinarily be caught dead in, all just to hear Theo and his jazz buddies belt out tunes worthy of Harlem's best.

It was still early evening, and the band wasn't up yet. Theo was on stage alone. He didn't often sing or play the piano, except when his closest friends were around. Jack watched from his bar stool, nursing a throat-singeing bourbon as Theo sang his heart out and put his own satirical lyrics to popular tunes. Tonight's victim was Bonnie Raitt and her 1991 R&B megahit, "I Can't Make You Love Me," a thoroughly depressing song in its own right about a woman who takes her cold-hearted boyfriend to bed one last time before getting dumped. Theo's shtick was to doctor it up and rename it, simply, "The Suicide Song."

Slit both my wrists.
Jump out the window.
Fire a bullet
into my brain.
Cuz you can't make me live
if I don't want to . . .

The audience was in stitches. Theo never failed to deliver. At least among drunks.

"Hey, Jacko!" Theo had finally spotted him, and, like it or not, his arrival had been announced to the entire crowd. Theo stepped down from the small stage and joined his friend at the bar.

"Funny gig," said Jack.

"You think suicide is funny?"

"I didn't say that."

"Wrong answer. Everything's funny, Jack. Until you learn that, I'm afraid I'm just gonna have to keep charging you double for rot-gut whiskey."

Theo signaled to the bartender, who quickly set up a round of drinks. Another bourbon for Jack, club soda for Theo. "Gotta play tonight," said Theo, as if apologizing for the soft drink.

"That's the whole reason I came here."

"Liar. After ten years, you think I don't know you? Jack Swyteck don't drink straight bourbon from the well unless he's been dumped, indicted, or both."

Jack gave a little smile, though it was somewhat disconcerting to be so transparent.

Theo was suddenly looking past him, and Jack followed his gaze across the bar, where his bass player was setting up for the evening gig. A crowd started gravitating toward the stage, staking out the good tables, and Jack knew he didn't have his friend's attention for long. But what else was new?

"So, what happened this time?" asked Theo.

"Two words for you: Jessie Merrill."

"Whoa. How weird is it to hear that name, right after I sang 'The Suicide Song'?"

"She's back."

"From the dead?"

"I didn't mean literally, moron."

Jack took a minute to bring him up to speed on Lindsey Hart. Theo wasn't a lawyer, but if Jack decided to take Lindsey's case, Theo would surely find his way into an investigative role, so it wasn't a breach of the attorney-client privilege. Besides, Jack needed to talk this out with someone, and Theo was one of the few people who knew the whole Jessie Merrill story. He was also the only client Jack had ever known to spend time on death row for a murder he didn't commit.

Theo let him finish, then smiled and shook his head. "For a guy who gets laid on about every other solar eclipse, you sure have a knack for squeezing the maximum fuck-up value out of relationships."

"Thanks. And for the record, that's every other *partial* solar eclipse."

"You're an animal, dude." Theo grabbed a handful of peanuts, munched as he spoke. "This Lindsey in deep shit?"

"Not sure. I tried to read the investigative report before I came over here, but my mind's all over the place."

"That talk about Jack Junior caught you a little off guard, huh?"

"A little? I've known about the adoption for a couple years now, ever since Jessie passed away. But I guess it really hit home when Lindsey showed me his picture. I actually have a kid out there."

"No, it's her kid. All you did was have sex with your girlfriend."

"It's not that simple, Theo. He looks just like me."

"Does he, really? Or do you just see it because his mother says so, and for some weird-ass Darwinian reason you want it to be true?"

"Trust me. There's a strong resemblance."

"Could have been worse, I suppose. Could have looked like one of your friends."

"Can you ever be serious?"

"No, but I can fake it." Theo took a drink. "So, you gonna be her lawyer?"

"I don't know yet."

"What's your gut tell you? She innocent?"

"Why should that matter? I've represented lots of clients who were guilty. I even thought *you* were guilty when I first took up your appeal."

"But I wasn't guilty."

"I would have fought just as hard even if you were."

"Maybe. But I sense that this case is different."

"You see the dilemma, too?"

"Yeah, except where I come from, we don't call it no dilemma. We call it gettin' caught in your own zipper."

"Ouch. But I guess it applies."

"Course it applies. Let's say your client is charged with murdering her husband and you agree to be her lawyer. Let's say she's guilty, but you're able to work your magic and convince the jury she's not. She walks. Where does that leave you?"

"Forget me. Where does it leave her son?"

"Living with a murderer, that's where."

Jack stared down into his bourbon and said, "Not something any self-respecting criminal defense lawyer should do to his own flesh and blood."

"On the other hand, if you don't take the case . . . Let's say she's innocent, but some boob of a lawyer blows it—like my trial lawyer did—and she gets convicted. The boy ends up losing both his mom and his dad, or at least the only mom and dad he ever knew. Can you live with that?"

"I'd say you've covered both horns of the dilemma."

"Fuck your dilemma. That's a thousand tiny metal teeth zipping right into your—"

"I got the picture, Theo. What do you think I should do?"

"Simple. Take her case. If you get into it and find out she's guilty, resign."

"That's dicey. Once a murder case gets going, you can't just withdraw. The judge won't let you out if the only grounds you have for withdrawing are that you suddenly think your client is guilty. If that were the standard, you'd have lawyers dropping out in the middle of trial every day."

"Then you gotta find a way to convince yourself that your client is innocent *before* you take the case. How about asking her to take a lie detector test?"

"I don't believe in them, especially with someone as emotionally distraught as she is. Might as well flip a coin."

"So, what are you telling me?"

"Bottom line, she could be indicted tomorrow, for all I know. I need a quick answer, and, as usual, there is none."

Theo took the drink from his friend's hand, placed it on the bar, and pushed it aside. "Then get off the fucking bar stool, go home, and read that investigative report. Read it the way you'd read it if that boy was just another boy."

His tone was stern, and Theo wasn't grinning, but Jack knew the words were coming from a friend.

Jack rose, then laid a five on the bar to cover the two drinks.

"Hey," said Theo. "I wasn't kidding."

"I know."

"I mean the tab, genius. Till you find that sense of humor, I'm charging you double, remember?"

Jack reached for his wallet and threw another bill on the bar. "Thanks for teaching me a lesson," he said with a chuckle. But as he zigzagged through the noisy crowd and headed for the exit, passing one pointless conversation after another, he couldn't help but wonder what all the forced laughter was about, and his smile faded.

He wished Theo were right. He wished to God everything were funny.

The following afternoon, Jack was on the fifth floor of the U.S. attorney's office in downtown Miami. He'd been up most of the night combing over a copy of the NCIS report Lindsey Hart had left with him. Jack had never seen an investigative report from the Naval Criminal Investigative Services before, but it was similar to scores of civilian homicide reports he'd examined over the years, with one major exception: the blacked-out information. It seemed that something—sometimes an entire paragraph, even an entire witness statement— was excised from each page, deemed by Naval Command to be too sensitive for civilian eyes.

Jack's first thought had been that the NCIS was withholding information from Lindsey because she was a murder suspect. He phoned a friend in the JAG Reserves, however, and discovered that it wasn't all that unusual for the family of slain military personnel to receive highly redacted investigative reports. Even when death was unrelated to combat—be it homicide, suicide, or accident—survivors didn't always have the privilege of knowing exactly what their loved one was doing when he died, whom he'd last spoken to, or even what he might have written in his diary just hours before a 9 mm slug shattered the back of his skull. To be sure, the military often had legitimate needs for secrecy, especially at a place like Guantánamo, the only remaining U.S. base on communist soil. But it was Jack's job to be skeptical.

"You know I wasn't being cute on the phone, right, Jack? I really do have absolutely nothing to do with the Hart case."

Gerry Chafetz was seated behind his desk, hands clasped behind his head, a posture Jack had seen him assume countless times when Gerry was his supervisor. Back then, they'd toil late into the evening, arguing over just about everything from whether the Miami Dolphins had won more football games wearing their aqua jerseys or their white jerseys to whether their star witness was a dead man with or without the federal witness protection program. Jack sometimes missed the old days, but he knew that even if he'd stayed, things could never have been the same. Gerry had worked his way up to chief assistant to the U.S. attorney, which would have made him a lot less fun to argue with, since now he knew everything.

"The case is here in Miami. Am I right?" asked Jack.

Gerry was stone silent. Jack said, "Look, it's no secret that Lindsey Hart is a civilian who can't stand trial in a military court. She's originally from Miami, so it doesn't take a breach of national security to figure out that if she's indicted for the murder of her husband, it will be right here in the Southern District of Florida."

Still no reply from Gerry.

A smile tugged at the corner of Jack's mouth. "Come on, Gerry. You won't even give me that much?"

"Let me put it this way: Theoretically, you'd be correct."

"Good. Theoretically, then, I'd like you to convey a message from me to the prosecutor assigned to this case. I've read the NCIS report. What there is of it anyway. Half of it was blacked out."

"Actually, Ms. Hart is pretty lucky to have a report at all."

"What makes you say that?"

"It can take as long as six months, at least, for the agency to issue a final report. This one moved very quickly. Your client should be happy about that."

Jack smiled to himself. Just as he'd thought: The chief assistant *did* know everything. Jack said, "Technically, she's not my client. Not yet anyway. Like I said on the phone, I'm still debating whether to take the case."

"How do you know there's going to be a case?"

"The NCIS ruled her husband's death a homicide."

"I meant a case against *her*."

Jack gave him an assessing look. "Are you telling me—"

"I'm not telling you anything. I thought I'd made that clear from the beginning."

"Okay. Right or wrong, Ms. Hart seems to think she's the prime suspect."

Gerry was deadpan, silent.

Jack said, "That's a pretty nerve-racking position to be in, for a woman who maintains her complete innocence."

"They all maintain their innocence. That's why I'm still sitting on this side of the desk. I respect you, Jack, but I sleep easier knowing that I don't defend the guilty."

Jack moved to the edge of his chair, locking eyes with his old boss. "That's why I'm here. I'm in a tough spot with this case. Lindsey Hart is—" He stopped himself, not wanting to say too much. Gerry was an old buddy, but he was still on the other side. "Let's just say she's a friend of a friend. Of a very close friend. I want to help her if I can. But I don't want to get involved in this if . . ."

"If what?" Gerry said, scoffing. "If she's guilty?"

Jack didn't return the smile. His expression was dead serious.

"Come on, Jack. You didn't expect me to look you in the eye and say, 'Yup, you're right buddy. Take the case. These investigators are breathing down the neck of the wrong suspect.' Or did you?"

"At this point, I just want to know how honest my own client is being with me. I need to verify something. It has to do with the time of death."

"Even if I knew the details of this case, which I don't, I couldn't comment on the investigation."

"Sure you could. It's just a question of whether you will or not."

"Give me one good reason why I should."

"Because I'm calling in every favor, every ounce of friendship that ever existed between us."

Gerry averted his eyes, as if the plea had made him uncomfortable. "You're making this awfully personal."

"For me, it doesn't get any more personal than this."

Gerry sat quietly for a moment, thinking. Finally, he looked at Jack and said, "What do you need?"

"There's a ton of information missing from the NCIS report, but one hole in particular has me scratching my head. Lindsey Hart says that her husband was alive when she left the house at five-thirty A.M. The medical examiner puts the time of death between three and five A.M."

"Not the first time the forensic evidence contradicts a suspect's version of events."

"Hear me out on this. The victim was shot in the head with his own weapon. The report makes no mention of a silencer. In fact, he was shot with his own gun, which was recovered in the bedroom just a few feet away from his body. No silencer in sight, no tattered pillow or blanket that was used to muffle the noise."

"So?"

"They had a ten-year-old son. If Lindsey Hart shot her husband between three and five A.M., don't you think their son would have heard the gun go off?"

"Depends on how big the house is."

"This is a military base. Even for officer housing, we're talking two bedrooms right next to each other, eleven hundred total square feet."

"What does the NCIS report say?"

"Nothing that I could find. Maybe it's on one of the pages that was blacked out."

"Maybe."

"Either way, I want to know how the investigators account for the sound of the gunshot. How is it that a woman fires off a 9 mm Beretta, and her ten-year-old son in the next room sleeps right through it?"

"Could be a sound sleeper."

"Sure. That could well be their explanation."

"And if it is?"

Jack paused, as if to underscore his words. "If that's the best they can come up with, Lindsey Hart may have just found herself a lawyer."

A weighty silence lingered between them. Finally, Gerry said, "I'll see what I can do. Keeping Jack Swyteck off the case might be just enough incentive for the lead prosecutor to cough up a little information."

"Wow. That may be the nicest thing you've ever said about me."

"Or maybe I just don't like women who murder their husbands and then run out and hire a sharp defense lawyer."

Jack nodded slowly, as if he'd deserved that. "The sooner the better on this, okay?"

"Like I said, I'll see what I can do."

"Sure." He rose and shook Gerry's hand, then thanked him and said good-bye. He knew the way out.

$$\frac{4}{.}$$

The answer came back sooner than anticipated. It was anything but what Jack had expected.

Jack had taken an easy weekend, a little boating on the bay with Theo, some work in the yard. Nothing could stop him from wondering how different his life might have been. At first, his attraction to Jessie Merrill had been overwhelmingly physical. She was a striking beauty, definitely not a prude, though the bad-girl image was mostly an act. She was easily as bright as any of the women he dated in law school, and if her impressive sphere of knowledge included knowing how to please, who was Jack to hold it against her? Unfortunately it hadn't occurred to him that she might be "The One" until after her flawless rendition of the time-honored "I don't deserve you, sure hope we can still be friends" speech. Jack would have given anything to get her back. Five months later, when she actually *did* come back, Jack had already fallen for Cindy Paige, the girl of his dreams, his bride to be, the woman he would eventually divorce and never speak to again.

Jessie graciously backed away and wished him well, never bothering to tell him that she was carrying their baby.

What if he'd never met Cindy? Would he and Jessie have gotten married? Would Jessie have avoided the life choices that had courted death at such a young age? Perhaps Jack would have a son to take to baseball games, to go fishing with, to viciously defend from the corrupting influences of Uncle Theo. By Sunday night, Jack had created the perfect little world, the three of them living happily ever after, the image of his son firmly in his head, everything about him as real as it could be—the sound of his voice, the smell of his hair, those skinny ten-year-old arms that wrapped around him as they wrestled on the floor.

Then came the Monday morning phone call from the U.S. attorney's office, the reminder that nothing in life was ever really perfect.

"Lindsey Hart's son is deaf," said Gerry Chavetz.

Jack could hardly speak, and he managed to utter only the obvious. "That's why he didn't hear the gunshot."

"That's why he can't hear anything," said the prosecutor.

Gerry continued to speak, and Jack gripped the phone tightly, as if fearful that it might drop from his hand. Jack should have probed for more information, and he would have kept Gerry talking all morning if the boy had been just another boy. But circumstances made it impossible for Jack to pretend that he didn't care, and his connection to Lindsey Hart's son was something Gerry and the rest of the world had no business knowing. He couldn't afford a slipup.

"Gerry, thanks a ton for the favor."

"Does this mean you're not going to defend her?"

"I have to think about that."

"But you said—"

"I know. I'm sorry, but I really have to run."

The phone landed with a little extra weight as he laid it in the cradle. He walked to the kitchen window and stared out toward Biscayne Bay, watching in silence as a warm southeasterly breeze carried in an endless roll of waves that gently lapped the seawall. It wasn't the overpowering force of nature, the kind of display that could strike fear in the soul. But it was unstoppable nonetheless, as unrelenting as the surge of emotions coursing through Jack's veins.

An image flashed in his mind, Jack standing in the hospital's nursery and holding a baby, the proud young father smiling ear to ear as a doctor slowly approaches, a serious expression on his face that robs Jack of his grin. It's obvious that the news is not going to be good, and Jack somehow realizes that the doctor is going to tell him that his son can't hear. Suddenly, the image transforms itself. Jack is no longer a father but a little baby in another man's arms. The man at the hospital is Jack's father, a young Harry Swyteck, and miraculously this sleepy little newborn named Jack can both hear *and understand* as the doctor lays his hand on Harry Swyteck's shoulder and says softly, "I'm very sorry, Mr. Swyteck. We did everything we could, but we could not save your wife." Jack feels himself falling as his father collapses into a chair, feels his father's body shake as the grim reality sets in, feels the young widower's embrace tighten as though he will never let this child go. Harry is saying something, trying hard to speak, his voice muffled, his face buried in the cotton blanket that is wrapped around his son. The words are a confusing mixture of love and anger, an anger both bitter and enduring. In his mind's eye, Jack is still wrapped in that blanket as the years are flying by. His father continues to speak, seemingly unaware that the boy is growing up, convinced that his son can't hear him anyway. Jack isn't exactly sure when it happens, but at some point the doctor returns. He refuses to look Jack or his father in the eye, as if he doesn't know which one should receive the distressing news.

"The boy is deaf," says the doctor, and it's Harry who sobs, though it pains Jack to know that it will take almost thirty years to get his hearing back, to understand what his father is trying to say to him.

Jack stepped away from the window and shook off the distorted memories, though they weren't memories at all, just painful images of a past that never seemed to stop haunting him, a past he had never let himself explore fully. The discovery of his own son wasn't going to make matters any easier.

Or would it?

As he reached for the telephone, he was suddenly a lawyer again. He dialed the InterContinental, put on his game voice, and told the hotel operator, "I'd like to speak to one of your guests, please. Her name's Lindsey Hart. It's urgent."

5

.

Jack met her in his office, face-to-face. He needed to judge Lindsey's credibility, and for that a phone call wouldn't do.

"Why didn't you tell me he was deaf?"

Lindsey stiffened at his accusatory tone, but she spoke calmly. "He was born that way. I thought you knew."

"Please, don't lie to me."

"That's the honest truth."

Jack considered her words but focused mostly on the body language. Her mouth was growing ever tighter. "I don't buy it," he said.

"Why would I deceive you about something like this?"

"All I know is that after I read the NCIS investigative report, I called and told you that I was troubled by the medical examiner's determination of the time of death. It didn't make sense to me that you allegedly fired off a gun in your house before five A.M., and yet there was no witness statement in the report from your son, no mention of him at all. It was inconceivable that he would have slept right through a shooting in the next room."

"And I agreed with you."

"But you left out the key fact."

"He can't *hear*, Jack. That doesn't make him an armchair. He can sense things."

"So when I called you and said there was a huge hole in the investigative report, *that's* what you thought I was talking about—that your son should have *sensed* a gunshot in the next room?"

"A door slamming, the panicky footsteps of the shooter scampering about the room. All that movement creates palpable sensations."

"Please, just answer my question. Is that really what you thought I was talking about?"

Jack wasn't happy about being so hard on her. But if there was one thing he couldn't handle, it was a client who lied to her lawyer.

"No," she said finally. "I knew exactly what you were thinking. Your assumption was that he should have heard the gunshot."

"You knew that. Yet, you still let me rush over to the U.S. attorney's office and argue that Lindsey Hart couldn't have shot her husband, not without the boy hearing it."

"I didn't know you were going to talk to the prosecutor. You said that you needed a little more time to think, that you'd let me know if you decided to take the case."

"So, it was okay to mislead me, so long as it was just between the two of us?"

She lowered her eyes and said, "I felt like I was

already unloading an awful lot on you without telling you that he was deaf."

She sounded sincere, but again her mouth was tightening in telltale fashion. Jack said, "I'm not sure that explains everything."

She spoke in a low, quiet voice, still no eye contact. "You have to understand. After you read the investigative report, when you called me, you sounded so high on the idea that the time of death proved me innocent. I . . . I just didn't want to shoot down the best thing I had going for me. Not right out of the gate."

"Did you think you could trick me into being your lawyer?"

She was suddenly trembling. Jack instinctively snatched the box of tissues from his desktop and gave her one.

"I'm innocent," she said, her voice quaking. "Do you have any idea what it's like to be accused of killing the father of your child, and to be innocent?"

"I can only imagine."

"Then don't you see? At the time, it didn't matter to me *why* you thought I was innocent. All that mattered was that you believed I didn't do it."

"Misleading me hardly reinforces that belief."

"If I could prove my innocence to you, then I wouldn't need you."

She dabbed away a tear, and Jack gave her a moment to compose herself. "Fair enough. But if you lie to me, you can't have me."

"I'm sorry. It won't happen again. Ever since this thing started, it's felt like no one is on my side. The police, everyone. They all seem to have their minds made up."

"Why do you think that's the case?"

"I think it's because of something I said to the *Gazette*."

"What's the *Gazette*?"

"It's the local paper down at the base. They asked me what I think happened to my husband, so I told them. And they printed it. From that day on, you'd think I was wearing a big stamp across my forehead that reads 'ENEMY COMBATANT.' "

"What did you say?"

She hesitated, as if she wasn't quite sure if Jack was ready to hear her theory. "My husband wasn't so much murdered as he was . . . eliminated."

"How do you mean, eliminated?"

"Silenced."

"By whom?"

She seemed unaware of it, but her hand had become a tight, angry fist around her tissue. "That NCIS investigative report has been completely sanitized. Doesn't it make you wonder what they're hiding?"

"From what I understand, that kind of redaction is not unique to this case."

"I'm sure it happens all the time. Whenever the navy has something to hide."

She was starting to sound paranoid, but Jack measured his words. "After all you've been through, you're certainly entitled to a certain amount of skepticism."

"You may not be aware of this, but the military's

track record on homicide investigations is less than stellar."

"That's a pretty sweeping indictment."

"I'm not saying they're incompetent. I'm saying that certain people in the military are not beyond a cover-up."

"And you know this because . . ."

"I was married to a career officer for twelve years. And I've done my homework. Did you know that the NCIS once tried to convince a mother and father that their son had shot himself in the head even though it was a scientific fact that he couldn't have produced the bullet trajectory unless he was standing on his head when he pulled the trigger?"

"That's appalling."

"It gets better. In another case, the NCIS issued a finding on July ninth that a Marine's wounds were self-inflicted. You know when they got the results back on ballistics, gunshot residue, and blood and tissue tests? August sixth."

"Obviously, you've looked into this. But this isn't a case of homicide covered up as suicide."

"The point is, they are capable of doing whatever suits their needs. They needed my husband out of the way, but no one would ever have believed that he had committed suicide. He loved life too much. So they did away with him, and instead of calling it suicide, they make it look like his wife did it. And then they issue this so-called investigative report that's completely full of holes. All meaningful information is blacked out in the name of protecting military secrets and national security."

Jack gave her a long, hard look. "For the sake of argument, let's assume a cover-up. You're saying that the military decided not to paint his death as suicide because they didn't think anyone would ever believe he killed himself."

"That's right."

"But for some reason the military came to the conclusion that no one would have any trouble believing that you would kill your husband."

She didn't answer right away, obviously uncomfortable with the way Jack had dissected things. "That's the essence of any frame-up," she said.

"A frame-up is a huge leap. Especially when you've shown me no motive."

"If you knew my husband, you'd understand my suspicions. We spent almost a third of our marriage on that little fenced-in chunk of Cuba. Year after year, I begged him to put in for a transfer. People are nice enough there, and it has a sense of community. But I hated the isolation. Oscar, on the other hand, was Mr. Guantánamo all the way. He wanted to rise as high as he possibly could right there on the island, no desire to go anywhere. Then, suddenly, that's all out the window. Two weeks before he was killed, completely out of the blue, he tells me he thinks it's time to leave."

"Change of heart, maybe?"

"No. It was a lot of little things—the way he lay awake at night, the fact that he was suddenly going to bed with a loaded gun in the nightstand. He probably didn't think I noticed these things, but I did. He was worried about something. He was suddenly acting like a man on the run. Like a man who knew something he wasn't supposed to know."

"Such as?"

"The military is full of secrets. And plenty of people have died trying to keep them."

"I need more than that."

"Then help me find it, damn it."

She was clearly frustrated, and Jack could understand it. He rose, walked around to the front of his desk, and took a more casual seat on the corner of it, no barriers between them. "Look, you're probably thinking that lawyers defend guilty clients all the time, so why is this guy so obsessed with guilt or innocence. But this case is—"

"Different," she said, finishing the thought for him. "I know."

"You understand why?"

"Of course. You want what's best for your," she caught herself, then said, "for my son. Just as I do. Which is why I would never—even if I'd wanted Oscar dead—I would *never* have shot him in our house while our son was sleeping in the next room. Deaf or not. Does that make any sense at all to you, Mr. Swyteck?"

Jack met her stare, and suddenly the silence between them was no longer uncomfortable. It was as if the proverbial light had finally come on. "Yes, it does, Lindsey. And I think it's probably time you started calling me Jack."

6

Alejandro Pintado was searching for good news.
Literally.

As usual, his search had taken him over the Straits
of Florida, a band of water some ninety miles wide
that connected the Gulf of Mexico to the Atlantic
Ocean, that separated Key West from Cuba, that
divided freedom from tyranny. For more than four
decades Cubans had fled Fidel Castro's oppressive
communist regime in makeshift rafts, leaky boats,
or even patched-up inner tubes. They risked their
lives on the high seas, many of them making it to
the United States, many others succumbing to tropical storms and walls of water, blistering sun and
dehydration, or sunken vessels and hungry sharks.
It was a tragedy that Alejandro had seen unfold with
his own eyes, starting with his first mission in 1992.
He'd made two passes over a small boat. On the first,
he counted nine bodies strewn this way and that, as
if they had simply collapsed. His second time around
a woman stirred at the bow, barely able to raise her
arm. She never moved again. As best the Coast

Guard could tell, a storm had washed their water and supplies overboard on the first night of their journey. In desperation they drank seawater. There were no survivors. It was no wonder that, to the exile community in Miami, the Straits of Florida were known as the Cuban Private Cemetery.

Despite the danger, they kept coming. So long as they were out there, Alejandro Pintado was determined to keep looking.

"Key West, this is Brother One," he said, speaking into his radio transmitter. "I have a visual."

"Copy that," came the reply.

Alejandro pushed forward on the yoke and dropped to an altitude of five hundred feet, his old single-engine Cessna whining as it picked up speed. The scene on the open waters below him was a familiar one, but it still made his heart race. Six- to eight-foot seas, foamy white-caps breaking against a vast ocean as blue as midnight, a thing of beauty if it weren't so dangerous. A small raft rising to the top of each swell, then disappearing between them, the white canvas sail tattered from winds much stronger than most rafters could anticipate. The craft was overloaded, of course, packed with three children, five women—one of them holding an infant—and six men. Some were standing, having spotted the plane, waving the oars frantically to get the pilot's attention.

You are almost home, thought Alejandro, smiling to himself.

His aircraft continued to descend. Three hundred feet. Two hundred. The rafters were jumping up and down, shouting with joy, as Alejandro sped past them. He waved from the cockpit, then began to circle around.

"Key West, this is Brother One," he said. "Looks like a happy group. Fairly good shape, considering."

Alejandro had definitely seen worse. He'd started in the early nineties as a pilot with Brothers to the Rescue, a group of Cuban exiles who formed their own search-and-rescue missions after a nine-year-old boy died of dehydration on his journey from Cuba. Not everyone agreed with the organization's hard-line anti-Castro stance, but it won international praise for an amazing recovery record. On average, the group saved one person every two hours of flight time, sparing thousands who might otherwise have perished at sea in their journey to freedom. The organization's focus seemed to shift, however, after Cuban MiGs shot down two of its planes in 1996. More and more resources went toward printing and distributing anti-Casto leaflets. That was when Alejandro broke off and formed his own group, Brothers for Freedom. Eventually, the better-known Brothers to the Rescue would stop flying altogether. But Alejandro had vowed never to give up. Rescue missions were costly, and private donations were hard to come by, so he used his own money. Brothers for Freedom—and the search for a free Cuba—went on.

"Brother One, this is Key West. Do you have a location yet?"

"Copy that. Let me make one more pass and—" He stared out the window toward the horizon, his anger rising at the unmistakable sight of a vessel headed toward the rafters. "Forget it," Alejandro said into the radio. "Coast Guard's on its way."

Alejandro could hear the disappointment in his own voice, and it seemed ironic even to him. In the early years, the sight of the Coast Guard was a blessing. In fact, he would have radioed for the Coast Guard upon sighting a raft. All that changed with the shift in U.S. immigration policy in 1996. Rafters intercepted at sea were no longer brought to the United States. They were either routed to another country or returned to Cuba. And if they went back to Cuba, it could mean five years in Castro's prison.

"Dirty sons of bitches got another one," said Alejandro.

"Sorry, Alejandro. You headed back?"

"Affirmative."

"Okay. By the way, I got a phone call about twenty minutes ago. There's a lawyer headed down from Miami to see you. His name is Jack Swyteck."

Alejandro adjusted his headset, making sure he'd heard correctly. "Swyteck? Any relation to Harry Swyteck, the former governor?"

"I believe it's his son."

"What does he want?"

"He said it's a legal matter. About your son."

Alejandro's throat tightened. Several weeks had passed since he'd received the kind of news that no parent should have to hear, but it still felt like yesterday. "How is he involved in this?"

"He was calling on behalf of Lindsey."

Lindsey. Lindsey *Hart*. The Anglo daughter-in-law who in twelve years of marriage had never taken her husband's Hispanic surname. "Don't tell me that woman has gone out and hired herself the son of the former governor," said Alejandro.

"I'm not sure. I got the sense he wants to talk to you before he takes her case. I told him to come by around two o'clock."

Alejandro didn't answer.

The radio crackled. "You want me to call him back and tell him to get lost?"

"No," said Alejandro. "I'll meet with him. I think he should hear what I have to say."

"Copy that. Be safe, Alejandro."

"Roger. See you in about forty minutes."

Alejandro stole one last look at the rafters below, his heart sinking as he watched them waving frantically at the rescue plane overhead. Surely they were convinced that they'd reached freedom's doorstep, that in a few hours they'd be safe and dry in the United States of America. But the U.S. Coast Guard had other designs, and once the border patrol interdicted rafters at sea, there was nothing Alejandro or anyone else could do. It sickened him to turn his plane away, knowing that their brief moment of hope would evaporate as his Cessna disappeared from sight.

Alejandro's hand trembled as he reached inside his collar. Hanging around his neck was a gold medallion of the Virgin of Charity of El Cobre, the patron saint of Cuba, a good-luck charm of sorts that Cuban relatives in Miami often sent to their relatives in Cuba to keep them safe on their journey to freedom. He'd worn it on his own crossing of the straits in a rowboat, thirty years earlier.

Sadly, he gave the medallion a kiss and headed home to Key West.

7
.

"I love this car," said Theo.

Jack glowered from the passenger seat. "It's mine, and it's not for sale."

Theo slammed it into gear, and the car nearly leaped from the pavement.

It was a good four hours from Miami to Key West, three if Theo was driving, and he had insisted on it. Owning a thirty-year-old Mustang convertible had its drawbacks, but a drive through the Keys was something any car lover lived for. Mile after mile, U.S. 1 was a scenic ribbon of asphalt that connected one Florida Key to the next, slicing through turquoise waters and one-stoplight towns that seemed to sprout from the mangroves. Plenty of warm sunshine on your face, amazing blue skies, a sea breeze like velvet. The deal was that Theo would drive down and Jack would drive back. A fair compromise, Jack figured, if for nothing else than the sheer entertainment value of having Theo come along.

"What did you say?" asked Jack. Theo's mouth

was moving, but it was drowned out by the rumble of the engine and whistle of the wind.

Theo shouted, "If you won't sell your wheels, at least leave 'em to me."

"What do you mean, 'leave'?"

"In your will, dude."

"I don't even have a will."

"A lawyer with no will? That's like a hooker with no condoms."

"What do I need a will for? I'm a single guy with no kids."

They exchanged glances, as if Jack's mention of "no kids" suddenly had a footnote next to it.

"Screw the will," said Theo. "Take it with you. God would love this car."

Jack turned back to his reading. Before leaving Miami, he'd jumped on-line and pulled down some background information about the U.S. naval base at Guantánamo Bay, just enough to know what he was talking about when he interviewed Lindsey's father-in-law. Theo left him alone until they reached the Stockton Bridge, about a mile from Key West International Airport.

"So, you gonna have to go to Camp Geronimo?"

"Guantánamo, not Geronimo. It's a naval base, not an Indian burial ground."

"How is it we got a naval base in Cuba anyway?"

Jack checked one of the web pages he'd printed. "Says here we lease it."

"Castro is our landlord?"

"Technically, yes."

"Shit, what does a guy like Castro do if you're late on the rent? Kill your entire family?"

"Actually, he's never cashed one of our rent checks. The lease was signed long before he came into power, and he refuses to recognize it as valid."

"Guess he's not about to try and evict us."

"Not unless he wants a made-in-America boot up his communist ass."

"So we stay there for free. But for how long?"

"The lease says we can stay there as long as we want."

"Damn. Whoever drafted that document must be in the lawyers' hall of fame."

They entered the airport off Roosevelt Road and headed toward the general aviation hangars, following the instructions that Jack had gotten over the telephone. A security guard directed them to a fenced parking area. The Brothers for Freedom office was a little box at one of the end hangars that barely had enough room for a desk and two chairs. The man inside escorted them toward the tarmac. A flock of hungry seagulls followed them. Just three feet above sea level, Key West International was notorious for its birds, many of which met the aeronautical version of the Veg-O-Matic with the constant coming and going of prop planes. Jack and Theo passed several rows of private aircraft, everything from seaplanes to Learjets. Finally they spotted Alejandro Pintado tending to his reliable old Cessna. Jack probably could have found the plane without any help at all, as it seemed to be held together by bumper stickers that proclaimed such telling messages as FREE CUBA, NO CASTRO, NO PROBLEM, and I DON'T BELIEVE THE *MIAMI TRIBUNE*—the latter being a swipe at the "liberal media," which sometimes criticized the tactics of exiles when it came to fighting Castro.

"Mr. Pintado?" said Jack.

A portly man with silver hair dropped his cleaning rag in the bucket, then emerged from beneath the wing. "You must be Jack Swyteck."

"That's right."

"Who's your friend here? Barry Bonds on steroids?"

"This is—"

"Mikhail Baryshnikov," said Theo, shaking hands.

"My investigator, Theo Knight."

Alejandro did his best to get his chest out, but the belly was still more prominent. "I hear you want to defend my daughter-in-law."

"I'm considering it," said Jack. "Can we sit down and talk?"

"I don't think that's necessary. This isn't going to take long."

Jack rocked on his heels. More hostile than he'd hoped. "First of all, I want to say that I'm very sorry about your son."

"Then why do you want to represent the woman who killed him?"

"Mainly because I haven't come to the conclusion that she did it."

"That pretty much makes you the only one."

"Is there something you can tell me, maybe enlighten me a little?"

Pintado glanced suspiciously at Theo, then back at Jack. "I'm not going to tell you two jokers anything. You aren't here to help me. All you want to do is get her off."

"Mr. Pintado, I'm not going to lie to you. I've represented some guilty people before. But this is an unusual case for me. I'm being completely honest when I say that I have no interest in representing Lindsey Hart if she's guilty."

"Good. Then you should fold your tent right now and go home."

"I can't do that."

"Why not?"

"Because I've met Lindsey. She's raised some serious questions in my mind. Lindsey says she's being framed. She thinks the NCIS report is a cover-up."

"She's been saying that for weeks. What else *can* she say?"

"So, you don't buy into the theory that your son may have been murdered by someone with a hidden agenda?"

"What are you implying?"

"Nothing. I'm just asking a question."

"I am sick and tired of people suggesting that my son was murdered because of the life of resistance I've led. It is not my fault that my son was killed."

Jack was taken aback by the defensiveness. "Look, I didn't come here to lay blame on anyone."

"I think you did. So let me clear this up right now. I know why Lindsey killed my son."

A commercial jet cruised overhead, the deafening screech of its engines seeming to punctuate the man's words. Finally, the noise subsided, and they could talk again.

"You want to tell me why she did it?" said Jack.

"It's pretty obvious, really, once you know

something about me, my family. I came to this country in a rowboat, not a penny to my name. My first job was washing dishes at the Biscayne Cafeteria. Twenty years later I was a millionaire, owner of thirty-seven restaurants. You've heard of them, no? Los Platos de Pintado."

"I've eaten there," said Jack. He knew the Pintado success story, too. It was printed on the back of the menu, including the quaint explanation of how the chain bore a tongue-in-cheek name that harkened back to his humble beginnings as a dishwasher: *Los Platos de Pintado* meant "Pintado's dishes."

Theo said, "Your restaurants are great, dude. But what's that got to do with your son's death?"

"It's not the restaurants. It's the money. We may not show it, but I've made a lot of it. Each of my children has a trust fund. I don't want to get into specifics, but the principal is seven figures."

"That's big bucks," said Jack.

"More money than most people can handle, if you ask me. So my children earn interest only starting at age twenty-one. The principal is theirs to keep when they turn thirty-five."

"So your son was a millionaire?" said Jack.

"Yes. For almost three years." He lowered his eyes and said, "He would have been thirty-eight next month."

"So, you think Lindsey killed him because . . ."

"Because they didn't live like millionaires. Oscar was a lot like me. Money wasn't that important. He wanted to serve his country. Six months ago, he signed on for another stint at Guantánamo."

"Interesting," said Jack. "Lindsey was married to

a millionaire who lived the simple life of a soldier on a military base."

"That's correct. So long as he was alive."

"And if he was dead?"

"She could live anywhere she wanted, with enough money in the bank to live any way she wanted to live."

Jack stood silent for a moment, thinking.

Pintado's eyes narrowed as he said, "And I guess she can afford to go hire herself a pretty fancy lawyer, too."

Jack said, "I'm not in this case for the money."

"Yeah, right."

Jack heard the crank of an engine. Another private plane slowly emerged from the hangar, its whirling propellers practically invisible.

Pintado grabbed his flight bag, threw it over his shoulder. "Now, if you'll excuse me, I've got another flight plan to chart out."

"One more thing," said Jack.

"Enough," he said, waving him off. "I've already told you more than I should."

"I was just wondering about your grandson."

That got his attention. "What about him?"

"Since you're so convinced of Lindsey's guilt, how do you feel about Brian staying with her?"

Pintado's eyes closed, then opened, as if he needed to blink back his anger. "You can't imagine how that makes me feel."

Jack studied the old man's pained expression, then looked off toward the runway. "You might be surprised," he said quietly. "Thanks again for your time, sir."

8

That night, Jack went bowling. He hadn't bowled in about five hundred years, but anytime he got together with his father, they seemed to end up doing something that made Harry Swyteck shake his head and say, "You don't get out much, do you, son?" Last time it was golf, and Jack was thankful that this time at least there were gutters to keep his balls from hitting the other players.

"You owe me thirty-two thousand seven hundred and sixty-eight dollars," said Harry.

Double-or-nothing wagers could add up in a hurry. Especially when you sucked. "I'll race you home for it," said Jack.

"You expect me to go double or nothing on a foot-race?" Harry said with a chuckle.

"I promise not to trip you."

"Whattaya say we just save your old man the heart attack and call it even?"

"Oh, all right. But only because it's your birth-day."

Harry slapped his arm around his son's shoulder,

and they walked out together to the car. Harry was turning sixty, and it didn't seem to bother him a bit, so long as he could spend a chunk of time celebrating alone with his son. As Jack drove him home, he couldn't help thinking what a difference ten years made. Jack hadn't been part of the fiftieth birthday celebration. It had been a huge party in the governor's mansion, but back then he and Governor Swyteck had not even been on speaking terms. Some thought it was because Jack was working for the Freedom Institute, defending death row inmates, while his father was signing death warrants faster than any other governor in Florida history. That philosophical disagreement probably hadn't helped matters, but the rift between them had existed for years. In hindsight, neither one of them fully understood it, but the important thing was that they'd finally gotten past it. Still, it made Jack wonder what this father and son might have been like, how different it would have been for Jack growing up, if his mother, Harry's young and beautiful first wife, hadn't died bringing Jack into the world.

They reached the Swyteck residence at eight P.M., right on schedule. Jack was just about to invite himself inside to say hello to his stepmother when Harry beat him to the punch.

"So, you coming inside for the surprise party?" said Harry.

Jack hesitated. It had been his job to get his father out of the house and back precisely at eight P.M. "What party?" he said lamely.

"Jack, really now. Have you ever known Agnes to keep a secret?"

"Good point." They got out of the car and followed the walkway to the front door. Harry opened
it and stepped inside. Jack was right behind him.

"Surprise!" they shouted in unison, a houseful of
friends erupting in one loud cheer.

Harry took a half step back, as if overwhelmed.
His wife came to him, smiling east to west. They'd
been out of the governor's mansion for nearly four
years, but she still carried herself like the First
Lady. "Got you this time, didn't I, Harry?"

He hugged her and said, "Sure did, darling." Then
he winked at Jack, as if to say, No one outfoxes the
fox. "A total surprise."

It was wall-to-wall people, the guest list having
grown from two hundred of the former governor's
closest personal friends to more than five hundred
"must invites." Drinks were flowing, platters of
tasty hors d'oeuvres were circulating, and it seemed
that within every circle of conversation someone
was telling stories about Harry at twenty, Harry at
thirty, and so on. It was fun for Jack to hear the old
tales, especially ones from the part of Harry's life
that Jack had missed by his own choosing, and to his
later regret.

The band was starting to play outside by the swimming pool. Jack was slated to give a little toast before
the cake and candles, and even though he was no
stranger to speaking before a crowd, he was feeling a
few butterflies. He kept going back and forth in his
mind, trying to decide between a speech from the
heart or a lighter speech that tickled the funny bone.
The choice, he realized, was preordained. No matter
how close he and his father became, they would al-

ways be Swytecks. There would always be things left unsaid.

"Jack, I want you to meet someone," said Harry.

Jack turned to see his father standing beside a distinguished Latin gentleman, his silver and black hair slicked straight back, almost as if he'd just emerged from the swimming pool. Harry's arm was draped around the man's shoulder affectionately. "Jack, this is Hector Torres. He's south Florida's new—"

"U.S. attorney. I know, Dad. I'm a criminal defense lawyer, remember?"

"Don't be so hard on the old man," said Torres, smiling. "I was the one who asked to be introduced. We've never formally met, Jack, but I feel like I know you, I've heard so much about you."

"You mean from my days as a prosecutor?" asked Jack.

"More from your old man. He and I go way back. I remember his *thirtieth* birthday party."

"Boy, that's some memory."

"Hey, watch that, son."

They shared a laugh, then Torres turned more serious. "I don't think your father ever ran for office without my backing. Can you think of anything, Harry?"

"Nope. You were always there."

"That's true. I was always there for you." He paused, as if to let the reminder hang in the air for a moment. Then he looked at Jack and said, "In all seriousness, your reputation is still sound at the office. I understand you're quite an exceptional lawyer."

"Depends on who you talk to," said Jack.

"Actually, I've been talking to a lot of people recently. Matter of fact, just a couple of hours ago I was speaking with Alejandro Pintado about you."

It was an awkward moment, such a festive atmosphere and yet such a stoic expression on the face of one of Harry's oldest friends.

Harry grimaced. "Ah, poor Alejandro. I read about his son, and I've been meaning to drop him a note. Terrible thing."

"Yes," said Torres, but he was looking straight at Jack. "A terrible, terrible thing."

"How's he handling it?" asked Harry.

"About as well as can be expected." Again he looked at Jack, then added, "Of course, he has his setbacks every now and then."

"Well, give him my best," said Harry.

"I will. Actually, I left him in pretty good spirits. I can't get into details—grand jury secrecy and all—but I think we're pretty close to an indictment. With the victim's family in south Florida, the case has been assigned to the Miami office."

"I was wondering about that," said Jack.

"Yes. Alejandro asked me to handle the case personally. It's sort of unusual for the U.S. attorney to actually try a case. But Alejandro's a good friend. I told him I would."

"That's nice of you," said Jack.

"Least I can do," said Torres.

Outside the house on the back patio, on the other side of the opened California doors, the band suddenly stopped playing. The lead singer grabbed the microphone and announced, "We're about ready for cake. Could the birthday boy start making his way toward the stage, please?"

"I guess that's our cue," said Harry. "Great to see you again, Hector. Thanks for coming."

"I wouldn't have missed it."

Jack said, "And thanks again for the nice words."

Harry started away, and Jack was about to follow when Torres grabbed him by the sleeve and stopped him. He spoke slightly above a whisper, softly enough so that no one but Jack could hear him amid the party noises. "I hate to have to say this at your father's birthday, but it needs to be said. Stay the hell out of the Pintado case."

"Is that coming from you or Alejandro?"

"Both. And if need be, I'll make sure you hear it from your father, too."

Jack chuckled lightly. "You really think *that's* going to stop me?"

"Only if you're as smart as he says you are."

"You're out of line, Mr. Torres."

"And you're out of your league, Mr. Swyteck."

Jack met his stare, finding not so much as a trace of a smile on the prosecutor's face. "We'll see about that."

Jack turned and worked his way through the crowd, passing one smiling well-wisher after another as he headed toward his father on stage. He wondered if Torres knew something—if somehow he'd discovered Jack's personal stake in defending Lindsey Hart. Or was he just protecting his old friend Pintado, playing the typical prosecutor's mind game, trying to screw with the mind of the opposition? It wasn't clear.

His stepmother hugged him as he reached the stage. Jack hugged her back, but he turned her body just so, allowing himself one last glimpse of Hector Torres amid a jubilant crowd.

The man still wasn't smiling.

9

Jack met Lindsey for breakfast at Deli Lane, a popular sidewalk café in South Miami. The street and sidewalk were paved with Chicago brick, and a tidy row of young oaks, each of identical height and limb span, planted at regular-spaced intervals, lent a Disney-like precision to the thoroughfare. The humidity had driven most customers inside, but they chose an outdoor table beneath the shade of a broad umbrella. Every few minutes, an exercise enthusiast jogged or walked past them, while a hungry stray terrier sniffed around for fallen scraps of bacon or French toast. Jack couldn't help overhearing the cosmetically enhanced supermoms at the next table, one of whom wanted to sue her plastic surgeon for making her a full cup size larger than she'd requested, and she was just, like, so totally pissed, darling, because her husband had blown her entire malpractice claim by sending the doc a two-page thank-you letter and a bottle of Dom.

The women finally finished off their three hundred calories for the day, divided the bill down to the last penny, and sped away in their respective gas-guzzling SUVs, leaving Jack and Lindsey in sufficient isolation to talk privately. Over coffee, Jack laid his concerns on the table.

"Everyone tells me you're guilty."

"I told you they would," said Lindsey. "It's because they don't know what they're talking about."

"Oscar's father got pretty specific."

"Pardon my language, but Oscar's father is an asshole."

"I don't know enough about him to debate you on that point. But he does know some influential people. And he doesn't want me representing you."

"Of course not. He never fights fair."

"He did lose his son, which can skew your perception of fairness. I'm not saying he's in the right, but he does seem genuinely concerned about his grandson."

Her voice shook as she said, "He's evil, Jack. I don't think Alejandro has come right out and told him that I did it, but it seems like every time he sees Brian, I end up having to explain to my own child why so many people are saying that I killed his father."

Jack drew a breath, reminding himself that every homicide was really about the innocent victims. And there was always more than one victim. "How is Brian doing?"

"Brian is a great kid. He's like his dad. He'll be fine."

For a split second, Jack thought she was paying him a compliment, but then he realized that she'd meant Oscar. Or had she?

"Has to be tough on him," said Jack.

"More than you know. Not only did he lose his dad, but then Guantánamo gave us the boot. Bad for morale to have a homicidal wife on the base, you know. So Brian doesn't even have any friends to lean on."

"Have you found a place to live yet?"

"Yeah. I got a month-to-month rental in Kendall. Brian will be starting middle school next week. We even went to Disney World a couple days ago. Thought that might help take his mind off things."

"How did he like it?"

"He loved it. I survived it. Don't take this the wrong way, but in certain respects I think that's the one place on earth that's actually better if you're deaf."

"I know what you're saying." He started humming "It's a Small World After All."

She actually smiled, and Jack noticed a little sparkle to her personality that, to this point, had been non-existent. It suited her well.

Jack said, "Now that you've brought it up, I guess we'll need someone to sign when I speak with Brian."

"I can do it. I did it when the military police questioned him."

"I'd rather meet with him out of your presence."

She did a quick double take. "Why?"

"Getting a child out from under the influence of his mother is just a sensible interview strategy. It has nothing to do with you or me or our circumstances. It's the way I'd do it in any case."

She didn't immediately take to the suggestion, but his point slowly seemed to register. "Okay, but . . ."

"But what?"

"Give me a day or so to sort some things out."

"What things?"

"Look in the mirror, Jack. I showed you his photograph at our first meeting. Brian is bound to see the resemblance. And then he's going to start asking questions."

"Does he have any idea that he was adopted?"

"No. Oscar and I never told him. I think I should have a long talk with him before he meets you and figures it out for himself."

"Okay. It's not my place to tell you how to handle that. But it is my job to tell you that we have to move fast. I think an indictment is coming down soon, so I need to make a decision about representing you."

She pushed aside her egg-white omelet. She hadn't taken a bite. "Which way are you leaning?"

"Brian is the only person who was in the house at the alleged time of your husband's death. So I need to talk to him."

"You didn't answer my question."

Jack surrendered his last piece of toast to a golden retriever that had been staring at him for the past five minutes with the eyes of a starving child. The dog left, and Lindsey was still locked onto him like radar from across the table, waiting for her answer. "Lindsey, I told you at the outset: I don't want to represent Brian's mother if it looks like she killed Brian's father."

"Does that mean you're not going to represent me?"

"Your father-in-law gave me some troubling information. Seems Oscar had a trust fund worth seven figures. It kicked in when he was thirty-five, but he was career military. He thinks you killed him to get off the base and get your hands on the money."

"That is so typical of him," she said, her voice taking on an edge.

"Did Oscar leave you his trust money in his will?"

"Yes."

"How much?"

"Two million and change."

"So it's in your name now?"

"No. The estate won't release the funds to me. Not until it's established that I didn't kill him."

"Damn it, Lindsey. Why didn't you tell me about this before?"

"Because I didn't want you to take on my criminal case just to get a big fat contingency fee in the probate matter. I'm more than happy to pay your usual criminal retainer, but mostly I want you to do this for Brian."

"Oh, come off it. This is crucial to your criminal case. Two million dollars is plenty motivation for you to kill your husband."

"Sure it is. If I'd known about it. But I didn't know anything about it until after Oscar was dead."

"Oscar never told you?"

"No."

"I find that hard to believe."

"It's true. The Pintado family is a strange one. They are very, very protective of their own. I'm sure you've noticed that I'm Lindsey *Hart*. Not Lindsey *Pintado*. Do you know why? Because Alejandro Pintado wouldn't let his son give me his name. That man never liked me, and for one reason: I'm not Cuban. And when I couldn't get pregnant and at the very least give him a half-Cuban grandchild, well, then I was truly worthless."

"I'm sorry about that. But before you start railing against Cubans in general, I should warn you. I'm half Cuban."

"Yeah, right."

"It's true. My mother was Cuban. I wasn't raised Cuban, but—"

"Then you're not Cuban. Kid yourself all you want, but if you weren't raised in that community, you are *not* part of that community. I spent my entire marriage trying to fit in, and as far as that man Alejandro is concerned, I might as well be from outer space."

"Lindsey, let's not get off track here. I'm talking about me representing you."

"That's exactly what I'm talking about, too. You're afraid to represent me. You're afraid of Alejandro Pintado. You're afraid that if you defend the woman who is accused of murdering his beloved son, it will push you further and further away from being a part of a community that you can never be a part of."

"That is totally unfair."

"Don't talk to me about fairness. Ask my husband how fair this is."

Jack took the blow, though Lindsey seemed to regret having said it. "Believe me," he said, "I couldn't be more sorry about what happened to your family, and I am committed to doing what's best for your son."

"That's very nice to hear. But let me tell you something about commitment. It's a lot more than words."

Now there was a speech he'd heard before. "I'm not just saying it to appease you. I mean it. The most important thing here is Brian."

"And to hell with Lindsey," she said, scoffing.

"I didn't say that."

"You didn't have to. So why don't you just go to hell yourself, Jack."

"What was that for?"

"Because you're acting as if I have no one else to turn to. I'm not some know-nothing wife who followed her husband around the world from one military base to the next. I've met some very interesting people—people I would call friends." She pulled her cell phone from her purse and started scrolling down the list of names in the address book feature. "Look, right here," she said, showing the names and numbers to Jack. "I could call Jamie Dutton. She works in the State Department. Nancy Milama. She's married to Tony Milama, chairman of the Joint Chiefs of Staff. People like that. I could call them, if I had to. They would help me."

"Then call them."

"I didn't want to call them. I called you because I thought you were right for the job. I thought you might do the right thing, stand up to a guy like Alejandro Pintado and find out who really killed your son's adoptive father. But it turns out you don't even have the courage to reach up under your skirt and find your own balls."

He tried to contain his anger, tried to understand this was a woman accused of murdering the father of her son. But he wasn't Job. "Lindsey, get a grip on yourself right now, or you and I are done."

She looked straight at him, her eyes clouded with a swirl of emotion. Anger. Disappointment. Then anger again. "I held my tongue before, Jack, but I'll say it now."

"Make it good. Because this may be the last time I'll listen."

She seemed about to explode. "I know you were playing games with me the other day when you said you didn't know Brian was deaf."

"It was no game. I had no idea."

"Even with all the joy that Brian brought to me and Oscar, every now and then I still had these awful thoughts."

"About Brian?"

"No. Never about Brian. About his birth parents. I wondered, Did they know their baby was deaf? And was *that* the reason they gave him up for adoption? It seemed like such a terrible thing to think about the people who had shared such a beautiful gift. I felt guilty for letting it even cross my mind. But now that I've met you face-to-face, now that I've gotten to know you and find out what you're really like, I have to say: That sense of guilt is gone."

Jack wanted to defend himself, but his thoughts were drifting back to Jessie. Beautiful, brilliant, and incredibly egocentric Jessie. He hated to think it, too. But maybe that *was* the reason she had opted for adoption.

And he had a little better understanding of Lindsey's resentment.

She rose and threw a ten-dollar bill on the table to cover her share of the bill. "Good-bye, Mr. Swyteck. And congratulations. I think there's probably just enough room for both you and Mr. Pintado in your self-absorbed little world."

Jack sat in silence, staring at nothing, not sure what had just hit him as Lindsey turned and walked away.

10

"**S**he is totally yanking your chain," said Theo. "You think?" said Jack.

"How many times did I fire your ass when I was on death row?"

"About every other week."

"See. Ten years later, I still can't get rid of you."

Jack was about to point out that this was his house, they were cooking his food, and Theo had his carcass parked on Jack's couch every weekend, all of which raised some pretty serious questions as to who couldn't get rid of whom. But Jack decided to leave it alone.

Theo turned his attention back to the stove. He was searing two thick tuna steaks in a crispy coating of lemon pepper, sesame seeds, and ginger. He looked like a short-order cook, spatula in hand, greasy white apron wrapped around his waist. To most people, Theo came across as the kind of guy whose idea of a seven-course meal was a six-pack and a bag of chips, but he was actually quite a good cook, and he enjoyed it. And like most good cooks, he hated meddlers in the kitchen.

"What are you doing?" he asked Jack.

Jack was standing at the sink, washing the mixing bowl. "Cleaning up," he said.

"Can't it wait?"

"I suppose. But I guess it's sort of an old habit."

"We talking about your ex again?"

"Yeah. Cindy never used to let me near the kitchen unless I cleaned up as I went along."

Theo looked at him as if he were from another planet. "Clean up while you're cooking? That's like stopping in the middle of sex to do the fucking laundry."

Jack shut off the water, considering it. "I think Cindy actually did that once."

"Jacko, that's one woman you don't need back in your life. But this Lindsey, she'll be back. Trust me."

"Aw, the hell with it. I'm better off without her." He shook his head. "But then there's Brian. I mean, what if his mother is innocent? He's getting the worst of it at both ends."

Theo smiled knowingly as he flipped the tuna steaks. "She's manipulatin' you, man."

"If she is, she's doing one heck of a good job of it."

"Which sort of makes you wonder, don't it?"

"Wonder what?"

Theo lifted the pan from the flame, then slid the steaks onto dinner plates. "Maybe you should be listening to that Mr. Potato."

"Pintado."

"Whatever. My point is this: Just maybe—she's not innocent."

Theo grabbed the plates and started toward the family room. Jack stood frozen at the kitchen counter. He'd had his doubts, to be sure. But coming from Theo's lips, just hearing it out loud, gave it an entirely different impact.

"You coming?" said Theo.

Jack was sifting through a stack of mail at the kitchen counter.

"Hey, Clarence Darrow. I said it's time to eat."

Jack held up a large manila envelope. "It's from Lindsey."

"Wow. That is the fastest 'I still love you' card in the history of the U.S. Postal Service."

"No. It's postmarked three days ago. Before our blowup."

Theo laid the plates of fish on the table. "This should be interesting."

"It's addressed to me, Theo. Not us."

"I slave all day, cook your meals, and this is the thanks I get?"

"Go away."

"Fine." He took both plates of tuna and threw his nose into the air, a bit like an all-pro linebacker pretending to be a ticked-off housewife. "There's Cheerios in the cupboard."

Unless you already ate them, thought Jack.

He waited for Theo to sink into the couch and lose himself in ESPN before opening the letter with a kitchen knife. He hesitated, then reached inside and pulled out a handful of photographs. He sifted through the stack quickly, then went through them again more slowly. They were all snapshots of Brian, some of them quite old, others more recent. A picture of Brian with his soccer team. A picture of Brian and his mother. Another one of Brian and his dad. They were saluting the flag. Oscar was wearing his khaki Marine uniform.

The last photograph was of Brian as a newborn. His mother and father were with him, locked in the awkward and tangled embrace that was so typical of new parents who had no idea how to hold a tiny infant. Jack couldn't be certain, but it appeared to be Brian's first day with his adoptive parents. They looked so happy together, which gave him a good feeling. But then he wondered how Jessie must have felt at that very same moment, the birth mother all alone, far removed from any celebration. Jack's sense of joy faded, and it vanished altogether as he thought about his own life on that day. By the time young Brian had looked into the eyes of his proud adoptive parents, Jack had completely moved on from Jessie, unaware that she was even pregnant. He'd already attained a remarkable level of self-delusion, having convinced himself that Jessie was not "The One," that Cindy Paige would spend the rest of her life as Cindy Swyteck.

Jack put the photographs aside and removed the letter from the envelope. He unfolded it slowly, not sure what to expect. It was handwritten in smooth, beautiful cursive.

Dear Jack,
I wanted you to have these photographs of
Brian. He is a special little boy, and he's becoming

*a young man in a hurry. I know that one day he
will be so grateful for everything you are doing to
help keep our family together, now that Oscar is
gone.*

*Jack, I know it's important to you that I be
innocent. Believe me, I understand that. And I
respect it, too. I would have no right to raise my
son if the things people are saying about me were
true. I don't know how to give you the comfort you
need, but if it would help, I would be more than
happy to take a lie detector test. Just let me know
when and where.*

*Thank you again for being there for us. Fondly,
Lindsey.*

Jack started to read it again, then quickly laid it
facedown on the counter as Theo returned to the
kitchen. His friend nearly broke two fishless dinner
plates as he dropped them into the sink. In less than
five minutes he'd eaten enough seared tuna to feed a
Tokyo suburb.

"What's the matter with you?" said Theo.

"Lindsey sent me some photos."

Theo raised an eyebrow. "We talkin' hot-moms-
dot-com material?"

"No, pervert. Photographs of her son. And a
letter."

"What she say?"

"She offered to take a polygraph. And remember,
this was written before our fight today."

"Heh. Ain't that a kick in the head?"

"Yeah."

"I thought you don't believe in polygraphs."

"I don't. But I tend to believe a recent widow and single mother who offers to take one. Especially when she says you pick the time, you pick the place, you pick the tester. You see the difference?"

"Yeah, I do. So, now what?"

"I don't know. You got any suggestions?"

"Yeah," he said as he walked toward the fridge. "How 'bout dessert?"

Jack stared at the letter, hopelessly confused. Finally, he looked at Theo and said, "That's the best damn idea I've heard in a long time."

11

Jack went food shopping with *Abuela*. This wasn't just the dutiful grandson taking his grandmother to the grocery store. This was Jack's biweekly lesson in Cuban culture.

"What you like for eating, *mi vida*?"

Mi vida. Literally it meant "my life," and Jack loved being her *vida*. "*Camarones?*" he said.

"*Ah*, shreemp. *Muy bien*."

It was part of their routine, Jack speaking bad Spanish, *Abuela* answering in bad English. Jack did the best he could for a half-Cuban kid who'd been raised one hundred percent gringo, which, of course, was the point of their little visits together to the grocery store. Mario's on Douglas Road was the neighborhood market in an area that began to establish itself as Cuban American with the first wave of immigrants in the 1960s. More than three decades later the conversion was complete, and Mario's Market was virtually unchanged, owned and operated since 1968 by a smiling old man named Kiko (there never was a Mario, he just liked the alliteration). A cup of *café con leche* was still just thirty-five cents at the breakfast counter in front. Nine aisles of food were stuffed with the basic essentials of life, including twenty-pound sacks of long-grain rice, *bistec palamillo* sliced to order, delicious caramel flan topping, an assortment of cooking wines to satisfy the most discerning chefs, and glass-encased candles painted with the holy images of Santa Bárbara and San Lázaro. Established customers could buy on credit, and the best Cuban bread in town, baked on the premises, could be purchased straight from the hot ovens in back. All you had to do was follow your nose, or for the olfactory deprived, follow the signs and arrows marked *PAN CALIENTE*. Jack had driven past the store a thousand times on his way downtown, and he would have kept right on driving for the rest of his life had his grandmother not come to the United States and opened a whole new set of doors for him. Twice a month they visited Mario's together to select the freshest ingredients, and then *Abuela* would come over to Jack's kitchen and demonstrate the old family recipes.

Abuela was a phenomenal cook. She always seemed to be preparing a meal or planning the next one, as if on a mission to make up for thirty-eight years of living under Castro with virtually nothing to cook and nothing to eat. Almost five years had passed since Jack's father called to tell him that *Abuela* was coming to Miami, and *Abuela* became Jack's window to the past—to his mother's roots. Of course there would always be the gap that no one could fill, the gaping hole of a life that was never lived, the tragedy of a mother who died bringing her son into the world. Jack's father had told him stories about Ana Maria, the beautiful young Cuban girl with whom Harry had fallen head over heels in love. Jack knew how they'd met, he knew about the fresh yellow flower she used to wear in her long brown hair, he knew how jaws would drop when she walked into a party, and he knew that when someone told a joke, she was the first to laugh and the last to stop. All of those things mattered to Jack, but even on those rare occasions when his father did open up and talk about the wife he'd lost, he could offer Jack only a snippet of her life, just the handful of those final years in Miami. *Abuela* was the rest of the story. When she talked of her sweet, young daughter, her aging eyes would light up with so much magic that Jack could be certain that Ana Maria had truly lived. And *Abuela* could be certain that she *still* lived, the way only a grandmother could be certain of such things, the kind of certainty that came when you took a grandchild by the hand, or looked into his eyes, or cupped his cheek in your hand, and the generations seemed to blur.

Abuela placed a loaf of Cuban bread in their shopping cart, then continued down the aisle. "So, who is the young lady?"

"What young lady?"

"I see you at Deli Lane the other day. Very pretty young lady with you."

Jack realized she was talking about Lindsey. Obviously she'd spotted them before things had turned nasty. "Her name is Lindsey."

"She live here?"

"She does now. She moved here from Guantá-namo Bay."

"Cuba?" she said, her eyes sparkling. "She Cuban?"

Jack smiled, knowing that nothing would have made *Abuela* happier than for her grandson to meet a nice Cuban girl. "No, she just lived in Cuba."

"Not Cuban, but she lived in Cuba," said *Abuela*. "Maybe I can live with that. She good friend?"

"She's actually more of a client than a friend." An ex-client, but Jack didn't want to get into that.

"She have trouble?"

"Yes."

"What kind?"

"They say she killed her husband."

Abuela's mouth was agape. "She kill her husband?"

"No. She's accused of it."

"*Dios mío!*" she said with a shudder. Then she did a double take. "That's her, no? That your friend Lindsey?"

The man behind the checkout counter was watching a small portable television, and *Abuela* was pointing in that direction. Sure enough, Lindsey's image was on the screen, the lead story on one of the Spanish-language news stations. Jack understood the language much better than he spoke it, so he stepped closer to catch the report in progress.

"Lindsey Hart, the daughter-in-law of Brothers for Freedom founder and president Alejandro Pintado, surrendered to federal marshals this afternoon after a grand jury returned an indictment charging her with murder in the first degree. Ms. Hart allegedly shot her husband, Oscar Pintado, a captain in the United States Marine Corps. Captain Pintado, the thirty-seven-year-old son of the well-known Cuban-exile leader, was found shot to death in his home on the U.S. Naval Air Station at Guantánamo Bay, Cuba. At a press conference today, United States Attorney Hector Torres announced that he, personally, would see to it that his office would commit whatever resources were necessary to ensure that justice was done in this matter. Mr. Pintado is reportedly pleased by today's developments and was unavailable for comment. However, Sofia Suarez, the attorney for Lindsey Hart, had this to say about the indictment—"

"Her *attorney*?" Jack said, his words coming like a reflex.

The on-screen image switched to an attractive female attorney, standing on the courthouse steps and speaking to a bouquet of microphones. "My client is shocked by today's indictment. Lindsey Hart is completely innocent. I cannot get into the details of our defense at this time, but suffice it to say that we smell a cover-up. We are convinced that Captain Pintado was murdered for reasons that this indictment does not even begin to describe, and we intend to prove that the military has something to hide here."

Jack had no idea who this Sofia Suarez was, or when Lindsey had even hired her. But the whole idea of taking on the U.S. military from the get-go seemed a bit over the top.

The anchorman returned to the screen and said, "Ms. Hart entered a plea of not guilty at her arraignment late this afternoon. She was denied bail and will remain in custody pending trial."

The newscast switched to another story, and Jack turned away from the television set. He'd known for some time that an indictment was looming, and it certainly wasn't unusual for the accused to be denied bail in a case of first-degree murder. But the thought of young Brian having to deal with his mother's incarceration was still difficult for Jack to stomach.

Abuela grabbed his hand and said, "Listen to me, *mi vida*. I saw how this Lindsey look at you in the restaurant. It seem nice, when I thought she maybe was good for you."

"Looking at me how? She was a client."

"*Aye*, you are so blind. That woman is big trouble. You forget that one. Understand me? Forget that one."

He was still reeling from the news of the indictment, but *Abuela*'s words struck a chord. *Forget that one.* People were so quick to judge, and Lindsey was getting it from everyone—from people she once considered friends at the naval base, and from people she'd never even met, like *Abuela*. Who could blame her for having been so angry at the restaurant, after her own lawyer had laid on a hefty dose of doubt?

"Forget about her, you say?" said Jack.

"*Sí, sí.* Forget her."

Jack shook his head, his thoughts still with Lindsey's son. His son. "It's not that easy."

12

They made it through the checkout line without too much financial damage, and Jack drove them to his house. *Abuela* had a fine kitchen, but nothing seemed to give her quite as much pleasure as taking over someone else's. In minutes she had unpacked the groceries and set up various food-preparation stations around Jack's kitchen counters and stove.

Jack went straight to the television and switched on *Action News at Six*. The feed-in for the lead story was basically the same report that Jack had watched in Spanish. As a bonus, however, the anchorwoman had somehow snagged an exclusive live interview with Alejandro Pintado from his mega-mansion in Journey's End, one of south Florida's most exclusive communities.

"Mr. Pintado, we understand that your son and daughter-in-law had just one child, a ten-year-old son. What will become of him now that his mother has been indicted and denied bail?"

Pintado spoke in a solemn voice, his wife seated at his side on the couch. "The loss of our son is a terrible tragedy, but we are determined to avoid more harm to our family. Our grandson has decided that he wants to stay with us while his mother is in jail, and Lindsey's attorney has indicated her agreement to that arrangement."

"Will that become permanent if your daughter-in-law is convicted of murder?"

"We expect that it will, yes."

The anchorwoman tried to get him to talk about the evidence against Lindsey, but Pintado wisely declined, probably at the behind-the-scenes direction of the prosecutor. She thanked him and brought the interview to a close.

Jack looked up from the set and saw his grandmother shooting him a reproving look. "What?" he said.

"You going to help, or you going to watch TV?"

"I'll help." He walked to the kitchen counter, gathered up the dirty mixing bowls, and started toward the sink. Another glare from *Abuela* stopped him cold.

"Who taught you to clean while you cook?" she said.

"Sorry," said Jack. Obviously she and his buddy Theo were of the same school when it came to the joy of cooking.

"Go sit over there," she said. "Watch and learn."

Abuela was singing something in Spanish as she cooked, and watching and hearing her gave Jack an idea. He pulled down an atlas from the bookshelf and turned to a map of Cuba. Suddenly, *Abuela* was looking over his shoulder, as if she were equipped with homeland radar.

"Bejucal," she said, pointing to a tiny black dot of a town near Havana. "Is where your mother grew up."

Jack sat in silence. He'd heard the stories of how his mother had come to Miami after the Cuban revolution. Focused on that spot on the map, he could imagine his mother and grandmother hugging and kissing each other for the very last time. *Abuela* had made the heart-wrenching decision to send her teenage daughter to the United States without her, knowing that it was better for her to live in freedom, and hoping that they would soon find a way to reunite. Unfortunately, it wasn't until long after her daughter's passing that *Abuela* was finally able to make the trip.

Like any escape route, the one from Havana was fraught with personal tragedies, *Abuela* and Jack's mother just one of thousands. In the broader annals of U.S. immigration history, however, the Cubans were an amazing success, particularly in Miami. There had been setbacks, of course, and any comparison of the first wave of immigration in the 1960s to some of the later refugees was bound to raise a few eyebrows, even among Cuban Americans. You could argue about that one till the *vacas* came home. The bottom line, however, was that both the city and county commissions were controlled by Cubans, the city mayor was Cuban, the county mayor was Cuban, three of south Florida's five congressional representatives were Cuban, and many of the most successful banks, businesses, law firms, brokerage houses, and so on were headed by Cubans. Unlike most Latino groups, Cuban Americans were largely Republican, not Democrat, and not just because Democrats were perceived as too soft on Castro. It was because so many Cuban Americans—Alejandro Pintado among them—had accumulated more than enough honest wealth to be counted among the GOP's biggest campaign contributors. Yet, with all those accomplishments, many still talked of someday going back to Cuba, if not to live, then at least to help rebuild the economy after Castro's long-awaited fall.

Jack had never really gotten caught up in all that "back to Cuba" talk. He hadn't been raised Cuban, he spoke stilted Spanish, and he hadn't really circulated in Latin social circles. Most people had no idea his mother was Cuban, so it wasn't unusual for him to find himself privy to a gathering of Anglos plotting their imminent departure from the "third-world country" that Miami was becoming. If enough liquor was flowing, some pretty respectable people were more than willing to buddy-up with an apparent gringo named Swyteck and reveal their secret wish to look their Cuban neighbor in the eye and say, "Hey, José, if you want to go back to Cuba so damn bad, then do us all a favor and get back on your fucking banana boat and get the hell out of here." Sometimes Jack would buck up and say something; sometimes he figured it wasn't worth his effort. But deep down he knew that what really bugged the loudest complainers was that, if all these so-called "Josés" did go back to Cuba, they wouldn't be traveling by banana boat. In fact, a good many of them would fly their children home from college at Harvard or Yale, hop on the eighty-foot yacht that was docked behind their three-million-dollar mansion in Gables Estates, and make a nice family trip out of it, soaking up sun and sipping cold *mojitos* served by one of their three Honduran housemaids.

"I should go to Bejucal," said Jack.

"What?"

"If I get back into this case for my friend Lindsey, I'll have to travel to Cuba. I should take a side trip to Bejucal."

Abuela said nothing. Jack asked, "What was it like there when my mother left?"

Abuela took a deep breath, let it out. Then she answered in Spanish. "It was exactly the way it was when I left, thirty-eight years later."

"Really?"

"Yes. And it was totally different, too."

Jack's gaze returned to the map. Bejucal was a fair distance from Guantánamo, but in Jack's mind the two cities were forever linked. One made him think of himself, the young boy who had never known his mother. The other made him think of another boy, an adopted child who had never met his biological parents. It wasn't the same thing, not by a long stretch, yet Jack found it slightly ironic that they shared the same option. They could try to learn about the person who had brought them into the world. Or they could leave it alone.

For Jack, the choice was suddenly clearer than ever before. He looked at his grandmother and said, "I want to go."

Jack looked for some sign of approval in her expression, but he could only watch in confusion as *Abuela* turned and retreated to the kitchen.

"Do you not want me to go?" he said.

She didn't answer. She was at the stove, tending to her cooking. Jack was fully aware that a journey back to Cuba was an emotional issue for many Cuban Americans, especially the elders, but he expected more of a *mix* of emotions from *Abuela*. Instead, there was just silence.

The telephone rang, and Jack decided to let the answering machine get it. He was still trying to figure out *Abuela*'s reaction, but *Abuela* was too clever for him. She answered it herself. Jack waved his arms at her, as if to say, Whoever it is, tell them I'm not here. *Abuela* ignored his silent pleas, obviously not wishing to discuss Jack's trip to Cuba any further.

"Yes, Jack is right here next to me," she told the caller.

Jack groaned and took the phone. "Hello?"

"Is this Jack Swyteck?" It was a woman on the line, a voice he didn't recognize.

"Yes, that's me. Who is this?"

"My name is Sofia Suarez." She paused, as if Jack should recognize the name. Then she added, "I represent Lindsey Hart."

Jack stepped out of the kitchen, away from the clatter of *Abuela*'s cooking. "Yes, I saw you on television."

"Oh, I hate cameras, but with all that media, I felt like I had to say something. How do you think it played?"

Jack didn't see the point in trashing her conspiracy theory just yet. "Hard to say."

"It sucked. I know. I sounded like one of those 'the world is out to get me' nutcases."

"It wasn't that bad."

"You're just being kind. Listen, I'm calling because . . . well, for a couple of reasons. One, Lindsey asked me to call."

"She did?"

"Yes. I heard all about the way she told you off the other day, and she is so sorry. She is under so much stress right now. I know that's not an excuse, but it certainly explains a lot."

"What does she want?"

"She's afraid to ask you to come back and represent her. But believe me, in her heart, she is begging for your forgiveness. She needs you, and the only person who knows that more than Lindsey is me."

"What do you mean?"

She chuckled mirthlessly and said, "I am so over my head here. I'm not a criminal lawyer. Lindsey hired me to handle her probate matter. The estate won't distribute Oscar's trust fund to her."

"I know. She told me about that. Finally."

"That's right up my alley. But a murder trial, no way. So please, I'm hoping that you can put aside what happened the other day and do the right thing. Obviously there will be plenty of money to pay you when this probate matter gets straightened out."

"It was never about the money," said Jack.

"I know. Lindsey told me about . . . you know, about you and Brian."

Jack stepped farther away from the kitchen, careful not to let *Abuela* overhear anything. "What did she tell you?"

"That you're the father."

Jack paused. It was strange, but somehow the fact that this Sofia knew his secret made him feel more connected to her. "I saw Lindsey's father-in-law on television. Did you agree to let Brian stay with his grandparents?"

Her sigh crackled over the line. "It was a hard decision. Lindsey's sister would have been glad to take him. But Brian truly wanted the Pintados, and Lindsey didn't want to drag him through a court fight over who should care for him while she's in custody."

Jack knew how Lindsey felt about Pintado. He had to respect a mother who would honor her son's wishes under those circumstances. "Well, hopefully it will all work out for the best in the end."

"Yes, if she's acquitted. Which, again, is where you come in."

"It's a complicated decision," said Jack.

"I'm sure it is. And I hate to push, but I need a commitment from you quickly. I'm scheduled to leave for Guantánamo in the morning."

"What for?"

"Interviews. On-site inspections. It's not easy for civilians to arrange a visit to the naval base. If I don't grab tomorrow's opening, it could be weeks before I'm able to schedule another trip."

Jack was thinking aloud. "I should be a part of that, if I'm going to be lead counsel."

"Definitely. So what do you say?"

"Let me sleep on it."

"Jack, I really need an answer. If you're not going to help me on this Guantánamo trip, I need to find a real criminal lawyer who will."

"I understand."

"No, I don't think you do. Have you seen the indictment yet?"

"No."

"It's a capital case. They're asking for the death penalty."

Jack went cold.

"She needs you, Jack. She *really* needs you."

Jack considered it. A probate lawyer in a death penalty case? Lindsey didn't have a chance. He wasn't one hundred percent convinced of her innocence, but she had offered to take a polygraph. She probably deserved better than the hand she'd been dealt so far.

Brian definitely deserved better—which was enough to swing the balance.

"Okay," said Jack. "I'm in."

13

•

The next morning Jack and Sofia Suarez met at the airport.

Getting into the U.S. naval air station at Guantánamo Bay had never been easy, and the nation's war on terrorism had made it nearly as tough as getting into a South Beach nightclub dressed in last year's fashion. A midmorning commercial flight took them from Miami to Norfolk, Virginia. It was up to them to find ground transportation to the naval air station for their Air Mobility Command flight to Guantánamo, which didn't leave until six P.M. Jack was actually looking forward to a little shut-eye on the plane. Following their initial phone conversation, Sofia had arranged for a courier to deliver a boxful of grand jury transcripts, witness statements, and other evidence upon which the prosecutor had relied to secure Lindsey's indictment. Jack had spent almost the entire night reviewing them, and it was now taking its toll. Despite his unstoppable yawns, Sofia seemed determined to talk strategy every step of the way to Guantánamo.

"You want to do the interviews, or you think maybe I should?" said Sofia.

"Wasn't that the whole point of my coming on board so quickly? So that I could take the lead?"

"It was, but then I got to thinking. We'll be talking mostly to men, and most of them have been trapped on a military base with a lot of other men for a very long time."

"So you're thinking . . . what?"

"Who are they more likely to spill their guts to? You?" she said, batting her eyes, just to make her point. "Or a total Latin babe?"

She was pouring it on for effect, but with her long black hair and perfect olive skin, the Latin babe thing wasn't a stretch. If Jack was going to be sandwiched between Lindsey and Sofia at trial, he was going to have to give some serious thought toward gunning for an all-male jury.

This is going to be interesting.

They had about an hour to kill before heading over to the military terminal, so they found a couple of stools at the end of the bar in a relatively uncrowded pub-style restaurant. Sofia was hungry, but Jack had been force-fed by *Abuela* before leaving the house and would have no use for food for perhaps two or three days. Sofia ordered a Cobb salad, and Jack had coffee.

"You ever been to Cuba before, Jack?"

"No, but I'm curious to see it. My mother was born in Cuba."

"Really? How does she feel about your defending the woman who is accused of killing the only son of the esteemed Cuban exile Alejandro Pintado?"

"My mother passed away a long time ago. But my grandmother is still alive and as opinionated as ever. She's not exactly crazy about it."

"Sounds like my father. He's Alpha Sixty-six—Bay of Pigs survivor. I'm proud of him, of course, but he is a bit extreme. For the past forty years he's spent two Saturdays a month dressed in camouflage, crawling around on his belly in the Florida Everglades, getting ready for the next armed invasion of Cuba. When I told him I was representing Lindsey Hart, I think he would actually have petitioned to have me disbarred if it hadn't cost him so much to put me through law school."

"Obviously his objections don't bother you."

"Nah. I'll be dancing in the streets along with everyone else when Castro falls, but it's not my life's work. In the eyes of men like my father and Alejandro Pintado, I suppose that makes me a communist. When it comes to politics, we just have to agree to disagree."

"I can relate to that," said Jack.

"Yeah, I seem to remember an article about you and your old man in *Tropic* magazine some years back. 'Why Can't the Governor Win His Own Son's Vote?' or something like that."

"A lot has changed since then." He smiled and added, "Though I'm still not sure I'd vote for him."

Sofia didn't seem to realize that he was kidding. She was picking the bits of hard-boiled egg out of her salad, adding them to a growing pile of suspicious perishables on a side plate. Finally she looked up and said, "So, are you wondering how I got this case?"

"As a matter of fact, I am. How do you know Lindsey?"

"We were lovers in college."

"What!"

"Gotchya," she said with a smile. "Man, you're easy. Actually, we shared an apartment our senior year at FSU. Kept in touch a few years after that. Then we lost contact, until her husband died. She needed a lawyer, and I guess she remembered that I'd somehow managed to get into law school. I got a phone call a couple of months ago."

"What did she tell you?"

"Well, she told me about Oscar. We cried together a little. Then she told me about the trust fund he'd left her, and how her father-in-law didn't want her to have it."

"Is that how she put it—that Alejandro Pintado didn't want her to have the family money?"

"Yes. Right from the beginning, she thought that Oscar's father would stop at nothing to keep her from getting that money. Even if it meant accusing her of murder."

"I've seen plenty of nasty things done for the sake of litigation posturing in my day. But actually pushing for a murder indictment takes the art of saber rattling to new heights, don't you think?"

"For most people, sure. For Alejandro Pintado . . . maybe not."

The waitress came and refilled Jack's coffee cup. When she was gone, Jack said, "Have you met her son, Brian, yet?"

"We met for the first time about three days ago.

I told Lindsey I needed to interview him if I was going to get involved in the criminal case."

"I told her the same thing. Didn't get me very far."

"She's very protective of him. If you ask me, she's truly devastated by what happened to her husband. The last thing she wants is her son getting dragged through the system and ending up with a screwed-up head."

"I can understand that. How did the interview go?"

"Fine. He's a wonderful kid. You'll like him."

Jack emptied a packet of sugar into his coffee. "What did he tell you about the night his father was shot?"

"Same thing he told the police. Didn't notice anything unusual during the night. He woke a little earlier than usual. He wasn't sure why. Something just didn't feel right. Got out of bed to go to the bathroom. His mom was already at work, but the door to the master bedroom was open. He saw the blood on the bed, then he saw the body."

"And that was when he called his mother at work?"

"Yes. Well, it was actually a digital page that he typed out. They have a special phone for the hearing impaired."

"I read the police report last night. Brian was pretty unclear about the exact wording of the message. Has his memory improved on that?"

"All he recalls is that he said something to the effect of 'Mom, come home, now—emergency!'"

"She came right home?"

"Yeah."

"Then what?"

Sofia finished off a chunk of avocado. "That's pretty much all the information he has. His mom sent him to his room and wouldn't let him out until the police came."

"Does he have any recollection of Lindsey saying anything like, 'Oh, my God, your father shot himself'—anything like that?"

"I don't think I asked him that."

Jack hesitated, then asked, "Did you ask him if *he* shot his father?"

"Not directly. I asked in a more general way if he knew who shot his father, and he said, 'No.'"

"Do you believe him?"

"Yes."

"Why?"

"I'd know if he was lying."

"How can you be so sure?"

"I'm a thirty-four-year-old single woman. How many times you think *I've* been lied to? Brian's ten. He's no match for me."

"Hard to argue with that," said Jack.

"The biggest problem with Brian is not that he hurts Lindsey's case, but that he's just not able to help her. He's deaf, so he's not going to be able to tell us that he heard his mother definitely leave for work at a certain time, or that he heard noises of a possible intruder. He can't even tell us what time he heard the gun go off."

"Disadvantage for us. Advantage for the killer."

Sofia nodded, seeming to follow his logic. "Which probably means that the killer was fully aware of Brian's deafness."

"I'd say so."

"I guess that's one of the things you'll want to establish with some of the witnesses you talk to at Guantánamo: Who knew that Brian was deaf, unable to hear a thing?"

"That's one of the things on my list," said Jack.

"What else you got on your list?"

"It's a work in progress."

"Oh, come on. What's right up there at the top? What do you want to know most?"

"What I want to know most is probably something that only Lindsey can tell me."

"What's that?"

He thumbed through the forensic report, which he'd read for the first time that morning. "How did her fingerprints end up on the murder weapon?"

Sofia didn't respond. Jack closed up the report and checked his watch. If they were going to make their AMC flight, it was time to get moving. They pooled their money to cover the tab and left the restaurant together.

14
.

The first thing Jack noticed were the stars. Millions of them seemed to pop from the sky the moment he stepped off the airplane. It was the kind of celestial brilliance never seen in the city. You had to be out on the ocean, far from civilization and city lights, floating in the middle of nowhere.

Or in Guantánamo Bay.

The sense of isolation at GTMO (pronounced "Gitmo") was a product of both geography and military might. The bay itself was a pouch-shaped enclave on the southeastern coast of Cuba, twelve miles long and six miles across at its widest point. The surrounding area was primarily agricultural, mostly sugarcane and coffee. The Cuzco Hills to the south and east and the Sierra Maestra Mountains to the north provided a certain natural shelter. Throw in a five-service task force, a few warships, fighter jets, some well-armed guard towers, and about eight gazillion miles of razor wire, and—*voila!*—you've got a perfect safe haven for many of the indigenous plants and animals that Cuban farmers and developers had virtually wiped out elsewhere on the island. As crazy as it sounded, some of the most unspoiled land in all of Cuba was at the U.S. naval air station. Many a serviceman and -woman had left GTMO thinking that it did indeed belong to iguanas and cactus plants, which only reinforced its reputation as "the least worst place." That feeling was certainly understandable around the airstrip, which was on the opposite side of the bay from the main base.

Jack and Sofia grabbed their bags, which had been laid out for them on the runway. It was too dark to see much of anything beyond the lighted pathway that led to a green Humvee parked by a large hangar along the airstrip. Lights from the control tower blinked in the distance. Some of the higher hilltops were ghostly silhouettes, backlit by a setting moon. The bay was not far off, Jack knew, not because he could see or hear it, but because he could almost taste the salt in the gentle breezes. Even in the middle of the night, it was mild enough to go without a jacket, and having come from Miami and all its humidity, Jack was pleasantly surprised by the arid climate.

"How'd you sleep?" Sofia asked as they followed a Marine toward the Humvee.

"Like a baby," said Jack. "Up every forty-five minutes and mad as hell about it." Jack had never had much luck trying to sleep on airplanes.

It was roughly a half-hour ferry ride across the bay. Jupiter rose on the horizon, outshining even the brightest star, as they left Leeward Point Field and departed from the dock. The inner harbor served commercial vessels. The ferry puttered across the outer harbor, toward the naval reserve boundary, and then docked at a landing that butted up against the main pier and wharf facilities between Cori-nasco Point and Deer Point. They were met by two members of the Marine military police who assured Jack that their vicious-looking German shepherd was completely under their control. Explosives dogs were a part of life here, and they weren't trained to be your friend. Jack and Sofia's bags passed the smell test, and then another Marine met them at the foot of the pier.

"You guys eat on the plane?" said the Marine.

"Not really," said Jack.

"McDonald's is still open, if you're hungry."

Jack recalled that Lindsey had mentioned McDonald's in their first meeting. It seemed to be a source of local pride. "My first trip to Cuba, and the first place I'm going to eat is at McDonald's?"

The Marine said, "You're in Cuba, but you're not really in Cuba. If you know what I mean, sir."

The irony of the remark amused Jack. How many times in his life had he heard people say he was Cuban, but he was not really Cuban? "Yes," said Jack. "I definitely know what you mean."

With a full schedule of interviews for the follow-ing day, Jack opted for sleep over food. They spent the night in separate guest cottages, and the driver picked them up at six A.M. Jack expected Sofia to be one of those perky morning-type personalities, but she was far outdone by their Marine escort, who probably ran five miles and peeled off four hundred sit-ups before his alarm clock even rang. They drove past a golf course, a Little League field, a shopping mall, and some tidy town-house subdivisions, all of which struck Jack as more akin to 1950s suburbia than a strategic naval base. Even the military buildings had a certain quaintness about them, mostly low-slung structures made of wood or cinder block, painted yellow with brown trim. Utility poles were stained forest green, perhaps to compensate for the scarcity of trees, let alone an actual forest.

They stopped for coffee at the Iguana Crossing Coffee Shop, and their journey ended at the "White House," the tongue-in-cheek name given to the impressive white building that housed the Marine command suite at the base. It was an inspiring sight, a simple white-frame structure set against the backdrop of a bright blue sky, the American flag flying proudly in the warm Cuban breeze. Their escort took them inside to a conference room. The walls were paneled with white wainscoting, and white Bahama shutters covered the windows. The blurred reflection of a whirling white paddle fan shined in the highly polished top of a long mahogany table.

A navy JAG lawyer stepped forward to greet them. "Captain Donald Kessinger," he said.

Sofia and Jack shook his hand and introduced themselves, though Jack noticed that the captain's eyes were still on Sofia even as he was shaking Jack's hand. A long travel day and an abbreviated night's sleep on a military bunk had knocked her down a peg or two on the eye-popping chart, but she was still quite a welcome sight on a military base. Finally, the captain looked at Jack and offered seats to his guests on the opposite side of the rectangular table, their backs to the windows.

"Thank you for agreeing to meet with us," said Jack.

"You're welcome. How was the trip down?"

"I think Dorothy had a smoother ride to Oz," said Sofia.

"Ooh, that's nasty. But you made it. So how can I help you?"

Jack laid his dossier on the table before him and removed a sheet of paper. "First thing I'd like to do is run down the list of potential witnesses that I faxed you from the airport yesterday."

"I have a copy right here," he said, flattening it out before him.

"My preference is to start the interviews with the military police officer who was first on scene in response to Lindsey Hart's nine-one-one call."

"I'm sorry. He's not available."

"Why not?"

"I'm not authorized to tell you why not."

"Where is he?"

"Reassigned."

"To where?"

"Can't tell you."

Jack penned in a little *X* before the first name on his list. "The NCIS report indicated that there were three other officers on the scene. I'd like to talk to them."

"They work as a unit," said the captain. "I'm afraid they've all been reassigned."

"So they're unavailable, too?"

"Completely."

Jack marked another *X*, then moved on. "Let's

talk about personnel in the surrounding area, people who simply may have seen anything unusual."

"Okay."

"I noticed guard towers all over the place here. I'd like to speak with the guard who was posted nearest to the crime scene."

"Mmmmmm. That would be PFC Frank Novich. Once again, sorry."

"Not available?"

"No."

"Reassigned?"

"Shipped out yesterday. You just missed him. Tough break."

"Where is he?"

"I believe he's in . . . well, I'm not at liberty to say."

Jack leaned into the table, doing his best to put some fire behind his tired eyes. "Captain, let's do this another way. Is there *anyone* on my list who has not been reassigned and relocated?"

"I seem to recall there was someone."

"Perhaps the captain's direct commanding officer?"

"No, I'm afraid she's gone."

"How about the three Marines he was with the night before his death?"

"Gone as well."

"So, exactly who did Ms. Suarez and I come down here to interview?"

"Looks like it's going to be Lieutenant Damont Johnson."

"Of the sixteen people I've asked to interview, you're giving me one?"

"Actually, I'm not giving you anything. Lieutenant Johnson is with the United States Coast Guard, and he is still here on the base."

"That's it? We came all this way to talk to one witness?"

"It's well worth the trip, I'd say. Lieutenant Johnson was Oscar Pintado's best friend."

"Oscar's best friend, or Lindsey's worst enemy?"

He didn't seem to appreciate the sarcasm. "Mr. Swyteck, I shouldn't have to remind a former federal prosecutor that these witnesses are under no obligation to meet with you before trial. The U.S. government has gone beyond the call of duty by arranging for you to talk to Lieutenant Johnson."

"I know the rules. But I can't help but smell a rat with these sudden reassignments."

"Reassignments happen all the time in the military."

"Some of them even for valid reasons, I'm sure."

The captain's expression soured. "Mr. Swyteck, I'm sure you're aware of the statements your client made to the local paper after her husband's death— her ridiculous suggestions that Captain Pintado was effectively rubbed out by someone here on the base because he knew too much about a top-secret matter. I also read statements to the same effect that your cocounsel here, Ms. Suarez, made on television after Lindsey's arrest. So let me put this in terms you can understand. I have no interest in helping a couple of slick Miami lawyers get their client off the hook by building a cockeyed big-government conspiracy theory. Pardon me if I seem unreasonable. But I owe that much to the victim's family."

"My client *is* the victim's family. So do me a favor, would you? Stop the speeches and bring me Lieutenant Johnson."

Their eyes locked, and finally the captain blinked. Jack watched as he pushed away from the table and left the room in silence. The door closed behind him.

Sofia said, "What kind of crap is this? They make us fly all the way down here for just one interview?"

"Yeah," said Jack. "Better make it count."

15

•

"**W**e are the front line in the battle for regional security," said Lieutenant Damont Johnson.

It sounded like the opening line from a presidential speech, and the lieutenant did have the air of a young leader about him. A handsome and articulate African American, obviously intelligent, the kind of guy you wanted on your side. He might have had a future in politics, if he could tone down the arrogance.

Jack and Sofia were seated on one side of the conference table. The lieutenant and the JAG lawyer, Captain Kessinger, were on the other. Kessinger wasn't the lieutenant's personal attorney, but he was there to make sure that nothing happened to "compromise the government's interests"—however those interests were defined.

"What does that mean?" asked Jack. "The front line in the battle for regional security?"

"It means we're in Castro's backyard. Or," he said as he glanced at the framed map on the wall, "if you envision the island as a big Cuban iguana with its tail cut off, some people say we're crawling straight up its asshole."

"And as America's ambassadors to proctology, what's your mission here?"

The lieutenant almost smiled. He seemed to like the way Jack stayed with him, blow for blow.

"I'm not sure how to answer that," said Johnson. "The Coast Guard conducts daily operations in the Caribbean theater, many of them out of Guantánamo. By doing that, we protect the United States of America from its two biggest external threats. Drug trafficking and terrorism."

"Which of those two matters are you personally involved in most?"

"I'd say my time is divided several ways. The two I just mentioned being a big part of my job. Immigration and rescue-recovery matters being equally important."

"By *immigration* you mean illegal immigration matters, I assume."

"Depends how you define *illegal*."

"You're not there to give away green cards, are you?"

The JAG lawyer grumbled. "Mr. Swyteck, I realize that this is not a formal deposition, but I don't think there's any need for sarcasm. The lieutenant is here on his own time, on a volunteer basis. You could at least be polite."

"Fair enough," said Jack. "Lieutenant Johnson, if I've offended you, I apologize. But let me go about it this way. You're Coast Guard. Oscar Pintado was a Marine. Correct?"

"That's right."

"And you guys were friends?"

"That's right. Best friends."

"Right. Best friends. Now, that's probably not as unusual as a joint tailgate party between a midshipman and a West Point cadet at the annual Army-Navy football game, but it still strikes me as a little out of the ordinary that two guys in two different branches of service would become best friends."

"We hit it off. What can I say?"

"How? What is it that made you guys such good friends?"

"I don't know. What makes anybody friends?"

Jack shrugged. "Common interests?"

Again the JAG lawyer mumbled. "Mr. Swyteck, I don't represent Lieutenant Johnson here, but I feel compelled to point out that the man is taking time off duty for this interview. He has more important things to do than ponder the essence of friendship. I mean, this isn't *Oprah*."

"Here's my point," said Jack. "Oscar Pintado's father is the founder of Brothers for Freedom. He has flown thousands of hours over the Florida Straits looking for Cuban rafters, hoping to bring them to America. You are an officer in the Coast Guard. You look for rafters every day, trying to return them to Cuba. Am I stating this fairly?"

"Basically, yes."

"Yet, you and the son of Alejandro Pintado became best friends. What's that all about?"

"You're analyzing it too much. Oscar and I would go out, have a few beers, shoot some pool. When you're surrounded by razor wire all day long, you don't usually talk about the world's problems when you get some R and R."

"Did you ever meet Oscar's father?"

"Nah."

"You know he's a very wealthy man, right?"

"Yeah, I heard that."

"If someone were to say that Lieutenant Johnson was buddying up to Oscar Pintado just because he likes to have rich friends, how would you respond?"

"I'd say that sounds like Lindsey Hart talking."

"How so?"

The JAG lawyer spoke up. "Excuse me, but Lieutenant Johnson volunteered to tell what he knows about the death of Captain Pintado. Why is it that you seem interested in talking to him about anything but that?"

"Why is it that you seem interested only in reminding him every five minutes that he's here on a volunteer basis and doesn't have to answer my questions?"

"Because he's a busy man, and he should be made aware of his options."

"He's aware. Now, I'd appreciate it if you'd sit tight and let me get answers to the questions I'd like to ask."

"Fine. Ask away."

"What was the question?" asked the lieutenant.

Jack said, "I'm just trying to get a sense for how you felt about the captain's wife."

The lieutenant said, "You mean before or after she shot her husband?"

"You think she shot him?"

The JAG lawyer grimaced. "Mr. Swyteck, come on. He has no way of knowing one way or the other. And I don't think it's appropriate to ask him to speculate on that matter."

"I think he's doing just fine," said Jack. "Lieutenant, is there some reason you don't want to answer my question? Do you think Lindsey Hart shot her husband?"

"Yeah, I think she shot him. Everybody thinks she shot him. That's why I was glad to hear she got indicted."

"Why do you think Lindsey Hart shot her husband?"

The JAG lawyer slapped his palm on the table. "This is going beyond speculation. You're asking him to make wild guesses about very serious matters, and I don't see how any of this is helpful to the investigation. I'm not his lawyer, but frankly, if I were, Lieutenant Johnson and I would be on our way out the door."

The lawyer rose from his seat, as if expecting the lieutenant to join him.

Jack looked at the lieutenant and said, "You gonna listen to the lawyer who's not your lawyer, or you gonna answer my question?"

"I don't see how he could responsibly answer that question," said the JAG lawyer.

"No, no," said the lieutenant. "I want to answer."

"You don't have to," said Kessinger.

"And you don't have to stay," the lieutenant told him.

Captain Kessinger slowly returned to his seat beside the witness. Then the lieutenant looked at Jack and said, "I actually liked Lindsey Hart. When she was on her medication."

"Her medication?"

"Yeah. She misses a few pills and—whoa. Goodbye."

"Medication for what?"

"Not sure. Oscar never told me anything specific, but if you want my opinion, I'd say the woman is bipolar or something."

"What makes you think that?"

"Many, many things. But let me give you just one example that you can probably relate to. Did she do that thing with her cell phone for you yet?"

"Cell phone?"

"Yeah. When she flips open her phone and points to the numbers stored in her address book. All those important people she says she could call in a heartbeat."

Jack didn't answer, but he couldn't help the look on his face.

The lieutenant smiled and said, "She *did* do it for you. I knew it. Admittedly, it wouldn't have the same impact on you in Miami as it did on me here in Cuba. Cell phones aren't much use in Guantánamo, so it was weird enough that she was walking around with one. But that Nancy Milama connection was truly special. Oh yeah, as if Lindsey Hart is going to pick up her cell phone and call Nancy Milama. Do you know who Nancy Milama is?"

"Lindsey told me that she was married to the chairman of the Joint Chiefs of Staff."

"Yeah. *Was* married."

"They're divorced?" asked Jack.

"Uh-uh. Tony Milama is a widower. His wife, Nancy, died three years ago."

Jack was speechless.

"So let me make this clear to you, Mr. Swyteck. It's a terrible thing that happened to my friend Oscar. But truthfully, I'm more scared for his son, stuck living with that wack-job mother of his."

Jack still couldn't speak.

The lieutenant looked at the JAG lawyer and said, "Now I think it's time for me to get back to work." He pushed away from the table, and the lawyer followed.

"Thanks for your time," said Jack.

The lieutenant stopped at the door and said, "You're welcome." He seemed ready to move on, then added, "You want a little free advice, Mr. Swyteck?"

"Sure."

"Not sure what you expected to find when you came down here. But we have two basic rules here at Guantánamo. First, the important stuff is always simple."

"What's the second?"

He smiled wryly and said, "The simple things are always hard."

Jack added a silent "Amen" to that, keeping his thoughts to himself as the two officers shared a little laugh and left the conference room.

16

Hector Torres waited at the end of the pier at the marina. The prosecutor needed to meet with Alejandro Pintado, which was never as easy as summoning him to the U.S. attorney's office. A man like Pintado didn't come to you. He made you come to him, even if you were prosecuting the woman accused of murdering his son. Equally power conscious, Torres was unwilling to get in his ten-year-old Ford and drive to Pintado's waterfront castle like a common servant to Miami's undisputed king of Cuban restaurants. They agreed to meet halfway, but it was Pintado who arrived in style.

A Hatteras 86 Convertible pulled up alongside the dock, eighty-six feet of yachting pleasure that was many times over the value of the prosecutor's modest Hialeah home. One of the crew helped Torres climb aboard and led him across the aft deck into the salon. It was technically a fishing boat, but the feel was more like a custom-built mansion, complete with a mirrored ceiling, club chairs, polished maple coffee table, and a wet bar with hand-crafted teak cabinetry. Pintado was seated on a curved, sectional sofa that faced the entertainment center. He switched off the flat-screen television with the remote and rose to greet his guest.

"Hector, very good to see you."

"Likewise."

They shook hands and patted each other on the shoulder, as close as two men ever seemed to come to hugging each other. Torres could easily have allowed himself to be envious of Pintado's wealth. They were both tireless workers, but Torres had chosen the life of politics and public service, leaving himself far fewer toys to play with as they neared the end of their respective careers. But six years on the Miami-Dade County commission and two terms as mayor had established him as a real player in the local political arena. After a short stint as chief assistant to the U.S. attorney, he cashed in his political chits to become south Florida's top federal prosecutor. Being U.S. attorney was more management than trial work, so the thought of actually getting back in the courtroom to prosecute Lindsey Hart had revitalized him, made him realize that there was nothing in the world more thrilling than trying a big case and winning it. For all his success, Pintado would never experience that high. He might as well die a virgin.

"So how is the case going?" Pintado asked as he filled two glasses with some kind of fancy-pants water that came in a blue bottle. He offered one to his guest and returned to the couch.

Torres said, "The case is going well. It was going

even better before you spoke to Jack Swyteck in Key West. That's why I'm here."

"You're not going to scold me, are you?"

Torres did not return the smile. "You told him about the trust fund."

"Says who?"

"Your personal attorney. I phoned him this morning to let him know that Swyteck was on the case. I reminded him that if Swyteck starts poking around into family financial affairs, don't reveal any details about the trust fund. But he said you'd already let the cat out of the bag."

"So, what's the big deal anyway?"

"That is a key part of our case. It's Lindsey's motive for killing her husband."

"I understand that."

"You needlessly tipped our hand, Alejandro. I purposely did not mention the trust fund to the grand jury so that we could surprise Swyteck with that information at trial."

"Oh, come on. Surely Lindsey would have told him about it before trial."

"You're assuming that his client is being completely forthcoming with him. That's not always the case."

"Well, hell. Okay, I slipped and said something I shouldn't have said. He came to see me, and, frankly, his whole approach bugged me. He tried to bullshit me with this idea that he wants to figure out if his client is innocent before he represents her. So I felt like hitting him between the eyes. I told him about the trust fund. And I have to tell you, the look on his face was worth it."

"No, it's not worth anything. I want the jury to see that look, not you."

"I still believe that he was bound to figure it out sooner or later."

"Then let it be later. I want him to figure out *everything* later. That's the way I'm playing this case. Jack Swyteck is a damn good lawyer. The way to beat him is to make sure he doesn't see what's coming."

"*Bueno.* I'm sorry I said anything. I can't take it back now."

"No, you can't undo it. But I need a commitment from you, Alejandro. I want you to take a vow of silence."

"*No problema.* I'll say not another word to Jack Swyteck."

"I want you to say nothing more to anybody. Unless I tell you to say it."

Pintado poured himself more water, shaking his head. "This is what I left Cuba for, to be able to say what I think."

"Talk all you want—after the case is over. Before then, everything that comes out of your mouth will only help the defense. Unless you clear it with me."

"You make this Swyteck sound like Superman."

"Do you want your daughter-in-law convicted or don't you?" said Torres.

"Of course I do."

"Then work with me."

Pintado took a breath, as if reluctant to yield any kind of control to anyone. "*Bueno.* We'll try it your way."

"You'll be happy you did. Just two simple rules. Always surprise the enemy. And never surprise me."

"I can do that."

"Perfect. So let's have it."

"Have what?"

"You've given me only half of what I need. You agreed not to talk without my blessing. That will make sure we surprise the enemy."

"What else do you want?"

"I just told you. I want no surprises. So I need the skinny on your son."

"My son was a Marine's Marine. There's no dirt on him."

"I've done some checking up. The last thing I need is for Jack Swyteck to figure this out before I do, so tell me something, and tell it to me straight."

"Sure. What do you want to know?"

The prosecutor turned stone-cold serious. "How did your son get to be so buddy-buddy with a slime bucket like Lieutenant Damont Johnson?"

17

Jack and Sofia had a late lunch of rice and beans in the Havana airport. The chef could have used a few pointers from Jack's grandmother, though it was a bit unfair to single him out, since even the Food Network could have used a pointer or two from *Abuela*, whether they wanted help or not.

Havana was an unexpected route home, but they had been given no choice. The next charter flight to Norfolk was two days away, far longer than the navy cared to have two civilian lawyers snooping around the base. At Guantánamo's behest, the Department of the Treasury immediately issued the licenses needed for U.S. citizens to travel lawfully within Cuba—proof positive that the bureaucracy could move when the bureaucrats wanted it to—and Jack and Sofia were whisked away on a commuter flight from Guantánamo City to Havana.

For all the travel, they'd managed just one witness interview and a twenty-minute visit to the crime scene. Amazing as it seemed, the interview was the most productive part of the trip. Lindsey's old house had been completely sanitized—repainted, recarpeted, the works. A young officer and his new bride had been living there for the past three weeks. The military wasn't exactly making it easy for Lindsey's lawyers to follow the investigative trail.

"I want to apologize," said Sofia as they walked to their gate.

"For what?" said Jack.

"For making this trip so difficult."

"What are you talking about? You didn't do anything."

"Sure I did. I got their backs up before we even got here. That JAG lawyer specifically mentioned the comments I made on television after Lindsey's indictment. They clearly are being more difficult because of my suggestion that Oscar may have been killed as part of a government cover-up."

"Don't beat yourself up over that."

"I should have just kept my mouth shut."

"The decision to transfer all those potential witnesses to another base was made at a very high level. Even if you hadn't said anything, they'd be playing these games. An officer in the United States Marine Corps was murdered, and you and I defend the woman whom they believe is the killer. That's all the reason they need to launch into combat readiness."

She gave him a tight smile, as if still embarrassed by her television performance but grateful for Jack's words.

They found a couple of open seats near the gate. Sofia read a magazine, but Jack was thinking about Lindsey Hart. After all, it was Lindsey, in her newspaper interview with the *Guantánamo Gazette*, who'd first gone public with the theory that Oscar was murdered because he "knew too much." In Jack's eyes, that theory had been a stretch from the get-go.

It was even more of a stretch if Lindsey was dialing for dead people on her cell phone.

"Gum?" said Sofia.

"Thanks," said Jack.

At three P.M., they were still waiting at the gate in Havana. Jack had brought a few books and magazines from Miami for the flight, but with the detour through Havana, he'd purposely left them in the path of a janitor and his broom. The guy probably couldn't read English, and he looked too proud for handouts, but he had a wedding ring on his finger and dirt under his nails, so Jack figured he could probably use the Treasury Department–issued Andrew Jackson bookmarks that Jack had left inside.

Nothing to read. No CNN on the tube. No cell phones or laptop computer to check e-mails. The chewing gum lost its flavor in thirty seconds, and Jack kept himself busy folding the empty foil back into its original rectangular shape and trying to re-insert it into the paper sleeve. The flight to Cancún was already more than an hour late in boarding. Once in Mexico, they'd catch another flight for the final leg to Miami. Jack was sitting close enough to the check-in counter to notice dozens of other Americans with the same itinerary, all with great suntans, all *without* travel licenses—and all in defiance of the U.S. government's trade embargo against Cuba.

"Lots of *yanquis* here," said Jack.

Sofia had her nose in her magazine. "What did you expect?"

"I don't understand it. How do they not get into trouble when they pass through U.S. customs with 'Cuba' stamped in their passport?"

"Simple. You fly to Cancún, then you hop another flight to Havana. The Cuban immigration guys know enough not to stamp your passport, but just make sure you put a ten-dollar bill inside when you hand it to them. You fly back to Cancún when you're done, then back to the States. The U.S. government has no way of knowing that you were partying till dawn every night at the Copacabana. They think you were in Cancún. Honest to God, it's that easy."

"Sounds like the only idiots who get caught are the ones who come back with one of those goofy souvenirs that says, 'My parents went to Cuba and all I got was this stupid T-shirt.'"

"Pretty much. Why do you think this trade embargo is such a joke?"

"Just bugs me," said Jack. "People like those two slobs over there."

"What about them?"

"I was listening to them when I bought my coffee. They were practically tripping over their own tongues, talking about how cheap and beautiful the girls are in Havana. Of course they're cheap, you morons. Their own government is starving them to death."

"You surprise me, Swyteck. It's refreshing to know somebody who actually gives a rat's ass about the girls with no choice but to come to the big city and sell their bodies to tourists."

"I surprise a lot of people. My mother was Cuban."

"Really? *Tú hablas español?*" Do you speak Spanish?

"*Sí. Lo aprendí cuando yo era un escurridero.*" Yes, I learned it when I was a drainpipe.

She chuckled and said, "I think you meant, when you were a schoolboy."

"What did I say?"

She was still smiling. "You said it exactly right. I wouldn't change a word of it."

He knew she was lying, and he felt the urge to redeem himself by telling her that he understood the language better than he spoke it. But he let it go.

Sofia said, "Funny, I voted against your old man in two gubernatorial elections. I don't recall hearing anything about his being married to a Latina."

"My mother passed away when I was young. Just a few hours old, actually."

"Oh, how awful. I'm sorry."

"It's okay. Obviously it was a long time ago."

"Was she born in Cuba?"

"Yes. A little town called Bejucal."

"I've heard of it. That's actually not far from here."

"I know. I checked the map before coming over."

"You ever consider going there?"

"Every now and then. Only lately have I gotten serious about it." Jack opened his carry-on bag and removed a photograph from inside a zipped pouch. "This is her," he said as he offered it to Sofia.

"You brought a photograph?"

"I have a few keepsakes that my father and grandmother gave me. Not sure why I brought it. Coming to Cuba for the first time, it just seemed right to have her with me."

"She's beautiful. Just a teenager here, I would guess."

"Yes. Seventeen. It was the last picture taken of her in Cuba."

"Who's that with her?"

"On the back it says 'Celia Méndez.' One look at the picture tells you they were best friends, but I don't know anything more than that. My grandmother doesn't seem to want to talk about Celia very much. I get the impression that she didn't approve of the friendship."

"*Abuelas*," she said, smiling and shaking her head. "They all have their quirks, don't they?"

"Some more than others," said Jack.

A voice over the loudspeaker announced that their plane was finally boarding. Jack and Sofia rose and walked toward the gate with the other ticketed passengers. Twenty minutes later they were inside the plane and in their seats. A few passengers were trying to stuff luggage into the overhead compartments, but nearly everyone had settled in for the flight. Jack was just getting comfortable when he heard his name over the speaker. The message was in Spanish.

"Passengers Sofia Suarez and John Lawrence Swyteck, please identify yourselves by pushing the flight attendant call button."

They looked at each other, not sure what to think. Then Jack reached up and pushed the button. The flight attendant came to them. "Please come with me," she said in Spanish.

"Both of us?"

"Yes."

They rose, but as they started up the aisle the flight attendant stopped and said, "Please, bring your carry-on luggage with you."

"What's this about?" asked Sofia.

"Please, gather your things and come with me."

She was pleasant enough, but the vibes weren't good. Heads turned with suspicion as they proceeded up the long, narrow aisle. The flight attendant led them completely off the plane, and they continued walking toward the gate.

"I told you not to hand out money to janitors," Sofia muttered.

"Something tells me that's not what this is about," said Jack.

Three men dressed in military uniforms were waiting at the gate. Each was carrying an impressive large-caliber pistol in a black leather holster. The two younger men also bore automatic rifles. The flight attendant handed over the passengers to the leader, a more mature-looking man who appeared to be of some higher rank that Jack was unable to pinpoint. He asked to see their passports, which they presented. As he inspected their documents, the airplane backed out of the gate and started toward the runway. The soldier kept their passports and said, "This way, please."

Evidently, they weren't leaving Cuba anytime soon.

Jack and Sofia followed directly behind the older man, and the two younger soldiers flanked them on either side. They walked for several minutes through the busy airport, three pairs of military boot heels clicking on the tile floors. They exited the main terminal through a long and hot hallway, passing through several sets of doors along the way, the last of which bore a sign that read in Spanish, RESTRICTED AREA—AUTHORIZED PERSONNEL ONLY. The lead officer opened it with a key, and the group continued its journey with hardly a break in stride. There was another long hallway, and they walked straight to the door at the other end. The man knocked once and said, "Excuse me, Colonel. I have the Americans."

The voice on the other side replied, "Enter."

He opened the door and then immediately assumed the rigid pose of a military salute. A simple command from the man inside put him at ease, and he nudged the Americans forward.

Sofia shot Jack a look as if to say that "ladies first" was for lifeboats and cocktail parties. Jack entered, and she followed.

Jack's eyes had to adjust to the lights, which were shining straight at his face. The room was windowless, but there was a large mirror built into the wall, undoubtedly a one-way gizmo that concealed the observers on the other side. The floors were unfinished concrete. The walls were cinder blocks that had been painted a bright white. Two uncomfortable wooden chairs were situated in the middle of the room, side by side, facing the lights. Even if he hadn't been nervous, Jack would have been sweating. It was one of those interrogation rooms that could just as easily serve as a torture chamber, the kind of place from which you'd expect both screams and confessions to flow freely.

A man dressed in simple green combat fatigues

stepped forward. His uniform was wholly unimpressive, yet he seemed to exude confidence as he spoke to the Americans in near-perfect English.

"Please, sit," he said in a voice that sounded way too friendly to be sincere. "The people of Cuba are eager to speak to you about your case."

18

"**A**re those lights really necessary?" said Jack, shielding his eyes.

The colonel walked around the table and flipped a wall switch. The spotlights went out, and the sudden contrast from bright light to normal made the room seem much darker than it actually was. The colonel pulled a ten-inch cigar from his shirt pocket, and another man immediately stepped forward to light it. The man was so quick and obsequious that he could only have been the colonel's personal aide. The colonel puffed hard on one end, rolling the other across a six-inch flame. Jack and Sofia were soon shrouded in a cloud of cigar smoke.

"My name is Colonel Raúl Jiménez," he said as the thick smoke poured from his nostrils. "The people of Cuba thank you for coming."

Jack glanced left, then right. "Funny, I don't see them here."

The colonel smiled, but it faded quickly. "You're looking at them."

With the wave of his hand, the armed soldiers

left the room. The colonel's aide remained at attention, standing off to the side.

"*Gracias*," said Sofia.

At first Jack wasn't sure why she was thanking him, but he too felt more comfortable with the automatic weapons out of the room.

"My purpose here is not to frighten you," said the colonel. "I wish only to do you a favor."

"Why do I doubt that?" said Jack.

"You are such a skeptic, *Señor* Swyteck."

"I can't help it. I'm a lawyer."

"True, very true. Tell me. How did your interview with Lieutenant Johnson go this morning?"

Jack and Sofia looked at each other, not sure how he knew.

The colonel said, "You don't think anything happens on that base that we don't know about, do you?"

"I haven't given it much thought," said Jack.

"We're sitting right on the other side of the razor wire. We watch them; they watch us. It's the way the game is played in Guantánamo. Has been for forty years. So tell me: How did your little talk with the lieutenant go?"

"You don't really expect me to discuss that with you, do you?"

He laughed heartily. "Just as I thought. He told you *nada*."

"Colonel, what is it that you want from us?"

"Just a few minutes of your time." He rose and started to pace, waving his cigar as he spoke. "Let me make a few educated assumptions here. One, the U.S. government didn't let you talk to anyone but Lieutenant Johnson, did they?"

Jack didn't answer.

"Two," said the colonel, "anyone who might know anything about the murder of Captain Pintado has been reassigned, no? Persian Gulf, maybe? Or perhaps Guam?"

He glanced at Sofia and then at Jack. It was clear he didn't expect an answer, but he didn't seem to need one. "Seems to me that you are getting the brick house here."

"Stonewall," said his aide.

"Stonewall, yes. Brick house is something else entirely, no?" He was looking at Sofia with that last remark. Women served extensively in the Cuban military, but machismo was still alive and kicking.

Jack said, "Colonel, unless you're going to put bamboo shoots under our fingernails, we're not going to tell you what was said at the naval base. Even then, I'd just make it all up."

"There's nothing you need to tell me, *Señor* Swyteck. All you have to do is listen."

"Okay. My ears are open."

"Like I said, we know you met with Lieutenant Johnson, because we are watching that base constantly. Twenty-four/seven."

"I would expect nothing less."

"Then it should come as no surprise that we saw—how shall I put this? We saw things of interest at your client's home on the night the captain left this world."

Jack's interest was suddenly piqued. "I'd like to hear about it."

The colonel flashed a sly smile, the smoldering cigar clenched between his teeth. "I bet you would."

"Come on, Colonel. I hope you didn't invite us in here just to play the 'I know a secret' game. What do you have?"

"A vigilant Cuban soldier. Watching from a guard tower through night-vision binoculars."

"What did he see?"

"Something that can prove that your client did not murder her husband."

Jack's pulse quickened. *Could this be true?* "I need specifics," said Jack.

"Not so fast. Before I offer up one of my own soldiers on a silver platter, I need to know: What are you offering in exchange?"

"Colonel, I'm in no position to deal with the Cuban military for the testimony of one of its soldiers."

"I'm confident that the son of Florida's former governor will find something to please us."

"I'm not looking to please you. And even if I were, the testimony of a Cuban soldier in a Miami courtroom will have huge repercussions. Need I remind you, Colonel, that this community nearly exploded over the return of a seven-year-old boy named Elián to his Cuban father?"

"*Claro*," he said. "You simply have to ask yourself up front: Is the woman accused of killing the son of a powerful Cuban exile willing to stake her defense on the sworn testimony of Fidel Castro's loyal soldier?"

The question nearly knocked Jack off his chair. The colonel had framed it perfectly. "I need some time to think this through," said Jack.

"*Bueno.* You have twenty-four hours."

"I'd like more than that."

"I'm not offering more than that. Take it or leave it."

Jack glanced at Sofia, and they quickly came to a silent understanding. Jack said, "All right, Colonel. Let's talk again at tomorrow's end."

"Good. You've already missed your flight, so enjoy your little overnight visit in beautiful Havana. You are the honored guests of the people of Cuba."

"Meaning you?" said Jack.

He smiled broadly, sucking on his cigar. "*Sí.* Meaning me."

19

Four decades of communism had not robbed Havana of its heart. But it was badly in need of angioplasty.

Everywhere Jack looked, he could find things old, things broken, things that seemed straight out of a world that had existed before he was even born. They rode in a taxi that had the hood of a 1956 Chevrolet, the back end of a 1959 Ford, and the interior of something just a cut above an ox cart. Their driver was a surgeon who earned more in tips than practicing medicine. He gave Jack and Sofia a driving tour of La Habana Vieja (Old Havana), a historic section of a magnificent city that could be either charming or appalling, depending on how closely you looked. Jack tried to envision it as his mother might have seen it as a teenager, an architectural marvel that boasted some of the most impressive cathedrals, plazas, and colonial mansions in the Caribbean. Over eight hundred of its historically significant structures were built *before* the twentieth century, some dating back to the 1500s. But after

decades of neglect, many of these irreplaceable structures had suffered irreversible damage, and recent
restoration efforts aimed at bolstering tourism were
simply too little, too late. Despite some convincing
paint jobs and face-lifts, it was impossible to ignore
the many sagging roofs and crumbling walls. Some
parts of south La Habana Vieja resembled Berlin in
late 1944, whole sections of walls missing, buildings
on the verge of collapse but for the tenuous support
of wood scaffolding, entire neighborhoods seemingly held together by crisscrossing ropes and wires
from which residents hung the morning laundry.

An old woman on a third-floor balcony was haul-
ing up a bucket on a rope.

"No plumbing?" Jack asked the the cabdriver.

"Not here, *señor*. If you go for walking, is *muy
importante* that you look over you head. Is not so bad
if you get spill from buckets going up. But the ones
coming down . . ."

"*Yo comprendo*," said Jack. I understand.

They continued west along the waterfront on the
broad and busy Avenida Maceo, stopping at the Hotel Nacional. The driver would have been more
than happy to continue the city tour, but Jack tipped
him extra to cut it short.

"*Gracias*," Jack said as he handed him a couple of
twenties. It was about a month's worth of wages for
a physician.

Hotel Nacional was the vintage 1930 grand dame
of Havana hotels, perched on a bluff with postcard
views of Havana Harbor. Its architect had also designed the famous Breakers Hotel in Palm Beach,
and it was built in a similar Spanish style, entered

via a long driveway that was lined with slender Royal Palms. The lobby screamed of opulence if not ostentatiousness, with mosaic floors, Moorish arches, and lofty, beamed ceilings. Jack looked around, saw the tourists at the bar sipping lime daiquiris and rum *mojitos*. He spotted another group of businessmen feasting on shrimp as big as their fists and lobster with drawn butter. He heard *salsa* music from the nightclub, the laughter of people dancing, the chatter of wealthy Europeans on holiday.

And then he heard the desk clerk's reminder: "One last thing, *señor*. Locals are not permitted in the hotel. It's the law, and I'm required to tell you that. So please don't bring them here."

"Sure thing," said Jack. With bitter irony he was reminded of an old Miami tourism slogan: "Miami—See It Like a Native." Here, the slogan should have been "Cuba—See It Like ANYTHING BUT a Native."

Jack and Sofia took separate rooms on the recently refurbished sixth floor. Jack pulled back the curtains and opened the window to take in the view. A warm, gentle breeze caressed his face. Looking east he saw Havana Harbor, where the explosion of the *Maine* had sparked the Spanish-American War. Somewhere to the west, he knew, was the town of Mariel, the launching point for the infamous boatlift that had brought a quarter of a million Cubans—"Marielitos"—to Miami in the early 1980s. Most had assimilated just fine, but twenty-five thousand of them had come from Castro's prisons, and at least one of them was convicted of murder again and had ended up on Florida's death row. Jack knew that one well, because the young and only son of Governor Harold Swyteck had been his lawyer—until he was executed in the electric chair.

Jack felt a slight queasiness in his belly.

The phone rang. He stepped back inside and answered it. The woman spoke in Spanish.

"Are you lonely, handsome?"

It took Jack a moment to translate in his head, and he wasn't sure he'd heard her correctly. Then he chuckled and said, "Cut it out, Sofia."

"My name is not Sofia. But I can be Sofia if you want me to be. I can be anyone at all. I can do whatever you want, whenever you want, however many times you want. Have you ever had a girl of sixteen? All you have to do is—"

Jack hung up. Obviously the bellboy or the doorman or someone had passed the word that an American man was alone in room 603. The desk clerk's admonition—no locals in the hotel—echoed in his mind.

Yeah, right. And drugs are strictly prohibited in Miami Beach nightclubs.

Jack took a seat on the edge of the bed—the very edge. He wondered how many sixteen-year-old Cuban girls had lain across these sheets, and then he recalled those two pigs in the airport talking about how cheap and gorgeous the women were here. He grabbed the phone and dialed Sofia's room. She answered on the third ring.

"Sofia, hey. It's Jack."

"What's up?"

"I wanted to let you know: I'm checking out of here."

"You don't like your room?"

"The room's fine. I just don't want to stay here."

"Where do you want to go?"

He didn't answer right away. His mind flashed with visions of his grandmother living in some dumpy house for thirty-eight years with hardly anything to eat. He thought of *Abuela* saying good-bye to his mother, spiriting her away to Miami, unaware at the time that she'd never see her teenage daughter again. He thought of the rum-guzzling, shrimp-gorging, cigar-smoking tourists and the young girls who became whores.

But the one image Jack couldn't conjure up was that of a little Havana suburb, the town in which the mother he'd never known had lived most of her too-short life.

"I'm going to Bejucal," he said.

20

·

Two hours later Jack and Sofia were in a rental car approaching the outskirts of Bejucal.

"You didn't have to come," said Jack.

"How were you planning to get around without me?" asked Sofia.

"My Spanish is fairly functional."

"I've heard you speak, Jack. And while it's very impressive that you were able to learn Spanish while you were a drainpipe, it probably wouldn't get you very far in a small town."

"A drainpipe? Is that what I said?"

She smiled. "It's okay. Your Spanish is really pretty good."

"How good?"

"Probably just good enough to get you beat up and ripped off. Which is why I came along."

"Oh, so you're here to protect me, are you?"

"No. I came to *watch* you get beat up and ripped off. Beats the heck out of Cuban television."

Touché, he thought.

The actual driving time from Havana was only

thirty minutes, and they reached Bejucal around dinnertime. *Abuela* had often told him that it was the prettiest town in all of Havana Province, and she was probably right. There were colonial facades everywhere, and just enough of them were freshly painted to allow the imagination to color in the rest. In the heart of town was a quaint little square with an ocher-colored colonial church. It was precious enough in its own right, but for Jack, just the sight of the old church took his breath away. His mother had been baptized there. The Cine Martí was nearby, and Jack wondered if his mother had ever gone there with her friends, or maybe even a boyfriend, dreaming of being an American movie star. Then his gaze drifted toward a billboard at the end of the square that read, *SOCIALISMO O MUERTE* (Socialism or death), and at once he understood *Abuela*'s comment about Bejucal: It was exactly as it was forty years ago; and it was totally different.

"You okay?" asked Sofia.

Jack had been unaware, but they'd spent that last few minutes stopped at an intersection for no apparent reason. He'd been absorbing it all. "Yeah," he said, shaking it off. "Just spacing out a bit there."

"You hungry? The Restaurante El Gallo looks pretty good."

"Sure," said Jack.

Jack parked the car, and they walked to the restaurant and took a table near the window. The house specialized in *criollo* dishes, so Jack ordered roasted chicken and *plátanos a puñetazos*. The waitress was extremely friendly, and naturally she recognized them as tourists. She insisted that they visit Plaza Martí, which she claimed was the setting for the movie *Paradiso*, based on the novel by José Lezama Lima. Jack didn't know if that was true or not, but it made him smile to hear it, as if it had been his own small town featured in a motion picture. In a way, it *was* his town.

Dinner was pleasant enough, and their waitress brought them mango slices for dessert. She seemed to take a genuine interest in making sure that they enjoyed their visit to Bejucal, so Jack thought he'd push his luck.

"Have you ever heard of a woman named Celia Méndez?" he asked.

She scrunched her face, thinking. "I know a couple of Méndez families. But not a Celia Méndez. How old is she?"

Jack pulled the old photograph of his mother and Celia Méndez from his pocket. It made him nervous to play this hand. All these years, he'd figured that Celia Méndez, his mother's best friend in Cuba, would be his best source of information about his mother. But what if it didn't pan out?

He showed the snapshot to the waitress and said, "This was taken over forty years ago. So I'd guess she's probably close to sixty."

The waitress shook her head, no recognition. "Sorry. Can't help you. But there is a Méndez who runs a *casa particular* over on Calle Martí. That family has lived in Bejucal for years. Why don't you stop by there? Maybe they can help you."

"Thanks. We'll do that."

She wrote down the address for them. Jack paid the bill in U.S. dollars, the only currency that seemed to matter in "communist" Cuba, and they left.

The literal translation of *casa particular* was "private home," and for many travelers there was no better accommodation in Cuba than to rent a room from a Cuban family. It had been illegal to rent housing in Cuba after the revolution, but all that changed with the fall of the Soviet Union and the Cuban government's need to find a new "superpower" (read: tourism) to prop up its failing economy. A new law in 1996 allowed Cubans to rent out one or two rooms in their homes, and soon afterward thousands of *casas particulares* popped up across the country, providing a hefty sum in tax revenues to a dictator who was clearly more interested in self-perpetuation than communist principle.

La Casa Méndez was a simple but tidy house facing a cobblestone street. A plump woman with dark skin and a bright yellow headband in her hair greeted them at the door. She was at most fifty, Jack surmised, too young to be his mother's friend Celia. She introduced herself as Felicia Méndez Ortiz. Rather than diving into his detective role with a slew of questions about Celia Méndez, Jack decided to break the ice with a simple business inquiry.

"Do you have a room available?"

"Yes," she said in a pleasant voice. "Just one."

"May we see it, please?"

"Of course. Come in."

The room was in the back of the house near the kitchen. There were two twin beds, a dresser, and an old rug on the floor. The annoying glow from a lamp with no shade was the only light in the room. They had walked past the living room and two other bedrooms to get there. Jack counted eleven people in the house, seven adults and four children. The Cuban woman explained that the big advantage of staying at a *casa particular* was that you get to live with a Cuban family, but the big disadvantage was that you get to live with a Cuban family.

"We'll take it," said Sofia.

"What?" said Jack.

She switched to English, for Jack's ears only. "If you're really good, I'll let you push the beds together. But don't count on it."

He knew she was kidding. "I was only being polite when I asked to see the room. I wasn't actually planning on staying here."

"You want to give this nice family your money, or you want to go back to Hotel Nacional?"

"You sure you're okay with this?"

"I had a male roommate all through law school. Nothing ever happened, and he was even cuter than you."

Jack wasn't sure if that was a compliment or an insult, but it didn't matter. "Okay. If you're up for it, we'll stay." He looked at the woman and said in Spanish, "We'll take it."

She smiled and led them to the kitchen. They sat around the table, and she recorded their names and passport numbers. And, of course, she offered them something to eat. It was a genetic thing, Jack decided, this Cuban compulsion to offer food to a guest even when there was none in the house. Jack and Sofia declined, but they did take the *café*. It was hot and strong, and the smell of roasted beans reminded Jack of *Abuela*'s kitchen. Jack had just about finished his cup when he decided it was time to share the photograph.

He laid it on the table and asked, "Do you happen to know a woman named Celia Méndez?"

The woman set her cup on the table. A smile crept to her lips as she examined the photograph. "You know Celia?"

"No. My mother did."

"Don't tell me your mother was Ana," she said.

Jack's heart thumped. *She knew!* "Yes. Ana Maria Fuentes."

She studied Jack's face, then glanced back at the photograph. She brought a hand to her mouth, as if astonished that so much time had passed. "Now I see it. You look very much like your beautiful mother. Celia and she were the best, best of friends. It broke her heart when she heard that she passed away. Such a shame." She shuddered, seemingly embarrassed by her own insensitivity. "Forgive me. I am sorry for your loss, as well, of course."

"Thank you. Did you know my mother?"

"A little. I was only seven—no, eight—years old when Ana left for America. Celia was my oldest sister."

Again, his pulse quickened. "Where can I find Celia?"

She blinked twice, then lowered her eyes. "Celia is dead."

Jack's heart sank, and his "Oh, no" was involuntary.

"She passed away last March. It was very sudden. Heart attack."

"I'm sorry. I know it may be difficult for you to talk about her, but if there's anything you remember about Celia and my mother, I would love to hear about them."

"I have some things, yes. But it's hard for me to know what I remember and what I remember Celia telling me, if you see the difference."

"Yes, I do. Whatever you can tell me, that's all I want to know."

The sadness seemed to drain away. Thinking of a much younger Celia was lifting the woman's spirits. "Celia and Ana were inseparable," she said with a nostalgic grin. "They did everything together. It was Celia who introduced your mother to her first boyfriend."

"Do you remember his name?"

"No, I don't. But Ana's mother—your grand-mother—didn't like him one bit. She didn't like Celia, either. Mostly because it was Celia who in-troduced this boy to her daughter."

"What was wrong with him?"

"Nothing, as far as I know."

"Why was my grandmother so against him?"

She winced a little. "Your grandmother has never talked to you about Ana's boyfriend, has she?"

"No. Tell me."

"Are you sure you want to know everything?"

"Yes. Believe me, I wouldn't have come here if I weren't sure."

She took a deep breath, then said, "Your mother got pregnant."

Jack went cold.

She nodded toward the photograph and said,

"She's probably with child in that photograph. She was just seventeen when it happened."

"Are you sure?" asked Jack.

"Oh, yes. I'm not mistaken about this. We're talking over forty years ago. A teenage girl, pregnant? This was quite the scandal in Bejucal. I don't remember everything that happened when I was eight years old. But I remember that."

"Did she—" Jack hesitated, afraid to ask. "Did my mother have the child?"

"I'm not sure I ever knew exactly what happened. I remember hearing that she was pregnant. I heard people talk about it. And it wasn't the next day, but it was pretty soon afterward that Ana Maria was on her way to Miami."

"Was she pregnant when she left?"

"I don't know. Really, I don't."

They sat in silence for a moment, Jack staring into his empty cup. The woman rose, as if sensing Jack's sudden need for some time to himself. "Excuse me, but I must check on the grandchild," she said, and she left the room.

Sofia stayed with him for a minute, and finally he looked at her. She seemed on the verge of saying something, then simply gave him a thin but sad smile of support, patted the back of his hand, and left him alone at the table.

The streetlight outside their bedroom window shined through slatted Venetian blinds, casting zebralike stripes across the twin beds. Jack was nearest the door. Sofia lay in the bed by the window. The room had no clock, but Jack knew it was late. He hadn't been able to close his eyes, let alone fall asleep.

"Jack?" Sofia said in the darkness. "You up?"

"Mmm-hmm."

"Are you okay? I mean, about what Felicia told you?"

He chuckled without heart. "Not exactly what I expected to hear."

"I know."

Silence returned. A car passed outside their window, and the headlights swept across the wall.

"Jack?"

"Yes?"

"Does this feel weird to you?"

"Does what feel weird?"

"Sleeping in the same room with me."

"Uhm. A little."

"When's the last time you slept in twin beds?"

He thought about it, then realized that it was with his ex-wife, one of the last trips they had taken together. Separate beds. The beginning of the end. "I don't really remember."

"I'm not trying to get weird on you, but for some strange reason this reminds me of when I was a teenager. My sister and I shared a room with twin beds. We would stay up at night and talk about all kinds of things. Boys. Soccer. Clothes. Mostly boys."

"Are you saying I remind you of your sister?"

"Hardly. I'm not sure why that popped into my head. I guess I was just reminded of how much I miss those days. Something made me think of it."

"Maybe it was the fact that no one bothered to tell me that I might have a brother or sister."

She propped herself up on one elbow, and even in the dim light Jack could see the horrified expression on her face. "Oh, I'm sorry. I didn't mention my sister in order to . . . I wasn't comparing your situation to—"

"It's okay," he said.

She lowered her head back onto the pillow. She was lying on her side, the thin, white bedsheet clinging to the gentle curve of her hip, the narrow band of light coming through the Venetian blinds reflecting on her hair. Jack rolled on his side, facing her, the gap between the twin beds separating them. But in the darkness, it was almost as if the gap weren't there.

"Funny," said Jack.

"What?"

"This thing with my mother. In my mind, I'd built this lofty image of a young woman in search of freedom. She leaves her family behind, leaves her friends behind, leaves everything behind, and somehow finds the courage to face a completely new world."

"No one has taken that image away. It just has a new twist to it."

"At least now I understand why my grandmother never wanted to talk about it."

"She's an old woman. It's natural for someone of her generation to sweep it under the rug. It must have hurt her terribly to hear people say her daughter was a troubled teen running away from her problems."

"But at some point I have a right to know, don't I?"

"A right to know what?"

Jack looked off to the middle distance, to the darkness beyond Sofia. "About my half sibling—the child she left behind."

"You don't know for sure that your mother had the child."

"You're right. But I still want to know."

"I suppose there's one person who could tell you."

Jack thought for a moment, then said, "All I have to do is figure out a way to ask without slicing *Abuela*'s heart to ribbons."

"Good luck," said Sofia as she rolled onto her back.

Jack fluffed his pillow and said, "Don't let me oversleep."

There was just enough light for Jack to see the smile on her lips.

"What?" he said.

"We're sharing a house with eleven Cubans. If that doesn't wake you, I'll be sure to notify your next of kin."

"Good point."

"Good night, Jack."

"Good night, Sofia."

21

A t nine o'clock the following morning Jack and Sofia were on the third floor of one of the many architecturally unremarkable buildings on the Plaza de la Revolución. The plaza was the hub of Cuban government. Through the window, Jack could see the headquarters for the powerful Ministry of the Interior, from which a monumental image of Ché was positioned perfectly to watch the endless political rallies that took place periodically on the vast square. Ché looked a little bored, thought Jack, which was fitting, since some of Castro's speeches had been known to stretch as long as fourteen hours. The plaza was quiet this morning, and Jack and Sofia sat alone in an office, waiting.

Colonel Raúl Jiménez entered the room with an officer's confidence, greeted them cordially, and took a seat behind his desk. "Have you made a decision?"

"Yes," said Jack. "I'm willing to listen to what your soldier has to say. But I'm not making any promises in return."

"That's a shame. It isn't often that I'm able to make such a generous offer."

"I appreciate that. But we are forced to deal with certain realities. Let's be honest. From the standpoint of pure trial strategy, eliciting testimony from one of Castro's soldiers could easily turn a jury against my client. Simple mathematics dictates that at least half the jury could be Cuban Americans."

"Yes, and the other half will not be Cuban American. I'm no lawyer, but isn't it a fact that you are required to convince only *one* juror that your client is innocent? That's all it takes for your client to be found not guilty, no?"

"True. But even without speaking to my client, I know she's not going to be doing cartwheels at the thought of putting her own fate in the hands of a Cuban soldier."

"How does she feel about death by lethal injection?"

"You ask good questions, Colonel."

He leaned back in his chair, hands clasped behind his head. The green uniform was darkened with sweat beneath his armpits. "I'm not asking for much in return, Mr. Swyteck. Just offer me something to make it worth our trouble to send one of our soldiers to testify in Miami."

"Is it money you want?"

"Not at all."

"Then spell it out. What are you after?"

The colonel leaned closer, his eyes narrowing. "After Captain Pintado was shot, we heard your client talking on a radio show out of Guantánamo. She was quite outspoken. She said she believes that her husband was killed because of something he knew. Something that was going on at the base that the government did not want the world to know about."

"That's been her position all along."

"Then, there it is," said the colonel. "We want to know: What secret did Captain Pintado know?"

"I can't promise to deliver something like that."

"Why not?"

"For a lot of reasons. Most importantly, because I'm not going to barter with you for testimony. Putting a Cuban soldier on the witness stand presents a ton of credibility problems as it is. Throw in a side deal—whatever it might be—and those credibility issues become insurmountable."

"No one is saying that we must disclose our agreement."

"Easy for you to say, Colonel. It's not your bar license on the line."

"So, is that your position? No deal?"

"I'm willing to call your soldier as a witness. I'm not willing to compensate you in any way, shape, or form for his testimony."

"Perhaps your client will feel differently once she understands the nature of his testimony."

Jack hesitated, then asked, "What will he say?"

The colonel leaned into his desk. His dark eyes glistened beneath the fluorescent lighting. "In general terms, he will testify as follows. On the morning of Captain Pintado's death, he saw your client leave for work. Ten to fifteen minutes later, he saw a man come to the house, go inside, then leave in a hurry."

Jack was silent, but Sofia said, "That's incredibly helpful."

"That's not all," said the colonel. "He will tell you who that man is."

"You mean to tell me that your soldier can identify this person by name?"

"That's exactly what I'm saying."

It was as if the air had suddenly been sucked from the room. Jack looked askance at Sofia, but she seemed stunned into silence. Finally, Jack said, "I'm worried about this."

"What is there to be worried about?"

"Your motivations."

"Meaning what?"

"It all comes back to the victim. He's the son of Alejandro Pintado. It's no secret that Mr. Pintado has been a burr under Castro's saddle. He's even been accused of invading Cuban airspace to drop anti-Castro leaflets over Havana. Seems to me that Castro wouldn't mind giving Mr. Pintado a little indigestion at trial to go along with his grief over the death of his son."

"That's not what this is about."

"But that's exactly the way it will play in Miami. Wouldn't it be just oh so clever for Castro to inject one of his own soldiers into the trial of the accused killer of Alejandro Pintado's son and get her off scot free?"

"Just because El Presidente holds no love for Mr. Pintado does not make the soldier's testimony false."

They were suddenly locked in a tense triangle of silence—Jack, Sofia, the colonel.

Sofia said, "Maybe we should speak to our client."

The colonel offered the telephone, sliding it across his desktop.

"Thanks, but no thanks," said Jack. "My position is firm: I'll take the testimony, but I'm not cutting any deals with the Cuban government."

"You drive a hard bargain, Mr. Swyteck."

"It's the only way to get this done."

The colonel shrugged and said, "Then it won't get done."

"What?" said Sofia. She appeared to be on the verge of begging for reconsideration, but Jack rose, and she followed his lead.

"I guess we have nothing more to talk about," said the colonel.

"I guess not," said Jack.

The colonel gave him a flat, respectful grin, as if he'd met a worthy opponent. He offered his hand, and Sofia shook it. Jack didn't.

"Have a safe trip home," said the colonel.

Jack said good-bye and left the office, following the colonel's aide to the exit.

22

•

Not since his ex-wife had dragged him to the Valentine's Day "red dress ball" had Jack seen so many women dressed alike. Dozens of them, most between the ages of twenty-five and thirty-four, many college educated. The vast majority had gotten into trouble with drugs, which was yet another similarity to that high-class charity ball that Jack was strangely reminded of, except that no one here had a doctor's prescription.

Lindsey Hart was seated at a small Formica table, wearing the orange prison garb of the Federal Detention Center of Miami, an administrative facility for men and women. A guard took Jack to the private cubicle reserved for attorney-client communications. The instant the door closed and the two of them were alone, Lindsey was on her feet, hugging Jack tightly.

"I'm so glad you're here," she said.

Jack hadn't expected that. He had his briefcase in one hand and patted her on the back with the other.

She pulled away and brushed her hair out of her face, sniffling back tears.

"I'm sorry," she said. "I didn't mean to make you feel awkward. This place is just so awful."

"I understand."

"I mean truly awful," she said, her voice quaking. "If you're not bored out of your mind, you're terrified to death. Some women don't like the way you look. Some don't like the way you talk. Some smell like they haven't bathed since childhood. The woman in the next cell is bucking for an insanity defense and keeps playing with her feces, which, believe it or not, doesn't stink half as bad as last night's dinner. Boiled cabbage. Who the hell can live on boiled cabbage? I just don't know if I can take this. The noises, the tension, the other women watching me in the showers. I feel like the new piece of ass on the market, and all the lifers are deciding which one gets to trade up for the fresh goods. Some of the guards are even worse."

Jack listened, but what could he say—that she'd get used to it? That he'd have her out of here in no time, don't worry about it? He just let her vent.

"I miss Brian so much."

She seemed on the verge of major tears. Her hands covered her face, and Jack noticed that she'd been biting several of her fingernails—something he hadn't noticed before. On impulse, Jack gave *her* a hug this time. It seemed to help. She blinked back her emotion, pulled herself together. They took seats on opposite sides of the table.

"I'm sorry I wasn't able to apologize to you in person for the way I fired you," she said with one last sniffle. "But apparently Sofia conveyed my feelings to you."

"She did," said Jack. "So, let's put that behind us, all right?"

"Okay, deal. I'm dying to hear how the trip went. Tell me about your meeting with the esteemed Lieutenant Damont Johnson."

"He had nice things to say about your husband."

"Of course he did. Oscar always bought his beer."

Jack paused to choose his words. "He was less kind in his remarks about you."

"What do you expect? Everyone at the base thinks I killed my husband."

"It went beyond that. He said he's concerned for your son. He thinks you're not equipped to raise him on your own."

Her expression tightened, and Jack could see the anger fighting to escape from somewhere deep within. But she kept control. "What does he mean, 'not equipped'?"

"Those were my words, not his. He believes you're bipolar."

She fell silent. Jack waited for a response, then asked gently, "Are you?"

"What if I am?"

"I'm not making a judgment. I'm just gathering facts."

"No. I'm not bipolar."

"Are you on any kind of medication?"

"Did Lieutenant Johnson say I was?"

"I think the way he put it was that you're a nice person so long as you take your medication."

She pursed her lips and said, "I had a prescription

for some anti-anxiety medication. I took it for about two years. I haven't taken it since I left Guantánamo."

"Why did you stop?"

"I didn't need it anymore."

Jack recalled the drastic change in temperament between the day she'd hired him and the day she'd fired him, which made him wonder about the self-diagnosis. "That's kind of curious," he said.

"What?"

"I'm thinking like a prosecutor. You felt that you needed anti-anxiety medication while your husband was alive. You don't need it now that he's dead."

"Oscar wasn't my source of anxiety. It was about life in Guantánamo."

"Anything in particular?"

"Oh, I don't know," she said with a touch of sarcasm. "Maybe it's because I lived on a communist island that is controlled by the longest-living dictator of the twentieth century, a man who hates Americans with a passion. Or maybe it's because I used to wake up every day wondering if today was the day the chemical weapons would come flying over the razor wire or the Hazmat team would find anthrax in my son's classroom. Or could it have possibly been that six hundred of the world's most dangerous terrorists were in a detention camp right down the road from my house? Or because my husband had a job that required him to put his life on the line every day of the year? You pick one."

"Did your husband have any idea how much you hated it there?"

"I didn't hate it. But Oscar loved it. At least until the very end."

"I guess it's fair to say that you were going to be living in fear—as long as Oscar was alive."

"I didn't kill my husband in order to get off the island, if that's your implication."

"It's not my implication. But it does tie in nicely with your motivation to get your hands on Oscar's trust fund and to get off the island and enjoy life. We should expect the prosecution to play that angle."

"It won't work. Like I said, Oscar was beginning to have a change of heart before he died. He was making more and more comments about how it might be time for us to leave Guantánamo. Why would I kill him when he finally started to talk about leaving?"

"Did he put in for a formal transfer?"

"No."

"Is there anyone but you who can substantiate the fact that he was thinking about leaving Guantánamo?"

"Not that I know of."

"Did you mention it to one of your friends? Maybe your friend in Washington? Nancy what's her name. The one who is married to the chairman of the Joint Chiefs of Staff."

Lindsey bristled, seeming to realize that he was testing her. "I haven't spoken to her in a very long time."

"Good thing," said Jack. "She's dead."

She averted her eyes and said, "I found that out only after I put on that little show for you at Deli Lane."

"Lieutenant Johnson says you did the same show

for him in Guantánamo. What's it all about, Lindsey?"

She sighed, seemingly embarrassed. "Truth is, I did meet her once. And she did give me her phone number. We weren't exactly girlfriends, and I admit, I did throw her name around a little, just for effect. It was wrong of me to do it, but . . . I don't know. The military can be such a 'who you know' environment, and an officer's spouse can feel like such an ornament. It does strange things to your self-esteem. Makes you do stupid things to try to impress people. I guess I did it with you, too. I'm sorry about that."

"Lieutenant Johnson would have had me believe that you were walking around Guantánamo talking to dead people on your cell phone."

"He's such a jerk. First of all, I don't talk to dead people. Second, it's just like him to twist the story and say it was a cell phone, which is his way of making me look even crazier. Last time I checked, civilian cell phones aren't much good in Guantánamo. It was a Palm Pilot, not a cell phone. But that's the way he operates. Whenever he has something to hide, he goes on the offensive."

"You've seen him do that before?"

"Sure. Here's a perfect example. After Oscar was killed, I decided to stay at Guantánamo as long as possible. I wanted to be there, eyes and ears open, until I found out who the bastard was who came into our home and shot him. Lieutenant Johnson was one of the first to complain to Oscar's commanding officer and say I should be kicked off the base because I was bad for morale."

"It's pretty clear that he thinks you shot your husband."

"No kidding. But did he tell you why he wanted me off the base *before* the NCIS report came back? Hell, he wanted me off the base before Oscar's body was cold."

"Maybe he knew what the report was going to say."

She raised an eyebrow, and Jack realized the implications of his observation. Lindsey said, "I'm so glad to hear you say that. Nice to know I'm not the only one who understands that the fix was in when that report named me the chief suspect. What else did Lieutenant Johnson have to say for himself?"

"I didn't get to ask him many questions about your husband's death. Every five minutes the JAG lawyer kept reminding him that he could leave any time he wanted, and he finally picked up on the hint."

"Who else did you get to talk to?"

"No one. Everyone else on my witness list has been transferred to another base."

"Unbelievable. Did you at least get to visit my house?"

"Only for a few minutes. The investigators released the crime scene two weeks ago. Someone else is living there now. The place has been scrubbed and repainted."

"That was it, then? You went all the way down there, and all you got was one partial interview and a quick stop at a cleaned-up crime scene?"

"Afraid so. From the moment we met with Lieutenant Johnson, it seemed they couldn't get Sofia and me off the base fast enough."

Lindsey ran her fingers through her hair, head down. "This supports everything I've been saying all along. They're circling the wagons. They're afraid you're going to find out why Oscar was really killed."

"That's going to be tough to prove, but we may have an important lead in that direction. Sofia and I were stopped by the Cuban government on our way out of Havana. There's a Cuban tower guard who may offer some helpful testimony."

"A Cuban soldier?"

"Yeah. The Cubans and Americans are watching each other constantly down there. It's not a total shock that someone on the other side of the razor wire might see something."

"What did he see?"

"I haven't interviewed him yet, so I don't want to get your hopes up too much. But according to the colonel we met with, one of the Cuban guards saw you leave your house for work, just as you say you did. And, more important, he saw someone else go in."

Lindsey's mouth was agape. "Oh, my God. That's fantastic! Did he see who it was?"

"They claim to be able to identify him. But they haven't given me a name yet."

"Why not?"

"Because they want me to cut a deal with them. They'll give me the Cuban soldier as a witness, but only if I give them something in return."

"Well, give it to them! What do they want?"

"It doesn't matter what they want. If there's any kind of deal at all, the prosecutor will destroy us in front of the jury. The only way we can bring a Cuban soldier into a Miami courtroom to testify on your behalf is if it's completely clean, no deals, no strings attached."

"Says who?"

"Trust me on this. It's my best judgment."

"But it's *my* life. I'm staring straight at the death penalty, and you're telling me to walk away from a witness who will testify that he saw an intruder enter my house because I might offend a few Cuban Americans on the jury?"

"I think the Cuban government will come around on this, if we play our cards right."

"So what did you tell them?"

"That I wasn't making any deals."

"You *what*?"

"Don't get angry."

"I'm not angry, I'm furious!" She leaped up from her chair and began to pace. "You should have called me before making a decision like that."

"You expect me to make a confidential phone call from a Cuban military office to a United States prison? I got a better idea. Why don't we just conduct our attorney-client conversations on *The Tonight Show*?"

She stopped pacing and returned to her chair. Jack could see the worry in her face, the lack of sleep in her eyes. She seemed broken, and she spoke without heart. "I don't have the stomach for this, Jack."

"That's why you hired me."

"You still don't seem to understand what I'm feeling."

"I do."

"No, you can't. The thought of never seeing my son again is tearing me to shreds. The thought of his wondering if his mother killed his father, I—" She stopped, unable to finish. "You can't possibly know how that feels."

Jack considered it, but it wasn't the first time he'd heard a parent tell him that until you've had children, you can't possibly know. "I suppose you're right."

"Unless . . ."

"Unless what?" said Jack.

"Unless you have a personal stake in the outcome."

"Brian is my biological son. Isn't that personal?"

"Not if there's no consequences to you if you lose."

"Brian loses his mother if I lose the case. Those are serious consequences."

"For Brian, not for you."

"I don't distinguish between the two. I'm doing this for his benefit."

"Are you? Or do you sit back and think, Oh well, if I lose this case, I'll look after Brian. I'll make sure he's raised properly. I'll have my own life with Brian."

"I haven't thought anything of the sort. If his mother's innocent, I want to get her acquitted."

"And if you lose, you should lose the same thing I'm losing."

"Meaning what?"

She leaned closer and said, "If I lose, I lose Brian. If you lose, then you should lose Brian, too."

Jack chuckled nervously. "This is crazy."

Her eyes brightened, as if she were suddenly on to something. "No, it's not crazy. You lawyers can be so dispassionate about the life-and-death decisions you make for other people. Maybe it's time you feel the way your clients feel."

"Exactly what are you saying?"

"I have two lawyers now, you and Sofia. I want Sofia to be the one who deals with Brian, not you. You get to meet Brian if, and only if, you win the case."

"I can't operate under those rules."

"What did you expect? That I would pull you aside at trial and say, 'Oh, Jack, promise me one thing: If I don't get out of prison, please make sure that Brian is well taken care of'? That's fairy tales. I want you to have everything riding on winning."

"You're using your own son as a carrot on a stick."

"I'm doing everything I possibly can to make sure the mother who loves him will be there to raise him. What's so terrible about that?"

"This isn't what's best for Brian. It's what's best for you."

"Like you said before. I don't see the distinction between the two."

"It's not going to make me win your case."

"No. But it might keep you from losing it."

"It also might keep me from being your lawyer."

"What are you going to do, quit?"

"Yeah," said Jack, rising. "I quit."

"Wait a minute. You can't quit. Once the case starts, a criminal lawyer needs the judge's permission to quit."

"But as you so happily pointed out earlier, you

have two lawyers now. That means the judge will let one of us quit whenever we want. You still have a lawyer, so it won't delay the case."

Her expression fell. Jack walked toward the door.

"Jack, please."

"No, you've made your decision. I'm outta here." He pushed the button near the door, and a buzzer sounded for the guard.

"Wait!" she said, her voice shaking. "I'll make a deal with you. You can make all the strategy decisions you want. The Cuban soldier as witness, all that stuff. It's your bailiwick."

"What about Brian?"

"We agree to do what's best for him."

"Which means what?"

"This is how I see it. Brian shouldn't meet you when I say so. He shouldn't meet you when you say so. I'd like him to meet you when he asks to see his biological father. I can't think of a better way to know when he's ready."

"You told him he was adopted?"

"Yes. I told him. Before I was arrested."

Jack didn't say anything.

She said, "That would be the ideal way to handle it, don't you think?"

"A murder trial is hardly an ideal situation. What if I need to talk to him before then?"

"I'll take you at your word. If Sofia can do as good a job as you can, you'll let Sofia interview him. Only if you think it's absolutely necessary to talk to him directly do you have any direct contact with Brian."

Jack considered it. The restriction seemed silly,

almost pointless, except that it was just enough to let her feel as though she was standing her ground and saving a little dignity—which went a long way in prison. "All right," said Jack. "You have my word on that."

"Thank you. I'll tell Sofia the same thing, so she knows what we agreed to."

"I'll tell her," said Jack.

The guard was at the door. Before Jack pushed the buzzer again to open it, Lindsey looked at Jack and said, "In case you're wondering, finding out that he was adopted . . . it didn't ease the pain of losing his father. Not a bit."

In another tone of voice, it could have sounded harsh, but there wasn't an ounce of malice in Lindsey's delivery. It was just a statement of fact, perhaps a not-so-subtle reminder that Jack shouldn't expect too much out of his first meeting with Brian.

"I'd still like to meet him someday. Under better circumstances, I mean."

"That's kind of up to you, isn't it, Counselor?"

Jack was about to punch the door buzzer, then stopped. He turned and gave Lindsey a serious look. "Tell me one more thing."

"What?"

"The forensic report. It says your fingerprints were found on the murder weapon."

"Does that surprise you?"

"Only if you don't have a good explanation."

She shrugged, as if it were nothing. "Of course my prints were on it. The gun was in our house. Do you think I was going to have a gun in my home and not know how to use it?"

"So you handled the gun before?"

"Oscar and I shot it together. Many times."

"He didn't clean it?"

"Of course he cleaned it. But I guess he missed a print or two."

Jack nodded. It would have been difficult to script a better answer. And perhaps that was what concerned him.

Jack pushed the button, the buzzer sounded, and the door opened. He said good-bye to his client, then headed down the corridor with the guard, the sound of shoe leather on concrete echoing off the prison walls. It hadn't been exactly the meeting he'd hoped for, but it had turned out all right, he supposed. Still, he was worried. Worried about Brian. Worried about future outbursts from Lindsey.

And somewhere, in the deepest corners of his mind, he was worried about whose number Lindsey might be dialing at that very moment on her magic cell phone.

23
.

On Friday morning, Jack was in court. The prosecutor wasn't happy to be there, and Jack probably would have preferred to soak his feet in kerosene and walk across flaming embers. But at some point he was going to have to bring it to the court's attention that the star witness for the defense might well be a Cuban soldier. Today was the day.

"All rise!" said the bailiff as the judge entered the courtroom.

Jack and Sofia rose. So did the prosecutors. There was no one else. The hearing was closed to the public because it involved a "sensitive" matter, not quite on the level of national security, but something akin thereto. Not even Jack's client was allowed in the courtroom. By court order, Jack's motion would be argued *in camera*, for the eyes and ears of the lawyers only.

"Good morning," said the judge as he settled into his chair. Judge Garcia was one of the oldest federal judges in south Florida, a Reagan appointee whose confirmation had slipped through the U.S. Senate while his would-be opponents were obsessed with keeping the *less* conservative Robert Bork off the Supreme Court. Miami was one of those strange places where drawing an Hispanic judge was more often than not the kiss of death for any lawyer advancing the traditional agenda of Hispanic Democrats. Jack was just glad he wasn't here on an affirmative-action case.

The lawyers greeted him and announced their appearances. Hector Torres, as U.S. attorney, staked out his position as lead trial counsel. With him was a lawyer from the Justice Department. A Washington connection—no surprise there.

The judge cleared his throat and said, "I've read the papers that the defense filed under seal. The transcript of this hearing will also be kept under seal. And I'm issuing a gag order that prevents anyone from discussing this hearing outside of this courtroom. Is that understood?"

"Yes, Your Honor," the lawyers replied.

"Good. Now, let me turn to the merits." He removed his reading glasses, as if to look Jack straight in the eye. "Mr. Swyteck, I have to tell you. When I reached the part of your motion where you claim that Fidel Castro is willing to send one of his soldiers into this courtroom to testify on your client's behalf—well, I nearly lost my lunch."

Loast my loanch. When he got angry or excited, the accent kicked in.

"Sorry, Your Honor, but—"

"Let me finish. Either this is the most surprising witness to a homicide in the history of Miami jurisprudence, or your motion is the most incendiary work of fiction I've read in my twenty-plus years on the bench."

"I assure you, it's not fiction."

Torres rose and said, "Judge, not to point out the obvious, but simply because a colonel in the Cuban army told Mr. Swyteck that a Cuban soldier can offer exculpatory testimony does not mean that any such witness actually exists. I'm not questioning the fact that he may have told this story to defense counsel, but this is so far from being established as truth that it hardly belongs in a courtroom. It's hearsay, and it's probably the worst kind of hearsay, since the source is a representative of a hostile government that has lied about the United States for over four decades."

"I understand your point, Counsel. And frankly, I couldn't have said it better."

This was exactly the reaction Jack had feared. "Judge, this is precisely the reason for our motion. Before we build up any expectations at trial, and before we run the risk of prejudicing a jury against us for calling a Cuban soldier as a witness, we want to get to the bottom of this as a pretrial matter. We want the opportunity to take a videotaped deposition of the Cuban soldier before trial. The government will have the right to cross-examine."

The judge chuckled, obviously skeptical. "And just how do you propose to get the Cuban government to submit one of its soldiers to a videotaped deposition?"

"It would be voluntary on their part, of course.

But I believe we have made enough of a showing to ask this court to give us the time we need to at least attempt to arrange for the deposition."

"How much time do you want?" asked the judge.

"This is a complicated process. It could be six or seven weeks, easily."

Torres groaned and said, "Now we see what this is all about, Judge. Delay."

"It's not about delay," said Jack. "This is a crucial witness."

"Nonsense," said Torres. "This is so transparent. It's the same old story every time the U.S. attorney's office pursues a high-profile case. The defense does everything it can to delay the trial, speedy trial be damned, all in the hope that the hoopla will die down before its client stands trial. What's next, Mr. Swyteck? A motion for change of venue?"

"Actually, if we are able to secure the testimony of a Cuban soldier, we may ask that the case be moved to Jacksonville or Tampa."

"See, Judge?" said Torres. "It's going to be one game after another."

"I assure you," said Jack, "this is no game. My client is sitting in jail."

"I understand that," the judge said. "But Mr. Torres has a point. I don't want delays."

Torres took a half step toward the bench, as if to underscore his plea. "Your Honor, I've been holding my tongue so far, but the problem with Mr. Swyteck's motion isn't just delay. This is outrageous, plain and simple. The victim in this case is the son of Alejandro Pintado. Mr. Pintado is a prominent Cuban exile, an outspoken critic of the Castro regime.

We all know how Castro feels about Mr. Pintado. Judge, you must resist any invitation to allow Fidel Castro to manipulate this trial and thereby exonerate the woman who murdered Mr. Pintado's son."

"I take serious offense at that," said Jack.

"Then you shouldn't have brought the motion," said the judge.

Jack was taken aback. "Excuse me?"

The judge looked down sternly. "If you take offense at being accused of allowing Castro to manipulate you, then you should not have brought the motion."

"Sorry you feel that way, Judge."

"Well, I *do* feel that way. To say the least, I am completely unamused by your attempt to leverage Fidel Castro's political propaganda into a legal entitlement to depose a Cuban soldier who may or may not have seen anything. Indeed, we don't even have his name, so we don't even know if he exists. The motion of the defense to postpone the trial date until it can secure the deposition of this unspecified Cuban witness is denied. Trial is set to commence three weeks from today. We're adjourned," he said with a bang of his gavel.

The lawyers rose and watched in silence as he disappeared through a side door to his chambers. After a disaster like this, Jack felt the need to get out of the courtroom as quickly as possible. He packed his trial bag and started for the exit.

"See you around, Jack," said Hector Torres. The prosecutor was glowing.

"Yeah. Take care."

Sofia caught up with him, but Jack only walked

faster. She kept pace, as if determined to make him say something. He refused, having learned not to talk when he was boiling mad.

The elevator came, and they entered together. It was still just the two of them. Jack watched the lighted numbers over the closed doors.

"How did I delude myself into thinking that a man like Judge Garcia would give this motion a fair shot?"

Sofia said, "We're still in the first inning. It's just one motion."

"No, it's deeper than that. If a federal judge has that visceral a reaction against a Cuban soldier as a witness for the defense, imagine how it's going to play to the jury. How's it going to play to someone whose husband spent twenty-six years in one of Castro's political prisons for criticizing the government? Or to some guy who brought his family to this country on a rubber raft, only to have his daughter drown on the way over?"

"They can still be fair."

"Yeah, sure. Whatever fair is."

The elevator doors opened. Jack stepped out. Sofia paused for a moment, then hurried to catch up as they crossed the main lobby and headed for the exit.

"What do we do now?"

"Damage control."

"That should be minimal. It was a closed hearing. There's a gag order. There shouldn't be too much backlash from the me—" She stopped as they reached the revolving doors. "—media," she said, finishing her thought.

Jack froze. On the other side of the glass doors, the media were waiting in throngs—camera crews, reporters with microphones, and the general sense of confusion that seemed to follow the media wherever they went. Most of the station logos were from Spanish-language radio and television.

"*Señor Swyteck!*"

They'd spotted him, so there was no turning back. Jack continued through the revolving door and met the mob head-on at the top of the granite steps near the courthouse entrance. An assortment of microphones was suddenly thrust toward his face. Jack tried to keep walking, but he could manage only baby steps. One of the crewmen on the fringe lowered a boom with a dangling microphone that clobbered him atop the head. He shoved it aside and forged his way forward.

A reporter asked, "Is it true that your client will be calling a Cuban soldier to the witness stand?"

The question nearly knocked Jack over. So much for the closed hearing. Courthouses weren't quite the sieves that police stations were, but someone had tipped off the press already. The same question was coming from everywhere. Scores of reporters, each one wanting the scoop on the Cuban soldier.

"Is it true, Mr. Swyteck?"

Jack hated to respond with "no comment," but he was still under a gag order, and the judge was mad enough at the defense as it was. He didn't dare push it. "I'm sorry, but I can't answer any of your questions at this time."

His refusal to answer seemed only to feed the growing frenzy. The questions kept coming, dozens at a time, each one somewhere between a bark and an angry shout.

"What's his name?"

"What will he say?"

"Will he defect?"

"Es usted comunista?"

Jack shot a look—*Am I a communist?*—and the camera flashed in his face. That last question had been purely a plant, designed to get him to look at the camera. It was like trying to wade through the muck of the Everglades, but Jack was slowly making his way down the steps, and the media went with him. Someone had taken hold of his jacket to keep him from moving too fast. He glanced over his shoulder and saw Sofia several steps behind, well within the mob's nucleus. Finally, they reached the sidewalk, and with one last surge they pushed beyond the curb and squeezed into the backseat of a cab. Jack went first. Sofia jumped in after him, slamming the door behind her.

"Coral Gables," Jack told the driver.

The many faces of the media were sliding across the passenger-side windows as the car pulled away. Sofia brushed her tangled hair out of her eyes. Jack straightened his jacket. It was as if they'd run through the gauntlet.

"No media backlash, huh?" said Jack as the car started down Miami Avenue.

"It'll blow over," said Sofia in a breathless voice.

"Yeah, sure." *In about a hundred years.*

24

"CASTRO'S PAWNS?" That was the banner headline for the Latin evening news.

It was an ingenious cover-your-ass tactic that the libel defense bar had concocted, this badly abused practice of disparaging the hell out of someone and then disclaiming all liability by putting a simple question mark after the attack.

"Castro's Pawns?"

"Drug Addict?"

"Toe-Sucking, Panty-Sniffing Loser Who Actually Dials the Phone Numbers in Men's Room Stalls?"

Thankfully the nonsense had stopped at "Castro's Pawns," which was bad enough. Much of it rolled off Jack's back, especially the attacks from an extreme journalist who would assail Jack's Cuban witness this week, and then next week call for a ban on nursery rhymes that promoted homosexual lifestyles. (*Rub-a-dub-dub, three men in a tub.*) Whatever the source, he didn't want to be home when the phone started to ring off the hook with calls from the media. Nor did he want *Abuela* to die of embarrassment when she turned on the evening news. So he watched at his grandmother's town house, poised for on-the-spot damage control.

"*Dios mio!*" she said, groaning.

"I'm sorry," said Jack.

"I no mad with you," she said, her emotions fraying her command of English. "I mad with them. A Cuban soldier for witness? *Es loco.*"

Jack didn't say anything. It did seem like a long shot, but he wasn't quite ready to dismiss as "crazy" the idea of a Cuban soldier coming forward to testify in his case.

"Look," said *Abuela* as she pointed to the television. "Is *Señor* Pintado."

The judge had issued a gag order, so Jack's first reaction was that the station was broadcasting file footage. But it wasn't. Alejandro was making a statement from his home. He and his wife were standing on the inside of the tall iron gate at the entrance to his walled estate. Various members of the media had gathered on the other side, their ranks spilling across the sidewalk and into the residential street. Pintado silenced them with a wave of his hand. Then he looked into the camera and addressed the television audience in his native tongue.

"I say this to Cuban Americans, to the people of Cuba, to the whole world. Fidel Castro will regret the day that he sends one of his soldiers into a Miami courtroom to defend the woman who murdered my son."

"Good for you," said *Abuela*.

Oh, boy, thought Jack.

Pintado thanked the crowd, then kissed his wife and started back toward the house. The newscaster gave a quick recap of what had just happened, repeating over and over again what Pintado had just said, analyzing it to death, proving that Hispanic news was, in this respect, no different than traditional network journalism. The more Jack thought about what he'd just seen, however, the more the day's events were beginning to make sense to him. The U.S. attorney may well be a close friend of his father's, but Jack wasn't about to be pushed around for the entire trial. He stepped out of the room, away from *Abuela*, then picked up the phone and dialed Torres at home.

"Hector, it's Jack Swyteck here."

"What can I do for you, son?"

"I'm not your son, and what you can do for me is explain that little stunt I just watched Mr. Pintado pull off on television."

"Stunt? Whatever do you mean?"

"The judge issued a gag order. No one is supposed to be talking about the possibility of a Cuban soldier testifying on my client's behalf."

"Oh, lighten up, please. Gag order or not, you surely aren't going to ask the judge to hold a grieving father in contempt for a one-sentence defense of his dead son."

"That's exactly what you were banking on, isn't it?" said Jack.

"I don't know what you're talking about."

"Cut the crap, Hector. I know your reputation. You choreograph everything. Alejandro Pintado isn't saying anything to the media without your prior blessing."

"Are you accusing me of circumventing the court's gag order?"

That was exactly what Jack was doing, and ten years earlier, the old Jack Swyteck would have crawled through the phone line and spit right in the prosecutor's eye. But experience had taught him to take a less accusatory approach. "Let me just say this. I found it quite surprising that the media was all over this story before any of us had even left the courtroom this afternoon. After all, my motion had been filed under seal. The only people who knew anything about the Cuban soldier were me, Sofia, the judge, and your office."

"And the clerk's office, of course. You know how careless those civil servants can be."

"Yeah," Jack said with sarcasm. "I'm sure it was the clerk's office that leaked it."

"Or maybe it was Castro who leaked it. Did you ever think of that, Jack? After all, you are his pawn."

"'Castro's pawn.' Interesting choice of words. Did you take them from the evening news, or did you also write the news script?"

"My dinner's getting cold. It's been nice chatting with you, Jack."

"Sure. I'm glad we cleared this up. At least now I know what I'm up against."

They exchanged a clipped good-night, and Jack hung up and returned to the television.

Abuela was still on the couch, riveted by the newscast. The coverage on Pintado was finally wrapping up, and the anchorman yielded to a meteorologist who looked like a high school intern from fashion school. Jack switched off the set. *Abuela* continued

to stare at the blackened screen, as if not quite believing what she'd just watched.

"Are you okay?" asked Jack.

Her lips quivered ever so slightly. "I wish *Señor*
Pintado had said something in your defense."

"In *my* defense? I'm not on trial."

"Is just that . . . my friends. What do I tell them?"

"No Castro, no problem?"

"You think this is joke? Many peoples will ask me
questions. What do I say?"

"Tell them that your grandson is doing his job.
And it's going just fine."

She sat up straight, as if searching for the forti-
tude to ask the next question. "Are you talking with
the Cuban government?"

"*Abuela*, that's privileged information. It's between me and my client."

"That sounds like 'yes' to me."

"It's not a yes. I just can't talk about it with you."

"There's nothing you cannot talk about with your
abuela."

"Believe me, there are certain things—" He
stopped. *Abuela* was giving him one of her pat-
ented looks, and Jack was suddenly struck with
an idea. "There's nothing we can't talk about, you
say?"

"*Nada*," she said firmly.

"Okay. I want to talk about Bejucal."

"What about Bejucal?"

"I went there. When Sofia and I were in Cuba."

Her expression fell. "Why didn't you tell me?"

"Because . . ." A slight pang of guilt gnawed from
the inside. He felt as if he were about to drop an

anvil on her head. "Because I met with Celia Méndez's younger sister."

Abuela went white. Her voice tightened. "Did you have a nice talk?"

"Very nice."

"What did you talk about?"

"My mother."

"Why would you do that?" She had switched to Spanish, and Jack answered in kind.

"Because I want to know about her."

"Jack, you don't have to go to the Méndez family to find out about your mother. Everything you need to know about your mother, I can tell you."

Their eyes locked, and Jack was suddenly drowning in a roiling mess of mixed emotions. He was angry that she hadn't told him everything. Yet he felt sorry for this sweet old woman who was so proud, so Catholic, and so deeply entrenched in the moral dogma of another generation that she had no alternative but to lie to her own grandson, lest he think his own mother had been a loose woman. He leaned forward and softened his voice. *"Abuela,* I love you. I would never do anything to hurt you. But I want to know the truth."

"What truth?" she said.

He was straining his limited knowledge of Spanish, but he wanted to put the question to her as softly as possible. Finally, he found the words, looked her in the eye, and asked, "Do I have a half brother or half sister in Cuba?"

Abuela caught her breath. Her bosom swelled, and for a moment Jack thought he might have to dial 911.

"Who told you that?"

"Felicia Méndez. Celia's younger sister."

"Why would you ask her about something like that?"

"I didn't ask, I just—"

"Why are you doing this, digging up such stories?" she said in a shrill, racing voice. "Your poor mother, God rest her soul, what would she think? Why must her own son dishonor her memory?"

"I'm honoring her memory. I'm just trying to find out who she really was."

Tears were streaming down *Abuela*'s cheeks, the wrinkles and worry lines directing the flow of her sorrow this way then that. Her voice quaked as she said, "I want you to stop this."

"Stop what?"

She rose quickly, her arms waving. Her fist bounced off her chest as she somehow found a voice that scorched him. "I want you to stop breaking your grandmother's heart!"

Jack wanted to say something, but he could come up with nothing. He watched in agony as she stormed out of the room, weeping. The door slammed when she reached her bedroom.

His gaze slid across the living room, toward the end table, until it finally settled on an old photograph of *Abuela* and Jack's mother. They were hugging each other, smiling widely, turquoise surf and brightly colored beach umbrellas in the background. It was a happy photograph, a joyous time. But as the silence lingered, Jack felt a tightness in his chest that was already beginning to feel like lifelong regret. His mind kept coming back to the same thought.

Abuela had denied none of it.

I'm no longer an only child.

25

As the case drew closer to trial, Jack found himself spending more and more time with Sofia. It was agreed that Jack would be the lead trial counsel, but Sofia still had a major role in the preparation, especially since Jack had given Lindsey his word that Sofia would be the point person for any direct communication with Brian.

"Any luck setting up an interview?" asked Jack.

Sofia took a seat at the conference table. "Same old story. I call Mr. Pintado. He promises to get back to me right away with a date when I can meet with his grandson. And then I never hear from him again."

"We're ten days from trial," said Jack. "We have to talk with him."

"We may have to go to the judge."

"I hate to do that. It makes us seem like the bad guys."

"I know Lindsey won't like it either," said Sofia. "Just from the standpoint of what it does to Brian."

There was a knock at the door. Jack's secretary

entered with their food delivery. Orange beef and cashew chicken from New Chinatown restaurant. Jack pushed aside the papers to make room for the food.

"Want to know one of the world's best-kept culinary secrets?" said Jack.

"What?" his secretary asked as she placed the cartons on the table.

"White rice. Cuban Americans make it better than the Chinese."

"I wouldn't argue with that. But how was the rice when you went to Cuba?"

"Rationed. Like everything else. Unless you're a tourist. But don't get me started." Jack served himself some orange beef. "You care to join us, Maria?"

"No, thanks. I'll let you two legal scholars get your brain food. But stop being such a slave driver, Jack. Take the girl out once in a while, won't you?"

Jack and Sofia exchanged glances, then offered a simultaneous, "Good night, Maria."

The door closed, and for the third evening in a row, it was just the two of them. Sofia poked at her food with a chopstick, then put the carton atop the desk.

"I wonder what Lindsey's eating tonight," she said wistfully.

"Probably the same thing she ate last night," said Jack.

"Do you think she'll ever get out?"

Jack coughed on an orange peel, not expecting such a direct question. "Are you asking if I think she's guilty, or if I think she'll be acquitted?"

"Do those questions have different answers?"

Jack didn't respond, at least not directly. "She has some serious problems, no doubt about it. You start with her statement that she was at work when her husband was shot. The medical examiner's estimated time of death says otherwise."

"But her son told the police that he found the body and called her at work."

"Hopefully he'll confirm that. If his grandfather ever lets him talk to us."

Sofia opened a diet soda. "Of course, Brian isn't going to save the day. He was sleeping when his father was shot. So Lindsey could have shot her husband, and then gone to work."

"Unless there was an intruder," said Jack.

"But there is no sign of break-in. Nothing of value was taken. So if it was an intruder, it was someone who came for no other reason than to kill Captain Pintado."

"Or someone who got scared off before he could take anything of value."

Sofia got a cup of ice, poured herself some soda, and gave the rest to Jack. "Which brings us right back to our original problem. We have only one witness who puts an intruder at the scene."

"And he happens to wear the wrong nation's uniform," said Jack.

The words seemed to take the fizz right out of their Diet Coke. "What are we going to do about that?" she asked. "You plan to call him to the witness stand or not?"

"I'm still pondering it."

"Well, I think I might let you ponder that one alone tonight."

"You're punching out already?"

"I figure my social life will go completely to hell once the trial actually starts. So I have a date tonight."

"I didn't know you had a boyfriend."

"I didn't say I had a boyfriend. I said I had a date."

"So you date women?"

"No," she said with a playful smile. "Now get the hell out of your cross-examination mode, and mind your own business."

"No problem. Have fun."

"See you tomorrow." She grabbed her bag and headed out the door. She'd parked in a metered spot right outside Jack's office, and Jack watched through the window as she walked to her car. She glanced over her shoulder and caught him peeking through the blinds.

"Just wanted to make sure you got there safe," said Jack, though he felt a little foolish. Not only couldn't she hear him, but she'd walked all of fifty feet to her car down a pedestrian-filled sidewalk. Hardly a dangerous journey.

So she caught me watching. Is that a crime?

Sofia waved, got in her car, and drove away. Jack glanced from the empty parking space to the sidewalk across the street. A woman was leaving the ice-cream shop with a young boy who looked to be about ten. He reminded Jack of Brian, and for a minute the woman resembled not Lindsey but Jack's old girlfriend, Jessie. Then he came to his senses. Jessie was dead. Lindsey was in jail. Brian was living with his grandparents.

And Jack was alone, wondering what to do next.

He got out the phone book, found the number, and dialed the Pintado residence. One lonely ring after another pulsed in his ear. He wondered what he'd do if Brian answered, which he realized wasn't likely, since the boy was deaf.

"Hello." It was a woman.

Jack said, "Is this Mrs. Pintado?"

"Yes. Who is this?"

"My name is Jack Swyteck. I'm the attorney for Lindsey Hart."

There was silence on the line. Jack said, "Please, don't hang up. I'm sorry to disturb you, but it's very important that we schedule a time and a place where I can meet with your grandson. His mother has that right."

"Brian is sick."

Jack had his doubts, and his tone conveyed it. "Is that so?"

"It's true. Brian has been throwing up since this afternoon. I don't know what it is. I guess maybe the flu. I've been running around with towels and buckets while waiting on a callback from the pediatrician. If I can't keep him hydrated, the nurse wants me to take him to the emergency room for an IV."

If she was lying, she definitely subscribed to the "Big Lie" school of thought. Jack said, "Is there anything I can do?"

"No, no. Of course not. But obviously I'm in no position to schedule an interview with him. Now, please, leave us alone."

Jack heard a retching noise in the background, which only confirmed that Mrs. Pintado wasn't making up stories. "Is that him?" asked Jack.

"Yes, yes. I told you he was sick. I have to go."

"I understand. Take care of your grandson."

"Thank you. Good night."

"Good night." Jack hung up. He was concerned about Brian's illness, but a sardonic smile slipped across his lips. He'd seen photographs of the boy, and Lindsey had told him a little bit about him. But this was the first time Jack had ever heard him. And he was puking his guts out.

Kids. Gotta love 'em.

Then he thought about going home to no one, and suddenly schlepping towels and buckets and making late-night runs to the emergency room didn't sound quite so bad.

He cleaned up the empty food cartons, then went to his desk to check his mail. It took him an hour to get to the bottom of the inbox. He had other cases, but none seemed quite as important as this one. This evening, however, he didn't have another late night in him. He packed up his briefcase, switched off the lights, and locked up the office.

The main lobby was locked, so he left the building through the nighttime exit. His car was parked in the garage across the street. He walked up the ramp to level Red 2. The parking garage catered to a working crowd, so most of the cars had gone already. The lighting was dim, several bulbs burned out. The lonely click of his heels echoed off walls of unfinished concrete. As he reached for his keys, he heard footsteps behind him, but he had no time to react.

"Don't turn around," the man said.

Jack froze. He started to put his hands in the air,

but the man's gruff voice stopped him. "Don't make a move. Don't do anything."

"What do you want?" said Jack.

"I'm not a robber. I'm not going to hurt you. I work for the government of Cuba."

A Cuban operative in Miami? Pretty good reason not to let anyone see your face. "What's this about?"

"Colonel Jiménez sent me. I have a message for you."

It took an extra moment for Jack to process that thought. It almost seemed too bizarre, but if the guy knew about Colonel Jiménez, he had to be for real. "Tell me."

"He wants you to know that he has something for you. He says you'll be pleased."

"Fine. How does Colonel Jiménez intend to get this 'whatever it is' to me?"

"He doesn't. If you want it, you come to Cuba and get it."

"When?"

"Your plane leaves tonight for Cancún. From there you fly to Havana."

Jack scoffed. "You expect me to get on a plane and fly illegally to Cuba just because some guy who claims to work for the Cuban government tells me to?"

"It's your choice. If you go, it's your client who benefits. If you don't go, it's your relatives back in Cuba who suffer."

Jack felt as if he'd been punched in the chest. "How do you know I even have relatives in Cuba?"

"Your father was the governor of Florida. We have a long file on you, Mr. Swyteck."

Jack didn't want to play into his hands, but his curiosity was getting the best of him. Could this man possibly know about his half sibling? Or was he talking about second and third cousins twice removed? "Exactly what relatives are you talking about?"

"Get on the plane, and Colonel Jiménez will be glad to tell you. Or don't get on the plane, and live with the knowledge that every last one of your relatives in Cuba will be treated as *gusanos*."

Gusanos. Worms. It was the label Castro used for the "traitors" who fled to Miami or otherwise betrayed the government. The backlash was never pretty. Food rations were cut. Employment was impossible. Their own neighbors might spit on them in the street.

Jack swallowed hard, but if this man had planned to hurt him, Jack would have been facedown on the pavement by now. There was a big potential upside in going. Having just visited Cuba and seen its hardships—and with the possibility of a half sibling living there—the downside of not going was too much to bear.

"All right," said Jack. "I'll go."

"I'll leave your plane tickets on the ground behind you. Count to twenty, then turn around and pick them up. I'll be long gone. You understand?"

Not even remotely. "Sure," he said, his head spinning, "I understand perfectly."

26

M orning came quickly. Jack was dressed and ready to go when he answered the knock at the cottage door.

Morning came quickly. Jack was dressed and ready to go when he answered the knock at the cottage door.

"Colonel Jiménez will see you now," said the man, standing in the open doorway.

Jack checked his watch. A driver had met him at the airport the previous night and told him to be ready at eight o'clock. It was closer to nine now, but Jack had lived in Miami long enough to know all about Cuban time.

"Right on schedule," said Jack.

Jack wasn't sure of his exact location, except that he knew he was in Havana and that this wasn't a hotel. His driver had taken him to a relatively quiet neighborhood in the Vedado section, west of central Havana, and Jack spent the night in a one-room cottage behind a main house. His room had no television, no radio, and no telephone. He'd had no time to pack before leaving Miami, just time enough to grab his passport and go. But the cottage came with a toiletry kit and a clean pair of socks and underwear, compliments of the Cuban government. He assumed he was staying in another *casa particular*, undoubtedly owned by someone loyal to the regime. He'd conducted himself under the assumption that he was under constant surveillance, which basically meant that he went to the bathroom in the dark.

His escort this morning was dressed in the civilian clothes of a house servant. He led Jack down a cobblestone walkway to the main house. It was an old neoclassical mansion, not so grand in design as old Havana's decaying three-story gems, but undoubtedly one of the many prerevolution homes that had been taken from Havana's wealthy, its owner either shot dead on the front steps or sent fleeing to Miami—perhaps someone Jack had even met. The grounds were small but well maintained. Tiny pink and purple flowers gathered like butterflies on the tangled vines of bougainvillea, and tall hibiscus hedges bore larger blossoms of bright red and yellow. The walkway led to a central courtyard, a traditional nineteenth-century layout where all rooms exited to the outdoors. Some windows still had original stained glass, which was not only beautiful but helped to filter the punishing tropical sun. It had been well after midnight when Jack arrived from Havana Airport, so he hadn't noticed how charming the place was. He also hadn't noticed the armed soldiers posted at each corner of the walled-in property.

"Who lives here?" Jack asked in Spanish.

"Colonel Jiménez, of course."

A guest of the colonel, himself. Communism suited him well, Jack thought.

Jack followed the man along a covered walkway, then upstairs to the second floor. At the end of the hall was a pair of massive wooden doors, each one carved elaborately and adorned with large brass knockers. The grand entrance seemed to trumpet the fact that someone important was waiting inside, an impression that was reinforced by the armed soldiers standing like pillars on either side of the doorway. Without a word, and with all the personality of the Queen's Guard at Buckingham Palace, the soldier on the left turned, knocked, and announced Jack's arrival.

"Send him in," came the reply. Jack recognized the voice as the colonel's.

The soldier opened the door and escorted Jack into a spacious, dark-paneled library. With a click of his heels the soldier retreated, leaving Jack alone with the colonel, who rose, smiled pleasantly, and offered Jack a seat. The colonel seemed to have learned from their previous meeting that Jack had no interest in shaking his hand.

"*Café?*" asked the colonel.

"*No, gracias.*"

The colonel shifted to English, which was exactly what most Spanish speakers did as soon as they heard Jack massacre their language.

"Thank you for coming on such short notice."

"Sure. Thanks for threatening my Cuban relatives."

The colonel offered a strained show of sympathy. "*Aye*, did he really do that to you? I swear, I send my men to Miami, and they become so rude. What is it about that city?"

Jack dodged the small talk. "Your messenger said you have something for me."

"Yes, I do. I think you are going to be very pleased."

"That's what I used to tell my clients when their execution date got moved from Monday to Thursday."

"You're a very funny man," he said, but his smile seemed insincere.

"Whattaya got, Colonel?"

The colonel picked up the phone, punched a few buttons, then spoke in very abrupt Spanish. Just seconds after he hung up, a side door opened, one that Jack hadn't even noticed because of the way it blended into the paneled walls. Two soldiers entered, only one of them armed. The one without a gun took a seat facing the colonel, his body angled toward Jack. The armed soldier left the room.

The colonel said, "This is Private Felipe Castillo."

Castillo nodded once toward Jack, who returned the gesture.

The colonel said, "Private Castillo is part of the surveillance team at Guantánamo Bay. He is one of many soldiers on Cuban soil whose primary responsibility is to monitor activity at the U.S. naval base. We have towers posted all along—well, I'm not going to tell you how many or where they are. Not that it's a secret. Both sides are constantly watching each other down there."

"Do you mean to tell me that Private Castillo saw the intruder enter my client's house?"

"I think I'll let Private Castillo speak for himself. He speaks no English, so I will translate for him."

"That's not necessary," said Jack. "I'll let you know if I miss something."

"Fine." The colonel addressed the soldier in Spanish. "Private Castillo, I've already explained to Mr. Swtyeck that you are part of our surveillance team at Guantánamo Bay. In general terms, explain what you do and when you do it."

"I'm part of the third eight-hour shift. I work midnight to eight A.M."

"So, you work both nighttime and daylight hours?"

"Yes. Mostly night, obviously. Which means I use infrared binoculars. After sunrise, I use regular binoculars."

"What portion of the base do you watch?"

"The permanent housing section of the main base. Mainly the officers."

The colonel said, "Private Castillo, you know why Mr. Swyteck is here, correct?"

"Yes."

"You know the nature of the charges against his client?"

"Yes, that was explained to me."

"Do you have any information that might be of help to Mr. Swyteck's client?"

"Yes, I do."

"Would you please tell that information to Mr. Swyteck now?"

"Yes, of course." He drew a breath, and he seemed to be fighting a bad case of dry mouth. The colonel poured him a glass of water, and the young man's hand shook as he drank, causing a trickle to run from the corner of his mouth. Jack didn't take it as a sign of deception. Any soldier of his rank would have been nervous in front of the colonel.

Castillo said, "Most of my nights are uneventful, but the most unusual thing that occurred on this particular night was somewhere between five-thirty and six A.M."

"What happened?"

"Part of the area I watch includes the housing for U.S. Marine officers. I noticed a soldier arrive at one of the houses."

"What made this event at all memorable?"

"Because it wasn't his house. But he walked straight in, no knock or anything."

"Before six o'clock in the morning?"

"That's correct."

"What house did you see him enter?"

"The house of Captain Oscar Pintado."

Jack's heart was pounding. "I'm sorry. What date are you talking about?"

"The seventeenth of June."

That was the day Oscar Pintado was shot. Jack was almost afraid to ask the next question, as if testimony this good just had to unravel. "Did you see who the man was who entered the house?"

"Please," said the colonel, "allow me to ask the questions. Your Spanish is not—"

"I think he understands me fine," said Jack.

The colonel considered it, then acquiesced. "Fine. You may ask your questions."

Jack was unaware of it, but he'd instinctively scooted to the edge of his seat. He didn't want to be combative, but he did have some serious probing to do. "Did you get a good look at the man who entered the house?"

"Yes, I did."

"Who was it?"

"Lieutenant Damont Johnson, United States Coast Guard."

"How can you be sure it was Lieutenant Johnson?"

"Because I've seen him at the Pintado house many times before."

"And how is it that you've seen him go to that house on so many different occasions?"

"This was my quadrant. I have a map and a chart that lists all the buildings, all the occupants."

"So it's part of your job to survey certain areas of the base."

"Yes," he said, then shrugged. "But, to be honest, everyone on the surveillance team had an eye on the Pintado house."

"Because of who his father was?"

"No." He smiled a little, as if embarrassed. "It was our entertainment."

"Your entertainment?"

"Yes. We spend long hours looking at nothing. When we got bored, we would always scan over to the Pintado house and see what was going on."

Jack watched his expression closely, searching for innuendo. "What kind of things went on there?"

"Well, like I said, I saw Mr. Johnson there many times."

"And you found him entertaining?"

"Oh, yes. Very."

"You mean when he went over to visit Captain Pintado?"

"Not so much then. I'd say he was most entertaining when he went over there to visit Captain Pintado's wife."

Jack tried not to show his surprise. "You mean Lindsey Hart?"

"Yes."

"How often did you see Lieutenant Johnson and Mrs. Hart together at the Pintado house?"

"Many times."

"Now, you told me earlier that you were part of the midnight to eight A.M. shift. So, I want you to think about this carefully. Are you sure you saw Lindsey Hart together with Lieutenant Johnson many times between midnight and eight o'clock?"

"Oh, yes. I saw them. Usually more like between two A.M. and five A.M."

"You actually saw them together inside the house?"

"Sure. We have sophisticated equipment. A tiny slit in the blinds is all we need to see into the bedroom."

"The bedroom," said Jack, his words almost involuntary.

"Yes. The bedroom."

"I hate to sound stupid, but what was Lieutenant Johnson doing in the bedroom with Captain Pintado's wife in the middle of the night?"

He smiled and said, "What do you think they were doing?"

"Nobody cares what you or I think they were doing. I want to know what you actually saw them doing."

Castillo glanced at the colonel, uttering a few words and expressions that Jack didn't understand.

The colonel looked at Jack and said in English, "They were going at it like a couple of porn stars."

Jack was silent, his eyes momentarily unable to focus. "How often did you see them together?"

"Maybe once a week."

"When was the first time you saw them together?"

"I'd say about two months before Captain Pintado's death."

"When was the last time you saw them together?"

"The night Captain Pintado died."

"They were together the night Captain Pintado was shot?"

"Yes. Lieutenant Johnson left the Pintado house around three A.M. Mrs. Hart left the house for work around five-thirty. Then about twenty minutes later, Lieutenant Johnson came back to the house and entered through the back door. He left about ten minutes later, and then the police arrived about sunrise. You know the rest."

Again, Jack fell silent. He'd expected to hear about an intruder, and instead he'd been whacked between the eyes with a sex scandal.

The colonel said, "Thank you, Private Castillo. That will be all for now."

"I have a few more questions," said Jack.

"That will be all for now," the colonel said, speaking as much to Jack as to the soldier.

The private rose and left the room. As the door closed, the colonel looked at Jack and said, "Surprised?"

Jack nodded, as if nothing came as a surprise any longer. "What do you expect me to do with this information from Private Castillo?"

"That's what I'm here to discuss. First, do you like what he had to say, or do you not like it?"

"I'm not sure," said Jack.

"It *is* one of those two-edged swords, isn't it? You have the lieutenant headed over to the Pintado residence right around the time of the murder. Or at least the time of the murder as established in the NCIS report, which I've seen, by the way."

"Naturally."

"So, you have the lieutenant at the Pintado house at the time of the murder. But you also have him involved in an affair with the victim's wife. They both have motive. They both have opportunity."

"You talk like a lawyer," said Jack.

"I watch a lot of *Law and Order*. American television is my one capitalist indulgence."

The opulent surroundings offered Jack plenty of opportunity to argue about the extent of the colonel's "capitalist indulgences," but he let it drop. Jack said, "Are you still offering to make Private Castillo available to testify at Lindsey Hart's trial in Miami?"

"That depends," said Colonel Jiménez. "If you like what he has to say, then yes: I am offering to make him available to you."

"No strings attached?"

"No strings."

Jack narrowed his eyes. "Why don't I believe you?"

The colonel took a cigar from the humidor on his desk, rolled it between his thumb and index finger. "I said it before, and I say it again. You are such a skeptic, Mr. Swyteck."

"I told you the last time we met: I'm not cutting any deals with the Cuban government."

"We are not after any deals."

"Then what's in this for you?"

"We have decided that it is delightful enough for us to show the world that Alejandro Pintado's son was married to a slut and was murdered by his best friend."

"And what if I decide to deny you that pleasure?"

"Meaning what?"

"What if I simply decline to call your soldier as a witness?"

"I suggest you think very hard about that. Or it's Lindsey Hart who suffers."

"Maybe Lindsey is willing to take that chance."

"Maybe. But perhaps there are others who do not have the luxury of choice." He reached into his drawer and removed an eight-by-ten photograph. He laid it on the desktop.

Jack examined it. A group of people were standing on the sidewalk, watching as men in dark green uniforms hauled their belongings into the street. Clothes were strewn in the gutter. Furniture had been busted into pieces. "What is this?" Jack asked.

"Look closely," said the colonel.

Jack tightened his gaze, and then he recognized it. Standing off to one side was Felicia Méndez, the Bejucal woman to whom Jack had spoken about his mother. She was sobbing into her husband's shoulder. Others in the photograph were crying, too, including two young girls, perhaps six and eight.

"This is Casa Méndez," said Jack.

The colonel sniffed his cigar, savoring the rich

tobacco. "Yes. I'm sorry to report that they lost their leasehold. Just happened yesterday. Thirteen people, no place to live now. Such a shame."

"You took their home away?"

"It's not like they can't get it back. Or should I say, it's not like *you* can't give it back to them."

"You son of a bitch. Is that what your boy in Miami meant when he said you'd treat my family like *gusanos?*"

"Indirectly, yes. Of course, we know that the Méndez family is not your family. But this is a good starting point."

"Are you implying that you have designs on actual blood relatives I may have here in Cuba?"

He nearly smiled, then his expression ran cold. "It wouldn't be much of an implication if I were to come right out and admit it. Would it, Mr. Swyteck?"

Jack didn't answer.

The colonel rose and pushed a button near his telephone. The double doors immediately opened, and the two soldiers posted outside his library entered.

"Thank you for coming, Mr. Swyteck. I'll give you a few days to consider your response."

"Colonel, I—"

Colonel Jiménez cut him off with a wave of his hand. "Talk to the dead captain's wife." He chuckled to himself and said, "*Aye*, would I love to be the fly on the wall for those conversations?"

Jack wanted to slug him, but he held his tongue. The more he kept talking, the more likely he was to say something about Jack's half sibling, and despite all the threats, it wasn't clear that the colonel knew anything about that. Jack didn't want to be the one to tell him.

"You'll hear from me. One way or another." Jack left the colonel's residence in the company of the two soldiers, saying not another word all the way to the airport.

27

Jack had five hours to kill at Havana Airport. The first leg of his circuitous Miami-via-Cancún journey wasn't scheduled to leave until dinnertime, so he found a seat at the restaurant and grabbed a demitasse of espresso, which made him only more restless. One more cup of this stuff, and he probably could swim home.

"More coffee?" the waitress asked.

"You don't happen to have decaffeinated, do you?"

She laughed and walked away. Coffee without caffeine? That was apparently the Cuban equivalent of stopping in the middle of sex to do the laundry.

Stimulants or not, Jack's anxiety level was up. Although Private Castillo had seemed truthful, Jack knew better than to accept at face value anything the Cuban government had to offer. His only shot at the whole truth was Lindsey herself. Was she having an affair with Lieutenant Johnson? Had they been together the night her husband was shot? It was up to Jack to get some straight answers out of his client. Or not. He'd defended plenty of accused murderers who had never told him the whole story. As a criminal defense lawyer, you dealt with it. The problem here, however, was that he wasn't only a criminal defense lawyer. He was Brian's biological father. And Jack wasn't exactly keen on the idea of his own flesh and blood being raised by the woman who had murdered the boy's adoptive father. As his friend Theo Knight had so aptly put it on day one, he was caught in his own zipper. Jack had to get the truth.

But first, he had to kill five hours.

He walked around the terminal, checked out the vending machines, and then found a bank of pay phones. In Cuba it was true that you never knew who was listening, but the risk of someone making any sense of Jack's voice-mail messages by eavesdropping on a pay phone seemed remote. Even so, he didn't call his office. He checked only his personal messages at home, which usually consisted of Theo bitching about some bogus call the ref had made in last night's Heat game or *Abuela* telling him about the nice Cuban checkout girl she'd met at Publix.

"You have one new message," announced the robotic voice on the answering machine.

Jack got a pen and a scrap of paper to jot it down, then relaxed at the sound of *Abuela*'s recorded voice.

"*Hola, mi vida.*"

There was a long pause, but Jack was relieved to hear her start with a term of endearment. Before leaving Miami, he'd called and told her he was headed for Cuba, just so someone would know where he was. Of course, he couldn't tell her why he was going to Cuba, which had only set her off all over again.

She was sure that Jack was going back to Bejucal to stir up more scandal about his mother. She'd actually hung up on him.

"I'm sorry." She said it in English, then switched to Spanish, so Jack knew that she had something important to say, something from the heart.

"I am so very sorry. I can't expect you to understand this, so all I can do is ask you to forgive me."

She sniffled, and Jack wished he could say something to her, but all he could do was listen to the message.

"When I sent your mother to Miami, lots of parents were sending their children away. The Catholic Church had the evacuation program—Pedro Pan. We've talked about that. Parents could send their children to live in freedom, and if all went well the family would hopefully reunite later. The important thing was to get the children out of the country before Castro and his rebels made it impossible to leave. I know that's why you think I sent your mother to Miami, but I—my situation was different. I sent your mother away because . . ."

His grip tightened on the phone, as he had the foreboding sense that she was about to tell him something that she could say only to an answering machine, that she could never say in person.

Abuela's voice faded, but Jack heard her say, "Because I was ashamed of her. She met that boy and—" She stopped herself, as if unable to say the word *pregnant* even after all these years. "—and I was ashamed of her."

Jack closed his eyes and absorbed the recorded sounds of her painful sobbing. He had never seen

Abuela cry, except tears of joy. In his mind's eye, he could see her agony, and it tore him up inside.

She was trying to compose herself, but her aged voice still quaked. "I sent Ana Maria away, and I told her I never wanted to see her again. I didn't mean it. I *swear* I didn't mean it. But I said it. Out of my own pride I said it right to her face. Pride can be such an awful thing. Out of pride, I sinned against God and my own daughter. And now . . . and for that, God has punished me. I never saw her again."

He could hear her weeping, and Jack's eyes welled with tears. Once again, his birth—his mother's death—had caused untold pain to someone he loved.

"You see, *mi vida*, it is not your fault she died. It was my fault. It was all my fault."

Jack wanted to hold her and shake her at the same time. It was no one's fault. *Why must there always be someone to blame?*

Abuela gathered her composure and said, "So, there was something I wanted to tell you. You asked about a sibling."

Jack put his emotions in check. *Abuela* had moved beyond the mea culpa. She had something more to tell him. She drew a breath and said, "You should do this now, while you are in Havana. Please, if you get this message, I want you to do it. Go to Zapata and Calle twelve. Look for L thirty-seven. Then, you will have all the answers you need. Good-bye, *mi vida*. I love you."

Jack stood motionless, the pay phone still in hand. "I love you, too," he said, though he knew she wasn't there.

28

"Are you sure this is the place?" Jack asked the taxidriver.

"Yes," he said, "Zapata and Calle twelve."

Jack peered out the open car window. He didn't doubt that the driver was correct, but he was having trouble processing the implications. They were parked on a street in the Vedado district, the commercial heart of Havana, not far from where Jack had spent the night as Colonel Jiménez's guest. Directly in front of them was an iron gate. A stone wall ran the length of the entire block. An engraved sign hung over the entrance, an impressive arc of weathered brass letters. It read NECRÓPOLIS CRISTÓBAL COLÓN.

"But this is a cemetery," said Jack.

"Sí. Cementerio de Colón."

"I'm looking for L thirty-seven, Zapata and Calle twelve. I presume that's a building or an apartment."

"There's nothing else at this address. Check with the groundskeeper inside. Maybe he can help you."

Jack paid the driver and stepped onto the sidewalk.

The door slammed, and the taxi pulled away, merging into traffic. Jack turned and studied the entrance, his mind churning. *Abuela* had sent him to a cemetery. L–37. Perhaps it was a building designation. Maybe he had an older brother or sister who worked here, maybe even lived on the property. But he didn't think so.

With heavy footsteps, he started toward the gate, pea gravel crunching beneath his feet. It was a warm, sunny afternoon, and Jack was squinting until he reached the shade of the jagüeys, broad and leafy trees that lined the streets of Vedado, their long and tangled aerial roots dropping to the ground like Caribbean dreadlocks. He stopped at the main entrance. The distant sounds of Havana were still about him—an occasional horn blasting, the drone of urban traffic—but noise seemed to dissipate as he peered through the iron bars toward the peaceful side of the cemetery wall. Green space was not exactly plentiful, but still he was struck by the vastness of the grounds. Looking left, right, or straight ahead, he spotted scores of major mausoleums, chapels, family vaults, and aboveground tombs. This place was to cemeteries what Manhattan was to skylines. Most of the memorials appeared quite old, many dating back to the nineteenth century. Jack grabbed a map at the entrance, deposited a small monetary donation, and ventured inside.

"Can I help you?" a man said in Spanish.

Jack stopped and looked up from his map. He was an older man, dressed in coveralls and a baseball cap. A thick mustache made it difficult to see his mouth, and crescents of sweat extended from the underarms of his T-shirt. From the dirt on the man's knees Jack assumed he was part of grounds maintenance.

"I'm looking for someone," he said. "An address, actually."

The man was clearly struggling with Jack's Spanish, but English was apparently not an option. "An address?" he said.

"Yes. My grandmother told me to go to L thirty-seven."

Jack offered his map. The man stepped closer, gave it a quick look, and said, "The cemetery is divided into many different rectangular blocks. The letter tells you the area. The number is the plot."

Jack's heart sank. L-37 was definitely not a building. So much for finding his half sibling alive. "Can you take me to it, please?"

"Sure," the man said.

Jack followed him down a wider path of pea gravel. They passed countless tombs, many adorned with angels, griffins, or cherubs. A few graves were brightened by fresh-cut flowers, but the most impressive splashes of pink, orange, and other flaming colors came from bougainvillea vines and hibiscus bushes that had been planted many years earlier, probably by mourners who had since found permanent rest here. Finally, they came to a tomb that was blanketed with fresh flowers, everything from begonias and orchids to African wild trumpet, scores of bouquets that had been laid neatly on top of the tomb and all around it. The man stopped, and Jack stood beside him. They watched in silence as a young woman laid a yellow bouquet of *corteza amarilla* near the headstone. Then she crossed herself, rose from her knees, and stepped away. She walked backward, which was odd, never turning her back on the tomb.

The man whispered, "This is *La Milagrosa*."

Jack had to think about the man's words for a moment, but he was pretty sure that they meant the Miraculous One. "Who is *La Milagrosa?*"

"She was a young woman who died in childbirth in 1901."

Jack felt a chill. His mother had died in childbirth. "Why all the flowers?"

"Because of the legend," the man said. "She was buried with her stillborn child at her feet. But many years later, when her tomb was opened, the baby was found cradled in her arms."

Jack glanced at the young woman stepping backward from the tomb. "Who is that?"

"Another young woman. One without children, for sure. For years they have come here to pay their respects, and to pray in hopes of having children of their own. But you must never turn your back on *La Milagrosa*. So she walks backward."

Jack watched a while longer, unable to feel anything but sorrow and pity. The woman seemed more pained than hopeful, but she continued to pray aloud as she put one foot behind the other in her reverent retreat. Finally, she disappeared behind a mausoleum.

"Is this L thirty-seven?" asked Jack.

"No, no. These graves are much older than the ones in Section L. Come."

They walked along a shaded path until they came to a small clearing. The groundskeeper paused, as if to get his bearings, then continued to the east. The stone markers became less impressive, newer than the ones in the previous sections but hardly new. Most of the departed here had died before Jack was born.

"Here it is," said the groundskeeper.

Jack stopped and looked down at the plain white headstone. It was about the size of a child's pillow, no carvings or embellishments of any kind. There was a first name but no last. No traditional born-on/died-on date, either. There was just one date. It read simply:

RAMÓN
17 FEBRERO 1961

It was a sobering moment. Jack read it over and over again, but there was only one way to read it. Slowly, almost without thinking about it, he got down on his knees. The coolness of green grass pressed through his trousers. His index finger ran along the grooves on the headstone, tracing the name and the date. He wasn't sure how he was supposed to feel. Mostly, he felt empty, drained of all emotion.

"Ramón," he whispered. That was his name. He'd lived all of one day.

Jack tried to conjure up an image of the infant, but it wouldn't come. He was powerless to envision this little person he had never known, but not because he didn't care. He was suddenly consumed by his own feelings for the mother he had never known, and there simply wasn't room in his heart for anything or anyone else. It was all so confusing. He knew her better now, having visited this place, but he didn't feel any better. Ana Maria had given birth to two children. Her first son died on the day he was born, but the mother lived. Her second son lived, but the mother died on the day of his birth.

Why? was all he could ask.

Perhaps it was the skeptical lawyer in him, or maybe it was just the anger of a boy who had lost his mother. But Jack couldn't decide if all this sadness was simply the cruelty of fate . . . or if something suspicious was at work.

"I will leave you alone now," said the grounds-keeper.

"Thank you," said Jack, but that word hung in the air. Alone. At that painful hour, it seemed to be right where Jack belonged.

Forever, alone.

29

It was the day before trial, and Jack was on the receiving end of a steely glare from Judge Garcia. If he didn't say something soon, those two burning lasers might zap him into legal oblivion. For the moment, however, he could only sit quietly as the U.S. attorney spoke to the judge in the crowded old courtroom.

"This is utterly an outrage, Your Honor," said Torres. "Brian Pintado is just ten years old. A very impressionable age. He has already suffered the untimely death of his father. Someday, he will have to come to terms with the fact that it was his own mother who took his father's life. In the meantime, his grandparents are doing the very best they can to provide a normal, nurturing environment for him. And yet, these defense lawyers"—he gestured accusingly toward Jack and Sofia, his tone filled with disdain—"these so-called officers of the court persist in contacting the Pintado household in their undying effort to coerce this child into meeting with them."

Jack rose and said, "Judge, if I may say something, please."

"Sit down, Mr. Swyteck! You'll have your turn."

Jack sank into his seat. It was humiliating under any circumstances to be rebuked by the judge, but it was especially demeaning in a courtroom that was overflowing with spectators. Worse still, most of them were the media.

The prosecutor seemed to swell with confidence. "Thank you, Judge. As I was saying, Brian Pintado has no desire to talk to these lawyers. Before her arraignment, Lindsey Hart agreed that her son could stay with his grandparents during her incarceration, and it is completely against their wishes that Brian meet with these lawyers. The rules of criminal procedure give the defense no right to depose this child. Nor do the rules require Brian to meet with the defense lawyers on an informal basis. Frankly, Judge, someone needs to send a message to Mr. Swyteck and his cocounsel that enough is enough. The answer is no. Go away. Good-bye. Brian Pintado is not going to talk to them."

The prosecutor cast one more disgusted look toward Jack, then returned to his seat.

The courtroom was silent, yet Jack had the distinct impression that if this had been the English House of Commons the backbenchers would have been shuffling their feet and muttering their approval with a resounding chorus of "Here, here!"

The judge said, "Mr. Swyteck, you're on. For your sake, I hope you can explain yourself."

Jack rose and stepped to the lectern. He didn't have to glance over his shoulder at the rapt audience to know that all eyes were upon him. "Your Honor, contrary to Mr. Torres's suggestion, we have not hounded Brian Pintado or his grandparents at every turn. We have made limited attempts to set up an interview, and we have been very discreet and polite in all our communications."

The judge scoffed. "I don't care if you hired Miss Manners to print up engraved invitations. If the boy doesn't want to meet with you, then you're just going to have to take no for an answer."

"I understand that. But this is the first time I've heard anyone say that he doesn't want to meet with us. Every time we've spoken to the Pintado family, the response has been along the lines of, 'Yes, he will meet with you, but now is not a good time.' Never did they say that it was *Brian*'s desire not to meet with us."

Torres sprang from his chair. "Judge, I resent the implication that we have somehow led the defense to believe that an interview with the boy was forthcoming. If Mr. Swyteck got that impression, it was his own mistake."

The judge removed his spectacles and rubbed his eyes, as if tired of the bickering. "Fine," he said from the bench. "Perhaps it was a misunderstanding. Or perhaps it was a case of the defense overstepping their bounds. As of this moment, however, I trust the air has been cleared. Has it not, Mr. Swyteck?"

Jack glanced at Sofia. It was a setback, to be sure, not to be able to interview Brian. But the judge was showing no sign of ruling that Lindsey's lawyers had a right to force an interview with her son. "If that's the way Brian feels," said Jack, "then we'll accept that."

"Good. There will be no more phone calls to the Pintado household. No more attempts to contact Brian Pintado. Agreed?"

Again Jack hesitated. The blow to their trial preparation was one thing, but his disappointment ran deeper. As absurd as it had once seemed for Lindsey to try to limit Jack's access to her son, it was even more bizarre that things were now playing out exactly as she had wished: Jack would never meet Brian—unless he won her acquittal.

"Mr. Swyteck," said the judge, "do I have your agreement on that?"

"Yes," he said without conviction. "Agreed."

The judge looked across the courtroom and said, "Is that satisfactory to you, Mr. Torres?"

"That should be fine, Judge. I'll simply hope against hope that Mr. Swyteck is as true to his word as his father is."

Jack shot a look of annoyance. *What a cheap shot, Torres.*

"Is there anything further that the court needs to take up?" asked the judge.

Jack heard the members of the media shuffling in the press gallery behind him. They were poised to run for the exits the minute the judge adjourned the proceeding.

But the prosecutor had one last surprise.

"There is one more thing," said Torres. "It has to do with that certain witness that is the subject of the court's gag order."

The judge practically rolled his eyes. "Consider

the gag order lifted. I don't think there's a reporter in this courtroom who doesn't already know more about that than I do."

A light rumble of laughter rolled across the courtroom, then silence.

Torres said, "In accordance with the court's pretrial order, the parties have already exchanged witness lists. Perhaps I missed it, but I did not see anywhere on the defense's list of witnesses the name of a Cuban soldier."

The judge flipped through the file and located the list of witnesses. Then he looked toward Jack and said, "Is he on your list or not, Mr. Swyteck?"

Jack hesitated. He wasn't being dishonest, but one of the oldest tricks in the book was perhaps about to backfire on him. "We didn't list him by name, Your Honor. But we did list our intention to call rebuttal witnesses."

The judge snorted. "You didn't really think you were going to slide a Cuban soldier in sideways over the transom by listing him generally under the category of 'rebuttal witnesses,' did you?"

"To be perfectly honest, Judge, we haven't decided whether or not to call the soldier as a witness at trial."

The prosecutor said, "In the interest of avoiding surprises, I would like the record to be very clear on this point. If Mr. Swyteck intends to call a Cuban soldier as witness, he should be required to disclose that fact here and now."

"I won't go that far," said the judge. "Mr. Swyteck can decide at a later time whether or not to actually call him to the stand. But if there is a Cuban soldier out there who claims to know something about this crime, I want to hear his name. If I don't hear it now, Mr. Swyteck, you've waived your right to call him."

Jack glanced toward the crowd. Many of the onlookers had quite literally moved to the edge of their seats. "Judge, we're in a public forum. I don't know what consequences might be visited upon this soldier or his family if I were to reveal his name in open court."

"Then don't call him as a witness. But if you want to preserve your rights, Mr. Swyteck, let's hear his name. *Now.*"

Jack paused, then said, "His name is Felipe Castillo."

Silence gave way to a growing murmur through the crowd. Jack could almost hear the pencils scratching across notepads in the press gallery behind him. Jack wasn't happy about giving up the soldier's name, but there was some satisfaction to be had in the astonished expression on the prosecutor's face. It was as if Torres had indeed thought that the defense was bluffing—as if, when push came to shove, Jack would be unable to deliver a name.

"All right," said the judge, his tone reflecting a little surprise of his own. "We have a name. Does that satisfy you, Mr. Torres?"

Again the prosecutor glanced at Jack, still unable to believe that there actually *was* a Cuban soldier who might soon be walking into the courtroom. "That'll do it, Judge."

"Then that concludes our pretrial conference. I will see you back here tomorrow morning, nine o'clock sharp. We'll pick a jury. Until then, this court is adjourned." The judge banged his gavel and left the courtroom through a side exit to his chambers, immediately unleashing the mad rush for the exits. No cameras were allowed in federal court, so the television journalists were leading the charge out the doors to their media vans to make their reports. Others charged toward the rail and fired questions at the lawyers.

"Is Felipe Castillo in Miami now?" one asked.

"Is it true that the soldier will be staying in your home, Mr. Swyteck?"

"Have you spoken directly to Fidel Castro?"

Jack wanted to respond, but with all the confusion and borderline hysteria, he feared that his answers would only be distorted in print. He looked at no one in particular and said, "We will issue a statement on this matter once we've made a final decision about this witness. That's all for now. Thank you."

The questions kept coming. Like it or not, Felipe Castillo was about to become a household name—at least a Latin household name—in all of south Florida. Jack and Sofia pushed toward the exit. It seemed to take forever, but they finally made it down the long aisle and out the double doors. Several more minutes passed before they could wind through the crowded corridor and reach the main exit. It was difficult for Jack to hear himself think, let alone to discern any one particular voice among the many that were coming at him. But somewhere above the ruckus he heard Hector Torres issue one last sound bite for the evening news.

"Watch carefully tomorrow," said Torres. "It won't be the prosecution that is systematically excluding Cuban Americans during jury selection."

Jack pushed through the revolving doors, and Sofia was at his side as they stepped into the afternoon sun. Compared to the mob outside the courthouse, the crowd inside had been a model of civility. A pretrial conference wasn't typically a spectacle, but it could be—particularly if someone as powerful as Alejandro Pintado had gotten wind from the prosecutor that he was going to force the defense to commit one way or another on the Cuban soldier as witness. Hector Torres was without question a friend to Jack's father. But he was proving himself no friend of Jack's.

"Looks like we have some more visitors," said Sofia. She was following closely behind him, like a running back behind a blocker.

A huge crowd had gathered on the sidewalk in front of the federal building. A few were the courthouse version of rubberneckers, simply drawn to all the commotion. Others were with the media, reviewing notes, toting cameras, and primping their hair, all of which was accomplished with the journalistic fancy footwork needed to keep from tripping over their own tangle of cords and wires. The largest numbers, and the obvious reason for the strong police showing, were those marching in protest. It was a mob scene, hundreds of people pushing toward the courthouse entrance. They were restrained by wooden barricades and row after row of police, some mounted on bicycles or horseback. One demonstrator had climbed halfway up a light-post, and as Jack and Sofia emerged from the building, he waved to the crowd and shouted something in Spanish that must have been the equivalent of "There they are!" Instantly, a sea of angry fists shot into the air, and the crowd began to shout the messages that were displayed on their signs and banners, most of which were in Spanish.

"Mr. Pintado, we love you!"

"We want Justice for Cubans, Not Lies from Cuban Soldiers!"

"Cuban Americans are AMERICANS!"

"No Castro, No Problema!"

Jack wasn't exactly sure how the last one fit in, but this was, after all, Miami.

"Holy cow," Sofia whispered into Jack's ear. It was an almost involuntary reaction to the gathering in the parking lot across the street. Dozens of mobile media vans were stationed there, many with microwave towers and satellite dishes. The call letters painted boldly on the vehicles identified about an equal number of English- and Spanish-language radio and television stations.

"Just keep walking," Jack told Sofia.

The crowd followed right on their heels, shouting and waving their signs as the defense team descended the granite stairs. Jack could feel their momentum gathering as they passed beneath the trees in the courtyard, and an armada of television cameras greeted them at the wide sidewalk. Questions and microphones popped up from everywhere.

Jack had anticipated a crowd, but nothing like *this*. Nonetheless, he stuck to his original plan and turned to face the television cameras. He wasn't the consummate politician that his father was, but he still showed signs of the Swyteck gift when addressing the media, a honed skill that made it seem as though he was looking the whole world directly in the eye when in reality he wasn't actually focused on anyone.

Jack said, "On the eve of this important trial, it is important for us all to remember that no one is grieving more for the loss of Captain Oscar Pintado than his son, Brian, and his wife of twelve years, Lindsey. Lindsey was extremely proud of her husband's service in the U.S. Marine Corps, and I'm proud to be her lawyer. We all look forward to her complete acquittal on all charges and the clearing of her good name. Thank you."

The reporters shouted a series of follow-up questions, but the moment Jack finished his statement, a sedan pulled up at the curb and stopped directly behind him and Sofia. The door flew open. Jack and Sofia offered no further comment as they climbed into the backseat. The door closed, and, had it not been for the police, the mob would have been climbing onto the hood. The vehicle inched forward, and crowd patrol finally managed to clear an opening. The sedan pulled away and headed for the expressway.

Theo was behind the wheel.

"Don't speed," said Jack. "But don't waste any time getting out of here."

"No problem, boss."

Sofia glanced through the rear window to check out the crowd they'd left behind. "Wow. I feel like a celebrity."

"Get used to it," said Jack.

"Does this mean there'll be groupies?" said Theo.

Jack rolled his eyes. "Just drive, Theo."

Theo managed to catch a string of green lights, and the car seemed to jump onto the expressway as they hit the on-ramp. In minutes they were cruising down I-95, away from downtown Miami, and then over to Key Biscayne via the Rickenbacker Causeway.

Key Biscayne was like another world, which was why Jack lived there. It was an island paradise, practically within the shadows of Miami's skyscrapers, yet far enough removed from the chaos that he could enjoy the city views without being constantly reminded of work. They rode in silence until Jack could decompress. There was no one better than Theo at figuring out when Jack was ready to talk, and by the same token, there was no one more blatant about not giving a shit whether Jack was ready to talk or not.

"So, how'd it go?" said Theo.

"How did it look?" said Jack.

"Like the *los quinces* party from hell," said Theo.

Sofia chuckled, recalling her own special fifteenth-birthday bash, which had been completely overdone in the grandest of Cuban traditions.

Jack wasn't laughing. He was focused on the emergency vehicles at the end of the otherwise quiet residential street. Two yellow fire trucks were blocking traffic. A tangle of rock-hard fire hoses were strewn across the wet pavement. Firefighters stood at the ready around the taped-off perimeter, and a menacing plume of black smoke billowed upward from the south side of the street. A team of four was aiming a fully activated hose and dousing an automobile with a powerful stream of water. Jack nearly gasped. The emergency was directly in front of his house.

"Shit!" said Theo. "That's your Mustang, Jack!"

Theo slammed on the brakes. The three of them jumped out of the sedan and ran to the edge of the street. Some onlookers had already gathered on the sidewalk. Jack pushed his way past them, but a police officer stopped him cold.

"That's my car!" said Jack.

The cop shrugged. "You mean *was* your car. Nothing you can do for it now, pal. Just stay back."

Jack couldn't move. He'd bought that old car with his first few paychecks out of law school. It was the only thing he'd gotten in his divorce from Cindy. It was the one thing in his lonely life that could pull him out of the office and force him, literally, to take the scenic route.

And now it was a flaming hot shell of charred metal.

He glanced at Theo, and he'd never seen such sadness in his friend's eyes. He was the only person on the planet who had loved that Mustang even more than Jack.

Jack stared in disbelief, saying nothing. Then he noticed something in the driveway alongside the car. He was watching from across the street, so he couldn't make it out at first. But after cutting the glare with his sunglasses he could plainly see that someone had spray-painted a message in red letters on the asphalt, presumably before they'd torched the vehicle. It took Jack a moment to read the upside-down letters, and then finally it clicked.

CASTRO LOVER was all it said.

Theo looked at him and said, "Son of a gun, the fun has begun."

The flames began to falter. The firefighters had the blaze under control, and they were just a few hundred gallons of water away from turning a spectacular bonfire into worthless remains.

"Yeah," said Jack. "Sure looks that way."

30

"The United States of America calls Alejandro Pintado."

With those ominous words from U.S. attorney Hector Torres, the case against Lindsey Hart was officially in high gear.

It had taken three days to select a jury. With over fifty percent of the county's population foreign-born, everything about Miami was a mix, and juries were no different. Not even Sigmund Freud could have divined the psychological interplay of race, culture, language, and politics. As a defense lawyer, you didn't try to be everything to everybody. You simply created enough reasonable doubt so that there was *something* for *somebody* to cling to, which was exactly the way Jack had played it during jury selection and his opening statement.

Now, it was show time.

"Mr. Pintado, please approach," said the judge.

A sea of heads turned as the victim's father made his way toward the witness box. The trial was in the central courtroom, which was filled to capacity.

The Mediterranean-style surroundings were impressive, with stone arches, frescoed ceilings, and plenty of high-polished mahogany. Only the center courtroom had a public seating area large enough to accommodate the overwhelming media interest. Despite the murmuring crowd of spectators, Jack could hear his client sigh in the seat beside him. She'd seemed dazed since the bailiff called the case at nine A.M. sharp. Jack understood. Nothing was more unsettling than to hear the words *"The United States of America versus"* followed by your own name.

Jack gave her hand a little squeeze. It was ice cold.

"I do," said Pintado, promising to tell the truth, the whole truth, and nothing but the truth.

"Please be seated," the judge said.

Pintado settled into the witness stand, which was situated opposite the jury. Judge Garcia was perched between the witness and the jury, a commanding figure in his own right, very judicial and even scholarly in his appearance and demeanor. Pintado was one of those rare witnesses who seemed to command even greater deference. Jack could see the respect and admiration in the eyes of several jurors.

"Good morning," the prosecutor said as he approached the witness. "First, let me express my condolences to you and Mrs. Pintado for the loss of your son."

"Thank you." The jury followed his gaze toward his wife in the first row of public seating. She was an attractive woman, smartly dressed, but her face spoke of many sleepless nights of grieving.

Predictably enough, the testimony began with the witness's impressive background—his childhood in

Cuba, his harrowing raft trip to Miami, his first job as a dishwasher, and his rise to fame as owner of a successful chain of Cuban restaurants. The prosecutor then steered him toward more pertinent matters.

"Mr. Pintado, would you please tell us about your son?"

He seemed to sigh at the size of the question. Pintado did not come across as the kind of man who was easily shaken, but his voice quaked just a bit as he answered. "Oscar was the kind of son every parent wants. He was a good boy, a good student in school. At Columbus High he was president of his senior class and played quarterback on the football team. We wanted him to go to college, but we were all very proud of him when he joined the Marines."

"Did he eventually go to college?"

"Yes. Right away, the Marine Corps recognized him as officer material. They steered him right, and he got his bachelor of science degree from the University of Miami. With honors, I might add. Then he went back in the corps on the junior officer track."

"It sounds like you loved your son very much."

"His mother and I both did. All our children, we love more than anything in the world."

"How long was Oscar stationed at the naval base in Guantánamo Bay, Cuba?"

"He made captain when he was transferred there. I'd say approximately four years ago."

"And he lived with his wife and son on the base, correct?

"That's correct."

"Can you tell us, sir, what kind of a father Oscar was?"

"He was absolutely terrific. His son is ten years old now. He lives with his grandmother and me. Brian is always asking about his father."

"Does he ask about his mother?"

Pintado speared his first glance in Lindsey's direction, but he didn't make direct eye contact. "Almost never."

The dagger wasn't even directed at him, yet Jack felt it. Lindsey leaned toward him and whispered, "That's so not true. See how he lies?"

The prosecutor asked, "What kind of a husband was Oscar?"

"He was a good husband. I have to say that he loved his wife very much."

"Based upon your own personal observations, would you say that she loved him?"

His lower lip protruded, the chin wrinkled. "No."

"Why do you say that?"

"From the very beginning, I felt that Lindsey was more interested in the Pintado family money than in Oscar."

Jack knew where this was headed, and he probably could have objected, but there was little to be gained by playing to the jury as an obstructionist lawyer who wouldn't even let a grieving father talk about his son.

The prosecutor said, "Did anything specific happen in the recent past to shape your views that Lindsey was after the family money?"

"Oscar had a trust fund. The money kicked in three years ago, on his thirty-fifth birthday."

"I hate to probe into your family finances, sir. But how much money are we talking about?"

He paused, then said, "It was in the millions."

"I suppose that buys a lot of beer nuts over at the officers' club in Guantánamo."

"That was exactly the point. There was really no place to spend that kind of money at Guantánamo. Oscar was a soldier. He lived like every other soldier." Again, he shot a quick glare at Lindsey. "And his wife lived like every other soldier's wife."

"What was their house like in Guantánamo? The physical structure, I mean."

"It was very modest. Built in the 1940s, I believe. Eleven hundred square feet. No garage, just a little carport on the side."

"Do you know how long your son planned to live there?"

"I suppose he could have been transferred to another base. But he was just a few birthdays away from twenty years with the Marines, and he had every intention of finishing out his career at Guantánamo."

"How do you know that?"

"We talked about it in connection with Brian's schooling. The military has never been willing to provide a Sign Exact English interpreter for Brian's classroom, so I called in some favors to find a good civilian interpreter who was willing to live on the base at the family's expense. It was long-term, at least until Brian started high school."

"So, for Oscar and Lindsey, that seven-bedroom dream home on the waterfront was at least a few years away."

"That's true. But Oscar could wait. He loved serving his country. He was a soldier, and he was happy to keep the money in the bank until his job was done."

"Was Lindsey happy?"

He glanced toward the jury, then back. "Maybe you should ask her."

"Thank you. No further questions," said Torres.

Jack rose and said, "I'd like a sidebar, Your Honor."

The judge waved the lawyers forward, and they huddled behind the bench on the side farthest from the jury. Jack said, "Judge, that last question and answer should make your skin crawl. It was so obviously choreographed to elicit the response Mr. Pintado gave: 'Maybe you should ask Lindsey.' The defendant is under no obligation to testify. It's completely inappropriate for Mr. Torres to use his own witnesses to plant a seed in the minds of jurors that my client needs to explain herself on the witness stand."

"I don't know what Mr. Swyteck is talking about, Judge. I simply asked a question, and the witness answered as best he could."

"Oh, please," said Jack. "You're talking to a former prosecutor. Are you trying to tell me that you ended the examination of your very first witness with a question that you didn't know the answer to?"

"All right, that's enough," said the judge. "I think Mr. Swyteck has a point. Watch yourself, Mr. Torres."

"No problem, Judge." As they turned and headed back to their places, Torres whispered in a voice only

Jack could hear, "Didn't know you were so afraid to put Lindsey up there, Jack."

"Didn't know you were so afraid to try and get a conviction without her," said Jack.

The prosecutor returned to his seat. Jack took his position before the witness. Cross-examining a local legend like Alejandro Pintado would be difficult under any circumstance. The fact that he was the victim's father made Jack's job even tougher.

"Mr. Pintado, I also would like to express my sympathy to you and your family."

The witness looked back at him coldly, no verbal response. Jack moved on. "I want to ask you about this trust agreement you mentioned."

"What about it?"

"That trust was established exclusively for your son. Not for him and his wife. Am I correct?"

"That's right."

"You never had any discussions with Lindsey about that trust, did you?"

"No. Lindsey and I didn't talk about money."

"You never sent her a copy of the trust instrument, did you?"

"No, of course not."

"You never heard her having any discussions about the trust."

"You mean with Oscar?"

"I mean with anyone."

Pintado thought for a moment, as if he was beginning to pick up Jack's implication. "No. Never heard her talk about it."

Jack would have liked to knock his point home and finish with a question like, So, as far as you know,

Lindsey never even knew about Oscar's trust. But he knew he'd probably get an answer like, Actually, Mr. Swyteck, my lawyer tells me that Lindsey called his office to ask about the trust four times a day for six weeks prior to Oscar's death.

Jack figured he'd leave well enough alone.

"Mr. Pintado, let's shift gears and talk about you for a minute. I understand that you're the founder and president of Brothers for Freedom."

"That's correct. One of my proudest achievements."

"Congratulations, sir. For the benefit of those in this courtroom who have never heard of it, how would you describe the purpose of your organization?"

"We fly humanitarian missions over the Straits of Florida in search of people trying to leave Cuba. Once we find them, we do everything within our legal rights to help bring them to safety in Florida."

Jack noticed three of the jurors nodding their heads in silent approval. It was hard not to admire what he was doing. But it was Jack's job to discredit him anyway.

"Mr. Pintado, I have here a copy of a newspaper article that appeared on page two-A of the *Miami Tribune* some eleven months ago. It talks about your role in Brothers for Freedom. Do you recall speaking to a reporter before this article appeared?"

"Yes."

"The article quotes you as follows: 'We don't want to be part of the Coast Guard's new agenda, which is to send Cubans back to Cuba. They have become Castro's border patrol.'"

Jack let the quote hang in the air. The silence in the courtroom was palpable.

"Yes, those were my words," said Pintado.

"You made that statement because the U.S. Coast Guard's current policy toward any Cuban refugees intercepted at sea is to return them to Cuba. Am I right?"

"That's right."

"That policy made you angry, did it not?"

"Of course it did. We're talking about sending people back to Fidel Castro, a ruthless murderer who once put a man on trial and executed him within five days of his return to Cuba. Many others are sitting in Castro's prisons, and their only crime is that they left Cuba in search of freedom and got stopped by the U.S. Coast Guard before reaching U.S. soil."

"I understand. So, the very idea that the Coast Guard would return rafters to Cuba made you and a lot of other people angry."

"Many, many people. That's right."

"It made your son angry, too, right?"

"Yes, it did."

"Is it fair to say that Captain Pintado felt the same way you did about the U.S. Coast Guard?"

"Objection," said the prosecutor. "There's no evidence that Captain Pintado ever referred to the U.S. Coast Guard as Castro's border patrol."

"Overruled. The witness may answer."

Pintado said, "On this particular issue, yes. I would say that my son felt the same as I did."

"Did he make his views known at the naval base?"

Pintado paused, careful with his response. "I

would hope not. There were hundreds of Coast Guard sailors stationed at Guantánamo."

"Yes. Hundreds. Which means, sir, that in the largest newspaper in the Coast Guard's Seventh District—which includes Miami and Guantánamo Bay—you called three thousand of your son's next-door neighbors 'Castro's border patrol.'"

"Objection," said the prosecutor. "Asked and answered."

It was the kind of objection Jack welcomed, as it only underscored Pintado's earlier response. "Yes, I guess it was asked and answered," said Jack. He squared himself to the witness and said, "Let me ask you this, sir: Is it fair to say that your 'Castro's border patrol' comment incited anger among Coast Guard personnel?"

Again, Pintado seemed cautious to agree with anything Jack said, but he couldn't deny this. "It made some people angry, sure."

Jack went back to his table, and Sofia handed him another exhibit. "In fact, let me read to you one of the many angry responses to your 'Castro's border patrol' comment. This is an actual letter to the editor that was printed in the *Miami Tribune* three days after your quote appeared in the newspaper. It reads, 'Dear Editor: As a World War Two Coast Guard veteran, I am outraged by Mr. Pintado's reference to our branch of service as "Castro's border patrol." I spent three years of my life on a destroyer in the South Pacific trying to outrun Japanese torpedos. I saw my friends literally blown out of the water as they transported American troops to the beaches on D day. If Mr. Pintado thinks that the Coast Guard works for a vicious dictator like Fidel Castro, then I volunteer to reenlist for duty so that I can personally transport Mr. Pintado back to Cuba.'"

Jack paused to give the jury time to feel the veteran's anger.

"Is there a question?" asked the prosecutor.

"My question is this," said Jack. "Mr. Pintado, did you feel at all concerned for your personal safety after seeing that kind of response to your comments?"

"I've always been outspoken. I'm used to that kind of thing."

"You're used to it, and you take precautions."

"I'm not sure I take your meaning."

"You have a bodyguard, do you not?" asked Jack.

"Yes."

"Your wife has a bodyguard as well, correct?"

"Yes."

"But your son—Oscar—he was on his own. No bodyguard. Living on the same base with hundreds of Coast Guard members whom you called 'Castro's border patrol.'"

Pintado struggled with his response, then simply brushed it aside. "Oscar obviously didn't have any problems. His best friend was in the Coast Guard."

"His best friend. That would be Lieutenant Damont Johnson, correct?"

"Yes."

Jack scoffed, seizing the opportunity to plant a seed of doubt in the jury's mind—and to give the prosecutor a dose of his own medicine about missing witnesses. "Well, perhaps Lieutenant Johnson will come here himself and tell us just how good a friend he *really* was."

"Objection."

"Sustained."

Jack weighed in his mind whether to push harder, but implying that a father was even indirectly responsible for his son's murder was touchy stuff. Jack could read the jury well enough to know that it was time to sit down.

"Thank you, Mr. Pintado. No further questions."

31

At the end of the day, Jack said good-bye to his client in the courtroom, handed her over to the federal marshals, and told her to keep her chin up on her journey back to prison.

That was the reality of a capital trial with no bail.

Jack knew that the routine had to be demoralizing for Lindsey. She'd trade her business suit for prison garb, her wristwatch for handcuffs. Instead of crawling into bed and giving her son a kiss, the best that she could hope for was that she would indeed sleep alone. She would lie awake and brainstorm about the next trial day, or play Monday morning quarterback as to each of the day's witnesses. Jailhouse snitches would try to befriend her, try to get her to talk about her case, all in hopes of unearthing some little gem that would curry favor with the prosecutor and earn them an early get-out-of-jail-free card. She'd keep to herself and search constantly for mindless forms of mental stimulation, anything to keep her from wondering if she'd rather die than spend the rest of her life in prison, wondering if death by lethal injection was truly painless. Her thoughts would be her only privacy, no one to share them with, not even her lawyers.

That left Jack and Sofia to handle the late-night planning sessions.

"How do you think it played today?" asked Jack. He was seated at his dining room table across from Sofia. Night after night in a law office could get old in a hurry, so he and Sofia agreed that the evening debriefings would alternate between his house and hers.

"You lost jurors number three and six, for sure. Probably number two as well. But we knew that before you even opened your mouth. Any one of them would make a strong good candidate for president of the Alejandro Pintado fan club."

Jack drew a breath, let it out. "I feel like I'm alienating the entire Cuban American population."

"Ironic, isn't it? After all you just went through, learning about your mother and your half-Cuban roots."

"When this case is over, I guess we'll probably both be moving to Iowa."

"Or I could finally make my mother happy. Get married, change my name, melt into suburbia."

"You're talking marriage now, huh? That must have been some date you had the other night."

"I was speaking theoretically."

"So, he was a dud?

"I didn't say he was a dud."

"He was definitely a dud. I can tell."

"And what makes you so smart?"

"I'm a trial lawyer. I have good instincts."

"Okay," she said with a smile. "So, not counting that charred Mustang sitting in front of your house, how many times have these awesome instincts gotten you totally burned?"

"Ooh. That was way harsh, Sofia. But . . . I was right, wasn't I? He's a dud?"

"Okay, you were right. But who are you to talk? Your friend Theo told me about that long-distance girlfriend of yours in Africa. What's her name—Ramapithecus or something?"

"Rene."

"Yes, Rene. The one who pops in for a visit every two or three months."

"She's a pediatrician. She does charity work over there. She comes back to Miami when she can."

"That's not exactly what Theo tells me. He says she flies in, breaks your bed, flies out."

"Theo told you that?"

"Yes. With a considerable amount of envy in his tone, I might add. But to the rest of the world, she doesn't sound like much of a girlfriend."

Jack wasn't sure how to come back. She was right. Rene wasn't much of a girlfriend. "At least she doesn't drive an El Camino. I mean, really: Who thinks *that* is a classic?"

She was half smiling, half aghast. "How did you know my date drives—"

A loud noise from outside the house gave them both a start. It sounded like someone banging pots and pans in Jack's driveway.

"What's going on out there?" asked Sofia.

"Theo. Ever since the police released the crime scene, he's been tinkering around."

"He doesn't actually think he can fix it, does he? The thing went up in flames."

"I don't know what he's doing. Sometimes with Theo you're better off if you just don't ask."

Jack cleared away the dinner remnants of prepackaged salads and pizza. They retired to the living room, where Sofia could review her trial notes and give Jack some feedback. Pintado's testimony had taken the entire morning, and the medical examiner had filled the afternoon. The prosecutor had done a decent job of getting the examiner to put the time of death within a range that was before Lindsey left for work. Jack had done his best to get him to concede that it was an estimate, that there was wiggle room.

The banging in the driveway continued, even louder than before. Jack looked up from his notes, annoyed. "What the *hell* is he doing out there? Building a cruise ship?"

"He's your friend. You tell me."

"Let me take care of this." Jack popped up from the couch and headed out the front door. The blackened shell of his Mustang was at the end of the driveway, right where it had gone up in flames. It was no longer a crime scene, but Theo had refused to let Jack have it towed away. He was dressed in dirty coveralls, crescent wrench in hand. Somehow, he'd actually managed to pry open the hood.

"Theo!" Jack shouted over all the racket. "We're trying to get some work done."

He stopped banging, stepped back from the car, and wiped the sweat from his brow. "So am I, man. Look what they did to my car."

"Hate to break this to you, but it's not your car."

Theo's mouth fell open, as if he were about to utter "Et tu, Brutus?" "Not *mine*? I washed this baby with my own hands. When it purred, I smiled. When it whined, I fixed it. What did you ever do? Put gas in it and pay the insurance? You wouldn't even buy it a garage. A fucking *porta cochere* is all you gave it. I think that's French for 'park your shitty Chevy Vega right here.'"

"You think I didn't love that car? I was the one who—"

"Boys!" said Sofia.

Jack and Theo turned to see her standing on the other side of the Mustang's charred remains. She walked around it, dragging her index finger across the soot-covered metal as she spoke. "Are you two grown men actually having an argument over who loved a car more? Hello-o-o-o. It's a car, guys. In the big scheme of things, how important is that?"

Silence fell over them. Finally, Theo looked at Jack, his expression deadpan. "Is she high?"

"She must be."

Sofia rolled her eyes and went back in the house.

They shared a little laugh, then Jack turned serious. "I mean it, Theo. It sounds like the musical cast from *Stomp* is out here. Can't you do whatever it is you're doing another time?"

"Do you want to find out who torched your Mustang or don't you?"

"Yeah, I do. That's what the police are for."

"The police. *Puh-lease*. Just tell the cops to stand back and let me do my job."

"You think you're going to figure out who torched my car, do you?"

"Yup. Just follow the parts."

"What are you talking about?"

Theo slid the wrench into his pocket and leaned against the car, his arms folded. "Here's the deal. For the past three days, I been askin' myself: How does a guy walk up to an amazing car like this and just burn it? It's such a waste."

"Some people love to watch things go up in flames."

"True. But more people love to make a quick buck."

"Meaning what?"

"The parts, Jacko. That's why I been banging away here. It's burned pretty bad, but I can tell you right now: Somebody walked off with some parts before they put a match to this baby. Definitely took your pony bucket seats. Probably got the rally pack gauges, wood steering wheel, shifter console. I can already see he got the four barrel carb and manifold from the engine compartment, and I'm just getting started in there."

"What would he do with all that stuff, sell it?"

"*Duh.* We're talking a vintage Mustang convertible. You can easily haul away a small fortune in parts."

"So the guy stole some parts? Where does that get you?"

"Like I said: Follow the parts. I just do some checking around with repair shops that specialize in collector cars. See if anyone unloaded some Mustang parts in the last few days."

Jack nodded, following his logic. "Actually, there aren't that many. At least not that many good ones. I can tell you that much from experience."

"Exactly. So, all I gotta do is go around shopping for the right parts. When I find the guy who has them, I just get him to tell me who sold him the parts."

"Sounds good on paper. But no grease monkey is going to tell you where he bought stolen parts."

"Wrong again, Jacko. No grease monkey is going to tell *you* where he bought the stolen parts." He slid the big wrench out of his pocket, then tapped it into his open palm as he spoke. "But he'll tell me. Trust me. He'll *beg* to tell me."

"I didn't hear that," said Jack.

"I never said it," said Theo.

32

•

The morning was all about bodily fluids. Jack had been expecting blood—crime-scene photos, spray-pattern analysis, that sort of thing. The prosecutor had something else entirely on tap.

Torres said, "Dr. Vandermeer, would you please introduce yourself to the jury?"

A small man with neatly cropped beard and mustache leaned toward the microphone. The witness box almost dwarfed him, and Jack had the sense that he should have been sitting on a phone book or something. He leaned toward Lindsey and whispered, "You know this guy?"

"Never seen him before," she said.

The witness cleared his throat and said, "My name is Timothy Vandermeer. I have a Ph.D. in psychology, and I am an M.D. who specializes in treatment of patients with problems of infertility."

"Are you board certified in this area?"

"Yes. I am an American Board of Obstetrics and Gynecology Certified Diplomate. I am also board

certified in the subspecialty of reproductive endo-
crinology."

"What other experience and education do you
have in this area?"

His response went on and on, everything from
his undergraduate dual major in biology and psychology to the numerous scholarly articles he had
written for medical journals around the country.
Jack stopped taking notes when Vandermeer mentioned a research piece entitled, "It's a Boy/It's a
Girl—The Joy of Spinning Sperm."

The prosecutor glanced toward the jury, as if to
make sure they were still with him. He seemed satisfied. "Doctor, you mentioned earlier that you have
a Ph.D. in psychology. Do psychological factors
ever come into play in your treatment of patients
with infertility problems?"

"Oh, yes, absolutely. You don't need a Ph.D. in
psychology to know that emotional factors, such as
stress, can affect one's ability to procreate."

"Does that hold true for both men and women?"

"Surely. It works both ways. Men, however, can
generally be less willing than women to talk about
these psychological factors. But that doesn't mean
they aren't there."

Again the prosecutor checked the jury, perhaps
to make sure he wasn't embarrassing anyone. Then
he shifted gears. "Doctor, was the defendant, Lindsey Hart, ever your patient?"

"No, she was not."

"Was her husband, Captain Oscar Pintado, ever
your patient?"

"Yes, he was."

There was a quiet rumbling in the courtroom, and the judge perked up a bit, too. Jack managed to cut his visible reaction to a sideways glance at his client. He could see in her eyes that she had no idea.

The prosecutor said, "Tell us how that came about, please."

"Captain Pintado first came to my office in Miami about a year ago. He was on military leave with his wife and son. But they weren't with him. In fact, I should point out that Captain Pintado specifically asked me not to tell his wife that he was consulting me."

"What was the purpose of his visit?"

"As he explained it, he and his wife had been trying to have a child for many years. They adopted a son, but they had not given up hope of getting pregnant. He told me that he and his wife had seen an infertility specialist together. Unfortunately, that doctor was unable to help them."

"Did he tell you why he came to see you?"

"Yes. His father recommended me. Alejandro Pintado—or perhaps Mrs. Pintado—happened to see me on a television talk show discussing my latest research on infertility issues."

"Briefly, Doctor, could you please describe the nature and findings of that research?"

His face lit up, as if he would have liked nothing better. "Gladly. In the most general sense, the nature of my research was sperm analysis. I compared two groups of men. In the first group, I analyzed the sperm of men who were in a completely monogamous relationship with a woman, either married or with a long-time partner. The other group was made up entirely of men who admitted to having sex with women who had multiple sexual partners."

"Let me make sure I understand this second group. It was not the man who had multiple sexual partners. It was the woman."

"That's correct. I was looking for a one-woman man, so to speak, where the woman had made no commitment of exclusivity to that particular man. Frankly, most of the men in this category were single men who were in a relationship with a married woman."

"All right. I assume you collected sperm samples from men in both groups."

"That's correct."

"What kind of analysis did you do?"

"The first step was a standard semen analysis. I wanted to make sure that I was dealing with sperm samples that fell within normal ranges. Particularly with respect to motility and forward motion."

"Would you explain those terms, please?"

"Motility refers to the extent to which sperm actually moves. Like the old macho saying, 'My guys can swim.' If they don't move, they're fairly useless. Swimming, however, is not the be-all and end-all. If your sperm is doing the backstroke, you're probably not going to fertilize the egg, either."

A little laughter wafted across the courtroom. Even the judge smiled. The prosecutor said, "So, forward motion is a separate component of motility?"

"That's right."

"That makes sense. What was the next step of your analysis?"

He grinned, as if too pleased with himself. "Not

to pat myself on the back too firmly, but this is where my analysis was somewhat groundbreaking. I examined the motility of sperm in two different environments. First, I looked at each man's sperm in isolation and took my measurements. Once I'd done that, I would introduce the sperm of another man into each man's sample. And I got the most interesting results."

"What did you find, Doctor?"

"In both groups of men, some of the motile sperm continued to swim forward, as if headed straight for the egg. Other motile sperm, however, swam directly toward the foreign sperm. These sperm attacked the invader, pummeled it, and destroyed it."

"What did this tell you, Doctor?"

"My conclusion is that men have two kinds of sperm. One has fertilization as a primary mission. The others act like soldiers, making sure that the invading sperm never reaches the egg. I call them assassin sperm."

"And you say this was true in both groups of men?"

"Yes, both groups had assassin sperm. But here is where the results became very interesting. The men who were paired in a monogamous relationship had relatively few assassin sperm. By comparison, men who were involved with women who had multiple sexual partners had far more assassin sperm."

"What accounted for this difference?"

"In my opinion, it is purely a psychological component—the man's state of mind. If he believed he was the only candidate in search of the egg, his assassin sperm count was low. But if he believed that he was in competition with another male, his body produced additional assassin sperm."

The prosecutor paused to allow the jury to absorb that crucial point. It wasn't clear that they understood where this was headed, but Jack knew—and he was planning his objection.

Torres said, "Let's get back to your examination of Captain Oscar Pintado. Did you do an analysis of his sperm?"

"Yes I did."

"What kind of analysis?"

"The same analysis I just described. I did a standard analysis first, which revealed that his semen fell within the normal ranges, including normal motility."

"Did you then test his sperm with . . . how should I put this? Invading sperm?"

"I did."

"What did you find?"

Jack was on his feet. "Objection. Sidebar, please, Your Honor."

The judge straightened in his chair, then waved them forward. They gathered out of earshot from the jury and witness.

Jack said, "Judge, first of all, I've never heard of this assassin sperm analysis. The very idea of a man's sperm doing kung fu on some other guy's business and then slapping microscopic high-fives all around sounds a little ridiculous."

"It's accepted science," said Torres.

"Maybe it is," said Jack. "But in this case, the doctor's testimony amounts to nothing more than a sneaky, backdoor effort to prove that my client was unfaithful to her husband."

"It's not the back door. We're talking about a scientific analysis of her husband's sperm. Captain Pintado had a high level of assassin sperm, which shows that he was married to a woman who had multiple sexual partners."

"Not even close," said Jack. "At best, it shows that *he believed* she had multiple sexual partners. I can see where evidence of infidelity might be probative of a wife's alleged motive to kill her husband. But mere evidence that the victim believed his wife was unfaithful doesn't add up to any motive on my client's part to commit murder."

"Mr. Swyteck may have a point," said the judge.

Torres grimaced, obviously frustrated. "Judge, could I have a word alone with Mr. Swyteck? I believe we can work this out, lawyer to lawyer."

"Fine. My bladder's calling anyway." He banged his gavel and switched on the microphone. "Court's in recess," he announced. "We'll resume in five minutes."

The judge made a beeline for the bathroom. The crowd broke into hundreds of small pockets of conversation. Jack signaled to Lindsey and Sofia back at the table, as if to say that all would be okay. Then he and the prosecutor hurried out the side door to a private room.

As soon as the door closed, the prosecutor looked at Jack and said, "I'll give you one chance to withdraw your objection."

"And why would I do that?"

"Because one way or another, I'm going to prove that your client was cheating on her husband, and that's part of the reason she killed him."

Jack showed no reaction. "I don't care what you hope to prove. At the moment, all I'm saying is that I'm not going to let you prove it this way."

"Then it's her kid who pays."

"What?"

"My first choice is to use Dr. Vandermeer to prove that Lindsey was cheating on her husband. But if you won't let me do that, then I'm going to call the kid to the stand. I'm going to ask him how many men he saw come and go from the house when his father wasn't home."

"You're bluffing," said Jack.

"No, I'm not. So it's your call, Jack. You can withdraw your objection and let Dr. Vandermeer testify. Or you can stand firm and make me put the boy on the stand. But don't kid yourself. Before this trial is over, the jury will fully understand that it was *you* who forced me to sit a ten-year-old child in the witness box so that he could tell the whole world that his mommy is a whore."

Jack struggled to show no reaction. Several strands of thought were weaving through his head, a tangled mess of conflicting information that seemed to wrap around his brain and choke off all ability to reason. Then he realized it wasn't thought or reason at all that was clouding the issue. It was emotion, pure and simple—his amorphous feelings for the biological son he'd never met. Meeting Brian for the very first time under circumstances such as these was something he didn't even want to consider.

"Let me talk to Lindsey" was all he could say.

33
.

At Jack's request, Judge Garcia stretched the five-minute recess into twenty. Jack watched from across the table as Lindsey massaged her temples, trying to nip a migraine in the bud. Sofia was seated at the short end of the rectangular table, perpendicular to Jack at her left and Lindsey at her right. It was just the three of them in the windowless conference room.

Lindsey's voice shook with anger as she said, "I can't believe that bastard would threaten to use my own son against me like that."

"I can," said Sofia.

Jack glanced at his cocounsel, as if to say *Let me handle this*. "Lindsey, as your lawyer, there's one thing I need to know: What would Brian's testimony be if the prosecutor called him to the stand?"

She stopped massaging and looked Jack in the eye. "You mean about these strange men coming to our house when Oscar was away?"

"That's exactly what I mean."

"It's absurd. If I were going to cheat on my

husband, do you think I would do it in my own house with my son in the next room?"

"Coincidentally, that's exactly what a certain Cuban soldier is going to say if we call him in your defense. You and Johnson were having sex while your son slept in the next room."

"I told you five times already, I was not having an affair with Damont Johnson. I wasn't having an affair with anyone."

Jack thought for a moment. "So, if Brian were to take the stand and say that a stream of strange men was parading toward your doorstep, he would be lying?"

"The prosecutor is bluffing. Brian would never say that."

"Can you be sure of that? Remember, he's been living with his grandparents for almost a month now."

Lindsey tugged nervously at a strand of her hair. "I don't know anymore. He's ten. He could be manipulated into saying just about anything, I suppose."

"Easily," said Jack, stepping into the role of prosecutor. "'Brian, did men ever come over to your house? Did they come with your father? Was your father there the whole time they stayed? Are you sure? Is it possible that your father left, and that the men stayed? Is it possible they came back later, after your father had left?' Before you know it, Torres has your son rattling off the names of a half-dozen soldiers who came to visit his mother."

"You can't let that creep do that to my son."

"There's only one thing we can do to avoid it."

Lindsey swallowed the lump in her throat. "Then that's what we should do. I'm not going to let my son be manipulated into testifying against me."

"You want me to withdraw my objection to Vandermeer's testimony?"

"If that's what it takes to keep him off the stand, yes."

"That's the way I'll pitch it to Torres. I'll let the doctor's testimony go to the jury only on the condition that he agree not to call Brian as a witness."

"Do it," said Lindsey.

"All right. But it does create another problem down the road. It's going to be that much harder for us to argue that the Cuban soldier is lying about you and Johnson."

"I told you, I was not having an affair."

"I know. And we agreed that if we put the Cuban on the stand, we would try to convince the jury that he was telling the truth about Johnson coming to your house the morning of the murder, but he was throwing in the spicy sex just to embarrass the Pintado family. But with Vandermeer in the equation, it's no longer your word against the word of a Cuban soldier."

"Then maybe we don't call the Cuban."

"Maybe we don't," said Jack. "I need to think more about that."

Lindsey seemed to be searching for words, then finally she looked at Sofia, then back at Jack. "Could I speak to Sofia alone for a minute?"

Jack said, "I'm your lawyer, too. This is all privileged."

"I would just feel more comfortable if Sofia and I were alone."

"We've got just two minutes left on this break," said Jack. "If there's something that needs to be aired, it needs to be aired among all of us."

A tense silence filled the room. "Okay," said Lindsey. She drew a breath, unable to look Jack in the eye as she spoke. "The Cuban soldier . . ."

Jack waited, but the silence continued. "The Cuban soldier what?"

Finally, she said, "He isn't lying."

Somehow, Jack had already known. But hearing it still felt like a mule kick. "You lied to me again, damn it."

"No, I didn't lie. Lieutenant Johnson and I weren't having an affair. It was . . ."

Again, she lapsed into silence. She was doing funny things with her lips, as if her mouth were at war with the words she was about to utter.

"It was what?" said Jack.

Her eyes closed, then opened, and her voice was barely audible as she said, "It was a good bit weirder than that."

Jack felt that mule kick again.

There was a knock at the door, and Sofia opened it. The bailiff stuck her head into the room. "Judge Garcia's back on the bench. He wants us back in the courtroom—*now*."

Jack was torn, but a federal judge was not the kind of person to keep waiting. "We'll finish this later," he said.

"There's nothing more to say." Her chin was on her chest, and she seemed to be biting back her shame, if not shutting down the flow of information.

"Like I said. We'll finish this later." Jack grabbed his briefcase, then took his client by the arm and led her back to the courtroom.

34

·

Theo Knight was on a shopping spree. The search was on for the stolen parts—and for the guy who'd torched Jack's Mustang.

As expected, relatively few shops specialized in classic-car parts, and many of those were highly specialized, dealing exclusively in Corvettes or foreign cars. A dozen phone calls produced no leads. Finally, a call to the Mustang Solution in Hialeah turned up the kind of bumper Theo was looking for. A personal visit to the shop confirmed that it was indeed Jack's. Theo had washed that car hundreds of times, knew every dent and ding. The rear bumper on Jack's car had a dimple to the right of the license plate mount. This one had the same dimple.

"How much you want for it?" Theo asked the shop owner.

"Four hundred."

Fucking thief, thought Theo. He peeled off five bills and said, "An extra hundred if you tell me where you got it."

"You a cop?"

"Cops take bills, dumbshit. They don't dish 'em out."

The owner smiled as he rolled up the cash and tucked it into his shirt pocket. "His name's Eduardo Gonzalez. Goes by Eddy. Known him since high school."

"Where do I find this Eddy?"

The guy made a cutesy face, as if he knew but wasn't telling. Theo laid another fifty on the counter, which did the trick.

"He's got his own welding shop or studio of some sort over on Flagler and Fifty-seventh. You'll see it. Says 'Eddy's Palace' on the door."

Twenty minutes later Theo was headed down Flagler Street with the rear bumper of a '67 Mustang convertible tied to his roof rack. He parked on a side street and walked up the block, past a liquor store, past a vacant theater, past one of those stores that sells everything you don't need for just one dollar. He stopped at an old storefront with a plate-glass window that bore the words EDDY'S PALACE.

He tried the door, but it was locked. The window looked as though it hadn't been washed in years. Theo wiped away a little dirt and peered inside. Just enough lights were burning to let him see a few things here and there. At first it looked like nothing but heaps of scrap metal, all shapes and sizes. As he looked closer, however, he could see that the pieces all fit together. They had form. They were sculptures. Eddy's Palace was an art studio.

Theo cupped his hands like blinders to cut down the glare. The forms came clearer. A huge, metal arm was reaching from the floor, like a hand from the grave. The man beside it was impaled on a lance, his gaping mouth exaggerated to emphasize his suffering. Several other figures seemed normal from the waist up, but the lower halves of their bodies were twisted and melted, overcome by metal tongues of fire. There were hundreds of other figures, some small, some larger than life, all with their mouths wide open, all with that same exaggerated expression of pain.

It looked like one man's version of hell.

Theo stepped away from the window, and he was about to give the door another try when he noticed a little sign near the doorbell. It read: DOORBELL BROKEN, PLEASE ENTER AT BACK DOOR.

Dusk was turning to dark, and even Theo was having second thoughts about walking down an alley in search of the back door to hell. The neighborhood was at best questionable. The windows on nearby buildings were covered with burglar bars, and Theo recognized the cigar shop across the street from a newscast about a month earlier. The owner had been shot dead in a robbery. But he'd come too far to back down from some metal-worker-turned-artist who didn't think twice about torching a true work of art, a classic Mustang convertible. Theo walked a few steps north and then turned down the alley.

It was a long, narrow alley, and with each step, Theo put the traffic noise from Flagler Street farther behind him. He was soon alone with the Dumpsters, deep into shadows so dark that he had to stop for a moment to let his eyes adjust. There was a street lamp overhead, and it should have clicked on by now. It had to be burned out. Theo took a few more steps, but then he stopped as he reached the end of the alley and rounded the corner to the back of the building. He heard something. It sounded like hissing.

A snake?

The thought made him shudder. Theo wasn't afraid of much, but he was definitely not a snake guy.

The hissing continued, and then Theo spotted the source. The door at the studio's rear entrance was open—wide open, not just unlocked. The hissing was coming from inside. Theo started toward the open door. It couldn't be a snake. The hissing was continuous. No snake hissed nonstop. He stopped at the open doorway and looked inside.

The back of Eddy's Palace was more like a metal shop than a studio. Eddy obviously created his sculptures right on the premises. A man—presumably Eddy—was busy at his welding table, his back to the door. He wore a metal visor over his head, the dark kind that protected the eyes from the intense glare of a welding iron. Theo could feel the heat escaping through the open door. Theo had done some welding himself, mostly on cars. He knew the arc could reach several thousand degrees. It was no wonder the door was open.

Theo watched for a minute or two. The artist was totally absorbed in his craft, shaping what appeared to be the all-important gaping mouth of another citizen from hell. Theo could have rolled through the back door in a tank and gone unnoticed.

Which gave him an idea.

Quietly, he stepped inside the studio. Eddy was

still focused on work, oblivious to anything else. The gas tanks were near the door. Another torch was hanging on a hook beside the tanks. Theo opened the valve on the extra torch. He could feel the gas coursing through the tubing. He had firepower, which made him smile a little. Then he turned the valve off on the torch Eddy was working with, and he gently closed the door.

The flame on Eddy's torch grew smaller and smaller until it finally went out. Eddy straightened up, as if ready to switch tanks. As he flipped up his visor and turned toward the tanks, Theo was on top of him like a *T. rex* on lunch. Eddy was facedown on the cement before he knew what had hit him. He squirmed for a moment, then a foot-long flame scorched the concrete floor just inches from his nose.

"Don't move," said Theo. He was sitting on Eddy's kidneys, pressing him into the floor.

Eddy's eyes were like silver dollars, his voice shaking. "Don't hurt me, man."

"Shut the fuck up, or I start cooking your nose from the inside out."

Eddy was shaking, but he didn't say a word.

"Good," said Theo. "Nice and quiet, and nobody gets hurt. I'm a real lover of the arts, so it would be a shame to toast you. I mean that. I really dig your work. Highly unusual pieces. Very reminiscent of . . . Oh, what am I thinking of?"

Sweat was pouring down Eddy's face. His breathing grew louder, but he didn't answer.

Theo tapped the head of the torch on the concrete, giving Eddy a start. "You can talk when I ask you a question, moron."

Eddy could barely keep his saliva in his mouth. "What was the question?"

"I said your work reminds me of something that I just can't put my finger on."

"Salvador Dalí?"

"Hmmm. Actually, I was gonna say mindfarts of a serial killer. But we can go with Dalí, if that makes you feel better."

"Just tell me what you want, man."

"I want information. Can you give me information, Eddy?"

"Whatever you want. Just don't hurt me, all right?"

"Sure. What I want to know is—" Theo stopped himself. This was too easy. Where was the fun? His gaze quickly swept the workshop, and a thin smile crept to his lips as he spotted the many half creations around him, all these suffering souls destined for hell. He was suddenly feeling spiritual. "You believe in God, Eddy?"

"I don't know, man. Do you want me to?"

"You must believe. All this hell around you. Can't be a hell if there's no God, right?"

"Sure, sure. I believe."

"Good. Because this is what I want to know. Hypothetically, let's say I'm God. This is just pretend now, okay? Don't be running to my momma's grave and tellin' her I think I'm God or something. So I'm God, and I've decided to grant my first interview. You got the scoop, Eddy, but you can ask only one question. Just one. So fire away. What do you want to ask God?"

"Huh?"

"There's no right or wrong here, pal. Just spit it out. It's just you and God in the back of your studio. For the moment, let's ignore the fact that God's packing a blowtorch that can melt your face into the concrete. Go ahead, ask your one question."

The punk could barely speak, he was so frightened. "Uhm—what's the meaning of life?"

Theo made a face, as if in pain. "What the hell kind of shitty question is that?"

"You said there was no right or wrong here."

Theo smacked him on the side of the head. "Did anybody ever fucking tell you to believe what I say?"

"No."

"Now ask another question. And make it good!"

He swallowed, but he didn't have anything to say.

"What are you, brain dead?" said Theo. "You can't think of one decent question? How about something like this: Why does cold water boil faster than hot water? You want to ask him that?"

He nodded tentatively.

"It doesn't, shithead. Who told you it was okay to ask God a trick question, huh?"

"Don't, don't!" He seemed to sense that the blowtorch was coming.

Theo squeezed the trigger, sending a tongue of flame onto the concrete. It was so close to Eddy that it singed his hair. The guy was about to crumble. "Give me a break, man, okay?"

Theo sighed and said, "Aw, shit. I gotta do everything around here. Okay, here's one last suggestion. I got God on the line, right? 'Yo, God, it's Theo. How you doin'? Got a question for you. Is there anything this poor slob here'—what's your name again?"

"Eddy."

" 'Is there anything poor Eddy here can possibly do to keep from getting scorched by a big, angry black guy who spent four years on death row after being wrongly convicted by a bunch of white jurors and one little Hispanic twit who looks a hell of a lot like Eddy?' "

It took a moment for the question to register, then Eddy gulped. "It wasn't me, man. I wasn't on no jury!"

Theo smacked the back of his head once more. "I know it wasn't you, asshole! But for the entire four years I spent in Florida State prison, my cellmates were Cindy Crawford and Whitney Houston. So if you think I don't got the power of imagination, then you got no fucking idea how bad this is gonna turn out for you."

"Please . . ." he said, now groveling. "Just tell me what you want."

Theo let him squirm for a moment, watched the tears run down a grown man's cheeks. Then he leaned forward and whispered into his ear. "Why did you torch Jack Swyteck's car?"

Eddy froze.

Theo said, "It was you, wasn't it?"

"It wasn't my idea," he said, shaking. "They told me to do it."

"Who told you?"

"Don't make me rat, man. They'll kill me. I swear, they'll kill me."

"Well, that's pretty funny, Eddy. If you tell me, they'll kill you. If you don't tell me, I'll kill you. It's like I once had to tell my old friend Jack: Looks like you're caught in your own zipper there, pal."

"I'm serious. They'll kill me."

Theo leaned closer, his nose nearly touching the nape of Eddy's neck. "*I'm* serious. *I'll* kill you." He gave the blowtorch a quick blast for added effect.

Eddy shivered, his voice racing. "Okay, okay. I'll tell you."

"Good boy, Eddy. I'm all ears."

Just after midnight, Jack thought he heard a knock at his front door. He was dressed in nylon jogging shorts and a T-shirt, foamy toothbrush in hand, preparing for bed. He rinsed his mouth and walked to the living room. It was dark, lighted only in places by the dim glow of an outdoor porch lamp that shined through the open slats in the draperies. He went to the front door and listened. Then he heard it again. A knock with rhythm.

DUH, duh-duh-duh-duh, DUH . . .

He stood in silence, waiting for the final *DUH, DUH.* Instead, there was a flurry of pounding, the signature psycho knock, and Jack thought he knew who it was. He turned the deadbolt and opened the door.

He barely got a look at her face before she burst across the threshold, threw her arms around his neck, and planted her lips on his. He was startled at first, but the passion was contagious, and in a moment he was kissing her back. Finally, she stopped for air.

"Hi, Jack."

"Hey, Rene," he said, breathless. "How you doing?"

Her expression turned serious. "It's been three months since you came to see me. I work in a West

African country so full of AIDS that I'm afraid to even *think* about sex." She grabbed his ass and said, "How do you think I'm doing?"

"I'm thinking maybe you'd like to come in?"

She closed the door with a hind kick, her eyes never leaving his. Jack looked away, scratching his head. It was a little overwhelming, especially since his mind had barely shut off from tomorrow's trial preparation. But that was Rene. Even after a transatlantic flight, she was drop-dead gorgeous. At least in Jack's eyes.

He walked to the couch and sat on the armrest. "It must be six weeks since I even got an e-mail from you. I'm pretty surprised to see you."

"I'm sorry about that. But first things first, okay? I'm presenting at a pediatric AIDS conference in Los Angeles tomorrow. My connecting flight leaves at six A.M."

"Not much of a window for good, quality vertical time."

"No. So lighten up, would you? A lot of guys would be envious of you right now."

"A lot of guys think the perfect woman is a twenty-year-old stripper with no gag reflex."

"Are you saying I'm not perfect?"

"No, I'm saying . . ." Jack paused.

There were two white columns at the entrance to Jack's living room. Rene tried to look at least half serious as she pressed her body against the nearest column, then wrapped her leg around it like an erotic pole dancer. "So I'm not twenty anymore. But two out of three's not bad."

Jack chuckled, and so did she. It was a nice combination, someone who could crack you up and turn you on at the same time. "Come here, you."

She went to him, nuzzling up to his neck.

"How long you been traveling?" he asked.

"Seventeen hours."

"How about a shower?"

"I'm wearing a thong."

"How about a quick shower?"

She kissed him about the face and said, "How about you shower with me?"

"Hmm. Very tempting, honey. But there's absolutely no way we'll get out of there without having sex, and sex in my teeny-tiny shower stall rates right up there with sex on a coffee table. Alluring in theory, but what the hell's the point when there's a perfectly good mattress twenty feet away?"

"You're such a putz."

"I know. It's a gift."

"Get your ass in the shower."

He smiled and said, "Yes, ma'am."

35

Jack was staring at the final witness for the prosecution. After a night with Rene, he was barely able to keep his eyes open. But it didn't take long to figure out that the prosecutor had saved the best for last.

Lieutenant Stephen Porter was the lead NCIS investigator on the case against Lindsey Hart. Motive had already been established: Alejandro Pintado and Dr. Vandermeer had painted Lindsey as an unfaithful wife who would gladly make herself a widow, if that's what it took to get off the naval base and inherit her husband's family money. The medical examiner had confirmed her opportunity to commit the crime: he placed the time of death before Lindsey left for work, though Jack had chipped away at his guesstimate. The final leg of the murder triangle was the means, which it was the investigator's chief function to establish.

"Did you consider the possibility of suicide?" the prosecutor asked.

Porter sat up straight, though he was already quite

rigid. He was alert, nicely groomed, and smartly dressed in his naval uniform, the antithesis of the typical chain-smoking, burned-out homicide detective on the civilian side. "Yes," he said. "We considered it. But the fact that the victim's gun was found with the safety on suggested that it wasn't suicide. Kind of hard to put on the safety after you kill yourself."

That drew a reverberation of mild amusement from the crowd.

Torres said, "Did you observe any blood-spray patterns or other evidence to indicate suicide?"

"No, and that's an important point. When someone takes his own life by firing a bullet into his head at close range, you would normally expect some back spray of blood and other matter onto the victim's own hand. I saw none with naked eye when I arrived on the scene, and I would add that no microscopic traces were noted in the autopsy report."

"What about fingerprints? If you are going to rule out suicide, it seems you would want to find some fingerprints on the gun that don't belong to the victim."

"We did find one extraneous fingerprint on the handle near the trigger."

"Did you establish a match for that fingerprint?"

"Yes, we did, with the FBI's assistance."

"Can you please tell the jury whose fingerprint it was?"

"It was the right index finger of Lindsey Hart."

Just that quickly, the prosecution had made its key points: Oscar Pintado's death was not a suicide, and a fingerprint from Lindsey's right hand—her firing hand—was on the gun. The only way for the defense to explain it was to put Lindsey on the stand. But they had a long way to go before the explaining would come, if it was to come at all. Lindsey didn't have to take the stand in her own defense, and Jack wasn't sure he wanted her to. So he needed to do some serious damage control before they broke for the weekend.

"Lieutenant Porter," Jack said as he approached the witness, "I'd like to hear more about this lack of back spray that you mentioned. First, let me make sure I understand this. Back spray occurs when a bullet is fired into the victim from extremely close range, correct?"

"That's right. It's generally referred to as a close-entry wound."

"Meaning a few inches or less?"

"Inches, or perhaps no separation at all between the gun and the victim's skin."

"We all agree that Captain Pintado suffered a close-entry wound, do we not?"

"No dispute on that."

"And we also agree that there was no back spray on Captain Pintado's hands, which weighs against a finding of suicide."

"That's correct."

Jack paused, then took a step closer. "What about Lindsey Hart's hands, Lieutenant? You didn't find any back spray on her hands, did you?"

He shifted in his chair. "No. But it's organic matter. All it takes is soap and water, and no more back spray."

"There was none in her hair, on her face, or on her clothes, was there?"

"None that we found. But there was plenty of time for her to shower, change clothes, even dump the blood-stained clothes in the hospital incinerator when she went to work that morning."

"Lieutenant, are you familiar with blood reagents, such as Luminol or Florescein?"

"Yes. Those are chemicals that react with blood."

"They can pick up traces of blood that may have been washed away or that are otherwise invisible to the naked eye, isn't that right?"

"Basically. Luminol turns it green, and Florescein makes it glow under UV light."

"You didn't use Luminol or Florescein to connect blood traces to my client, did you?"

"No," he said, seeming to reach deep for a prepared response. "Chemical reagents can destroy other evidence. So we didn't use them."

"Is that the reason you didn't use them, Lieutenant? Or was it because you knew that the results would only hurt your case against my client?"

"Objection."

"Sustained," said the judge. "The witness told you why he didn't use it. Move on, Mr. Swyteck."

"What about gunshot residue?" said Jack. "When the gun is fired at such close range, doesn't gunshot residue often blow back onto the trigger hand?"

"It can, yes. I assume you mean the nitrocellulose powder, which is the propellant that forces the bullet down the barrel."

"Your investigative team didn't collect any gunshot residue when it swabbed Lindsey Hart's hands, did it?"

"No, we didn't. But again, the weapon involved

here is an M9 9 mm Beretta pistol. There's less residue on the hands with an auto-loader, and it's much easier to wash off. It might require a couple of scrubbings, but still, all it takes is soap and water."

Jack went back to his table, and Sofia handed him the investigative report. He flipped through it just long enough to make the prosecutor wonder what he was up to, then he squared himself to the witness and said, "When I read the NCIS final report, Lieutenant, I didn't see any identification of witnesses who saw the defendant washing her hands."

"There are none listed."

"I didn't see any reference in your report to any abrasions or redness on the defendant's hands, or any strong soapy odors—anything which might suggest that she'd given her hands a vigorous scrubbing."

"None were noted."

"I didn't see any reference in your report as to whether the basin or tub were even wet, indicating recent usage."

"The report doesn't address that," the lieutenant said, his voice becoming softer.

"I didn't see any reference in your report to an examination of the plumbing to determine whether blood or other matter had been washed down the drain."

Again, the lieutenant's voice dropped. "We didn't do that."

"You could have done that, couldn't you? Your investigative and forensic team could have removed the plumbing and examined the insides of the pipes for traces of blood or gunshot residue."

"It's possible."

"But you didn't do it?"

"No."

"So, just to be clear on this. You and your investigative team can't say one way or the other whether Lindsey Hart was busily scrubbing her hands clean before the police arrived on the scene, can you?"

"No, we can't."

"And you and your investigative team can't say whether any blood or gunshot residue was washed down the drain."

"No, we can't."

"Nonetheless," he said, his voice rising, his pace quickening, "it's your position that Lindsey Hart fired a gun into her husband's head at close range, and then she wiped her hands squeaky clean?"

"Yes."

"She went to all that trouble—wiped all that blood off her hands, cleaned off every last bit of that gunshot residue—but then she left a big old fat fingerprint on the murder weapon. Is that your testimony, Lieutenant?"

He paused, obviously uncomfortable with Jack's spin on it. "It happens," he said.

"It happens," Jack said with a tinge of sarcasm. "Thanks, Lieutenant. I think we got it."

Jack turned his back on the witness and returned to his seat. Lindsey gave him a look of approval, though the worry in her eyes was still evident. It was way too premature to start celebrating, but his point had seemed to register with the jury.

"Mr. Torres," the judge said, "you may reexamine."

"Thank you, Your Honor." He buttoned his coat as he rose, but rather than approaching the witness he remained at his place behind the prosecution's table. "Very briefly, Lieutenant. You've handled a few homicide investigations in your career, have you not?"

"Many, many of them."

"In your experience as an NCIS investigator, how is it that you're able to nail those killers who take great pains to cover their tracks?"

"More often than not, it's because they made just one dumb mistake."

"Just one?"

"One is all it takes."

"Like forgetting to wipe a fingerprint off the gun?"

He nodded, then glanced toward the jury and said, "Like forgetting to wipe the gun."

"Thank you, Lieutenant. No further questions."

The high Jack had felt after his cross-examination had just taken a nosedive. Two of the jurors had even smiled and nodded, as if volunteering to carry the prosecutor's new mantra all the way back to the deliberations room: *One is all it takes.*

The judge said, "The witness may step down. Mr. Torres, do you have any more witnesses to call?"

Torres gave his witness a moment to get clear of the witness stand. He was ready to make a major announcement, and he wanted no distractions to take away from his spotlight. Finally, he said in a firm voice, "Your Honor. The government rests its case."

"Thank you," said the judge. All rose as the judge dismissed the jury. When the last of them had filed out of the courtroom, Lindsey, the lawyers, and spectators settled back into their seats.

The judge made some housekeeping announcements, then looked at Jack. "Mr. Swyteck, should your client choose to put on any evidence in her defense, I suggest you be ready to do so at nine o'clock Monday morning." He banged his gavel and said, "We're adjourned."

"All rise!" cried the bailiff.

The judge exited to his side chambers, and the rumble of the crowd filled the courtroom. Jack turned toward Lindsey and said, "Big weekend ahead, Lindsey. It's decision time."

"Decision time for what?"

Jack closed his briefcase and said, "Just about everything."

36

The reception at Mario's Market was ice cold.

The trial had come between Jack and his biweekly lesson in Cuban culture from his grandmother, so he was determined to take *Abuela* to the market on Saturday morning. She'd told him ten or eleven times over the telephone that it wasn't necessary, that it was really okay to skip their little shopping date just this once. Since his return from Cuba, she'd refused to speak about her tearful voice-mail message and Jack's visit to the cemetery. Jack promised not to raise it again, assuring her that this outing was purely for the fun of it. She still seemed wary, but Jack finally persuaded her. After just two minutes inside the store, however, he realized that her reluctance had nothing to do with Jack's mother and the child she'd lost.

"Do they really have to glare at us like that?" said Jack.

"Not us, *mi vida*. You."

The outrage in the Cuban community over the

possibility of Castro's soldier as a witness had seemed to peak with the torching of Jack's Mustang, but the hate mail and vicious attacks on Cuban talk radio had grown steadily since Jack's grilling of Alejandro Pintado on the witness stand. Having defended death row inmates for his first four years of practice, Jack could deal with critics. But Saturday morning at Mario's Market wasn't the faceless fury of strangers whose acceptance Jack neither sought nor needed. These were good people, regular folks, neighbors who played dominoes with his grandmother in the park. It was the woman behind the deli counter who used to have his coffee ready for him, exactly the way he liked it, before he even asked. It was the cashier selling Lotto tickets who had always insisted that some combination of Jack's and José Martí's birthdays was definitely the lucky number. It was the seventy-nine-year-old stock "boy" who would tell Jack about the gunfights on Eighth Street (long before it became "Calle Ocho") between Batista loyalists and the Castro supporters. And it was the butcher who used to laugh at Jack's terrible Spanish, tell him that it's a good thing his mother was from Bejucal because an accent like his wouldn't even earn him the distinction of "*honorary* Cuban." Jack expected the backlash from the Cuban community at large, and he was even getting used to some of it. But rejection from these folks was rejection on a whole different level.

"Let's get some bread," said Jack.

"I think we should just go home," said *Abuela*.

He could see the pain in her expression, but he

wasn't ready to retreat just yet. He kissed her on the forehead and said, "You wait here. I'll get the bread and take the dirty looks with me."

He walked to the end of the aisle and ducked beneath a sign that pointed the way to PAN CALIENTE. It was a back area separated from the main store by thick, clear plastic strips that hung in the doorway and kept the heat on the baking side. A man wearing white overalls and a white T-shirt was loading another tray of dough into the oven.

"Antonio, how are you today?"

Antonio was smiling until he connected the voice with the speaker. He turned back to his work, saying nothing as he slid the tray into the hot oven.

"How about a couple of loaves?" said Jack.

Antonio closed the oven door and put the tray aside. "We're out."

Jack could see six loaves sitting atop the oven, which was where the just-baked bread was stored and kept warm. It was one of the secrets that helped such a little store sell eight hundred loaves a week.

"Out, huh?" said Jack.

"*Sí*, all gone."

"What about those?" Jack said, pointing toward the oven.

"Those aren't for you."

"Antonio!" a man shouted. Jack turned and saw the owner, Kiko, stepping out of the storage room. He said something quickly in Spanish, too quick for Jack to pick up. But the baker promptly moved away. Kiko grabbed two hot loaves and laid them on the table.

"Sorry about that," he said.

"It's okay. I should be the one to apologize. Pretty foolish of me to come here in the middle of a trial like this one."

Kiko shrugged, as if he couldn't completely disagree. "It's an older clientele here, Jack. First generation mostly. Everyone here had their home stolen from them, and most of them know people who ended up in one of Castro's prisons just because they dared to complain about it. That can make you kind of emotional."

"I understand that. I'm not trying to stick my finger in anybody's eye. I'm just . . ."

"Doing your job?"

Jack looked away. It was the truth, but somehow it didn't sound like enough. "I don't know what the hell I'm doing anymore."

Kiko bagged the long loaves and handed them to Jack. "I meant to tell you, I enjoyed that article in yesterday's paper about you."

To mark the end of the first week of trial, the *Tribune* had run a feature story on the three main lawyers in the Guantánamo murder case—Jack and Sofia for the defense, and Hector Torres for the prosecution. It noted the Cuban roots of all three lawyers, with special emphasis on Jack, who was known by most people only as the son of a gringo former governor.

"Not too bad, was it?" said Jack. "They actually got everything right for once."

"Not everything," said Kiko, his expression turning serious.

"Is there something I should know?" said Jack.

"A lot of gossip passes through this store, but

I happened to hear something this week that I thought I should pass along. It's about your mother."

"What?"

His voice lowered, as if he were uncomfortable with what he was about to say. "I don't speak to your *abuela* about her daughter and Bejucal. Her friends have warned me that it's just something you don't speak to her about."

"Her friends are right," said Jack. He didn't bother with the specifics.

"Anyway, one of my customers—El Pidio, we call him—he's a good guy, been coming here for years. He's also from Bejucal. I don't think your grandmother knew him, but apparently he knew your mother."

"Really? Did he say something about her?"

"Well, that's why I mentioned the newspaper article. There was a twenty-year-old picture of Hector Torres in there. Page twelve, I think. El Pidio swears that when he saw that picture, he was sure that Hector Torres was once engaged to your mother back in Bejucal. Supposedly she broke it off and came to Miami."

"He must be mistaken. I've been told that my mother was—" Jack paused for the right words, not interested in getting into the details of the pregnancy. "She was seriously involved with a local boy when she left Bejucal. So it couldn't have been Torres. The article said he was from Havana. And I'm sure my grandmother would have recognized the name and said something if it was Hector Torres."

"According to El Pidio, the boy's name wasn't Hector Torres. It was Jorge Bustón."

Jack was at a loss for words, partly from hearing the name Bustón for the first time, but partly because he didn't understand. "That doesn't make sense. If his name was Jorge Bustón, then how does Hector Torres fit into this?"

"Take this for whatever you think it's worth, Jack. But based on that picture, my friend says he'd bet his whole life savings that Hector Torres was from Bejucal and was in love with your mother."

"Wait a minute. Is he saying that Torres is . . ."

"*Sí, sí. Exactamente.* Hector Torres is Jorge Bustón. That's what he thinks."

Jack suddenly realized he was crushing the loaves of bread. "That can't be."

"You're probably right. I'm sorry. I wasn't sure if I should say anything to you or not. The article mentions how Hector Torres and your father have been friends for over thirty years, how Torres helped Harry Swyteck get elected governor, all that stuff. I don't mean to stir anything up."

"Don't worry about it. Thanks for passing along the info. And double thanks for the bread."

Jack started to walk away, but Kiko caught him and slipped a business card into his hand. On the back was a handwritten number.

"El Pidio's phone number," said Kiko. "Like I say, maybe he's crazy. But maybe he's not."

Jack gave a little nod and he stuffed the card in his pocket. Kiko shook his hand firmly, as if to convey that they would speak of this no more. Then Jack left the bakery to track down *Abuela*.

37

J ack had an appointment at South Miami Hospital.

He knew he had to stay focused on Lindsey and her trial, and this latest information about Jack's mother and Hector Torres was already distracting enough. Even so, Jack was suddenly feeling the need to tackle at least one of the things that had been gnawing at him about Brian.

It had to do with Brian's biological mother.

Lindsey had seemed to be holding something over Jack's head from the day they'd met, her underlying accusation that both Jack and Jessie had decided to give up Brian because of his hearing impairment. Even though Jack hadn't even known about the baby, let alone his deafness, Lindsey's words were beginning to feel like a spot on his soul. Maybe it was the reason Jessie had decided not to tell him about the baby. Could she have thought he was so utterly shallow that he wouldn't have wanted any part of a child who was less than perfect? There was one way to rule out the possibility.

Jack met Jan Wackenhut in the hospital cafeteria on her lunch break. She was the head of the speech pathology and audiology department. Jack had gotten her name through a friend who, of course, couldn't help adding that Jan was a lively brunette and a terrific dancer. Jack got a lot of that from do-gooders who couldn't wait for him to rejoin the Married Farts Club, but this was all business. They sat on opposite sides of a little round table in the corner. Jack had an iced tea, and Jan picked at a small wedge of quiche as they spoke.

"When did you say the child was born?" asked Jan.

"Ten years ago."

She guzzled some ice water, dousing an over-nuked piece of broccoli that had apparently set her mouth on fire.

"I can tell you this," she said. "We do screen infants for hearing loss here at this hospital. But that wasn't the case at most hospitals in the country ten years ago. In fact, it's only been in the last two or three years that infant screening has caught on. I read something not long ago that said only twenty percent of newborns were tested as recently as 1999."

"So, ten years ago, it's unlikely that my friend would have discovered that her newborn was born deaf and then decided to give him up for adoption."

"Highly unlikely. Especially when you consider that most women make the decision to give up their child for adoption long before delivery. Your friend would have to have known that the baby was deaf before it was even born."

"Is that possible?" said Jack.

"Not really."

"What about prenatal testing?"

"How old was your friend when she gave birth?

"Young. Early twenties."

"At that age, she probably would have had only ultrasound, which is limited to identifying problems of a physical or structural nature. It can't detect problems of function—mental retardation, blindness, deafness. It can't detect chromosome abnormalities either, like Down syndrome, which can sometimes be accompanied by problems like deafness."

"What if she had some more extensive testing?"

"Even amniocentisis and CVS test for a specific number of chromosome, biochemical, and structural disorders. Deafness, blindness, and even some heart defects and some types of mental retardation just aren't picked up through prenatal testing. And even if you could test for deafness, you'd have to be looking for it to detect it. You can't just blanket test for every conceivable defect known to medical science. Not yet anyway—and definitely not ten years ago."

Jan finished off the rest of her quiche in three quick bites. "Time to get back to work," she said.

"Ditto," said Jack. He thanked her, then started down the long maze of freezing-cold hallways that eventually led him to the hospital exit and the parking garage. He wasted about five minutes looking for his Mustang, a mental lapse that ended with the realization that his car was gone for good and that he was driving a crappy rental.

As he climbed behind the wheel and switched on the A/C, he wasn't thinking about his car, his old girlfriend, or even Brian. He was thinking about Lindsey, how the mother of a deaf child probably should have known that deafness couldn't be detected through prenatal testing, and that ten years ago a newborn probably wouldn't have been screened.

Yet, she'd still looked him in the eye and accused him and Jessie of dumping their baby because he was less than perfect.

He felt a rush of bitterness toward Lindsey, but he pushed it aside. His heart was pounding. Jessie'd been gone such a long time. But somehow he hoped she could hear him nonetheless.

I'm so sorry, Jessie. I'm sorry I let myself think that about you.

At ten minutes past three Jack was surrounded by any number of women who could have kicked his ass. Fortunately, most of them were behind bars.

Jack and Sofia had a trial-strategy meeting with Lindsey at the detention center. He cleared security at the visitors' entrance, then passed through the main visitation area. It was one of the most depressing sights he'd ever seen on such a beautiful Saturday afternoon, a great day for the beach, the park, maybe a little barbecue with friends in the backyard. Teary-eyed wives slow-danced with their husbands, the music playing only in their heads. Mothers in prison garb hugged daughters in pigtails. Little boys giggled at the sound of a mother's voice, a sound less familiar with each passing month. Jack felt a tinge of sadness for Brian, thinking that someday he might have to come here to visit his mother. Then he felt the same sadness for Lindsey, realizing that Brian wasn't here today, right this very minute, because his grandparents had already convicted her and wouldn't allow him to visit.

Jack entered a quieter area that was reserved for attorney-client meetings. Sofia was waiting for him in Room B, but their client had not yet arrived.

"Lindsey on her way down?" said Jack.

"Actually, I just sent her back to her cell. We had a long talk."

"Without me?"

"Yes. You and I need to talk."

She invited him to sit with a wave of her hand, but Jack remained standing. *You and I need to talk.* Never in his life had he heard a woman utter those words and then follow up with good news. "What's going on here?" said Jack. "Why did you and Lindsey meet without me?"

"She's coming back, so cool down, okay? The three of us will have our full session together. But there was one thing she needed to speak to a woman about. It's nothing personal against you. There are certain things a woman can't say in front of a man. Even if the man is her lawyer."

"You gonna tell me what's going on, or do I have to guess?"

"It's about the Cuban soldier."

"The Cuban?" Jack said, incredulous. "How does that *not* involve me?"

"It does, and we'll talk more about it when Lindsey comes back. There's just an aspect of his testimony that's—well, frankly, highly embarrassing for Lindsey. So she and I talked it out first."

"Obviously you mean the part about her and Lieutenant Johnson in the bedroom."

"Obviously."

Jack laid his briefcase on the table and pulled up a chair. "There's no way around the embarrassing parts. If we call the Cuban to the stand, he's going to give us the good and the bad."

"Lindsey understands that. And, frankly, I don't see it as all that bad."

"You don't?"

"No. I've been watching that jury carefully. I see how they've been looking at Lindsey ever since that fertility doctor shared his assassin sperm theory. There is no doubt in my mind that every single one of those jurors has already labeled Lindsey an adulteress."

"I can't argue with that," said Jack. "But we certainly run the risk of reinforcing that impression by calling the Cuban soldier to the stand."

"That was my fear, too. Before I had this little talk with Lindsey."

"You think differently now, do you?"

"I do. I think the Cuban soldier may be the only way to prove that Lindsey isn't lying when she says she wasn't having an affair."

"Excuse me? The Cuban saw her having sex with Lieutenant Johnson. Going at it like porn stars, I think were his exact words."

"Things aren't always what they appear," said Sofia.

"Ah, yes. I see your point. It must have been one of those newfangled CPR classes. Groin-to-groin resuscitation."

"I understand your skepticism. But you haven't heard Lindsey's side of the story yet."

"And you have?"

"Yes."

"And?"

Sofia's expression was stone-cold serious, as serious as Jack had ever seen her. "You need to call the Cuban, Jack. He should be witness number one for the defense."

38

Security at the courthouse was extra tight on Monday morning. A ring of police cars surrounded the building. Plainclothes officers (some wired with headsets, some less conspicuous) wandered amid the onlookers. Miami Avenue was completely closed off, and hundreds of demonstrators had pushed their way up to the barricades, getting as close to the courthouse as the police would allow. They shouted in English and Spanish, not a single word of support in any language for the first witness for the defense.

The atmosphere inside was less charged but equally tense. Visitors, both media and nonmedia, were patted down and individually searched with electronic wands. Metal detectors at the entrance were set high enough to detect gold fillings. Bomb-sniffing dogs led their masters through the long corridors. Armed federal marshals were spaced at fifty-foot intervals.

It was every bit the spectacle that Jack had expected, yet it was in a strange way the first confirmation that this might actually happen. Jack had worried about it all weekend, ever since he'd placed the phone call to Colonel Jiménez on Saturday afternoon.

"We're on for Monday morning," Jack had told him.

"I'm very pleased to hear it," the colonel replied.

Because Jack had notified the U.S. government before trial that the defense might call a Cuban soldier as witness, a detailed procedure had been worked out through the State Department to bring him to Miami quickly and smoothly. While a typical Cuban migrant would be forced to pay the Cuban government approximately five years' salary in cash upon departure for the United States, all it took was Castro's blessing to get this particular Cuban soldier into Miami overnight. Still, Jack had his doubts. Would the soldier actually come? Would he defect when he reached U.S. soil, recant his testimony, and disappear into freedom? Those doubts followed him all the way into the courtroom.

One way or the other, he knew he didn't have long to wait.

Jack rose and said, "Your Honor, the defense calls Private Felipe Castillo."

A shrill cry pierced the courtroom, and a barrage of angry shouts erupted from the galley.

"Order!" the judge said with a bang of his gavel.

The shouting continued, all of it in rapid-fire Spanish. Each speaker had his own message, which made the collective impact indecipherable to Jack's ears. But he knew they weren't shouting, Go, team, go!

Federal marshals covered the disturbance immediately. A man and a woman went peaceably to the exit. Three other men had to be handcuffed, their shouts of protest still audible as they disappeared into the hallway. Some of the jurors watched the arrests, horrified. The others kept their eyes on Jack and his client, as if to say, How dare you.

The courtroom had more than its usual rumbling and shuffling of feet, which the judge quickly gaveled down. "That will be the end of that," the judge said sharply. "Any further outbursts, and I will close this courtroom to all but the media."

A stillness came over the courtroom, but the tension remained.

"Bailiff," the judge said, "bring in the witness."

The bailiff walked to a side door, opened it, and escorted a young Hispanic man into the courtroom. He was dressed in civilian clothes, a suit and tie, as if *that* would tone down the controversy. Lindsey squeezed Jack's hand. Spectators moved to the edge of their seats. Jurors sat up rigidly in their chairs. It was as if everyone suddenly realized that they were watching history in the making, or at least something pretty cool to talk about at cocktail parties.

Private Castillo stepped up to the witness stand to take the oath. The bailiff recited the familiar words in English, and then a translator spoke to the witness in Spanish.

"*Sí, lo juro.* Yes, I swear," he replied, and then he took a seat. His eyes darted from the judge, to the jury, to the audience. His gaze finally came to rest on Jack, the only familiar face, the least hostile expression in the courtroom.

Jack approached slowly. He wanted the witness to

feel comfortable enough to say all that needed to be said to help his client, but coddling him would brand both Jack and his client as Castro-loving communists in the eyes of the jury. He knew he was walking a fine line.

"Good morning, Private Castillo."

"*Buenós*," he said, which was translated to "Good morning." The translator seemed almost superfluous, since all but one of the jurors was bilingual, and one or two of them probably would have benefited more from an English-to-Spanish translator. It was yet another factor for a defense lawyer to throw into the mix: The jury for the most part would hear each question and answer not once, but twice. Any misstep was a fuckup times two.

Jack moved through Castillo's background quickly, or as quickly as possible with a translator. There was no way around the fact that he was an enemy soldier, but Jack did his best to downplay the man's love for the regime, continuing in the question-translation/answer-translation format.

Jack said, "Military service is required in Cuba, is it not?"

"Yes, in some form."

"When were you required to start your military service?"

"As soon as I finished my secondary education."

"If you had refused to serve, what would have happened to you?"

"Jail."

Jack purposely skimmed over his duties and responsibilities as a tower guard on the Cuban side of Guantánamo. This was one witness the jury would never warm up to, no matter how long Jack kept him on the stand and tried to personalize him. The best strategy was simply to hit the highlights and then send him home.

"Private Castillo, were you on duty on the seventeenth of June, which was the day of Captain Pintado's death?"

"Yes, I was."

"Did you notice anything unusual at the residence of Captain Pintado?"

"Yes, I did."

"Was this something you observed with the naked eye, or with aided vision?"

"Aided, of course. We have fairly sophisticated viewing equipment. Quite powerful."

"Would you describe what you saw, please?"

Through a series of questions and answers, the witness repeated the story exactly as he had told it to Jack in Colonel Jiménez's office. He was part of a surveillance team that watched a portion of the naval base that included officer housing for U.S. Marines. On the morning of Captain Pintado's death, around five-thirty A.M., he saw Lindsey Hart leave for work, as usual. About twenty minutes later, sometime before six A.M., he saw a man enter the Pintado residence. He didn't knock. He just went straight inside.

"Was that man wearing a uniform?" asked Jack.

"Yes, he was."

"What branch of service?"

"U.S. Coast Guard."

"Enlisted man or officer's uniform?"

"Officer, but not very high ranking."

"Can you describe any of his physical character-istics?"

"Fairly tall, definitely taller than Captain Pin-tado. Kind of muscular, big shoulders. And he was black."

"Would you recognize that man if you saw him again?" asked Jack.

"Yes, absolutely."

Jack returned to his table, and Sofia handed him a photograph. Jack had the clerk mark it as a defense exhibit, handed copies to the prosecutor and to the judge, and then approached the witness. "Private Castillo, I have here a group photograph of U.S. Coast Guard officers stationed at Guantánamo and several other locations within the Coast Guard's Seventh District. It was taken near the end of last year. I ask you to take a good look at the photograph and tell me this, please: Does the man you saw en-tering the residence of Captain Pintado on the sev-enteenth of June also appear in this photograph?"

Torres was on his feet. "I want to object, Judge. We've already heard testimony that the man is black. Handing the witness a photograph of mostly white officers and then asking him to pick out the black guy is a joke."

Jack said, "Your Honor, there are fifty-two black men in this photograph. If the witness can pick out the man he saw from among the fifty-two pictured, that's more reliable than most police lineups."

"Overruled. The jury shall decide for itself what weight to attach to any identification, or misidenti-fication, as the case may be."

The witness seemed somewhat confused with all

the translations, but then he focused. Jack said, "Sir, please examine the photograph and tell me if you see the man who entered the Pintado residence on the morning of June seventeenth."

His gaze roamed back and forth, taking in row after row. Then it moved up and down, as if he were examining the many faces from another angle. The whole process was taking much longer than Jack had expected.

"Private Castillo?" the judge said. "Is the man in that photograph, or isn't he?"

The translator put the question to him again, and he didn't react. Jack didn't show it, but he was beginning to sweat.

"Private Castillo?" the judge repeated.

"Do you see him?" said Jack.

The witness looked up from the photograph. "This is him."

Jack stepped forward, saw where he was pointing. "Let the record reflect that the witness selected the man in the third row, fifth from the left. Lieutenant Damont Johnson."

For an instant, the name seemed to take on a life of its own as members of the media scribbled it down simultaneously. Jack quietly breathed a sigh of relief. The witness had placed someone else at the scene of the crime near the time of the murder. Lindsey had reasonable doubt.

If the jury believed it.

The judge said, "Any further questions for this witness, Mr. Swyteck?"

Jack was tempted to end on the high note, but it would have been worse for the illicit sex to come out on cross-examination. Besides, he had a new angle on the so-called extramarital affair—the one that Lindsey had confided to Sofia, the one she'd been too embarrassed to share directly with Jack.

"One final line of questioning," said Jack. "Private Castillo, did you happen to see Lieutenant Johnson at Captain Pintado's house on any occasions other than the morning of June seventeenth?"

"Yes."

"How many times?"

"Many times."

The next question stuck in Jack's throat. Even though the prosecutor had already convinced the jury that Lindsey was a cheating spouse, graphic testimony from an eyewitness was bound to change the whole tenor of the trial. But Jack had to get through it.

If Sofia was right, this was their only way to explain what really went on in that bedroom.

"Sir, can you tell me who Lieutenant Johnson was with on those other occasions?"

"I saw him with Captain Pintado's wife."

A rumble worked its way through the crowd, and it seemed to crawl right up Jack's spine like a big, fat, collective, What did he say?

"Where were they?"

"In the bedroom."

The rumble turned to outright chatter. The judge banged his gavel. "Order!"

Jack couldn't bring himself to look at the jury, but he could almost feel their scowls. "What . . . were they doing?"

God, please, he thought. *Let him say anything but "Going at it like a couple of porn stars."*

"They were having sexual relations."

Suddenly it was as if the courtroom were a cocktail party, and the host had walked in naked. It seemed that everyone was talking, some mortified and indignant, others giddy and excited by this new wrinkle in the case.

Again the judge gaveled them down to silence. "This courtroom will come to order!"

Jack waited for the noise to subside, then continued. He was having second thoughts about this new strategy they'd developed, but there was no turning back now. Sex was in the case, and Jack had to put the defense's spin on it.

"Private Castillo, can you tell me if Lieutenant Johnson and Lindsey Hart were alone in the bedroom on those occasions you saw them together?"

"Objection," said the prosecutor.

"On what grounds?" said the judge.

Torres struggled, and it was clear that he couldn't quite put his finger on any strict legal theory. He just didn't like the feel of things. Then he found something. "Judge, I believe the witness's testimony should be limited to what he saw."

"Can you rephrase your question, Mr. Swyteck?"

"Certainly. Private Castillo, did you see anyone in the bedroom other than Lieutenant Johnson and Lindsey Hart?"

"You mean while . . ."

"Yes," said Jack, the clarification somewhat painful, "while they were engaged in sexual activity."

The witness considered the question, then said, "No. I can't say that I saw anyone else in the room."

Jack glanced back toward Sofia. She had enough of a poker face not to show her disappointment, but her theory wasn't playing out as they'd hoped. Jack took a few steps back, simply buying time, regrouping his thoughts. Then he took another shot. "Private Castillo, do you know what kind of vehicle Captain Pintado drove?"

"Yes. A red Chevy pickup, older model."

"I want you to think hard now, all right? Did you happen to notice Captain Pintado's pickup parked in the driveway on any of the occasions when you observed Lieutenant Johnson and the defendant in the bedroom together?"

"You mean while . . ."

"Yes," said Jack, again dreading the clarification, "while they were having sex."

The witness was silent for a moment, then the answer seemed to come to him. "Yes, it was there."

Pay dirt! "One time? Two times?"

"No. Every time. Every time I can remember."

Jack tried not to smile, but he was glowing on the inside. "Let me make sure I understand. Every time you observed the defendant having sex with Lieutenant Johnson in the Pintado bedroom, Captain Pintado's vehicle was parked in the driveway. Is that your testimony?"

"Objection," said the prosecutor. He finally seemed to realize that Jack was giving this love triangle some interesting new angles.

"Overruled," said the judge. "The witness may answer."

"Yes, that's correct. I didn't really think of it before. But now that you ask the question, I'm sure of it. I saw it. There were always two vehicles. Captain Pintado's pickup and Lieutenant Johnson's car."

"Thank you. No further questions." Jack returned to his seat.

"Mr. Torres, cross-examination?" said the judge.

"Oh, absolutely," he said as he approached the witness. He stopped a few feet away from him, saying nothing, simply allowing the witness to feel the presence of the United States government. Then he turned his back on him, shaking his head, mocking the soldier's response to Jack's final question. "You didn't really think of it before, but now that Mr. Swyteck has asked the question, you're sure of it. You saw two cars." He began to pace, allowing time for his skepticism to spread throughout the courtroom. "How convenient."

"Objection," said Jack. "Is there a question?"

"Sustained."

"What *else* didn't you think of until Mr. Swyteck asked the question? Lieutenant Johnson's convenient arrival at the murder scene on the morning of Captain Pintado's death, perhaps?"

The witness waited for the translation, then said, "I don't understand."

"Not important. I'm sure the jury does."

"Objection."

"Sustained. Let's have some questions, Mr. Torres."

"Yes, Your Honor. Private Castillo, I noticed that Mr. Swyteck didn't spend much time covering your job description. So let me ask you a few questions

about that. You're part of a unit that conducts surveillance over the naval base at Guantánamo, is that
correct?"

"Yes, generally."

"It's your job to keep track of what's going on
inside the base?"

"Yes."

"And it's also your job to keep track of anyone
trying to enter the base, right?"

"Trying to enter the base?" he said, confused.

"Let me clarify that. There is some distance between the perimeter of the U.S. naval base and the
area occupied by Cuban forces, is there not?"

"Yes, of course."

"And the Cuban government has placed many
obstacles in that area, isn't that right?"

"I'm not sure I understand."

"There are razor-wire fences in that area, aren't
there?"

"Yes."

"There's even a mine field in there, right?"

"Yes."

"Those obstacles were put there to prevent ordinary Cubans from reaching the base and seeking
freedom on U.S. soil."

"I don't think I understand."

"I think you do. Isn't it true that an important
part of your job is to keep ordinary Cubans from
reaching freedom?"

"Objection," said Jack.

"Sustained," said the judge, but the damage was
done. He'd driven home the point that the witness
was the enemy—one of Castro's goons who was in-

strumental in keeping families in exile from being united with the families they left behind in Cuba.

Torres said, "Now, let me ask you about these sexual relations you observed at the Pintado household. Earlier, you said that you saw the defendant cheating on her husband."

"Objection," said Jack. "I think we've raised a serious question as to whether it was 'cheating' or not, Your Honor."

"Rephrase the question, please," said the judge.

"You observed the defendant having sex with Lieutenant Johnson."

"Yes."

"And as Mr. Swyteck's objection just suggested, you are trying to imply that there was some kind of weird threesome going on here."

"I'm not trying to do anything but tell you what I saw."

"Oh, please, sir. You're here today to bring shame on the Pintado family and to embarrass Fidel Castro's archenemy in exile, Alejandro Pintado."

"Objection."

"Sustained. Questions, please, Mr. Torres."

The prosecutor stepped closer to the witness, his tone growing more aggressive. "You know that the victim's father is Alejandro Pintado, do you not?"

"Yes, I'm aware of that."

"You know who Alejandro Pintado is, don't you?"

"I've heard his name."

"He's one of the most vocal members of the anti-Castro exile community, isn't he, sir?"

"If you say so."

"No, it's not what I say. It's what *you know*. You

know exactly who Alejandro Pintado is, don't you, sir?"

"I know he's been very vocal against our government."

"Yes, you know that. And you wouldn't be here today if the victim's father weren't so vocal in his opposition to Fidel Castro, would you?"

"I don't know."

"Private Castillo, is it not true that Cuban regulations prohibit members of the military from obtaining exit visas until their compulsory service is completed?"

The witness did a double take upon the translation, as if he were surprised by the prosecutor's awareness of that restriction. "Yes, that's true."

"So, you're in this courtroom only because someone made a very important exception under the laws and regulations of Cuba."

"Yes."

"Then let's be honest, sir. You're here today *only* because Fidel Castro wants you here."

Jack considered an objection, but Torres already had the jurors in his hand, and no objection at this point was going to wrest them free from his control.

The witness shrugged and said, "I suppose."

"Thank you," the prosecutor said smugly. "That'll do it."

39

Jack met with Theo over the lunch break. He would have preferred to stay at the courthouse with Lindsey and Sofia, but Theo claimed to have something of ball-busting importance to talk about. A handful of protestors marched up and down the sidewalk outside the courthouse. Jack donned his darkest shades—six-dollar specials, the kind so cheap that you were guaranteed *never* to lose them—hoping not to be recognized as he made a quick dash for Theo's car at the corner.

"Whassup?" said Theo as Jack piled into the passenger seat.

Jack didn't actually hear him, just saw his lips move. The stereo was loud enough to shatter fine crystal, a mind-numbing blast of so-called music, one of the many kinds that Theo liked, one of the few that made Jack wonder how the two of them were actually friends. Jack switched it off.

"How do you listen to that crap?" said Jack.

"What's wrong with it?"

"Nothing, if you like songs where the most commonly rhymed words end with U-C-K."

"Like the world needs another fucking song about taking a little chance, doing a little dance, and finding a little romance."

Jack considered it. Maybe the guy had a point. *Maybe*.

"Got you some lunch," said Theo as he handed it to him.

"Thanks," said Jack, unwrapping it. "What is it?"

"The Felipe Castillo special."

Jack chewed off the corner of his Cuban sandwich—slices of ham, pork, cheese, and pickles on Cuban bread, pressed together with a sandwich iron. "Very funny, Theo."

"How'd it go this morning?" asked Theo.

"I don't know. I think it might have been a mistake to put him on the stand at all."

"You're probably right."

"You think?"

"Oh, yeah. Bad mistake, Jacko. Right up there with Napoleon charging into Waterloo, Hitler turning his tanks against Russia, Dustin Hoffman going to see Elaine's portrait."

"Dustin Hoffman *what*?"

"*The Graduate*, dumbshit. You know, when Mrs. Robinson asks Benji if he would like to go upstairs and see her daughter's—"

"I saw the flick. You equate a movie with a military decision that was probably the turning point of World War Two?"

"No. But I don't think a Cuban soldier in Miami

is in the category of earth-shattering, either. So get some perspective."

"Do you live to see me scratch my head? Is that what makes you tick?"

The car stopped at the traffic light. It was a ride to nowhere, just cruising around the block long enough to hold a completely private conversation before Jack returned to court. Theo looked at Jack and said, "I'm making some headway on your Mustang."

Jack opened his bag of chips. "You kidding me?"

His expression was deadpan. "I kid about sex. I kid about death. I kid about everything. Except cars."

"What'd you find out?"

"I found the guy who did it. Some little weasel. Not even Cuban. Couldn't give a shit about Castro."

"Then why did he burn my car and write 'Castro lover' on the pavement?"

"Because somebody told him to. Hired him to, I should say."

"Who?"

"Don't know yet."

"He wouldn't tell you?"

"He would have, if he knew. It was a very thorough interrogation. The guy still couldn't give me a name."

Jack winced at the thought of a "thorough" investigation. *Better not to know.* The traffic light changed, and Theo turned the corner back toward the courthouse.

"So what's your take?" said Jack. "Some anti-Castro group hired him through a go-between? Tried to scare me into not bringing the Cuban soldier into the courtroom?"

"Not sure it was an anti-Castro group."

Jack swallowed one last bite of sandwich. "What, then? You think the anti-Castro message was just window dressing? Something to make it look like the work of an exile group?"

Theo steered his car toward the curb. They were a half block from the courthouse, as close as any vehicle could get with the added security. "Maybe so."

"Who else would even care if a Cuban soldier came into the courtroom or not?"

"Maybe that's not the right question. Maybe the right question is: Who else would try to make the defense too scared to call its best witness?"

"Or even more to the point, who else would be perfectly happy to see Lindsey Hart take the fall for the murder of Oscar Pintado?" Jack thought about it, then crumpled his sandwich wrapper into a ball. "You got any leads?"

"One good one. The people who hired the little pyromaniac didn't pay him in cash."

"Don't tell me they wrote a check."

"No. They paid in cocaine."

Jack was reaching for the door handle, then stopped cold. "A drug connection?"

"Maybe."

"That could change everything."

"Yup."

"Stay on it, Theo."

"What are you gonna do?"

Jack glanced out the windshield, then looked at

Theo and said, "I'm thinking maybe it's time for another face-to-face with Alejandro Pintado."

Theo nodded once, no disagreement, and then gave Jack one of those closed-fist handshakes. Jack got out of the car, closed the door, and started down the sidewalk to the courthouse, ready to face yet again that ever-present group of Pintado-family supporters.

40

The return of Alejandro Pintado to the witness stand brought the courtroom to a complete hush. Technically, the prosecutor could have objected to Jack's attempted rematch with the government's star witness, but Torres held his tongue, apparently pleased to have an encore performance from the victim's father. The jurors watched with the same sympathy and respect they had shown earlier, their admiration perhaps even greater than before. The woman in the first row probably would have kissed his ring, had Pintado offered. Jack, too, approached with some level of respect.

Sometimes, even disembowelment had to be done politely.

"Mr. Pintado, isn't it true that Brothers for Freedom has given serious consideration to shutting down its operations?"

The witness gave him a quizzical look. "What time period are you talking about?"

"Over the last two years."

"We had some discussions," said Pintado. "Nothing definite. And as of late, there has been no talk of that at all. As long as Cubans come across the Florida Straits in search of freedom, our planes will be out there looking for them."

Jack let him have his moment, then checked his notes for the details. "Sir, would it surprise you to know that from January to December of last year the U.S. Coast Guard interdicted over one thousand undocumented Cuban migrants at sea?"

"That would not surprise me at all."

"How many Cubans did Brothers for Freedom rescue in that same year?"

He looked away awkwardly and said, "Two."

"The year before that, the Coast Guard interdicted nine hundred Cubans. How many did Brothers for Freedom rescue?"

"That year? I think none."

"In fact, if we exclude the current year and go back five years, Brothers for Freedom rescued a grand total of just eleven rafters. Isn't that true, sir?"

"Well, you have to remember, we spotted far more than that. Unfortunately, the Coast Guard got to them and returned them to Castro before we could help them. That's my whole objection to the wet-feet/dry-feet interdiction policy."

"By wet feet/dry feet, you mean that if the Coast Guard interdicts Cuban rafters at sea, they are returned to Cuba. But if—"

"If they make it to dry land, they make it to freedom. That's all my organization is trying to do. Get people safely to freedom."

"And that's why you referred to the U.S. Coast Guard as 'Castro's border patrol.'"

"I think their actions speak for themselves."

"Okay. Now let's get back to my original question. In five years, Brothers for Freedom rescued eleven Cuban rafters, correct?"

"That's correct."

"This year, things have been different, have they not? Particularly in the first six months?"

"We've had more success, yes."

"Much more success," said Jack. "Through June of this year, a period of just six months, Brothers for Freedom rescued thirty-seven rafters."

"Thirty-eight, actually. One of the women we rescued was eight months pregnant."

"You must be proud of that."

"I'm proud of all my people. We just keep getting better at what we do."

"And more efficient, too," said Jack. "Brothers for Freedom filed fewer FAA flight plans this year than in any previous year, has it not?"

"That's true."

"You purchased less fuel this year than in any previous year, correct?"

"That's right," said Pintado.

"And interestingly enough, according to INS estimates, the total number of rafters leaving Cuba is down by almost twenty percent this year when compared to previous years."

"I don't know the exact figures, but I can't argue with those numbers."

"So, even though you were flying less, and even though there were fewer rafters to be found, your rescues increased dramatically in the first six months of this year. All because you suddenly became better at what you were doing?"

"I think so, yes," said Pintado.

"Or was it because you simply had better information?"

"I'm sorry, I don't understand. Better information about what?"

"Better information about where the rafters were going to be . . . and where the Coast Guard *wasn't* going to be?"

"Objection, Your Honor," said the prosecutor. "There has been absolutely no evidence adduced at this trial to suggest that Mr. Pintado has a source at the U.S. Coast Guard."

"Objection sustained."

"Let me lay the proper foundation," said Jack. He took a step closer and said, "Mr. Pintado, you testified earlier that your son's best friend at the naval base was who?"

"Lieutenant Damont Johnson."

"And which branch of service is Lieutenant Johnson in?"

He glared at Jack, then said quietly, "Coast Guard."

Jack paused, not quite sure how far to press his point. Any jury had a low tolerance for bashing the victim's family, but the chances of getting this witness back for a third round of questioning was virtually nil. Jack had to take his shot.

"One last question, sir. Since your son died in June—in other words, since Captain Pintado's friendship with Lieutenant Johnson ended—how many undocumented Cuban migrants has Brothers for Freedom rescued at sea?"

Pintado seemed ready to strangle Jack. "None," he said quietly.

It was the answer the defense needed, yet Jack hardly felt vindicated. He genuinely felt sorry for him, even sympathized with his views, but someone may well have decided that Mr. Pintado's cause was a cause worth killing for, either in support or opposition. It was up to Jack to make the jury see that, even if he wasn't ready to plunge into Theo's drug theory.

But the groundwork had been laid.

"Thank you, sir," said Jack. "No further questions."

41

Trial ended midafternoon on Monday so that the judge could deal with an unspecified emergency, perhaps a crucial pretrial hearing in another case, perhaps a teenage daughter who'd locked her keys in the car. Jack stopped by the prosecutor's office before heading for the parking lot. Torres gave him ten minutes alone, just the two of them.

"What is she looking for?" asked Torres. He was seated behind his desk, not a single scrap of paper on it. He'd obviously swept it clean before allowing the enemy into his office. Jack had always taken the same precaution as a prosecutor. There wasn't a criminal defense lawyer in the business who couldn't speed-read upside-down and backward.

"Excuse me?" said Jack from his seat in the armchair.

"Your client. I assume that's why you're here. What's she looking for, manslaughter?"

"I'm not here to deal."

"Good. Because the best I can do is murder one with life imprisonment. I'll give up the death penalty."

"Life's a long time for an innocent woman."

Torres let out a deep chuckle.

Jack kept a straight face. "You got the wrong defendant."

"You got the wrong client."

"Where's Lieutenant Damont Johnson?"

Torres worked a pencil through his fingers like a miniature baton. "Your guess is as good as mine."

"Funny how his name keeps coming up at trial. Never in a good light. I'd love to give him the opportunity to explain himself."

"Not a chance."

"Why are you hiding him?"

"Why are you after him?"

"Because I think he can tell the jury who really killed Oscar Pintado."

Torres folded his hands atop his desk and looked straight at Jack. "I think the jury already knows who killed Oscar Pintado. Her name is Lindsey Hart."

"I hear Johnson is in Miami."

"What of it?"

"Are you holding him for rebuttal, or are you just trying to keep me from getting to him?"

"That's none of your business."

"It's totally my business," said Jack. "So far, you've kept Johnson away from me, and you've even managed to keep me from talking to my own—" He stopped himself short of saying "my own son." "Talking to my client's own son," he said, correcting himself. "Those are probably the two key witnesses in the case."

"You're free to put the boy on the stand. The

judge's order only prevents you from interviewing him, not calling him as a witness."

"I don't think either one of us wants to put the victim's child on the stand."

"We gotta do what we gotta do."

"That's what I'm telling you: I don't think I have to go anywhere near the boy, if you'll give me Johnson."

He smiled again. "Very creative, Swyteck. For the good of the child, you want me to give you Lieutenant Damont Johnson."

"There's no good reason for you to keep Johnson out of this."

"That may be true. But you're not giving me a good enough reason to put him in."

"Brian Pintado isn't a good enough reason?"

"Not even close."

Jack scoffed lightly, looked away. "Nice to know you care, Hector."

"Yeah, yeah. Shame on me for playing to win. If you'll excuse me now, I have a cross-examination to prepare for. I have a sneaking suspicion that a guilty defendant may soon be taking the stand in her own defense."

Jack rose and started toward the door, forcing himself to keep putting one foot in front of the other. He'd come here determined not to let this get personal, but it was the first time he'd been alone with the prosecutor since . . . he didn't know how long. Definitely since the eye-opening talk about his mother that he'd had with Kiko at Mario's Market.

"You ever been to Bejucal?" Jack's hand was on the knob, but the door was still closed.

The prosecutor's mouth was open, but no words followed. For a moment, it looked as if Jack had punched him in the chest.

"What?" he said finally.

"Bejucal, Cuba. Have you ever been there?"

"Who wants to know?"

"Ana Maria Fuentes's son."

Their eyes locked. Jack had resolved to put Bejucal aside until after the case was over, but something inside him wouldn't allow it. Maybe it was the fact that they were alone together, and that the meeting had gone badly. Maybe it was the fact that he seemed to have less respect for Torres with each passing day, and the thought of any intimacy between him and his mother was beyond any son's comprehension. Or maybe he was just curious.

"Sorry, Jack. Never been."

Neither man looked away. "Just thought I'd check."

"Glad you did."

"Me, too." Jack opened the door and started out.

"Hey, Jack."

He stopped and turned.

"Say hey to your old man for me."

Even if Torres wasn't rubbing the Swyteck noses in some sordid romantic history, the smugness in the prosecutor's tone made Jack want to bash in that phony smile and kick his teeth in. The Justice Department logo on the wall, however, was a quick reminder that it wasn't worth it. He said nothing as the left the U.S. attorney's office and closed the door behind him.

42

The farther Jack's rental car carried him away from downtown, the more convinced he was that Hector Torres was hiding something about his mother. But he had to put it out of his mind. For now.

The rented sedan provided ample distraction. Each time he pushed the clutch that wasn't there, reached in vain for the stick shift, anticipated the growl of the engine that was gone for good—it all made him wish that he could have been there for Theo's "thorough interrogation" of the slug who'd set his Mustang afire. As Jack left the business district and reached the residential high-rises on glitzy Brickell Avenue, he switched on the radio. It was preset to a Spanish-language talk station, courtesy of the previous renter. Jack's latest courtroom "attack" on Alejandro Pintado had set off a new round of Cuban talk-show fireworks, and the name Swyteck was at the center of it. He was glad that he and *Abuela* didn't share a surname.

"The Pintados are the victims here," said one

caller in Spanish. "Not that *jinetera* who married him."

Jinetera. Jack couldn't translate it. Then he remembered his trip to Cuba, the teenage girl who'd called his room at the Hotel Nacional and told him she could be anyone and do anything he wanted, all he had to do was ask—and pay. *Jinetera*.

Prostitute.

Talk radio brought out the extremists in any language. But Jack was beginning to think that, when all was said and done, the mood wasn't going to be much different in the jury room. He had to turn things around.

He checked the clock in the dashboard: four forty-four P.M. Tomorrow would be showtime for Lindsey, and it was going to take a lot of work to get her ready. Still, Jack had some time to kill before meeting Sofia at the jail for their client's all-important prep session. He reached for the missing stick shift, cursed his inability to downshift his rental, and pulled a U-turn just before the entrance to Key Biscayne.

In ten minutes he was outside the home of Alejandro Pintado.

He parked the car on the grass beside the sidewalk, but he didn't get out. At the cul-de-sac at the end of the street, a boy was riding his bicycle. Around and around in circles he went, laughing each time he jerked back on the handlebars. He was trying to pull wheelies. Jack smiled. He had been the king of wheelies when he was ten years old.

The boy was Brian.

He was playing the way Jack used to play, like any

other ten-year-old kid, even if the diamond-shaped road sign on the opposite side of the street did announce to the world, DEAF CHILD PLAYING. Jack could certainly see the good in warning passing motorists, but he couldn't deny his own sense of sadness as he wondered how it must have made Brian feel, each time he rode his bike, walked his dog, played in the yard, or simply looked out his bedroom window, to see that big, black-and-yellow reminder of the cruel hand his own birth had dealt him. The blame game was always pointless, especially so in the case of birth defects, but Jack suddenly found himself hoping and praying that if he'd given Brian this weakness, that he'd given him his every strength, too.

A security guard tapped on the glass, ending the reflective moment. Jack rolled down the driver's-side window.

"You can't park here," the guard said in Spanish.

"I'm here to see Alejandro Pintado."

"He didn't tell me about any meetings."

"Tell him that the lawyer for his daughter-in-law would like to speak to him. Off the record." He glanced down the street again, spotted the boy. "Tell him I want to do everything I can to keep his grandson off the witness stand."

The guard considered it. "Wait here," he said, then walked up the sidewalk. Jack waited for him to disappear inside the house, then dialed up Theo on his cell phone.

"Hey, it's me, Jack. You got any more information on our drug connection?" Jack immediately cringed. He couldn't believe he'd just said that on a nonsecure cell phone, but Theo was one step ahead of him.

"Uh, yeah, pal. I'll have that *aspirin* to you by to-morrow morning."

"Sorry, man."

"It's okay. Dumbshit."

"Seriously, you got any more leads on what we talked about yesterday?"

"Nothing. Why?"

"I'm about to have a little chat with Alejandro Pintado."

"Wish I could help you."

"It's okay. I think we got enough."

"Enough to what?"

The front door to the house opened, and Alejandro stepped onto the porch. "Bluff," said Jack into the phone, and then he disconnected.

Jack watched as Pintado crossed the lawn, headed up the driveway, and then climbed into the back of his Mercedes. The security guard came for Jack and led him to Pintado's car.

"What? Does Mr. Pintado think I bugged my car?"

"No," the guard said dryly. "But he *knows* you didn't bug his."

The guard opened the car door. Jack got inside and sank into the black leather seat. The door closed and the locks clicked shut automatically. Pintado shot him a cool expression from the other side of the car. He still had a distinguished air about him, even if he did seem to have aged just a bit since the commencement of trial.

Pintado said, "Pardon me for not inviting you inside the house, but after the way you treated me in court, my wife probably would have sicced the Dobermans on you."

"I was afraid you might feel the same way."

"Oh, I do. I came out only because you said it was about my grandson. Protecting him from this circus is very important to me."

"To Lindsey as well."

Pintado shot a look, as if he didn't quite believe it.

Jack said, "I don't like getting children involved if I don't have to."

"I respect that," said Pintado.

"How is Brian doing?"

He gave Jack a long look, as if wondering whether he really cared. "Brian's happy here. Happy as any kid can be who just lost his father. His grandmother and I are doing the best we can. As soon as this trial's over, we're sending him up to a camp in Dunedin for a week or so. It'll be good for him to be around other hearing-impaired kids who live with parents who can hear. For now, we just try to explain things as they happen."

"That has to be tough."

Pintado glanced out the window toward the guard in the driveway. "I've had to triple my security since this trial started. It's one thing for people to dog me all over town, but when they start after my grandson, I feel like cracking some heads."

"Brian's being hassled?"

"Last week. Don't know if it was an overzealous reporter or some pervert who followed Brian to school the other day. Snatched his backpack while he was out on the soccer field. Scared the hell out of us."

"People get crazy with any big trial. It's good that you're taking precautions, but it was probably just a souvenir hunter looking for stuff to sell on eBay."

"What kind of sicko would want a child's backpack?"

"The same idiot who hangs out at South Miami restaurants hoping to get his picture taken with O. J. Simpson and his latest girlfriend."

Pintado shook his head, then showed mild irritation in his tone. "I don't dislike you personally, but I don't appreciate the way you came after me on the witness stand."

"For what it's worth, I wouldn't have done it if I didn't think Lindsey was innocent."

"That's mostly a Cuban American jury. Attacking me and my family like that, I'd say you pretty much sealed Lindsey's fate."

"You're forgetting that I don't have to convince the whole jury. I have to give only one of them reasonable doubt."

"Trust me. That entire jury is ready to ride you and your client out of town on a rail."

"And I'll happily go, if that's what it takes to keep an innocent woman out of jail."

"What makes you so damn sure she's innocent?"

"What makes you so sure she's not?"

"You've heard the evidence. The family money she wanted. The extracurricular activities with Lieutenant Johnson. Hell, her fingerprint was on the murder weapon."

Jack paused, timing his approach. "Mr. Pintado, let me ask you this question. Do you want to find out who killed your son?"

"Don't patronize me."

"I'm not. I'm just curious: Doesn't it bother you that we haven't heard a word from Lieutenant Johnson?"

He looked away, saying nothing.

Jack said, "Johnson was your source, wasn't he? He was feeding your son information about Coast Guard routes. And Brothers for Freedom used that information to improve the flow of Cuban rafters to U.S. soil."

He looked at Jack and said, "I'm not the one on trial here."

"I couldn't agree more. That's why I would have much preferred to have Johnson on the witness stand than you."

"Look, I just don't see where you're going with this. I'm not admitting anything, mind you. But so what if Johnson was leaking Coast Guard information to help us bring Cuban rafters to shore? It doesn't give anyone a reason to kill my son."

"No, it doesn't. Not until you mix drugs into the equation."

His head snapped. "Drugs? What the hell are you talking about?"

"Think about it. It helped your operation immensely to know when and where Coast Guard cutters would be patrolling certain areas of the Florida Straits. You could tell rafters when to sail, where to sail, when to change course, where to look for help coming to shore. How valuable do you think that same information would be to a drug smuggler?"

"Are you accusing *me*—"

"No," Jack said firmly. "I'm not accusing anyone yet, because I honestly don't have the goods. But let me tell you what I think. I think Damont Johnson was taking the same information he gave to you and selling it to drug dealers. I think your son found out about it. And I think it got Oscar killed."

Pintado's eyes were as wide as saucers. "That's the first I've heard any such thing."

"It didn't come to me until recently. Not until I found out that drug people were the ones who torched my Mustang."

"Have you gone to the U.S. attorney with this information?"

"It's not information. It's a theory. Two-thirds of the way through trial, Torres isn't interested in helping the defense prove its theories."

"Why should I be interested?"

"Because a win is a win to an egomaniac like Hector Torres. But his win is your loss. If Lindsey is convicted, the person who killed your son is still walking the streets."

He took a breath. "This is . . . this is an awful lot you've just unloaded on me."

"I know it's late in the game. But I wouldn't have come if I didn't have some hope that you'd want to eliminate any possibility that the mother of your only grandson is an innocent woman."

"What are you asking for?"

"Lieutenant Damont Johnson."

"What about him?"

"I know he's in Miami. And I have a feeling you know where Torres is hiding him. Let me get a subpoena on him. Give me a shot at him on the witness stand, and I promise you, I won't call Brian to testify on his mother's behalf."

Pintado glanced out the window, and Jack followed his gaze toward the cul-de-sac at the end of the street, toward Brian racing around on his bicycle. "Thanks for your time, Mr. Swyteck."

"Will I hear back from you?"

He looked at Jack, answering in the same flat tone. "I said, thanks for your time."

Pintado flipped a switch that unlocked the car doors, then pointed with a nod toward the handle. Jack opened it and stepped out of the car, taking just one more distant glance at Brian as he closed the door and walked back to his rental.

43

It would forever remain a mystery, Jack figured. He was standing at the bathroom sink in Sofia's house, his hands dripping wet. His ex-wife used to have the same puzzling habit, always stocking the guest bathroom with linen-and-lace hand towels that were frilly enough for royalty and about as absorbent as Teflon. He'd always suspected that the towels you were actually *supposed* to use were hidden away in some secret drawer that only people who were raised "properly" knew how to find. He just didn't get it. One of life's little enigmas.

He wiped his hands on his pants.

"Jack, should I pour you some coffee?" Sofia asked from outside the closed door.

"Thanks, good idea," he said.

He was bracing himself against the countertop, palms down and elbows straight as he stared wearily at his reflection in the mirror. The in-prison prep session with Lindsey had delivered more than its usual share of surprises. They could have spent all night with her, but the guard had allowed them only an additional fifteen minutes beyond the end of visitation. Jack had hoped to get a good night's sleep before putting Lindsey on the stand, but he and Sofia had left the jailhouse with the same realization. They had a lot of work to do.

"I'm making espresso," said Sofia. Jack could tell she was no longer right outside the door but was shouting from somewhere near the kitchen. "You want some, or you still want coffee?"

"Double espresso," Jack shouted back.

It was funny how eighteen-hour workdays and late-night trial preparation bred such familiarity between coworkers. Sofia was actually carrying on a conversation with him while he was in the bathroom. For all she knew, he was seated on the proverbial throne, yet it didn't seem to faze her. Not even his ex-wife used to talk to him through the bathroom door, except for that one time. *Honey, hurry up, I'm ovulating!* As it turned out, the world was probably a better place for his decision to go right ahead and finish that *Sports Illustrated* article about Dan Marino and his record-setting passing season.

Jack was still staring into the mirror. He looked exhausted, bordering on burnout. Trials were always draining, but few lawyers had ever handled during their career a murder trial in which the stakes were as personal as they were for Jack in this one. Brian was his son, and no matter how much Jack tried to play that down as a mere biological fact, he couldn't erase it as irrelevant. So what if the law of adoption regarded him as insignificant? It had meaning *to him*, and so long as it had meaning, it mattered not only whether Lindsey was acquitted or convicted, but also whether she was truly guilty or truly innocent. The trial was nearing an end, and for all the ups and downs, ins and outs, he still didn't know whom to believe.

And tonight's session hadn't helped any.

He splashed cold water on his face, then again took stock of himself in the mirror.

It seemed like light-years ago, but earlier that same evening he'd been on a definite roll. His drug-running theory had finally gelled in his mind, and he was even beginning to believe it. It seemed entirely plausible that Lindsey had been right all along. Her husband had been murdered because he knew the wrong thing about the wrong person. Her theory seemed to fit nicely with his latest thinking that Captain Pintado had uncovered a connection between his Coast Guard source and a drug-smuggling scheme.

Then Lindsey dumped on him all over again.

"There's something you should know," Lindsey told him. She was seated on the opposite side of the table, dressed in prison coveralls. Her voice was flat, her expression grave.

"What?" asked Jack.

"There's a good reason my fingerprint was found on Oscar's gun."

"Right. You said it was because you and Oscar had shot the gun previously in target practice."

She shook her head. "That's not it."

Jack had the definite feeling that she was about to tell him something he should have heard much earlier. "All right. Tell me how your print really got there."

Her shoulders slumped, she looked down at the table. "You know how we've talked in the past about how Oscar's gun was found with the safety on, which meant his death probably wasn't suicide?"

"Yes."

There was a long silence, then finally she said quietly, "I was the one who put on the safety."

44

Jack kept one eye on the jury as his client passed before the judge and took a seat in the witness stand. He'd been wrong about jurors before, but it didn't take a mind reader to see that Lindsey had a long way to go with this group.

Lindsey appeared somewhat nervous, which was to be expected, but it didn't prevent her from capturing exactly the right look. Jack and Sofia had choreographed her image right down to the tiny American flag on the lapel of her navy blue business suit. Sofia had helped with her hair in the rest room, a conservative twist suitable for a single mother. They didn't want to overdo it with a too-traditional, Laura Ashley–inspired matronly look—that just wasn't Lindsey—but Jack had definite guidelines. Two-inch heels or less. No cleavage. No flashy jewelry; pearls preferred. Easy on the makeup. Tell the truth.

That last one was his only remaining worry.

"Good morning," said Jack. "Would you please introduce yourself to the jury?"

"My name is Lindsey Hart. I was married for twelve years to Captain Oscar Pintado, United States Marine Corps."

"Did you and Captain Pintado have any children?"

"We were unable to conceive, so we adopted a baby boy. Brian is ten years old now."

"Would you say you were a happy family?"

She hesitated, considering it. "We were at one time. For several years, yes, we were very happy."

"When did things start to change?"

"When Oscar was transferred to the naval station at Guantánamo. About four years ago."

"What was it about Guantánamo that had such a negative impact on your family?"

"I don't think it was anything specific about Guantánamo. Oscar simply started to change."

"How so?"

"Brian and I seemed to become less important to him."

"Was there something or someone else who became more important?"

"His friends, I would say."

"Any friend in particular?"

"Lieutenant Damont Johnson. He was with the Coast Guard. He was Oscar's best friend."

"Did you get along with Lieutenant Johnson?"

She averted her eyes. "No. Not in the least."

"Ms. Hart, you've heard testimony about a possible relationship you may have had with your husband's best friend. Did you have any kind of relationship with Lieutenant Johnson?"

"Yes."

Jack softened his tone, but it didn't make the

question any easier. "Was that relationship sexual in nature?"

"It was entirely sexual."

That raised a few eyebrows, including the judge's. Jack asked, "How long did this relationship go on?"

"Over a six-month period, I'd say."

"During that period, how often did you have sex with Lieutenant Johnson?"

She lowered her eyes and said, "As often as Oscar told me to."

If jaw-droppings could make a sound, there would have been a cacophony from the gallery of spectators. Jack let the answer settle upon the jurors, then said, "Tell us about the first time you and Lieutenant Johnson had sex."

"I've never had any recollection of it."

"You mean you've forgotten it?"

"Not in the sense that I once remembered and have now forgotten it. From the day it happened, I've never had any memory of it."

"Were you conscious when it happened?"

"No. I had been drugged."

"How do you know it occurred?"

"I know my body. I know when I've had sex. And if there was any doubt, Oscar showed me the photographs he took."

"Photographs of you and Lieutenant Johnson having sex?"

"Yes."

Again, Jack paused. The packed courtroom seemed to take a collective breath. Jack said, "You say you were drugged. How do you know you were drugged?"

"Because one moment I was feeling fine. Then Oscar brought me a glass of wine. I drank just half of it, and I'd never felt like that before. Dizzy, disoriented. Then I passed out. When I woke up, my body felt so strange. The only thing I can compare it to is when I had my appendix out and I came to after the anesthesia. And then . . ."

"Then what?"

"Then Oscar showed me the photographs."

"The ones of you and his friend having sex?"

Her eyes were beginning to well. Her voice shook as she said, "Yes."

Jack gave her a moment to compose herself. "Do you know who gave you the drug?"

"I assume it was—"

"Objection. The witness is clearly speculating."

"Sustained."

Jack asked, "Did you drug yourself?"

"No."

"So someone else gave it to you?"

"Clearly."

"Do you know what kind of drug it was?"

"No. I don't."

"Getting back to these photographs of you and Lieutenant Johnson, when your husband showed you those photographs, was Lieutenant Johnson with him?"

"No. It was just Oscar and me."

"Do you know who took the photographs?"

"All I can say is that when Oscar showed them to me, they were still on his digital camera. They weren't developed or printed out. He brought them up electronically on the LCD display."

"How did that make you feel, when you saw those photographs?"

Her eyes clouded over, and she reached for a tissue. "I was drugged and violated by my husband's best friend. And my husband took photographs. How do you think it made me feel?"

He gave her more time. "I'm sorry I have to ask these questions," said Jack. "Just a few more on this. Do you know what happened to those digital photographs?"

"No. Lord knows I searched the house for that camera. I wanted to destroy the images. But I never did find anything."

"Before this happened, would you describe your sexual relationship with your husband as normal?"

"No," she said, her voice quaking.

"I'm not prying for too much detail, but I have to ask this. What about it was not normal?"

She pulled herself together, took a breath. "After we were unable to conceive, Oscar took it as a blow to his manhood. It was a slow process, but he never really recovered. It was so irrational." She paused as if searching for strength to continue. "I felt so much anger coming from him every time we were intimate. It was a perversion of the Marine mentality, that if you suck it up and try harder, you'll succeed. But finally he had to accept that there was something wrong. We weren't going to have our own child. And like I say, that realization was a real blow to him. As time went on—I'm talking years, now—it became more and more difficult for him to . . . perform."

"When this incident with Lieutenant Johnson

took place, did you have any sexual relationship at all with your husband?"

"No," she said, staring down into her tissue. "Unless you call hiding in the closet and snapping photographs of your wife with another man a 'relationship.'"

"What did your husband do with these photographs?"

"He kept them."

"Do you know why?"

"He told me that—"

"Objection," said Torres. "We're getting into hearsay."

Jack said, "Judge, the testimony is offered simply to prove that the witness felt threatened. It's not offered to prove the truth of the matter asserted."

The judge made a face. He wasn't the sharpest tool in the shed when it came to evidentiary matters such as hearsay, and Jack had given him just enough to scare him away from excluding the testimony. "Overruled. The witness may answer."

Lindsey said, "Oscar told me that if I didn't continue to have sex with Lieutenant Johnson, he would divorce me and use the photographs to take Brian away from me. Prove I was an unfit mother, having sex with another man in my own bedroom while my deaf child slept in the next room."

"But the photographs showed that you were unconscious, didn't they?"

"It was hard to tell in the photographs. Lots of women close their eyes at some point while having sex."

"So what did you do?"

"I did what he wanted me to do." Her voice was barely audible.

The judge said, "Ms. Hart, you'll have to speak up."

"I did what he wanted me to do," she said. "I continued to have sex with Lieutenant Johnson."

"Were you drugged on those occasions?"

"No."

"Then why did you do it?"

"I didn't see a choice. I didn't want to lose my son."

"Are you saying that you were prepared to do this for the rest of your life?"

"No. But you have to understand. Oscar was from a very powerful family. He was a respected Marine on a military base. My word against his wasn't going to add up to much. Until I could figure something out and find help from someone I could trust, I had to go along with it."

"So, when that Cuban soldier came into this courtroom and testified that he saw you and Lieutenant Johnson together, that could very well have happened?"

"If he saw anything, he saw me yielding to my husband's threats. I was just going along with it."

Jack nodded, as if satisfied. But in his own mind, he couldn't help juxtaposing her "going along with it" against the soldier's "going at it like a couple of porn stars." Thankfully, those words never made it before the jury. "Ms. Hart, did you observe any impact that this 'threesome,' I'll call it, was having on the friendship between your husband and Lieutenant Johnson?"

"Toward the end, I did."

"What happened?"

"Lieutenant Johnson started showing up at my house alone, when Oscar wasn't there."

"Did you have sex with him when your husband wasn't there?"

"No, never."

"Did you tell your husband about Lieutenant Johnson's extra visits?"

"Yes."

"What was his reaction?"

"He was very angry. He told me that if he ever caught me and Lieutenant Johnson together, he'd kill us both."

"So it was okay to be with Lieutenant Johnson only so long as your husband was there to watch."

"Yeah. He was very much into control."

"Did you ever observe your husband have any cross words with Lieutenant Johnson over this?"

"Only once, and they took it outside. I'm not sure what was said."

"After this argument between the two men, did Lieutenant Johnson continue to come around, un-invited, so to speak?"

"No. He didn't."

"Did you tell your husband this?"

"No. In fact I told him the opposite. I told him that Johnson was continuing to come over asking for sex, just the two of us, no one taking pictures."

"You lied to him?"

"Yes. I was desperate. I saw a way out. If Oscar got mad at Johnson, I thought it might be the end of this nightmare."

"What happened after that?"

"I don't know."

"How soon after that did your husband turn up dead?"

"Objection," said Torres. "The question unfairly implies there's some linkage between the two."

"What kind of objection is that?" said the judge. "Overruled. The witness shall answer."

"Oscar was dead less than two weeks later."

Jack said, "Ms. Hart, you didn't tell anyone about the things your husband forced you to do with Lieutenant Johnson. Not even the police."

"No."

"Why not?"

"I was ashamed of it. I didn't think anyone would ever understand how trapped I felt. Mostly, I didn't want Brian ever to know it."

Jack listened like a lawyer, but her last answer hit him like a father. They'd rehearsed her testimony beforehand, but it was far different now, inside a packed courtroom with hundreds of sets of eyes and ears absorbing every detail. All those intimate secrets that Lindsey was too ashamed to share with anyone—even with her own lawyer, until it was almost too late—could now be gobbled up by any slob who could read a newspaper. It wouldn't happen today, maybe not even next month or next year. But someday, Brian would know everything.

Jack said, "Let's talk now about the specific morning of your husband's death. How did the day begin for you?"

"Like any other. I was sleeping in Brian's room when my alarm clock/radio went off."

"You normally slept with your son?"

"I did, ever since the thing with Lieutenant Johnson started."

"Did you check on your husband at all?"

"I wouldn't say I checked on him. He was sleeping in the bed when I went to the master to take a shower and get my clothes."

"Are you sure he was alive?"

"Yes. He was snoring."

"So you showered, dressed, then what?"

"Grabbed a banana and went to work."

"What time?"

"Usual time. Five-thirty. I worked at the hospital, and I liked the early shift, because I got home in time to meet Brian after school."

"Did everything go as usual at work?"

"Yes, until Brian sent me a digital page. It was almost six A.M."

"What was the message?"

"It said, 'Mom, come home, now!' The word *now* was in all capital letters. And there were three exclamation points."

"What did you do?"

"I hurried home."

"Did you call the police?"

"No. I'd gotten messages like this before. Usually it was Brian getting mad because his father punished him, or was making him do push-ups before school, something like that. I didn't want to involve the police. Oscar would have been furious with me."

"What did you find when you got home?"

"Brian was in his room, crying. He has some verbal ability, even though he's deaf, but he was way too shaken to come up with words. In sign he told me to check in the master bedroom. So I went."

"What did you find?"

"Oscar. He was in the bed, and there was a lot of blood on the sheets and pillow. I ran to him, knelt at his side. I could see that he'd been shot in the head. It was . . ." Her eyes closed, then opened. "It was an awful-looking wound. He had no pulse, wasn't breathing. I knew he was dead."

"What did you do?"

"I called the police."

"Anything else?"

"It was all such a blur. But I remember . . . I remember seeing his gun on the floor next to the bed."

"Did you touch it?"

"Yes."

"Why?"

She looked at the jury and said, "I put the safety on the gun."

A low murmur swept across the courtroom. The prosecutor looked puzzled, and several jurors straightened in their seats. The significance of the safety being on or off—homicide versus suicide—seemed to have been lost on no one.

Jack waited for silence, then asked, "Why did you put the safety on?"

"When I saw his body lying there, dead, my first thought was that Oscar had killed himself. He was alive when I had left for work. As far as I knew, no one had come by the house. His own gun was on the floor next to the bed. And that whole thing with Lieutenant Johnson had me convinced that he was disturbed or depressed."

"Let me ask you again: Why did you put the safety on the gun?"

She swallowed hard. "That's what I was explaining. I married a Marine. Brian's father was a captain, a leader. In a Marine's world, courage is everything. I knew that someday Brian would probably have to know the truth about his father. But at that moment, all I could think of was that I didn't want my ten-year-old boy to have to deal with the fact that his father was a coward who killed himself."

"So you put the safety on the gun?"

"Yes. I knew the police wouldn't think it was suicide if the safety was on."

"But, by doing that, you made yourself into a murder suspect."

"The thought of becoming a suspect didn't cross my mind at that particular moment. If anything, I didn't see how I could be a suspect. I was at work when Oscar was shot."

"Not according to the time of death established by the medical examiner. He placed the time of death sometime before you left for work."

"Well, all I can say is that the medical examiner is wrong."

Jack backed away from the lectern, taking a few casual steps closer to the jury. Lindsey looked drained. He knew it was time to wrap it up, lest she have nothing left to stave off the prosecutor's attack on cross-examination.

"Ms. Hart," he said in a firm, direct tone. "Did you kill your husband?"

"No. I did not."

Jack shot a quick glance at the jury, a gut check to

see if any of them looked persuaded. At best, they looked confused, not sure what to believe anymore. But for a criminal defense lawyer, that was sometimes enough.

"Thank you, Ms. Hart. I have no further questions, Your Honor."

45

Judge Garcia insisted on squeezing in Lindsey's cross-examination before the lunch break. The prosecutor pecked away at her testimony, trying to highlight inconsistencies for the jury. He finished exactly the way Jack had expected. He painted her as a liar from day one.

Torres stepped toward the witness, his questions like lances. "You never told the police that you were having sex with Lieutenant Johnson, did you?"

"No."

"You never told them that your husband had drugged you and forced you to have sex with another man."

"No."

"You never went to a battered women's shelter."

"No."

"You never sought any rape counseling."

"No."

"You never told the police that it was you who had put the safety on your husband's gun."

"No, I didn't."

"In fact, when the police asked you point-blank, you denied ever having *touched* the gun."

"That's true."

"When Captain Pintado's father asked you point-blank, you again denied that you had ever touched the gun."

"That's true, too."

"You lied to the police."

"Yes."

"You lied to your dead husband's father."

"I regret that."

"You probably even lied to your son."

"Objection," said Jack.

"Overruled."

Lindsey straightened in her seat, as if to strengthen her resolve. "No. I would never lie to Brian."

"You would never lie to your son?" the prosecutor asked, incredulous.

"No."

He scoffed, seemingly disgusted. "Ms. Hart, even *now*, when you finally admit that you put the safety on the gun, you tell us that you did it because you wanted to be able to *lie* to your own son about the cause of his father's death. Isn't that right, ma'am?"

She turned slightly pale, as if not sure how to handle that one. "I thought it was best that way."

"Lies, all lies," he said, voice booming. "Is that what you think is best?"

"Objection."

"Overruled."

She brought her hand to her brow, pained. "I don't know anymore."

The prosecutor stepped closer. Then he glanced

back at Jack, shooting him an accusatory glare, before asking the final question. "Ms. Hart. Is there *anyone* you haven't lied to?"

Jack was about to object, but there were times when a lawyer could do his client more harm in the jury's eyes by running to her defense. Lindsey was shaky, but she needed to handle this one on her own.

"I'm not a liar," she said. "And I've never lied to this jury."

Good answer, thought Jack.

But at this point, he wondered if even he believed it.

Trial broke for lunch, and Jack had time only for a quick bite and for a few phone calls. He made just one, in particular, about Brian.

It hadn't been a major part of her direct testimony, but Lindsey's mention of the fact that Brian possessed some verbal skills, even though he was deaf, had stuck in the back of Jack's mind. He recalled his conversation with Alejandro Pintado, who'd mentioned that Brian was going to camp for hearing-impaired children after the trial was over. The two statements weren't inconsistent, but they did have him thinking back to one of the first things Lindsey had told him about Brian's condition. He was born deaf, which was why Lindsey had insisted that Jack and Jessie had known about his deafness before giving him up for adoption. Jessie probably would have had no way of knowing, as Jack had discovered, but his present curiosity had a different bent, one that was completely unrelated to what Jessie might have known or not known.

It had more to do with just how many lies Lindsey had told him.

Jack didn't have unfettered access to Brian's medical records, but he was usually able to get what he needed when he put his mind to it. From a quiet spot in the attorneys' lounge in the courthouse, he checked with directory assistance and dialed the phone number for Florida's only camp for hearing-impaired children.

"Hello," said Jack. "I'm calling for some general information."

"What kind of information would you like, sir?" the woman asked.

Jack didn't want to lie outright to her, but he also didn't want her to know that he was fishing for information about a child already enrolled. He said, "I have a friend with a ten-year-old boy who I think would benefit from your camp."

"Most children benefit tremendously. What kind of hearing impairment does the boy have?"

Jack knew some specifics from his discussions with Lindsey, but he had to think for a moment to answer to the question correctly. "He has bilateral sensorineural hearing loss."

"To what degree?"

"I'm not an expert on the terminology, but I believe it's in the profound category."

"We consider profound to be in excess of ninety-one db, which means that he might not even be able to hear loud sounds without amplification."

"That's his situation."

"Is it congenital or acquired?"

"He was born that way."

The woman on the line hesitated, then asked, "Are you sure?"

"Well, yes. Like I said, it's sensorineural hearing loss."

"I don't mean to condescend, but it's called sensorineural hearing loss to distinguish it from conductive hearing loss. It simply means that the nerves are damaged, which is permanent and generally irreversible. But sensorineural has both congenital and acquired causes."

"I'm pretty sure it's congenital."

"The reason I ask is this. If it is congenital, this camp would not be the right place for your friend's child."

"Why not?"

"We're not staffed for prelingual deaf children. Any child who comes here developed some language skills before suffering an acquired hearing loss."

Jack gripped the phone more tightly. "Are you saying that you don't have any children at your camp who have congenital hearing loss?"

"Not in the profoundly deaf category. Like I said, we're not staffed for that type of impairment. This wouldn't be the appropriate place for such a child."

"I see," said Jack.

"If you check our website, there are links to some excellent alternatives."

"I'll do that. Thank you very much."

Jack hung up the phone. The camp director couldn't have been more specific. Lindsey had been equally clear in her assertion that Brian was congenitally deaf. Yet the Pintados had made arrangements to send their grandson to a camp that was not appropriate for a child like Brian. That left only two possibilities. The Pintados were sending Brian to the wrong camp, which didn't seem very likely. Or . . .

Jack turned toward the window, staring out at the street traffic five stories below. The prosecutor's cross-examination was suddenly replaying in his mind.

Lies, lies, all lies.

Jack tucked his cell phone into his pocket and headed to another conference room near the courtroom, where Sofia and Lindsey were having lunch. Since Lindsey was in custody, a guard was posted outside the door. He allowed Jack to enter.

Jack looked at Lindsey, eyes glowing. "How did Brian lose his hearing?"

She was about to answer, then stopped, seeming to have read the expression on Jack's face. "Who wants to know?"

"Is that the way you handle everything? Your answer depends on who wants to know?"

Sofia said, "Jack, what's wrong?"

Jack stepped farther into the room, but he did not sit down. "I'll tell you what's wrong. I'm tired of being lied to by my own client."

"I told the truth today," said Lindsey.

"Did you?" said Jack. "Or do you live in a world where the forecast is always the same: mostly cloudy, continued showers of bullshit."

"What are you talking about?" asked Lindsey. "I admit, I may have misled you in the past, but that's only because the truth is so painful. Do you think it's easy to walk into a courtroom full of people and tell them you had sex with a sailor while your husband took photographs? Can you blame me for not running into your office on the first day and saying, 'Hey, Jack, here's our defense. I'll tell the world that I was a sex slave.' The media doesn't publish the names of rape victims out of respect for their privacy, but if you're married to a pervert, your entire sex life is front-page news. How fair is that?"

"Don't change the subject, Lindsey. I'm talking about what you said to me under the cloak of the attorney-client privilege."

"So am I. It just took me a while to get comfortable with the idea of having to say these things not just to you but to the whole world. But I did it. I was honest with you, and I did not perjure myself. Everything I said on the witness stand was true."

"Why did you lie to me about the cause of Brian's hearing loss?"

"What?"

"You told me he was born deaf. He wasn't, was he?"

"What difference does it make? He's deaf."

"I don't understand why you would lie about something like that."

"It's . . . it's not important."

"Every untruth is important. Why would you lie about this?"

"I have my reasons, okay?"

"What the hell are they?"

"Because . . ." Her lips pursed, as if she were about to explode. "Because I didn't want you to think I was a bad mother, all right? But now you know. Brian has acquired deafness. You want to blame me? Great. Go right ahead and do it. Be just like Oscar, just like Oscar's parents, just like Oscar's friends. Blame Lindsey. Everybody has to blame Lindsey. Well, it wasn't my fucking fault, damn it!"

Her voice nearly shook the room. Jack was stunned into silence, not sure what to say as he watched Lindsey lower her head and cry. Sofia laid a hand on her shoulder, but her touch seemed only to trigger a deeper reaction from Lindsey. It was a veritable catharsis, perhaps months of pent-up emotion spilling onto the conference room table.

"I wasn't blaming you for anything," said Jack. "I just want to know the truth."

Lindsey dabbed her eyes with a tissue, pulled herself together. "No, you want so much more than that. You want to know everything there is to know about me and Brian. You don't have that right. Taking this case didn't make you Brian's father."

Jack could have argued genetics, but he knew what she meant. "No one said I wanted to be part of your family, Lindsey."

"I'm sorry. I didn't mean that. I don't want you to think I'm ungrateful for everything you've done."

There was a knock at the door. Jack opened it, and the guard said, "Trial reconvenes in two minutes." Jack thanked him, then turned back to his client.

Sofia said, "I guess we should get back."

Lindsey and Sofia rose, but Jack didn't move. Lindsey looked at him and said, "You are coming back, aren't you?"

Jack still didn't move.

Sofia said, "I can take it from here, Jack. If that's what you want."

"No!" said Lindsey, her voice racing. "You can't

quit. You promised to stay in this case as long as you believed I was innocent. A little lie about the cause of Brian's hearing loss doesn't change that."

"It's deeper than that," said Jack.

She grasped his arm and said, "Don't do this to me. That's not what I—that's not what *Brian* deserves."

Jack stared at her coolly, trying to take the emotion out of his decision. Finally he said, "That's the last time I'm going to let you play the Brian card. You understand me?"

"Yes," she said quietly, releasing him.

Jack opened the door and led the way back to the courtroom, putting a good ten feet of airspace between himself and his client.

46

At seven o'clock that night, Jack drove to Alice Wainwright Park just south of downtown Miami. Leaving the car, he followed the exercise trail toward the rock-lined edge of Biscayne Bay and took a seat on the wooden bench near a kiosk that faced the mangroves. He knew he was in the right place because he was seventy-five paces east of the graffiti-covered wall that proclaimed, MADONNA, YOUR GUARD IS AN ASSHOLE, a leftover complaint from years earlier when the singer lived in one of the exclusive waterfront mansions in the neighborhood.

And then he waited, exactly as he'd been instructed.

Trial had adjourned for the day at five P.M. The afternoon session was devoted to forensic experts whom Jack had hired to neutralize the testimony of the medical examiner, particularly with respect to Captain Pintado's time of death. All had gone well enough, but Jack had much higher expectations for what the evening might bring.

His cell phone rang, and he answered quickly. It was Sofia.

"Don't we have a meeting?" She was referring to their standard date for evening debriefings after each trial day.

"I may not make it tonight," said Jack.

"You still thinking of withdrawing as counsel? I can't say I'd blame you, if you did."

"No. Like Lindsey said, I promised to stay on the case as long as I believe she's innocent. And don't think I'm nuts, but I'm suddenly leaning that way again."

"What happened?"

"Alejandro Pintado called me back. He's supposed to meet me in about two minutes."

"What about?"

"After Lindsey testified this morning, he went home and sifted through some of his son's personal effects. I guess Lindsey was too distraught to deal with shipping his things from Guantánamo after his death, so Oscar's father took care of it and had everything shipped back to Miami. Anyway, guess what the old man found."

"No idea."

"The digital camera Lindsey testified about."

There was silence on the line. "Don't tell me . . ."

"Yup," said Jack. "Some very interesting photographs were still on it. I'll let you know how our meeting goes."

Jack hung up and tucked the cell phone into his pocket. He waited a few more minutes, then checked his watch. Quarter past seven. Pintado had told him to be at this particular bench no later than seven P.M.

He wasn't late yet, at least not by Miami standards. Jack watched a couple of shirtless college boys toss a Frisbee on the lawn, and it was hard to believe that just five thousand beers ago, he'd once had abs like that, too.

"Hello, Jack."

He turned and saw Alejandro Pintado seated at the other end of the bench, which startled him a bit. "What are you, the stealth bomber or something?"

"What?"

"Nothing. I'm glad you came."

"This was something I couldn't do over the phone."

Jack noticed the dossier tucked under Pintado's arm. "Is that for me?"

"Yes."

"Pictures?"

"No."

"No?" said Jack, surprised.

Pintado laid the dossier on the bench beside him. "It's in no one's interest for those photographs ever to see the light of day."

"Don't mean to quibble with you, Mr. Pintado. But those photographs are evidence."

"They are evidence of the fact that your client had sex with Oscar's best friend. She's admitted that. There's no need to show the world pictures of it."

"That's not the point. They were taken with your son's camera. Probably by your son."

"Probably," he said, then looked away. "When I went down to Guantánamo after Oscar died, I cleaned out his locker at the Officer's Club. Lindsey probably didn't even know about it. I guess that's why she never found the pictures. I didn't even think to download the images myself until she testified about the digital camera."

Jack gave him a moment, trying not to embarrass him. "Look, Mr. Pintado. I know this has to be awful for you. Your son is dead, and now you find out that he was taking these photographs of his wife. But this was no run-of-the-mill lovers' triangle. This was an abused woman caught between two men. I don't know what brought things to a head. Maybe Oscar didn't like the way Lieutenant Johnson started coming around the house when he wasn't there, pestering Lindsey for sex. Maybe in some sick way Johnson really started to like Lindsey, and he got tired of Oscar hanging around and taking pictures every time he had sex with her. Something went wrong, and Oscar got shot. Your grandson's father is dead. And now his mother is standing trial for a murder she didn't commit."

"You think it was Johnson," said Pintado. It wasn't a question, more like a statement.

"Don't you?" said Jack.

"I don't know. But I do know this much: I want to hear from the lieutenant."

"So do I. That's why the other day I asked you for any information you could give me about his whereabouts. I want to subpoena him."

A seagull landed at their feet. Pintado shooed it away. "You were right, you know. Johnson is in Miami. Torres wants to keep him out of the trial if he can. Says he wants him in town just in case he might need him for rebuttal. But I think he wants him here so that you never find him."

"I'm sure Torres is convinced that Lindsey did it.

He doesn't want me pecking away at Johnson on the witness stand and filling jurors' minds with reasonable doubt."

"I agreed with that strategy," said Pintado. "But I'm not sure I do anymore."

Jack glanced at the dossier. "You got something for me?"

"The address is inside here. You get your process server out there tonight, you'll have Johnson in trial tomorrow."

Jack reached for the dossier, but Pintado pulled back. "Not so fast."

"What's wrong?"

Pintado gave him a sideways glance, then held it. "Did Lindsey ever tell you how Brian became deaf?"

Jack reeled a bit, taken by the sudden shift in their conversation. "No. She just said it wasn't her fault."

"It doesn't surprise me that she'd keep it from you."

"Keep what?"

He patted the dossier and said, "There's a copy of Brian's medical history in here as well. It will tell you how he went deaf."

Jack wanted to know, but he wasn't sure what Pintado was trying to accomplish. "How did you get this?"

"My lawyer. As a grandparent I had no legal right to see it before. But now that Lindsey's in jail and my wife and I are Brian's custodians, the doctor had to hand it over to us. I got it just a few days ago."

"What do you want me to do with it?"

"Read it. And once you do, I think you'll agree with me."

"Agree with you on what?"

Pintado's eyes narrowed, his expression very serious. "No matter how this trial turns out—even if it turns out that Lindsey didn't kill Oscar—Brian belongs with his grandparents."

"I don't think I understand."

"Read the file, Jack. Then you will."

Their eyes remained locked for several long moments. Then Jack reached for the dossier, and this time Pintado didn't pull back. Jack took it from him and said, "All right. I'll read it. With interest."

47

A sly old trial lawyer from north Florida (the only part of Florida that was truly "the South") once told Jack, "Catchin' a gator is the easy part. It's lettin' him go that'll cost you fingers and toes. If it ain't the snapping jaws, it's the swoosh of the tail that gets ya." It was another way of saying to be careful what you wish for; you can wrestle a witness onto the stand, but once his mouth opens, it can be a buss or a bite. That old man's words echoed in Jack's mind as he prepared to do battle with Lieutenant Damont Johnson, knowing full well that this was one witness who'd be jamming him at every turn.

Jack had filled the morning session with other witnesses, most importantly an expert who testified that it wasn't uncommon for a physically or psychologically abused wife to keep her suffering to herself, even deny it to authorities. A subpoena wasn't slapped on Johnson till midmorning, and he was finally hauled into court as the last witness of the day.

"The defense calls Lieutenant Damont Johnson," Jack announced.

It was as if the collective pulse of the courtroom had suddenly quickened, the excitement palpable. Spectators stirred in their seats, jurors straightened to attention, and the media reached for pen and paper. The courthouse artist worked furiously at the lieutenant's likeness, as if utterly confident that this was evening-news material. For an instant, Jack had almost felt that it didn't matter what Johnson said, that it was worth the dumbfounded expression on the prosecutor's face just to bring Johnson into the courtroom. Soon enough, however, that initial excitement wore off.

"Lieutenant, was it you or Captain Pintado who drugged Lindsey Hart the first time you had sex with her?"

Johnson did a double take, but kept his composure. He was an imposing figure in his own right, dressed in the white uniform of an officer, his hat in his lap. It was hard to maintain a sense of dignity, given the nature of the questioning, but he was holding his own. "Excuse me, but neither one of us drugged her."

"You're saying she was a willing participant?"

"I'm saying it was her idea."

The prosecutor smiled, and to say that Jack was headed down the wrong track would have been the trial's grandest understatement. He knew better than to think that Johnson would admit to having forced Lindsey to have sex. He wasn't going to break down on the witness stand and tearfully confess that he killed Oscar Pintado. That kind of drama happened on television every week, but rarely in a real courtroom. Jack had to score the sure points in his direct examination, let Torres have a shot on cross, and then hope for a few strategic openings that he might capitalize on through redirect. That was the plan anyway.

Jack said, "Let's see what we *can* agree on, shall we, Lieutenant?"

"Sure."

"You had sex with Lindsey Hart, did you not?"

"Yes."

"Oscar Pintado saw you have sex with his wife?"

"That's true."

"He even took photographs?"

Johnson shifted, as if slightly uncomfortable with that notion. "Yes. He did."

"Do you also agree that this is something most husbands don't do?"

"Not the ones I know."

"Not even for their best friends?"

"Right again."

"You were Oscar Pintado's best friend, weren't you?"

"Best friend on the base. I wouldn't say I was his best friend in the world."

"All right. Am I correct in assuming that having sex with Oscar's wife wasn't part of your friendship from day one?"

"That's a fair assumption."

"That's something that developed after you two had been friends for a while, correct?"

"Right."

Jack paused, debating how to proceed. He could launch into a series of questions about how the sex got started, who suggested it, that sort of thing. But that strategy was likely to elicit only lies, or at the very least answers Jack didn't like. He took a safer approach.

"Oscar Pintado came from a very wealthy family, did he not?"

"That's my understanding."

"He's not the kind of guy who would be tempted by an offer of money from one of his friends."

"What are you trying to say?" he said, his eyes narrowing with suspicion.

"You didn't give him money to have sex with his wife, did you?"

"Of course not. Like I said, it was Lindsey's idea."

Jack stepped closer, doing little to mask his skepticism. "Her idea, huh? Let me ask you something, Lieutenant. How many men are on the naval base in Guantánamo at any one time?"

"I don't know. Several thousand, for sure."

"Most of them between the age of twenty and thirty?"

"Most of them, yeah."

"Most of them in pretty darn good shape? Physically, I mean."

"Sure."

"Most of them don't have wives or girlfriends with them on the base, do they?"

"Relatively few do."

"So, what you're telling us is this," said Jack as he walked toward his client, laying a reassuring hand on her shoulder. "While living on a Caribbean Island and surrounded by several thousand hard-bodied, twenty-something men—most of whom hadn't been intimate with a woman in quite some time—my extremely attractive client decided that she needed to have sex with *you* while her husband watched and took pictures. This was her great idea; is that what you're saying?"

A light chorus of chuckles emerged from the audience. Even one of the jurors smiled. The witness burrowed his tongue into his cheek, a sure sign that Jack was getting to him.

Jack said, "Is that what you're saying, Lieutenant?"

"Look, all I know is that Oscar told me she—"

"Whoa, objection!" shouted Torres. "What Oscar told him is hearsay, Judge."

"Sustained."

Jack said, "But, Judge—"

"I sustained the objection, Mr. Swyteck. Move on."

Jack could have argued about exceptions to the ruling, but it was clear that the judge had heard enough about sex, and he was in no mood to reconsider. Jack's point was made, nonetheless. It was time to wrap up.

"Lieutenant, just a couple more questions. Obviously you're an officer in the U.S. Coast Guard."

"That's right."

"If you wanted to know tomorrow's patrol routes for Coast Guard vessels in the Florida Straits, you'd know how to get that information, wouldn't you?"

"They don't give me that information."

"I didn't ask that. I said, you'd know how to get it, wouldn't you?"

"Just because I know how to get it doesn't mean—"

"Lieutenant, please. Just answer my question. You'd know how to get that information, right?"

Johnson fell silent, as if trying to figure out a way to deny it. Finally, he said, "Yeah. I'd know how to get it."

"Thank you. No further questions."

Jack returned to his seat. He didn't expect smiles from his client, but she looked positively ashen. It was understandable. They'd flirted with fire. But they'd come out ahead.

Thank God.

Torres approached the witness. "How nice to see you here today, Lieutenant." His voice had just a hint of sarcasm.

"Nice to see you, too."

All semblance of familiarity drained from Torres's face. His voice had a definite edge to it, somewhere between a police interrogator and drill sergeant. "Lieutenant, I want to take you back to the morning of June seventeenth, the day Captain Pintado died."

"All right."

"We've heard testimony in this case that sometime before six A.M. you went to Captain Pintado's house. Do you admit or deny you were there at that time?"

"I was there."

"We've also heard testimony that you entered the house without knocking. Do you admit or deny that?"

"I admit it."

"Finally, we heard testimony that you were seen running from the house a few minutes later. Do you admit or deny that?"

"I admit that also."

Jack looked on, confused. The witness was readily admitting the very things that Jack had thought he would never admit. Something wasn't right.

Torres said, "Lieutenant, would you please tell the jury *why* you went to Captain Pintado's house that morning?"

"Lindsey called me on the telephone. She told me to come over."

"Did she tell you why she wanted you to come over?"

"She told me that Oscar was gone. She said that he'd taken Brian fishing, so it could be just the two of us."

"What did you take that to mean?"

He shrugged, as if the answer was obvious. "That we could have sex without Oscar being around."

"Were you agreeable to that?"

"Yes, I was."

"Did she say anything else?"

"She said, 'I'll be waiting for you. I'll leave the door unlocked. Come straight to the bedroom. I have a big surprise for you.'"

"What did you do?"

"What do you think? Got in my car and drove over."

"What happened when you got there?"

"I did exactly as she told me. The door was unlocked and I went inside, straight back to the bedroom. That's when I found Oscar's body. He was still in bed, soaked in blood."

Torres was clearly energized, practically tripping over his own questions, so caught up in his own roll. "What did you do?"

"I ran through the house, made sure there weren't more bodies. That's when I found Brian in his room."

"Did you say anything to him?"

"Yes. You know, he's deaf, but he can read lips to a certain extent. I said, 'Brian, what happened to your father?'"

"Did he respond?"

Johnson said, "Brian started to cry. Then he looked at me and said—"

"Objection, hearsay," said Jack. There was a knot in Jack's stomach as he spoke. He wanted to hear the answer—perhaps he wanted to hear it more than anyone else in the courtroom—but the prosecutor's strategy was crystal clear. He was trying to convince the jury that Lindsey had set up Johnson for the murder she'd committed.

Torres said, "Your Honor, it's an excited utterance by a ten-year-old boy whose father has just been shot in their own home."

The judge considered it, then said, "I'll allow it. The witness may answer."

The lieutenant leaned closer to the microphone, and Jack suddenly felt the pain of Lindsey's finger-nails digging into his forearm. It was as if they both knew exactly what Johnson was going to say, knew that the killer would be revealed and that Lindsey's fate was sealed.

Johnson's mouth opened, and the words oozed like hot lava. "Brian looked at me and said, 'I shot him. I shot my dad.'"

Lindsey sprang to her feet. "That's a lie!"

A collective gasp swept across the courtroom.

"Order!" the judge shouted, the crack of his gavel rising above the outburst.

"That's a total lie!" said Lindsey, tears streaming down her cheeks.

"Mr. Swyteck, get your client under control, or I'll have her removed."

"It's a lie, Jack," she said, her voice breaking. "It's a total lie!"

Jack eased her back into her chair. She was shaking uncontrollably, and Jack was drawing every ounce of strength from within himself to stay composed. Sofia, too, was keeping it low-key, but the surprise was evident in her eyes. As tough as it was, Jack was quite certain that the defense didn't look half as stunned as the prosecutor did.

Torres stared at the witness, a gladiator's stance. "Excuse me, Lieutenant," he said firmly. "Perhaps I didn't hear you right. Did you mean to say that the boy's words were something to the effect that his mother had shot his father?"

"No. You heard me right. Brian told me that *he* had shot his father."

Lindsey's head was in her hands. Jack's gaze shifted back and forth from her to Johnson, still not quite believing.

The prosecutor did his best to seem indignant, strutted across the courtroom, his voice rising in anger. He was about to do what no lawyer ever wanted to do: impeach his own witness.

"Lieutenant Johnson," he said, his voice booming, "you and I had numerous conversations about this case, did we not?"

"Yes, sir."

"We even did some mock examinations, practice sessions, during which I asked you questions and you gave me answers. Isn't that right?"

"Yes, that's right."

"Not once in any of those conversations did you tell me about Brian's confession to you. Did you, Lieutenant?"

"No. I did not. But that's because—"

"That's enough," said Torres, cutting him off.

Johnson appealed to the judge, a look of anger and panic coming over him. "Your Honor, I have to explain this."

"There's no question pending," said Torres.

The judge scratched his chin, as if he himself was overwhelmed. "The witness always has a right to explain his answer. Lieutenant Johnson said no, he never told you that before. Let's hear why."

Torres retreated to his seat, clearly uneasy.

Johnson looked at Lindsey and said, "The reason I never said anything about Brian is that Lindsey made me promise not to. After Brian confessed to me and I ran out of the house, I tracked down Lindsey and had a few words with her. I accused Lindsey of calling me over there to set me up for a murder I didn't commit. She said she was sorry, that she was just trying to protect Brian. And then she asked me—she begged me—whatever I do, please don't tell anyone that Brian shot his father."

The courtroom was stone silent.

The judge leaned back in his chair, eyes raised toward the ceiling. "Any further questions, Mr. Torres?"

The prosecutor rose. Had this been a prizefight,

he would have been staggering. "Nothing further, Your Honor."

"Mr. Swyteck, any redirect?"

Jack could have put a finer point on it, but that was the beauty of reasonable doubt. No fine points were required. "Nothing, Your Honor."

"The witness is excused."

Jack watched, along with everyone else in the courtroom, as Lieutenant Johnson stepped down. He made eye contact with no one, his eyes forward in soldierlike fashion as he walked out.

The judge broke the silence. "Call your next witness, Mr. Swyteck."

The words hardly had meaning to him. Jack was still trying to absorb what had just happened. It did make logical sense, but the emotional impact on the judge, the jury, or anyone else in the courtroom was nothing compared to the kick between the eyes that it was for Jack. Certain things finally and suddenly began to explain themselves. Lindsey's refusal to let Jack talk with Brian. The grandparents seeking a court order to keep Jack away from Brian. From the very beginning, it was all about keeping anyone and everyone away from Brian.

And now Jack understood why.

"Mr. Swyteck, your next witness, please."

His client's earlier lies somehow seemed less devious now that Jack knew whom Lindsey had been protecting. Jack patted the back of her hand as he rose, trying to keep her from shaking. "Your Honor," he said, his voice carrying throughout the courtroom. "The defense rests."

48
·

Jack couldn't remember another good day that had felt so bad.

Before trial had even started, Jack had been well aware that the entire case could turn if he could just get Damont Johnson on the stand. But even as that first question for the lieutenant left his lips, Jack's highest hope was to convince the jury that a kinky arrangement had gone very wrong and that Lindsey's husband had ended up dead at the hand of his own best friend. Never had Jack figured that Johnson would hand him victory by fingering Lindsey's son.

Of course he was devastated. As much as Jack wanted to pretend that his decision to take this case was all about Lindsey and her son, all about keeping an innocent mother out of jail, his motivations had always run deeper than that. It was about Jack and his biological son. Jack wasn't sure what he'd expected to get out of this, even in the best of circumstances. At the very least, he had wanted to meet Brian, maybe get to know him on some level. It worried him that Brian would grow up without a father. It pained him that Brian might lose his mother, too. And it bugged him to no end that Brian might grow up with his grandparents in a tony, gated community where kids cried at their own birthday parties because Mommy had promised that Cirque du Soleil would be there and all she could pull off was a command performance by the traveling cast from the Broadway musical *The Lion King*.

The very fact that he hadn't suspected Brian, however, was troubling in its own right. Jack had crossed that line between personal interest and professional judgment. He was blinded by emotions, which told him that he never should have been in the case in the first place.

And now he knew exactly why Lindsey had hired him.

He popped open a can of beer with one hand, channel-surfed with the other, as the local television anchors delivered their punchy spin to a newsworthy day at the courthouse.

"A shocking development," said one.

"A monstrous blow to the prosecution," said another.

Jack switched back and forth between stations, checked all of them out in rapid-fire fashion. Then he did a double take. He'd moved two stations beyond it before the image triggered something in his brain, but he hurriedly scrolled back to one of the stations where he thought he'd seen Hector Torres speaking.

It *was* him. The footage was taped, but it was only a few minutes old. The prosecutor was fielding questions from the media as he left the courthouse. Jack increased the volume and listened. He handled the string of "What will the prosecution do now?" questions with ease, never breaking stride as he dished out such time-honored platitudes as, "We shall stay the course until justice prevails." One question, however, brought him to a dead halt.

"Mr. Torres, how do you answer charges from the defense team that you've known all along that Lindsey Hart was innocent?"

He shot an icy glare, then collected himself for the camera. Torres had made a career out of never losing his cool in public. "First of all, Lindsey Hart is not innocent. We'll prove that tomorrow in our rebuttal case. Secondly, I have never concealed evidence of a defendant's innocence in my life, so if I had such evidence, Jack Swyteck would have known about it."

The reporter persisted, pushing closer. "So why do you think the defense is making those accusations?"

What accusations? thought Jack. He hadn't spoken to anyone.

Torres seemed to compose a response in his mind before speaking. "I don't presume to vouch for Jack Swyteck's integrity, but I've been friends with his father for three decades. I have to assume that some of the old man's class has rubbed off, in which case Jack would never make a half-cocked accusation like that. So, until I actually hear it from the horse's mouth, I'm going to treat those alleged accusations as mere rumors that don't deserve a response."

The taped segment ended, and the anchorwoman

was back on-screen. Jack switched to another channel, then another, but they had all moved on to other news. He could have called Torres to assure him that those accusations from "the defense team" hadn't come from him, but he was content to leave it exactly the way Torres had played it: rumors.

He switched to ESPN, and the phone rang. It was Sofia. She'd seen the same broadcast, the same talk of accusations from the defense.

"Did you hold a press conference and forget to tell me about it?" she asked.

"No. Did you?"

"You know me better than that by now."

He did. His entire career, Jack had choreographed every aspect of trial, from the number of times the defendant looked at the jury during direct examination, to the exact words that any member of the defense team uttered to the press. Sofia wouldn't undermine him on this point.

Jack said, "I'm sure that reporter was just baiting him, attributing pure rumors to the defense team."

"Clearly," she said. "But I'm beginning to think that somebody should stand up and give Torres what he deserves."

"I couldn't agree with you more."

Sofia said, "You think Torres knew all along that the boy did it?"

"No. I think he knew that if Johnson was pushed, he'd blame it on the boy. That's why he kept Johnson hidden away from us. But he still doesn't believe that Brian did it. I'm sure of that."

"Do you want to get together tonight? Plan for Torres's rebuttal?"

"Not unless you were able to talk Lindsey into meeting with us."

"Sorry. She just wants to be alone tonight."

"Can't say I blame her. Everything she's worked for over the past two months, every lie she's ever told us, just came crashing down on her head. Or, I guess I should say Brian's head."

There was silence on the line, as if Sofia wasn't sure what to say. Finally, she said, "Are you going to be okay, Jack?"

Jack was staring at the television. Basketball on ESPN Classics. To think, just a few days earlier he'd harbored secret thoughts of taking Brian over to the gym, maybe a little game of one-on-one. It could have been fun to play with someone who didn't maul you on the way to the basket the way Theo did. *Not to be.*

"Sure," he said. "I'll be okay."

"Call me if you need anything. Or if you just want someone to talk to."

"Thanks. I'll see you tomorrow."

She said good-bye, and Jack hung up the phone. He drew a breath, but before he could exhale, the phone was ringing again. He picked it up and said, "Yes, Sofia?"

"You sure you're going to be okay?"

"Do I sound like I'm not okay?"

"You sound a little like someone who's trying too hard to sound okay, or someone who's okay now but who probably won't be once he sits down and really thinks about what happened."

Jack looked at the phone, incredulous. The last time he'd had a conversation like this, he was married. "I'm okay."

"Okay enough to do something?"

"Do something about what?"

"You ever been to Casa Tua's on the beach? They have a great tapas bar upstairs. I won't even talk about the case, if you don't want to. I feel so bad for you. What you went through today was just awful. Sitting at home alone is only going to bring you down even more."

"Thanks. Maybe another night."

"Okay. Give me a call if you change your mind."

"Sure. Good night."

He hung up, then closed his eyes as the cushy leather armchair almost swallowed him whole. The phone rang the instant his body came to rest. He answered with just a hint of annoyance in his tone.

"Sofia, I swear on my mother's grave I'm totally okay."

The caller hesitated, then said, "Is this Jack Swyteck?"

Jack straightened in his chair. "Yes, sorry. I thought you were someone else. Who is this?"

"My name is Maritza Rodriguez. Formerly Maritza Torres."

"You must be Hector's—"

"I'm Hector Torres's ex-wife."

Jack was going to guess daughter, just to be nice, though the voice sounded plenty old. "How can I help you?"

"I'd like to meet with you," she said.

"What about?"

"I've been following this trial from day one. I have to say, I've wondered all along if Hector had the right person. Then I saw the way he treated your client, and all doubts vanished. That poor woman. But that's just like Hector. Always treating the victim like the criminal, especially when it comes to an abused woman."

"Is there something you want to tell me about the case?"

"You might say that. I was just watching the evening news. When I saw my ex-husband mention his long-time friendship with your father, I couldn't take it anymore. I had to say something."

"About what, exactly?"

"About . . ." Her voice trailed off, as if she weren't sure how Jack would react. "It's about your mother."

Jack froze. He had plenty on his mind, and tomorrow he had to contend with whatever Torres deigned to throw at him in rebuttal. But he'd been around long enough to know that people who were eager to talk tonight weren't always willing to talk tomorrow.

"I'd love to talk to you, Mrs. Rodriguez. Just tell me where you want to meet."

49

Jack met Maritza Rodriguez at her house in Pine-crest.

South Florida wasn't the birthplace of "McMan-sions"—multimillion-dollar spreads so cookie cutter in design that they bordered on tract housing for the filthy rich—but it had certainly run with the concept. Whole neighborhoods had succumbed to the bulldozer, vintage 1950 shoe boxes replaced by nine-thousand-square-foot Mediterranean-style megahomes in which twenty-foot ceilings, walls of windows, and four-figure monthly A/C bills came standard.

Jack was seated on the leather couch in the great room. It was supposed to be the heart of the house, but like most of these new houses he'd visited, it had a sterile feeling—Saturnia floors, ecru walls, crown moldings so high that you needed a telescope to see the dentil details. Behind Mrs. Rodriguez was a shiny black grand piano, another McMansion staple, as if a musical instrument that no one in the house knew how to play would somehow warm up the icebox.

"My ex-husband had a thing for your mother," she said as she peered over the rim of her coffee cup.

Jack tried not to appear shocked. "That must have been a long time ago," said Jack. "My mother died when I was born."

"It was many, many years ago, before Hector and I even met. Before Hector came to this country."

"It's funny you mention this now," said Jack. "A friend recently told me that Hector bears a strong resemblance to my mother's old flame in Bejucal. The guy swears it was Hector Torres."

"He's probably right."

"Only problem is, the guy's name was Jorge Bustón. Not Hector Torres. Unless Hector changed his name."

"Not to my knowledge," she said. "People did do that, of course. Especially those who took a very vocal role against the Cuban government when they got here. If you left family back in Cuba, changing your name was a good way to keep your loved ones from being persecuted for your own anti-Castro activity waged in exile. But Hector never mentioned anything to me about changing his name."

"As far as you know, your ex has always been Hector Torres?"

"Yes. But now that you raise the issue, if someone changes his name, it's conceivable that he wouldn't tell anyone. It all depends on the reason for the name change, I suppose."

"I suppose," said Jack, thinking. He could have probed more, but he didn't want to get too far off the main point. "When you say your ex-husband had a thing for my mother, what do you mean?"

She sighed, as if not sure how to put it. "Let me start at the beginning. Hector and I met here in Miami in 1967, got married in 1968."

"My mother was already dead."

"Right. You were just a baby when Hector became friends with your father."

"Why would he become friends with my father if he had a thing for my mother?"

"That's what I wanted to know."

"Did you ask him?"

"Yes. He told me why, but the answer was obvious. He still loved her."

Jack shook his head, confused. "Wait a minute. He buddied up to my dad because he was still in love with my mother?"

"I can tell you for a fact that when Hector came to this country, even after he met me, he was determined to find your mother. When he learned that she was dead, he was devastated. Frankly, I think he became friends with your father for one reason. It was the only way he could find out what happened to the woman he really loved."

"But he and my father have been friends all my life."

"All I'm saying is that your mother was the reason they became friends in the first place. I didn't say she was the reason they remained friends over the years. I'm quite certain that, to this day, your father knows nothing about that relationship."

"So, what made you call me now, after all this time?"

"Like I said, it bugged me to see that hypocrite ex-husband of mine on television invoking his friendship with your father. Especially after the way he treated your client on the witness stand. After the way he treated me in our marriage. After the way I'm sure he treated your mother."

"What do you mean, the way he treated my mother?"

"Hector was—" She stopped herself, measuring her words. "I was married to Hector for only four years, but I know him well. Trust me, he's never had a healthy relationship with a woman in his life. He's not capable of it."

"Do you know something specific about my mother?"

"Only what I saw."

Jack blinked hard, even more confused. "Wait. You and Hector met after my mother was dead. So what could you have seen?"

"I saw a man consumed by the memory of a woman he couldn't live without."

"Lots of people carry a torch."

"I'd call it an obsession."

"He'd probably call it sentimental."

"There was nothing sentimental about it. The man scared the hell out of me. It's why I divorced him. I followed him one day," she said, her voice tightening.

"What?"

"He used to leave the house every Saturday, not tell me where he was going. So I followed him one day."

"Where'd he go?"

"The cemetery. Flagler Memorial Park."

"That's where my mother is buried. He visited her grave?"

"Yes. Every Saturday."

"Even after he was married to you?"

"That's right."

"That's why you divorced him?"

"It wasn't just the visiting that bothered me."

"What was it?"

"It was—it was just strange."

"I'd like to know."

"Like I said, I followed him to the cemetery. I hid behind a mausoleum so he couldn't see me. He looked around to make sure no one was watching. And then he . . ."

Jack felt his pulse quicken. "What?"

Her voice started to shake. "He lay down on top of her grave."

Jack went cold.

"And then he . . ." Her voice trailed off. She couldn't say the rest, and Jack didn't want to hear it anyway. Her eyes were cast down toward her coffee cup. Jack was looking at her face, but the image was suddenly a blur.

"So you divorced him," said Jack, his anger rising. "And he remained friends with my father all these years. Shook his hand, smiled to his face, went to his birthday parties, used him for whatever political capital my old man was worth."

"I didn't know that until I saw him on the news tonight. But when I heard that—well, I just had to call you. I'm sorry. This has to be a terrible thing to hear about your own mother."

"No need to apologize. You did the right thing."

They sat in silence, as if neither one knew exactly where to take the conversation from here. Maritza stirred her coffee, and the spoon shook in her hand. The outing of her ugly secret had only seemed to make things more awkward.

Jack checked his watch, then rose. "Trial tomorrow. I should be going."

She seemed relieved by the suggestion. She saw him to the foyer and opened the front door.

"Thanks again," said Jack.

She shook his hand, then a look of concern came over her. "Please don't tell Hector that I said any of this. I'm happy now. I've remarried, I have a nice life."

Jack looked into her eyes, and he could see beyond the concern. He saw traces of genuine fear—an old fear that had suddenly reared its head after all these years. For an instant, it was as if he were looking into his own mother's eyes, and he wondered if it was that same kind of fear that had driven her from Bejucal, that had carried her across an ocean. And then it suddenly came clear to him: *Abuela* may have bought her daughter a ticket to Miami, but Ana Maria hadn't boarded that Pedro Pan airplane because her mother told her to go. She hadn't left Cuba out of shame. She was indeed running for freedom, the kind of freedom that only Torres's ex-wife could understand.

"I won't say a word," he promised. He turned and started down the front steps, walking into the silence of night. As the door closed behind him, he turned for one last look, one final impression of the door too heavy on the house too big—and of the nervous woman inside, all too believable.

50

Whoever coined the phrase "There's no second bite at the apple" had obviously never heard of rebuttal.

Jack took his seat in the central courtroom knowing that a criminal trial rarely ended with the words "The defense rests." The prosecution always had the right to call witnesses to rebut the case presented by the defense, and Lieutenant Johnson had given Hector Torres no other choice. Jack was quite certain that the U.S. attorney would call at least one witness in rebuttal, and Jack didn't have to tell Lindsey who that one witness would likely be.

"Your Honor," said Torres in a voice that filled the courtroom, "the United States of America calls Brian Pintado."

The big double doors opened in the rear of the courtroom. At once, the eyes of the judge, the jury, and several hundred spectators were locked like radar on a ten-year-old boy.

"The witness will please come forward," said the judge.

Slowly, Brian made his way down the center aisle escorted by the bailiff. His eyes darted left and right, as if in search of a friendly face in the crowd. He appeared nervous, as anyone would, especially a child. But from a distance—if Jack squinted and ignored the difference in height between Brian and the bailiff—he seemed amazingly mature. Brian was a young man, not a boy, looking sharp in his dark blue suit and burgundy tie as he walked bravely down the aisle. Still, Jack's perception was clouded by vague and confusing memories of the child in the photographs Lindsey had showed him, Jack's first images of his biological son. He recalled that evening outside Alejandro Pintado's house, the first time he'd laid eyes on Brian in the flesh. He was just a carefree kid riding a bicycle at the end of a cul-de-sac, and Jack found himself wanting to cling to that image and never let go. This was a courtroom, however, not a playground, and Jack was beginning to feel like the proverbial parent who had blinked twice and missed it all—the first steps, the first words, the soccer games, the graduations, the whole shebang. Brian was growing up without him, as it should have been with adoption; but Jack couldn't help feeling that someone was being cheated, if not himself, then Lindsey—if not Lindsey, then Brian. Kids grew up too fast, even without a murdered parent, and putting Brian on the witness stand would surely bleed away the last remaining drops of innocence from a tattered childhood.

If the smile of anticipation on Hector Torres's lips was any indication, he didn't seem to give a damn.

"Please raise your right hand," the bailiff said.

Brian did as he was told, though he seemed slightly confused by the administration of the oath. The bailiff said it aloud, and a young woman signed it out for Brian, breaking down the barriers of lost hearing. Jack watched the woman's gestures with interest, all that gibberish about "the truth, the whole truth, and nothing but the truth." What could it possibly mean to a ten-year-old boy, be it in sign or the spoken word? It probably would have made more sense to pinky swear.

"I do," said Brian.

It was the first time Jack had heard his voice. The speech was understandable, though far from perfect. His response was somewhere between "I do" and "Ah duh."

"Please be seated," said the judge.

The courtroom was silent as the prosecutor stepped forward. Brian wasn't focused on Torres, or the jury, or the judge. Initially, it struck Jack as odd that the boy wasn't even seeking out his mother, but then he realized that Brian was riveted to the sign interpreter, his connection to what was going on in the courtroom. A trial was scary enough for a child with hearing. For the deaf, the anxiety had to be even higher. It was understandable, therefore, that Brian wasn't looking at his mother.

What was really odd was that Lindsey wasn't watching her son.

The judge said, "Young man, I know this is all new to you. If you get tired or confused or need a break, you speak up and let me know. You understand?"

Brian waited for the sign interpretation, then said, "Yes, sir."

The judge looked at the prosecutor and said, "Mr. Torres, proceed."

"Thank you, Your Honor." Torres unbuttoned his suit coat and buried a hand in his pants pocket. He was trying hard to be nonthreatening, the exact opposite of the way he normally handled witnesses. "Good morning, Brian."

"Good morning." That time, he didn't need the interpreter. He read Torres's lips.

"First, let me say how sorry I am about the loss of your father. I know this is extremely painful for you, so I will try to be brief."

There was a short pause for signing, then Brian thanked him. Torres took another step closer, now with both hands in his pockets. He spoke in a low voice, a hint of sadness in it, more paternal than prosecutorial. "Brian, is that your mother sitting over there?"

Again there was silence. Brian's gaze slowly shifted toward the defense table, finally coming to rest on Lindsey. Jack saw no anger in his eyes, no animosity. Brian seemed to be pleading with his mother, as if asking for forgiveness.

Still, Lindsey wouldn't look at him.

Brian said, "Yes, that's my mom."

"All right," said Torres. "You understand that you have to tell the truth in this courtroom. It doesn't matter who is watching."

Jack didn't like the implication that his client might encourage falsehoods, but he withheld his objection. There was no upside in jumping all over a kid who was merely acknowledging that he had to be truthful.

Brian said, "Yes, I will tell the truth."

Torres paused, as if an ominous stretch of silence was the appropriate buildup for his next question. Finally, he asked in a grave tone, "Brian, did you shoot your father?"

Brian looked at his mother, and for the first time since the young witness had entered the courtroom, Jack's client made direct eye contact with her son. It was almost imperceptible, and Jack wasn't sure if he was actually seeing it or imagining it. But he could have sworn that Lindsey—ever so slightly—had shaken her head.

The boy looked at the prosecutor, then spoke directly to the jury. "No, I did not kill my father."

"Thank you. No further questions."

Torres turned and took his seat. Brian seemed ready to get up and leave, but Jack was quickly on his feet, which sent a clear message that the ordeal wasn't over yet.

The judge said, "Mr. Swyteck, cross-examination?"

"Yes, Your Honor."

Jack could manage only half steps as he approached the witness, as if his feet were weighted in blocks of cement. Brian looked terrified, and it sickened Jack to think that this was how they would meet, this was how he would introduce himself to his own flesh and blood, the big bad defense lawyer staring down a ten-year-old boy on the witness stand. Jack wondered who had selected Brian's clothes, who had combed his hair, who had told him not to worry, that it would all be over soon. Jack wanted to cut through the tension and be a friend whom Brian could turn to. He wanted to wish away all the horrible things that had happened at the little house in Guantánamo. He wanted to lose the necktie, reach across the rail, and see if the kid wanted to arm wrestle him or do a round of rock, paper, scissors.

He wanted to do anything but what he had to do.

Jack took another step forward, pushing through that profound sense of dread, struggling to get a tighter grip on reality and find a stronger sense of purpose. This boy was a witness. Not just any witness, but a key witness for the prosecution. He was in this courtroom for one reason: to help the prosecutor put his mother in jail. It was Jack's job to keep Brian's mother out of jail, to keep Lindsey from taking the fall for her son.

"Good morning, Brian," said Jack.

Brian was silent. He clearly didn't want any part of Jack's pleasantries, and the mistrust written all over his face only added to the tension that filled the courtroom. No one could have possibly envied Jack's position, the lawyer forced to paint his client's young son as a murderer. Yet, no one outside the defense team knew the full depth of Jack's pain. No one else knew that Jack was up against *his own child*.

"Brian, how long have you been deaf?"

"A long time."

Jack nodded. It was a true answer, but an evasive one as well. The medical file that Brian's grandfather had shared with Jack had laid out all the details, putting Brian's deafness in an entirely new light. In fact, it wasn't until Jack learned the true cause of Brian's hearing loss that he came to see the case against Lindsey so very differently, which made it seem like the right place to start his cross-examination.

"How did you lose your hearing?" asked Jack.

The boy dipped a shoulder, as if embarrassed to answer.

Jack said, "All you have to do is tell the truth. That's all we want to hear. Just tell us the truth."

"It was an accident," said Brian.

"An accident," said Jack. "How did it happen?"

"I did it myself."

"You made yourself deaf?"

He nodded.

"How did you do that?"

Brian looked away. "Headphones."

"You were listening to loud music, isn't that right, Brian?"

"Yes."

"Over a period of many months, you put on the headphones, and you kept turning up the volume louder and louder. Right?"

Again he nodded.

"Each time you did it, you damaged your hearing a little more. By the time you were five years old, you were profoundly deaf."

Brian didn't answer, but Jack was saying it for the jury's benefit anyway. "Isn't that right, Brian?"

"Yes."

Jack moved closer. He was pretty sure he knew the answer, but he had to ask the question. It was time to test his theory, and he couldn't have been more sorry that it had to come at Brian's expense. "Why did you do that to yourself, Brian?"

The boy shook his head.

"Brian, did your mother and father argue a lot?"

He waited for the interpreter, then said, "Yes. All the time."

"Did your father ever hit your mother?"

Again he paused. He scanned the courtroom, seeming to search for help. Finally he answered, "Yes."

"Did she cry?"

He nodded.

"Did she scream?"

"Yes."

"How did it make you feel to hear your mother screaming and crying?"

"Not good."

"Bad?"

"Terrible."

"Bad enough so that you didn't want to hear anymore?" asked Jack.

"Yes."

"Bad enough to make yourself deaf?"

The prosecutor was on his feet. "Judge, I hated to call the defendant's son to the stand, but at least I kept it short. This is way beyond the scope of direct."

"Overruled. But, Mr. Swyteck, be sensitive."

Be sensitive, thought Jack. *If he only knew.* "Yes, Your Honor." Jack squared himself to the witness and said, "Brian, did you ever feel angry toward your father?"

"Sometimes."

"Did your father and mother have a fight on the night he died?"

"Yes."

"Was she screaming?"

"I couldn't hear it."

"But you saw them fighting, didn't you?" said Jack.

"Yes."

"Could you hear it in your head?"

A pained expression came over the boy's face. "Yes."

"So even though you're deaf, you still heard your mother's screams. In your head?"

He nodded.

"Did your father hit your mother that night?"

"I don't remember."

Jack sensed that he was lying. Then again, there were no bruises noted on Lindsey after the police came to the house and found Oscar's dead body. "Did your father do anything at all to your mother that night? Anything that made you mad?"

He began to tremble. "He made her do things. Like he always did."

"What kind of things?"

"With Lieutenant Johnson."

Jack drew a breath. He had to carry this line of questioning through to its conclusion, but he wasn't sure he could. "Brian," he said, his voice tightening. "Did you see the things that your father and Lieutenant Johnson did?"

"I know what they were doing."

"How do you know?"

"Because they took my mother in the bedroom. And they locked the door."

"Did you see them go into the bedroom?"

"Yes."

"How many times did you watch this happen? How many different nights?"

The child shrugged.

"More than once?"

"Yes."

"More than five times?"

"Yes."

"More than ten times?"

"Yes."

"This happened many times over a long period of time, didn't it, Brian?"

He nodded.

Jack was trying to be the good lawyer and stick to his cross-examination. But it was only human for him to empathize with a boy who had essentially lost his mother. Jack had felt that same anger, the way his own mother was taken from him. He often wished that there had been someone he could blame, someone who could be the object of his anger. In that sense, Brian had an advantage. He knew who had come between him and his mother. He knew exactly who to hold accountable.

The judge said, "Mr. Swyteck, do you have any further questions?"

Jack composed himself, brought himself back to the task at hand. Brian had already denied shooting his father, so there was no percentage in rehashing that ground. Jack, however, had another angle, good lawyer that he was. "Brian," he asked in a serious voice, "were there ever times you wished that your father was dead?"

Brian stared at Jack, then at the woman who was repeating the question in sign. He was just ten years old, but he seemed to know a trap when he saw one. Jack watched him squirm, watched him mull over in his mind the question that seemed to split him in two, the side that wanted to answer and the side that didn't.

Jack was dying inside, but he had to push it. "Brian, please answer me. Were there times you wished that your father was dead?"

Tears were streaming down the boy's cheeks. He nodded and said, "Many times."

Jack couldn't move. Another lawyer might have asked the next logical question, but Jack couldn't do it. He'd taken Brian far enough. He would leave it right there. "Thank you. No further questions, Judge."

Jack returned to the table for the defense. Lindsey had tears in her eyes, and she grasped Jack's shoulder the instant he took the seat beside her. He didn't dare look at her for fear that just one glance might set her off, a broken mother sobbing into her lawyer's pinstripes. Jack glanced at Sofia, who seemed entirely at a loss for words. In another case, with another witness, she might have leaned over and whispered, Excellent job, Jacko! But not in this case. Not with this witness.

Jack closed his eyes, then opened them. He didn't often think this way, at least not since he'd stopped defending death row inmates. The words were right there, tumbling around in his mouth, ready to be shouted out at the top of his lungs. They were bitter words, words so true that sucking them back was like swallowing a handful of rusty nails.

God, I hate this fucking job.

51

The case went to the jury just before noon.

Jack had some time on his hands, but he didn't know how much. The general rule was that a quick verdict was bad for the defense, which didn't really mean anything, except that it was a show of confidence for the prosecutor to hang around the courthouse while the jury deliberated, and it was a show of optimism for a defense lawyer to leave and go about his business. So Jack went.

He was doing his best to appear optimistic.

Jack hadn't identified a single misstep in the prosecutor's closing argument, especially the rebuttal— the last words to the jury. In his mind, Jack kept playing that crisp delivery over and over again, each time hoping to discern a flaw in the prosecutorial logic, some inconsistency, some semblance of reasonable doubt that a strong-minded juror could cling to and force the others to vote for Lindsey's acquittal. But Torres's words kept jabbing at him like a lance.

It wasn't every day that a federal prosecutor accused him of falsely painting his own son as the fall guy for murder.

"Blame it all on the child," Hector Torres said, repeating his mantra to a riveted jury. The courtroom was stone silent, as if the crowd knew that this was the prosecutor's last shot at reclaiming the momentum that he'd let slip away. "Does it surprise you, ladies and gentlemen, that the defense would adopt this eleventh-hour strategy? It shouldn't. These people will stop at nothing to bring shame on the Pintado family.

"Mr. Swyteck did his best to paint the child as a murderer, but let me remind you that I was the only one who asked Brian Pintado if he shot his father, and he denied it under oath. I could go on and on, but I'll leave you with these three thoughts.

"One," he said as he raised his index finger, counting off his final points. "It is undisputed that Lindsey Hart's fingerprints were found on the murder weapon.

"Two, it is undisputed that Lindsey Hart was having sex with a man who was not her husband.

"Three—remember the testimony of the government's expert witness, Dr. Vandermeer? He was the fertility doctor who told you that Oscar Pintado had a very high count of this 'assassin sperm,' which meant that he was a very jealous man. I find that quite interesting, and you should, too. When you go back to deliberate, ask yourself this question: If Oscar Pintado was *forcing* his wife to have sex with another man—if this threesome went down the way

Lindsey Hart said it did—then why was Oscar so jealous? If he enjoyed watching his wife have sex with another man, then why did it bother him so much that it had a scientifically measurable physiological effect on his body? *Why?* I'll tell you why."

The prosecutor paused, eyes narrowing as his gaze drifted toward the defendant. "Because Lindsey Hart is a liar and a murderer." He faced the jury and said, "Treat her like one."

A honking horn jolted Jack from his thoughts. Traffic was moving again, but just barely. Jack inched his car forward a few feet, then hit the brake, slowing to a dead stop in a forty-five-mile-per-hour zone. A long trail of orange taillights blinked on and off ahead of him. Enrique Iglesias sang his heart out on not one but three different stations that Jack tried on the radio. Latin dance music blasted from the boom box in the convertible that was caught in traffic beside him. Driving south out of downtown Miami after four o'clock in the afternoon was like getting stuck at the end of the world's longest conga line.

He turned off U.S. 1, wound his way behind a car dealership, and found himself next to Mario's, that little Cuban market where *Abuela* loved to shop—which got him to thinking.

He steered into a parking space and reached for his wallet. Tucked behind his driver's license was the business card that Kiko had given him when Jack and *Abuela* had visited the market in the middle of trial, though now it seemed like a thousand years ago. He removed it, then checked the name and the telephone number that Kiko had written for him on the backside.

El Pidio—the man who had told Kiko that Hector Torres looked like Jorge Bustón, the man who'd dated Jack's mother back in Cuba.

Jack had never followed up, too caught up in Lindsey's trial to be searching for additional distractions. Or maybe he was like *Abuela*, not sure that he wanted to know the truth. But the way this case had played out—or was about to play out—he felt as though he needed more truth in his life. If nothing else, his meeting with Torres's ex-wife had his curiosity about his own mother flowing once again. It bothered him that she'd used the word *obsessed* to describe Torres's attraction to his mother. The more he considered it, the more curious it seemed that his half brother—"Ramón," according to that gravestone back in Cuba—had died the day he was born. Jack's instincts continued to tell him that something was not quite right.

He flipped open his cell phone and dialed the number.

An old man answered in Spanish. Jack responded in kind, if you called Spanish with a John Wayne accent "in kind."

"Mr. El Pidio?"

"Not 'Mr. El Pidio,'" the man said, grousing. "Just El Pidio."

"This is Jack Swyteck. I'm—"

"Ah, Swyteck. I know who you are. Kiko told me you'd probably give me a call."

"I understand you knew my mother in Bejucal."

"Yes. I was her doctor. I delivered her baby."

Her doctor? So many questions were suddenly racing through Jack's head, but he got back to what was most important, the one thing that was almost too difficult to ask. "Then you must know. . . . How did my brother die?"

There was silence. Finally, his voice crackled as he breathed a heavy sigh and said, "That's a very complicated matter, young man."

52

At dusk, Jack caught up with his father at the Biltmore driving range. Harry was perched atop a grassy knoll, dressed in knickers, argyle socks, and a classic tweed golfer's cap, the kind of getup that a man didn't dare wear without a single-digit handicap. Jack watched from the bench as Harry, deep into his rhythm, popped one ball afer another onto the range. It looked as if manna had fallen from heaven, hundreds of little white balls scattered across the green grass before them.

"Dad?"

Harry halted in the middle of his backswing, slightly annoyed by his son's timing. "Yes?"

"Do you think there's anything a man shouldn't know about his wife?"

Harry paused, as if bowled over by the question. "If a man asks his wife a question, he should get the truth."

"What if he doesn't ask? Should someone tell him?"

"You mean should his wife tell him?"

"No. Let's say she can't. Should someone else tell him? Someone who knows the truth."

Harry seemed somewhere between confused and suspicious. "What's this about, son?"

Jack was speechless. What would he possibly tell his father? That Ana Maria had borne a son who died in Cuba? That she, herself, never would have died if Jack had never been born? That she would have known the dangers if it hadn't been for her obsessive old boyfriend—Harry's old friend, Hector Torres? Thirty-six-year-old memories were all Harry Swyteck had of his first wife. Jack was at a loss for any good reason to trample all over them, but he still wasn't sure how to handle it.

Jack said, "I've been thinking of Lindsey Hart, all the horrible things that came out at trial. The way Oscar treated her. If she's acquitted and remarries, would her new husband want to know all the details? Would he have a right to know?"

"I suppose that knowing those things could help him understand her fears, her moods. If it would make the new marriage stronger, then he should know."

"But knowing just for the sake of knowing—"

"What's the point? It's like looking your wife in the eye on your deathbed, after fifty years of marriage, and telling her that you kissed another woman forty-nine years ago. It doesn't accomplish anything, unless your goal is to break her heart."

"Exactly," said Jack, perhaps a little too enthusiastically. "So, if it were you, you wouldn't want to know all those details."

Harry laid his five iron aside. His confusion was

tipping more toward suspicion. "Is there something you're trying to tell me?"

Jack was searching for clues in his father's eyes— a need to know, a desire to know. He saw nothing of the sort. But Jack suddenly felt something from within, a realization that there comes a point in every child's life when it's no longer time for the parent to watch out for the child, that it's the child who protects the parent.

"No, nothing," said Jack. "Like I said, I've been giving a lot of thought to Brian Pintado and his mother."

"You sure that's what this is about?"

The answer didn't come right away, but Jack spoke as firmly as he could. "Yeah. I mean, the whole thing is such a mess, and it will only get more complicated as Brian gets older. What's he going to think about his mother a few years down the road?"

Harry studied his son's expression, as if sensing that Jack had subtly changed the subject from what a husband should know about his wife to a son's feelings toward his mother. But the older man let it go. "It will depend on what the jury's verdict is, I suppose."

"Hopefully, she'll be acquitted."

"Then what? Will the juvenile authorities come after Brian for murdering his father?"

Jack was silent. That was something he didn't want to think about. "Hard to say. It's not as if Brian came right out and confessed to the murder on the witness stand."

"You took him to the brink, though. Got him to admit that he wished his father was dead."

They exchanged glances. The estrangement was over between this father and son, but even the distant past never completely washed away. Neither one said a word, but Jack knew they were sharing the same thought: As a boy, how many times had Jack gotten angry at his old man and told him flat out, "I wish you were dead"?

"Kids have those thoughts and don't mean it," said Jack.

"Yes," said Harry. "That's true."

More silence. Then Harry took a half step closer and laid his hand on Jack's shoulder. "I'm proud of what you did in that courtroom. You took a tough case, and you did one hell of a job. However it turns out, you have nothing to be ashamed of."

"Thanks." Jack smiled flatly as he watched his father pick up his driver and tee up another ball. Harry hit a couple, and Jack was about to walk away. But there was one thing he just had to say. "Dad?"

"Hmm," said Harry. He was adjusting his stance, head down.

"Hector Torres is not your friend."

Harry swung through, never taking his eyes off the ball. "You think I don't know that?"

"You know?"

"I've known for over thirty years, Jack. Never been able to put my finger on it. But believe me, I know a phony-baloney when I see one."

He knew. But he didn't *know*.

Harry said, "Why do you mention it? Did Torres double-cross you or something?"

"You might say that."

"Well, don't hold back because you think he's my

old buddy. You tee right up and give him exactly what he deserves." Harry smacked the ball with all his might. It sailed on a rope and landed just in front of the two-hundred-fifty-yard marker.

"Thanks, Dad. I'll definitely do that."

53

•

Jack was alone at the counter at Joe Allen's Diner, eating a steak sandwich and fries for dinner, when his cell phone rang. It was Sofia.

"Jack, the jury's back."

He checked his watch: a few minutes past seven. The jury had been out nearly five hours. Marginal as to whether that was too quick to be good news. "Okay. I'll meet you at the courthouse."

He drove straight downtown and in fifteen minutes he was in the courtroom. The prosecutor was standing before the judge. Sofia was standing next to him. A few members of the media were in the public seating area, the die-hards who had decided to camp out at the courthouse until the jury returned its verdict. Jack started forward, but the judge was already stepping down from the bench and headed back to his chambers. Jack hurried down the aisle, and Sofia met him at the rail.

"False alarm," she said. "No verdict yet. The jury just had a question for the judge."

"What was it?"

"It had to do with the testimony of the Cuban soldier. They wanted to know what time of day he said it was when he saw Lieutenant Johnson go inside the Pintado house."

"The judge should tell them to rely on their own recollection."

"That's exactly what the judge said he was going to do. He just wanted to call us all together to tell us that the question had been asked. I guess it's a good thing they're asking questions."

Jack dismissed it. How many times in his years as a trial lawyer had he tried to divine whether it was a good or bad thing that a juror had asked a question, cracked a smile, nodded her head, or scratched his ass. "Yeah, I guess it's a good thing," said Jack.

"Lindsey's holding up pretty well," said Sofia, "considering."

"That's good," said Jack. He was more worried about Brian, but that was for another day. He glanced across the courtroom and saw Hector Torres packing up to leave. He excused himself from Sofia, then caught up with the prosecutor.

"Hector, you got a minute?"

"Sure."

"Let's go someplace where we can talk, all right?"

Torres followed Jack to an attorneys' conference room across the hall. Jack closed the door, but neither man took a seat. They stood on opposite sides of the table. "Your client want to plead?" said Torres.

"Depends on what you're offering."

"Same as before. Life in prison, no death penalty."

"Then no deal."

"Suit yourself. Nice and short meeting. Just the way I like them." Torres started for the door.

"One other thing," said Jack.

Torres stopped to face him. "What?"

Jack's mouth opened, but it was as if the words needed a little time to catch up with his thoughts. "I spoke with a man named El Pidio today."

"El Pidio?" he said, showing no recognition.

"It's a nickname. You might know him better as Dr. Blanco."

The expression drained from the prosecutor's face. His voice tightened, but he was suddenly unconvincing. "Why would I know that name?"

"Because he's the physician who delivered your child in Cuba. My mother's first child."

Torres averted his eyes, then took a half step back. A thin smile came to his lips, as if he were proud that he'd managed to keep his secret this long. "Have you spoken to your father yet?"

"No."

"You spoken to anyone?"

"I think it's my turn to ask the questions."

The prosecutor laid his briefcase on the table, and then he extended his arms outward, as if he were an open book. "What would you like to know?"

"Actually, there isn't all that much left to find out. Dr. Blanco was a wealth of information."

Jack saw through the cool veneer, saw the concern in the other man's eyes. Torres asked, "What did he tell you?"

"One of the things that has always haunted me was the fact that my mother died when I was born. So you can imagine how curious I must have been when I found out that her first child died on the day he was born. Seemed like a strange coincidence. Too strange."

"I don't know anything about that."

"I think you do, now that I've talked to Dr. Blanco. See, my mother died from preeclampsia. It's a condition that can be fatal to the mother or the child. If the pregnancy goes to full term—like my mother's did with me—it's more often fatal for the mother. If the baby is born premature—like my half brother—it's more often fatal for the baby."

"Well, congratulations. You've just solved a mystery that means nothing to anyone. Except you."

"And you," said Jack.

"This has nothing to do with me. Your mother was already dead when I came to Miami."

"That's the point. She didn't have to die. It was Dr. Blanco's opinion that my mother should have no more children after the death of her first. Her pregnancies were too high risk."

"Then she should have followed her doctor's advice."

Jack looked at him coldly. "He never gave her that advice."

"That's the doctor's problem, isn't it."

"No. It's yours. He said you wouldn't let him tell her."

"That's ridiculous."

"She was a teenager. Unmarried and pregnant. You told Dr. Blanco that you were the father, that you intended to marry her and make an honest woman out of her. But only if she could give you children, especially another son."

"I don't remember any of that."

"Well, maybe you'll remember this. He said that you put a knife to his throat and threatened to slit him open from ear to ear if he told my mother not to have any more children."

Torres shook his head, but his demeanor changed, as if he no longer saw the point of denial—at least not as long as it was just the two of them behind closed doors. "I was nineteen years old," he said, as if that was an excuse.

"My mother was twenty-three when she died."

Torres said nothing, showed no emotion.

Jack said, "I always thought she came to this country seeking freedom. She came here to get away from you, didn't she?"

"I loved your mother."

"No, you loved controlling her."

"I loved your mother and wanted to have a family with her. Is that a crime?"

"You followed her to Miami."

"I came here on my own."

"You befriended my father just so you could find out more about her."

"So what if I did? Big deal. I carried a torch."

"A *torch*? More like a flamethrower. You were obsessed."

"That's absurd."

"You visited her grave."

"Somebody needed to. God knows your father didn't."

"This isn't about my father."

"I put flowers on her grave. Big damn deal."

"Flowers my ass. I *know* what you did there."

Torres went rigid. He clearly had grasped the meaning of that last remark, knew that Jack had spoken to his ex-wife. "I don't have to listen to this crap."

Jack grabbed him by the lapel, shoved him against the wall.

"What are you gonna do, hit me? Is that what you want to do?"

Jack tightened his grip. He did want to hit him. He wanted to hit him hard enough to knock him back to Cuba.

Torres was having trouble breathing, Jack was pushing so hard against him. "What good would it have done?" the prosecutor said, his voice strained. "What if I had let that doctor tell your mother not to have any more children. Where would that leave *you*, huh, Jack? You would never have been born. You got nothing to hold against me. You should be thanking me."

There was truth in what he said, but not the kind of truth that made Jack want to forgive him. Jack, however, wasn't sure how it made him feel. There was just a surge of emotion. The sadness of his never having known his mother. The frustration of pulling snippets of information from his father and grand-mother over the years. The utter dismay of learning that he hardly knew anything important about her. But mostly he felt anger—anger over the fact that, with or without Hector Torres, there had never been a chance for Jack and his mother to enjoy any kind of happy ending. At least not in the 1960s. One of them was destined to be buried, Jack or his mother, his mother or Ramón. There was still no one to blame, no clear culprit. Just this pathetic excuse for a human being standing before him.

Jack cocked his arm, ready to paste one on that ugly puss. Torres recoiled—hardly a defense—but a quick knock on the door stopped Jack cold.

The door opened. Sofia entered, and her eyes widened with surprise. "What's going on?"

Jack released the older man. Torres straightened his wrinkled lapels and said, "Just a little disagreement, that's all."

Sofia looked confused, but she didn't pursue it. "Jury's back again. This time it's for real. They have a verdict."

It took a few seconds for the message to sink in, to bring them back to the reason they were there in the first place.

Torres grabbed his briefcase and started for the door. Then he stopped and looked back at Jack. "Just to finish up our conversation, Counselor. And I suppose this bit of advice applies equally well to the jury verdict as it does to what we were talking about earlier." His eyes darkened, and his expression turned very serious, almost threatening. "Live with it, Swyteck. You're just gonna have to."

It had been a long time since Jack had felt such hatred toward anyone. The prosecutor turned and was gone, but Jack could almost feel the heat rising from his own skin.

Sofia seemed reluctant to say anything, but finally she had to. "Jack, we should go. Lindsey's waiting."

He took a moment, then gathered himself. *Lindsey.*

How strange it felt just to hear her name. How strange it was to know that her fate had finally been decided.

Without another word, he started down the long corridor with Sofia at his side.

54

Jack returned to a packed courtroom. Someone had done a crack job of alerting the media of an impending verdict, and Jack suspected that his initials were H.T.

Hector Torres was seated at the table nearest the jury box, drumming his fingers expectantly on the tabletop. Lindsey sat impassively between her two lawyers, saying nothing. The galley was filled nearly to capacity, fuller than it had been on any day since the first day of trial. A few journalists had fired questions at Jack and Sofia as they entered the courtroom. How was their client doing? What was Jack's prediction? As if any of that mattered. The fat lady hadn't quite sung, but she was at least exercising her voice. Is was all over but for the reading of perhaps one, hopefully two, simple words from a slip of paper. The verdict was in the can. Lindsey's life was in the balance. The rest of Brian's life would be forever changed, one way or the other, for better or for worse.

Jack wished only that he knew with greater certainty which way was better and which way was worse.

"All rise!" shouted the bailiff.

The crowd was quickly on its feet, and the mull of numerous conversations ceased. A side door opened, and Judge Garcia entered the courtroom from his chambers. He climbed to the high-back leather chair atop the bench and instructed the bailiff to bring in the jury. Seven men and five women entered the courtroom in single file, each taking his or her assigned seat in the jury box.

"Please be seated," the judge told the rest of the courtroom.

Jack glanced over his shoulder as he took his seat. Alejandro Pintado and his wife were behind the prosecutor in the first row of public seating. They were holding hands and locking arms, so close together they were practically one person. Jack couldn't help but note the contrast: the pain and emotion all over the faces of the victim's parents, the complete lack of expression on the face of the accused. Jack knew it wasn't because Lindsey didn't care. She was emotionally and physically drained from too little sleep and too many worries. At some point, the body's defense mechanisms took over. Numbness was always the last defense, the place people landed when they were just too weary to fight any longer.

The judge said, "Madam forewoman, has the jury reached a verdict?"

A middle-aged woman in the first row stood and said, "We have, Your Honor."

A flurry of thoughts ran through Jack's mind. The jury had chosen a fore*woman*. A good thing or a bad? Less likely to convict in a death penalty case? More sympathetic to an abused wife? Full of venom for a slutty mom who cheated on her husband? It was pointless to speculate. It was simply time to hope for good news and to brace for bad.

Jack took Lindsey's hand, but she pulled away, as if she preferred to handle this on her own and in her own way.

The written verdict almost seemed to float across the courtroom, passed from the forewoman to the bailiff, from the bailiff to the judge. Judge Garcia adjusted his reading glasses, looked down, and read the verdict to himself. In hundreds of trials, Jack had never been able to tell which way a verdict had gone by reading the judge's face as he inspected the verdict. Judge Garcia was the typical model of stoicism. He passed the verdict back to the bailiff and said, "The defendant will please rise."

Lindsey was slow to find her footing. Jack stood on her left, Sofia on her right.

"Madam forewoman, please read the verdict."

The air in the courtroom suddenly seemed too thick to breathe. Jack glanced one last time at the Pintado family in the first row. Mrs. Pintado was leaning into her husband, unable to watch. Mr. Pintado was drawing short, anxious breaths. Most of all, however, Jack noticed that their grandson wasn't there.

A good thing, thought Jack. *Either way, that was a good thing.*

The forewoman took the verdict from the bailiff, unfolded it. Her hand shook as she read it aloud. "In the United States of America versus Lindsey Hart, Case Number 02-0937, we the jury find as follows. As to Count I, violation of chapter eighteen, United

States Code, murder in the first degree, we find the defendant . . ."

She paused, and Jack felt a lump swelling in his throat.

"Guilty."

Lindsey gasped as she collapsed into her chair. Jack went down with her, trying to hold her steady, though he too felt as if his knees had been cut out from under him. The courtroom was immediately abuzz with surprise, approval, and even some heart-felt dismay. Jack shot a quick glance toward the jurors, but none of them would look in his direction. Behind the prosecutor, tears were flowing. Oscar Pintado's mother had let out a shriek, neither of delight nor despair. It was just an outburst that seemed to tell the world that justice had been done.

"This can't be!" said Lindsey.

"Order!" the judge shouted as he banged his gavel. "Ladies and gentlemen of the jury, thank you for your service. You are hereby dismissed. Counsel, please contact my chambers for a sentencing date. This court is adjourned."

With a final crack of the gavel, it was over.

Jack looked out toward the crowd, people scampering for the exits, journalists sprinting to find a prime spot outside the courtroom where they could issue their live evening-news reports. It was all a blur, and Jack couldn't focus. Finally, he looked at Lindsey. Her eyes showed only shock and disbelief.

"This can't be happening," she said again and again.

But it was happening, and for Jack, it was one of those distressing moments in life when he didn't fully come to the conclusion that something shouldn't happen until he actually felt it happening. Yet, deep down, he wondered if he would have felt the same way if the verdict had been not guilty.

Jack felt a firm tug at his sleeve. Lindsey had taken hold of him. The federal marshals were at her side, ready to escort her to prison. It was the same marshals who had taken her away at the end of each day of trial for the past two weeks. This time, however, their presence had an entirely different feel, the verdict having stamped a daunting sense of permanence on her journey back behind bars.

"Jack, you have to do something!" she said.

Jack wanted to put her at ease, but all he could manage were a few halfhearted words of encouragement. "It isn't over yet," he told her, but it sounded hollow.

She glared at him through cloudy eyes, and Jack wasn't sure if she was ready to cry or to tear his head off. She kept looking at him, her chin reaching over her shoulder as the marshals took her out the side exit.

Jack drew a breath, his head pounding. Behind him, on the other side of the rail, reporters called out their barrage of questions. It was all just clatter.

Hector Torres approached the defense table, but he didn't offer a handshake. There was no smile on his lips, but Jack could see it in his eyes. The prosecutor said, "Well, I guess congratulations are in order. For me, at least. See you around, Jack."

"Shove it, jerk," said Sofia.

Jack raised a hand, quieting her as the prosecutor turned to face a flock of journalists just outside the rail. Jack showed them his back as he gathered up his briefcase.

"That man is such an idiot," said Sofia.

"Don't worry. What goes around, comes around."

"How do you mean?"

"You'll see."

Jack had a statement prepared for the press, but he had no inclination to give it. This was one time when he didn't feel the need to explain anything. He was content to let the U.S. attorney have his moment of fame. He lifted his briefcase and headed up the center aisle. Sofia followed. A few members of the press were right with them, but Jack's silence soon caused them to lose interest, particularly with the U.S. attorney holding journalistic court in the hallway. Jack exited through the double doors in the back of the courtroom. A circle of reporters had gathered around the prosecutor as he issued sound bite after sound bite. Jack watched with interest, wondering if he'd ever in his life seen a more pompous ass. Finally, nearly two minutes into his endlessly self-serving "I knew I would be vindicated" speech, the prosecutor was interrupted by a seasoned reporter who simply couldn't hold her question any longer.

"Mr. Torres, is it true that your name used to be Jorge Bustón?"

The prosecutor did a double take. "What?"

Another reporter chimed in. "Jorge Bustón. The same Jorge Bustón who worked in Havana in the early 1960s as a block warden for the *Comité para la Defensa de la Revolución*?"

"I . . . I . . ." The prosecutor kept stammering, and the questions kept coming.

"Sir," another journalist said pointedly, "isn't it true that you earned a commendation from the

Communist Party for ratting out so-called enemies of the revolution in your neighborhood?"

Torres's mouth hung open, and the feeding frenzy had begun.

"Mr. Torres—or should I say Mr. Bustón—aren't some of those political dissidents that you fingered still sitting in prison?"

"What was behind your fall from Castro's good graces in 1964?"

"Is that why you changed your name and became so vocal against Castro when you came to Miami? Because you were driven out of the party?"

The U.S. attorney was speechless, and all color had drained from his cheeks. He looked utterly confused, until finally he glanced across the hallway and picked out his adversary in the crowd. Jack was silent, moving not a muscle—except to offer a hint of a smile that confirmed the fact that old Dr. Blanco had indeed been a wealth of information, and that Jack, too, had placed a few choice calls to the media before the rendering of the verdict. Jack wanted to say it to the prosecutor's face, but he didn't have to. He was certain that, by now, Torres had fully realized what was going on, that he could hear Jack throwing his snide remark right back at him, even if no words were actually spoken.

Live with it, Jorge. You're just gonna have to.

Jack turned and headed for the elevator, hoping that perhaps, somewhere, a forever-young woman named Ana Maria was smiling.

55

Jack slept until nine-thirty the next morning.

The previous night, Theo had brought over a broad selection of wheat beers that he was debating whether to stock at Sparky's, figuring that a lost trial was the perfect occasion for Jack to sample all fourteen brands. It didn't seem all that funny now, but at about two A.M. it had busted Jack's gut to watch a lug like Theo turn into Truman Capote as he read aloud from the artsy-fartsy sales literature for each of the different German brews.

"*Ayinger Braü-Weisse*," he'd said. Then he took a little sip, smacking his lips at hummingbird speed. "Fruity, yet herbaceous."

Jack slowly lifted his head from the pillow. The great thing about wheat beer was that it never gave you a hangover. Another one of Theo's lies. It seemed to take forever, but finally Jack managed to sit upright on the edge of the bed. Then a friggin' trumpet blasted in his ear, but it was only his telephone. He snatched it up before it could ring a second time. It was Theo, jovial as ever, showing absolutely no signs of overindulgence. The man was the devil.

"Hey, Jack. Have you seen this morning's paper?"

"Only if it was printed on the inside of my eyelids."

"Here, let me read it to you."

Jack groaned. It was another of Theo's quirks. Perhaps it was because he'd never been read to as a child, or maybe he was a closet television newscaster, but for some reason Theo enjoyed reading aloud, with feeling—and with incredible volume. Far more volume than Jack's beer-soaked brain could handle. He held the phone about a foot away from his ear and listened.

Theo cleared his throat, mumbled through the introductory sentences, then skipped to the good part. "Says here, quote, 'Reportedly, Ms. Hart's conviction has been no small source of anxiety for her alleged lover, U.S. Coast Guard lieutenant Damont Johnson. Sources tell the *Tribune* that Lieutenant Johnson's biggest fear is that Ms. Hart, now convicted of murder, will break her silence and reveal the truth about her husband's shooting, which may well implicate Johnson. These same sources confirm that Lieutenant Johnson is in a race to beat her to the punch. In a telephone interview late last night, however, U.S. attorney Hector Torres would neither confirm nor deny that he is having any discussions with Lieutenant Johnson, and he declined to comment on whether the government is willing to cut a deal in exchange for the lieutenant's tell-all testimony.'"

Jack's head was pounding, but it wasn't the wheat beer. "Does it say who the source is?"

"No. One of those anonymous jobs. You want me to visit Johnson, try to find out?"

"No. Stay out of it."

"I don't really get the point of this anyway," said Theo. "Lindsey's already convicted. Why would the prosecutor want to deal for Johnson's testimony now?"

"We've still got a sentencing hearing. Torres wants a needle in her arm, and I'm trying to keep her alive."

"So Johnson is going to flip again and say it wasn't the kid who done it after all?"

"I don't know. This is just an article in a newspaper, with anonymous sources to boot. Who knows what's really going on? Could be true, or it could be someone with his own agenda who lied to an overeager reporter for his own purposes."

"Or this he could be a she."

"Yeah. Or that."

"Whatchya gonna do?"

Jack massaged his temples, trying to stop the throbbing. "Go straight to my only source. I'll talk to Lindsey."

Lindsey's pallor was as lifeless as the cold beige walls of the detention center. She looked the way Jack felt, and she hadn't been the one drinking all night. Her elbows were on the table, her head was in the palms of her hands. The newspaper article was spread out in front of her. They were alone, behind a locked door in a windowless room that was reserved for attorney-client communications.

"Who's the source for the article?" asked Lindsey.

"Don't know," said Jack.

"Who do you think it is?"

"No idea. I was listening to Cuban radio on the way over here. They think it's Castro."

"Very funny."

"I'm not kidding."

She got up from her chair and stepped away from the table. She began to pace slowly, just a few steps in each direction, as the room was small. "You think it could be true? You think Johnson is dealing with the U.S. attorney?"

"I phoned Hector Torres on the way over here. He wouldn't take my call."

"Then it must be true," she said, her voice quickening. "They're talking."

"I wouldn't jump to that conclusion."

"You don't know Damont. Deep down, he's a survivor."

"Survivor or not, he has a long way to go to earn the trust of a federal prosecutor."

"Torres is a slimeball. He won't care how slippery Johnson seems, as long as he wiggles in his direction."

"I don't know about that," said Jack. "If Johnson is going to be of any use at all to the prosecution, he has to say that you shot your husband. Problem is, he's already testified under oath that he was in your house that morning and that your son confessed to the crime. Those are hardly reconcilable."

She stopped pacing and looked Jack in the eye. "They're completely reconcilable."

Jack was taken aback by her glare. "How do you mean?"

"Brian confessed to the crime because . . ."

"Because why?"

"Because he thought he was covering for me."

Jack's pulse quickened. "Was he?"

She drew a breath and turned away

Jack said, "Was Brian covering for his mother, Lindsey?"

She still didn't answer, wouldn't look at him.

Jack's voice took on an edge. "I want the truth this time, damn it. No more lies. You tell me the truth, and maybe I can work something out with Torres. You keep on lying, I guarantee you'll die by lethal injection."

She turned and faced him, her eyes glistening with tears. "Brian didn't kill Oscar. But neither did I."

"Then what did happen?"

She drew a breath, collecting herself. "Most of what you heard about Oscar was true. He was an awful man, awful to me, awful to Brian. We fought a lot, and Brian was the one who suffered. The thing with the headphones and Brian's loss of hearing— that's all true."

"Is that where the truth ends? Everything else you told the jury was a lie?"

"No. Not by a long shot. The sex. Oscar and Johnson and me. I was telling the truth about that, too. He gave me a club drug or something. That's how it all got started."

"It wasn't something you wanted to do?"

"No. Not at all." She paused, then added, "Not at first."

Jack nearly had to shake his head, make sure he'd heard that right. "What do you mean, 'not at first'?"

She was suddenly less misty, more defensive. "What do you think it means, Jack? It means I didn't like it at first, but my feelings changed over time."

"So what are you saying? You were abused and fell into some low self-esteem psychological—"

"I'm not making any bullshit Stockholm syndrome excuses, Jack. My feelings never changed about the three-way stuff. My feelings toward Damont—that's what changed."

"You liked having sex with him?"

"It went beyond that. I liked *him*."

"How did Oscar feel about that?"

"Ask the fertility doctor, the government's expert. He told the jury all about Oscar's assassin sperm count, his jealousy over my infidelity. What the doctor didn't realize was that Oscar wasn't jealous in the normal sense. He just didn't like it that Damont and I started to do it on our own terms."

"It was something Oscar could no longer control. Was that it?"

She shook her head and chuckled, but it was mirthless. "The only time Oscar was ever happy was when he had everything and everybody under control. He got his rocks off watching Damont and me go at it. He scored points with his daddy by getting all Coast Guard routing information from Damont and feeding it to Brothers for Freedom. And I was the pornographic quid pro quo he used to pay back his buddy Damont for all that secret information."

"And then things fell apart," said Jack.

"Of course. But Damont is the one who came up with the solution, not me."

"You two had a plan?"

She nodded slowly. "I went to work at the hospital that morning, and I called Damont, just like he told the jury I did. But I wasn't trying to lure him over to the house and set him up for a murder that had already gone down. It was all just part of the plan. I told him, 'Go on over, Damont. Door's unlocked. Brian's asleep for another forty-five minutes. Oscar's asleep in the bedroom. Do what you gotta do.'"

Jack felt numb for a second. "So Johnson went?"

"Yeah. Just like that Cuban soldier said he did."

"Then what?"

"He went straight to the bedroom. He found Oscar's gun right where I told him it would be. And then . . ."

"He shot him?"

She seemed to struggle, then said, "Yeah. He shot him."

Jack paused. He wasn't sure why. It just seemed like the fitting thing to do upon the mention of someone's untimely death. "But wait a minute," said Jack. "At some point he talked to Brian, right?"

"Right. That was when things started to go wrong. See, Damont and I didn't think Brian would hear the gunshot. But something woke him. The vibration of footsteps on the wood floor, maybe a light going on. Whatever it was—Brian sensed that something was happening."

"But if Brian got up and he saw Johnson standing over Oscar's body, he would have known that Johnson shot him, right?"

"Except that he didn't see Johnson. Damont heard Brian's bedroom door open before Brian stepped into the hallway. Damont hid in the closet. All Brian saw when he came in the bedroom was Oscar all bloody and lying on the bed."

"Is that when Brian called you at work?"

"Yes. And then he went back in his room, too scared to come out until I got there."

"What did Johnson do?"

"When he heard Brian's door close, he came out of the closet and ran out of the house. But then, this is where he finally got clever. He waited a minute or two, then walked back in the house and went straight to Brian's room. He was acting all excited, told Brian that I had called him and asked him to come over, that something had happened to Oscar. Poor Brian, he just freaked. He didn't know what to do. He got all flustered and figured that *I* had shot Oscar. He knew how much Oscar and I had been fighting; he knew how abusive Oscar was. He knew if I'd done it, that Oscar had deserved it."

"So Brian told Johnson—"

"Right," said Lindsey. "Brian said he had done it. I guess he figured a ten-year-old boy wouldn't go to jail. But his mommy would. He thought he was protecting me." She was leaning against the wall, as if exhausted, her eyes cast downward. "That's the truth, Jack. That's the way it really happened. Damont and I weren't sure which one of us might eventually get charged. But we agreed up front, if either of us was, we wouldn't point the finger at the other. If push came to shove . . ."

"You'd blame it on Brian."

She folded her arms tightly, withdrawing a bit, as if Jack had hit below the belt by saying it aloud.

Jack said, "That was all just a dance that you and

Johnson did in the courtroom. His accusing Brian, your breaking down and saying it was all a lie. Nice touch, Lindsey. All the more believable if the mother stands up and defends her son."

"I'm not proud of that," she said.

Jack looked off to the middle distance. He could have gone through the entire alphabet, A to Z, listing the things she shouldn't have been proud of. But he wasn't here to lecture. He was here to keep her off death row. "What brought it all to a head anyway?" said Jack. "How did Johnson finally decide that it was time for Oscar to go?"

She seemed relieved to have another question, anything to release her from the painful silence of self-reflection. She forced a little smile and said, "Ah, now that's where the story gets very Miami."

Jack went straight from the prison to Theo's apartment. His friend was just about ready to head down to Sparky's Tavern to set up for the lunch crowd when Jack caught up with him. Theo sat on a bar stool at the kitchen counter and listened for almost ten minutes without interruption—a record for him—as Jack recounted his entire conversation with Lindsey. Since Theo was his investigator, Jack didn't have to worry about breaching any privileges. More important, he was able to give his friend complete vindication on his theory about who torched Jack's Mustang.

"Johnson was definitely in with druggies," said Jack.

"I knew it!" said Theo as he slapped the countertop.

"He was feeding information about Coast Guard routes to Oscar, who then passed it along to his old man."

"Don't tell me Alejandro Pintado is a trafficker

Jack went straight from the prison to Theo's apartment. His friend was just about ready to head down to Sparky's Tavern to set up for the lunch crowd when Jack caught up with him. Theo sat on a bar stool at the kitchen counter and listened for almost ten minutes without interruption—a record for him—as Jack recounted his entire conversation with Lindsey. Since Theo was his investigator, Jack didn't have to worry about breaching any privileges. More important, he was able to give his friend complete vindication on his theory about who torched Jack's Mustang.

"Johnson was definitely in with druggies," said Jack.

"I knew it!" said Theo as he slapped the countertop.

"He was feeding information about Coast Guard routes to Oscar, who then passed it along to his old man."

"Don't tell me Alejandro Pintado is a trafficker."

"No, no way. Two totally distinct things were going on here. Pintado used Johnson's information strictly to avoid border patrol and help Cuban rafters get to shore. But it was Johnson who realized that the drug trade would pay handsomely for the same information. So he started selling it to them."

Theo nodded, seeing where this was headed. "And Oscar found out about it."

"Yup."

"And then Oscar had to go."

"You got it," said Jack. "To think I nearly played the drug card at trial. I probably would have, had I thought the jury wouldn't lynch me for calling the Pintados a bunch of cocaine traffickers. Turns out Oscar got himself killed doing the honorable thing, saying no to drugs. Go figure."

"Hindsight, Jacko. It all works out in the end." Theo popped another mini-doughnut into his mouth, his tenth since Jack had started talking. Powdered sugar was everywhere. All this talk of drugs, the countertop was beginning to look like a snort fest in a South Beach nightclub.

"Still not sure 'bout sumptin'," said Theo, his mouth still full. "Why'd the drug folks torch your car?"

"Well, we knew from the start that whoever it was didn't want to see Lindsey acquitted."

"Why would the druggies care?"

"All I can figure is that they were happier to see Lindsey go down for murder than Lieutenant Johnson. Keeping Johnson out of jail was the only way to make sure he kept feeding them the information they needed."

"Interesting," said Theo, mulling it all over. "So bottom line is, Oscar might still be alive if he didn't go snooping around and find out what else his friend Damont was doing with the Coast Guard secrets."

"That's about the size of it. Tough break for Captain Pintado."

"You kidding me?" said Theo. "He's the lucky one."

"How do you mean?"

"That article in today's newspaper—don't you remember? It said Lieutenant Johnson is talking to the U.S. attorney, looking to tell all. What do you think these drug folks are gonna do when they read that? Sit around and wait to see if dumbass Damont names some names or not?"

Jack almost smiled. He hadn't thought of that, but it was the kind of thing Theo was usually right about. "Guess I wouldn't want to be Lieutenant Damont Johnson right now."

"Shee-it," said Theo. "You don't want to *know* Lieutenant Damont Johnson right now."

One gentle wave after another broke about twenty yards offshore. Thin sheets of emerald green water rolled up like a tarp onto Hallandale Beach, churned into white foam where the wet sand gave way to powder, and then retreated into the Atlantic. It was six A.M., and Marvin Schwartz was up with the sun, dressed in his usual Sunday morning uniform: rubber-soled sandals, white cotton chinos rolled up to the knee, long-sleeved gossamer shirt, broad-rimmed straw hat. Early Sunday morning was usually his best hunting time; Saturday night revelers had been known to leave behind everything from pocket change to Rolex watches. Actually, it wasn't a *real* Rolex, but the boys back at the Golden Beach condo didn't know a good knockoff from the real McCoy anyway.

The chirping of seagulls gave way to the beep of his metal detector. He marked the spot mentally, then knelt down and dug away the sand with a serving spoon he'd borrowed from the cole slaw bin at Pumpernickel's Deli in 1986.

The disappointment was etched all over his sunweathered face. A bottle cap. The ninth one this morning. Not a good day so far.

"Mah-vin. You find my diamond earrings yet?" It was his wife shouting from her chaise lounge at the cabana. She looked like a big beach ball from this distance, five feet wide and five feet tall.

"No, dear," he mumbled, making no effort to speak in a voice loud enough to be heard.

"Ten years you been lookin'. Still no diamond earrings?"

"No, dear."

Diamond earrings, he thought, scoffing. *She wants diamond earrings, she should have listened to her mother and married Dr. Moneybags.*

He was climbing over a big clump of seaweed when the metal detector suddenly went berserk, chirping and beeping wildly. He moved the wand to the left, and the chirping stopped. He moved it back to the right, and it was sounding off like a carnival again. He smiled, his heart racing with excitement. He poked through the strands of seaweed. Barnacles and other shellfish were all over the place. A piece of driftwood was all he could find, but there had to be something metal in there somewhere. He pushed away more seaweed, then stopped. The morning sun caught the gold, and the utter beauty of that reflection sent chills down his spine.

A ring!

He knelt down for a closer look. It looked like a Super Bowl ring at first, so big and ostentatious. As he reached to pick it up, he noticed the engraving on the side, and the prominent "U.S." insignia told him that it was from one of the academies.

A Coast Guard ring.

He grabbed it, lifted it, then dropped it on the spot, recoiling quickly. The ring was still attached to a finger. The finger was still attached to a blackish-purple hand.

The hand had been severed at the wrist.

"Sheila!" He dropped his metal detector, jumped to his feet, and wobbled back to the cabana as fast as his bony legs would carry him, shouting over and over again at the top of his lungs, *"SHEEEI-LAH!"*

Epilogue

•

The Miami-Dade County medical examiner described it as "Foreign matter, triangular-shaped cartilaginous material, 2.5 cm × 2.3 cm × 2.7 cm, embedded in the palm of the left hand of an African-American male." A marine biologist confirmed that it was a shark's tooth. Fingerprint and DNA analysis confirmed that it was in the left hand of Lieutenant Damont Johnson. No other body parts were recovered, so the rest of the story was conjecture. But the possibilities weren't exactly endless: Either he'd decided to swim with a school of hammerheads, or someone had used him for shark bait.

Lindsey told the prosecutor all that she knew about Johnson's drug trafficker connections. Jack made sure that her proffer implicated only the guilty parties, namely her and Lieutenant Johnson, and not Brothers for Freedom or the Pintado family. Since she hadn't dealt directly with the druggies, she wasn't able to offer any specifics that might help law enforcement track down Johnson's killers. Still, it was useful enough to persuade the prosecutor to back away from the death penalty. Judge Garcia followed the government's recommendation and sentenced Lindsey to life in prison. Lindsey didn't seem to think a life sentence was fair, since she wasn't the trigger person, but she'd have a chance to draw her nice distinctions between murder and conspiracy to commit murder at her parole hearing in about sixteen years.

Jack decided to have no contact with Brian or the Pintado family until he felt that the time was right. On the first Saturday morning after Lindsey's sentencing, that time had come. He and Theo drove to Coral Reef Park, where Brian played intramural soccer.

"You sure you want to do this?" asked Theo as they walked across the parking lot.

"Positive," said Jack.

They followed the wood-chip footpath past several playing fields. Jack glanced at the different games that were being played simultaneously, one field after another. It was like a stroll through the sporting life of a child, everything from the four- to six-year-olds, where a few kids hustled after the ball while others picked flowers, to the middle-schoolers, who were already starting to play like future Olympians. Jack and Theo stopped at the south field.

Jack spotted Alejandro Pintado seated in a lawn chair on the sidelines, and he knew he was in the right place. He and Theo found a spot about twenty yards down the line and watched some of the game, blue jerseys versus yellow jerseys.

"That's Brian over there, isn't it?" said Theo. "Goalie for the blue team?"

Jack looked toward the net, and he smiled. "Yeah. That's him." Jack watched him make a couple of nice saves, then turned at the sound of Alejandro's voice, startled to see that he'd come over to talk.

"You just a big soccer fan, Jack?" said Alejandro. "Or do you have a kid out here, too?"

Jack wondered if he had any idea how ironic the question was. "Actually, I came to see you."

"In the middle of my grandson's soccer game?"

"I wanted to catch you at a time and place where I could see Brian do something other than testify in a courtroom. Hope you don't mind."

"Depends on what it's about."

The referee's whistle blew. A boy in a blue jersey was down. A group of parents on the opposite sideline was about to have a cow, but the kids just kept playing. Theo wandered off quietly, allowing Jack to have a little one-on-one time with Alejandro.

Jack said, "It's about a couple things. One is just something I'm curious about. You remember that newspaper article that came out in the *Tribune* right after the trial? The one with the anonymous source?"

Alejandro was watching the game, not so much as glancing at Jack. But Jack could tell he was listening. Jack continued, "I thought that article was a stroke of genius. It prompted Lindsey to talk to the prosecutor, because it made her think that Johnson was on the verge of turning state's evidence. At the same time, it effectively put a target on Johnson's back, since it made the drug people think he was going to rat them out. In hindsight, I have a sneaking suspicion that none of it was true. Johnson had no intention of going to the U.S. attorney. Somebody had a very well-conceived plan, and he got the whole thing in motion by burning a favor with a reporter who was willing to work with an 'anonymous source.'"

Alejandro lit a cigar, saying nothing.

Jack said, "You think I'm on to something? Or am I totally off base, Alejandro?"

They watched the kids battle for the ball in the near corner, then Brian made another save. Pintado said, "The boy's good, isn't he?"

"Yeah, he is," said Jack.

"Being deaf's a disadvantage most of the time. But out here, it shuts out all the noise and distractions, lets Brian focus on the ball. In some ways I think it makes him a better goalie."

"Could be," said Jack.

Finally, he looked right at Jack and said, "It's like everything else in life. You keep your eye on the ball at all times. You identify your strengths, and you use them. Whatever they are. You know what I mean, Jack?"

Jack considered it, but not for long. He didn't even want to think about what he might do if his own son were murdered, even if his son had been a lousy husband and an even worse father. "Yeah," said Jack. "I think I know what you mean."

They turned their attention back to the soccer game. Then Pintado said, "You said there were two things. What's the other thing you wanted to talk to me about?"

"Brian," said Jack.

His expression turned more serious. "What about him?"

"I just wanted to let you know that I think he

landed where he belongs. Plenty of bad things have happened to him, but that's all in the past. I think he'll have a good life. And I'm happy about that."

He looked at Jack curiously, as if wondering why he cared. "I appreciate that."

"Good luck to you."

"Thanks. Same to you."

They shook hands, then Jack walked away, leaving Alejandro alone on the sideline to cheer on his grandson.

Jack caught up with Theo a couple of fields away. He was watching the four-year-old players, laughing it up with an attractive mom on the sidelines. He tucked something into his pocket, probably her phone number, then gave her a little wave good-bye as he hurried over to catch up with Jack. They talked as they walked down the tree-lined path that led back toward the parking lot.

"Did you tell him?" asked Theo.

"Tell him what?"

"That Brian isn't your kid?"

"Didn't have to. No one ever told him he was mine. Not me, not Lindsey."

Theo put a hand on Jack's shoulder, giving him a friendly shove. "Hey, man, I'm sorry it turned out like this."

"No problem. I'm okay with it."

Jack had been glad to find out the truth, though he didn't condone Theo's tactics. When Jack had visited the Pintado house during the trial, Alejandro had told him how worried they'd been for Brian's safety after some fool had stolen his backpack. That fool turned out to be Theo. Unbeknownst to

Jack, Theo'd snatched the boy's backpack from under the bleachers at soccer practice. Inside, there was a goaltender's protective mouthpiece, which contained more than enough traces of saliva for a DNA test. It took weeks to get the lab results, and Theo didn't tell Jack about it until after they were in.

"I've been wondering," said Jack. "The lab needed my DNA to make the comparison. What'd you end up giving them? Or should I say, what did you end up taking from me?"

"Well, uh . . ."

"What?"

"I actually got your sample first. Sort of had a doctor help me out with that."

"A doctor?" Jack stopped cold. Just one night in town on her way from Africa to L.A., and Dr. Wham-Bam-Thank-You-Jack was suddenly in the middle of it all. "Damn it, Theo. Why'd you go and drag Rene into this?"

"What are friends for?"

Jack considered it, as if it were high time someone actually answered that question. "Let me get back to you on that one, okay, buddy?"

They walked in silence for a moment, then Theo seemed to read Jack's mind. "You knew even before I told you about it, didn't you, Jack? You knew Brian wasn't yours."

"I wouldn't say that. Lindsey had me pretty convinced."

"Personally, I never saw that much of a resemblance between you and Brian. I think you wanted it to be true, so you saw it when she showed you those pictures."

"Maybe. But I still had my moments of doubt. I suppose that's why I never told her that Jessie had left a nice inheritance for the boy she'd given up for adoption."

"Nice?" said Theo, his voice almost shrill. "As I recall, she left him everything she had, including that settlement on her life insurance policy. That's more than nice."

The shady footpath gave way to sun-baked asphalt. Jack looked around for his car. Even after all this time, he half expected to see the old Mustang.

Theo said, "So, now what do you do, Jacko? Even though Brian's not your son, he's still Jessie's. Which means he's still entitled to her inheritance."

"I know."

"So when do you tell Alejandro about the cash windfall?"

"I'll let Jessie's estate handle that. I'll call the lawyer on Monday. And tell her we finally found Jessie's heir."

Jack opened the car, got inside. Theo slid into the passenger seat, and their doors closed simultaneously.

"You think Jessie knew all along that the kid wasn't yours?"

Jack considered it. "No. I think she managed to convince herself that he was mine. For whatever reason."

Theo flipped down the sun visor and checked his reflection. He seemed utterly fascinated with the fact that Jack's rental car had a light-up mirror that worked. "Why don't we ask God what He thinks?"

"What?" said Jack as he started the car.

"It's a special offer, limited time only. The last guy to get a chance like this totally blew it, so don't you screw up. God has decided to let you ask Him just one question. What's it going to be?"

"What are you talking about?"

"Maybe you want to ask Him something like, 'Did Jessie know you weren't the father when she filled out that birth certificate, or didn't she?'"

"I don't like this game."

"Then think of something else to ask. Come on. What's your one question?"

"Okay. How about, Why did my mother have to die?"

Theo made a face, as if he'd just sucked lemons. "Shee-it, man. You're such a fucking downer sometimes, you know that, Swyteck?"

"You're the one who brought it up."

"Yeah, but—*damn*. A few more people like you in the world, poor God's gonna end up on Prozac."

"Okay, smart ass. What would your one question be?"

"Whattaya havin'?"

"Huh?"

"Whattaya havin'? As in to drink, moron. That's what I'd ask Him."

"God gives you one question, and all you want to know is what He'd like to drink?"

"Isn't that the way all great conversations get started?"

Jack shook his head and backed the car out of the parking spot.

Theo looked at him and said, "So, Jack: Whattaya havin'?"

Jack hit the brake, then shifted into gear. "It's eleven o'clock in the morning."

"True, true. It's getting late. But if we start with tequila for lunch, we could easily be talking to God by dinnertime. With any luck, you could have an answer to that one question before sunset."

Jack shot him a bemused expression. "You're a sick man, Theo."

Theo checked the light-up mirror one more time, smiling at himself as Jack drove out of the parking lot. "Yeah. I am, ain't I?"

Acknowledgments

•

August 2004 marks the tenth anniversary of the publication of my first novel, *The Pardon*. I'm old school, and I think relationships matter. So, nine novels later I feel lucky to say that they were all published by the same publisher (HarperCollins), represented by the same agents (Richard Pine and, now in spirit, Artie Pine), and shaped by editors I like and respect (the last seven by Carolyn Marino, who adopted this orphan).

Even more important, 2004 marks the tenth anniversary of marriage to a woman who was willing to take a ride with a lawyer who wanted to be a writer. I probably never would have had the guts to quit my day job, so thank God that the love of my life turned out to be an English literature major who simply said "Go for it, honey." So I did. And so did you, Tiff. I'd say "All's well that ends well," but this will never end.

I'm also grateful to many others who answered my cries for help in writing and researching *Hear No Evil*, including the American Speech-Language

432 Acknowledgments

Hearing Association; the Cuban-American National Federation; Carlos Sires (interviews and translation); Steve Sawatzky (Mustang expert); Tito at Galiano's Market (Cuban food); Dr. Gloria M. Grippando and Eleanor Rayner (manuscript comments); and Michelle Starke, M.D. (obstetrics). Others prefer to remain anonymous, but I'm equally grateful to them.

In support of a good cause, I've named a character in *Hear No Evil* after Janis Wackenhut, the winner of a fund-raising auction for the Gold-Diggers, Inc. The Gold-Diggers is a nonprofit organization that has raised over one million dollars for the benefit of the Leukemia and Lymphoma Society of America, Inc., Southern Florida Chapter, and the Food for Life Network. It's a beautiful thing when the arts can feed the hungry and fight disease.

Turn the page for an excerpt from

James Grippando's

NEED YOU NOW

It was too good to be true: A Wall Street whiz whose performance was the statistical equivalent of a baseball player with a career batting average of .962. For years, critics had voiced their skepticism. Whistleblowers had laid out dozens of red flags for the Securities Exchange Commission. Yet no one would listen. The entire law-enforcement arm of the U.S. government—tireless teams of federal agents and prosecutors who had dedicated their careers to fighting sophisticated financial crimes—was just a bunch of incompetent, bumbling fools who couldn't spot a massive Ponzi scheme that had unfolded right under their regulatory nose for more than a decade. It was the Wall Street version of the Keystone cops.

Or so the world was led to believe.

I sure bought into it, hook, line, and sinker. Perhaps a financial advisor—even a relative newbie in his twenties—should have been more skeptical.

I worked in private wealth management at the midtown Manhattan office of the International Bank of Switzerland—that's "BOS," mind you, as the German-speaking founders of this century-old juggernaut were quick to appreciate the unfortunate English-language connotation of bankers with business cards that read "I.B.S." Over the decades, bright minds and bank secrecy had swelled the bank's total invested assets to two trillion dollars. I was the junior member on a team of high-net-worth specialists that managed a nine-figure piece of that pie. Clients counted on us to know fraud from legit. I never steered a dime of their money toward Cushman, but it wasn't because I *knew* anything. My reaction to Cushman's scheme was like everyone else's. I was stunned as the estimated losses climbed ever higher—thirty-billion, forty-billion, sixty-billion dollars. I felt sorry for the innocent victims. I wondered if I knew any of them. I wondered who else was a crook. I joined in speculation around the water cooler as to where in the world all that money had gone. And then I went home at night, switched on cable news, and nodded off as politicians debated whether Wall Street needed tighter regulation. I was convinced that nothing would really change—until somebody did something from the inside. So I did something. Something a little crazy. I'm still not sure I learned the truth. But I did learn something *about* the truth, especially where unimaginable sums of money were involved. The truth can get you killed. Or worse.

The epiphany came right after my return from Singapore.

I'd been away from New York longer than planned—months longer. Asia was a BOS stronghold, even stronger than Europe. Our weakness was in the United States, where the bank was generally regarded as a mere shadow of itself. "Uncertainty" had been the market watchword before my gig in Singapore. A new management team was about to change all that, if the BOS press releases were to be believed. Wall Street wasn't exactly whistling with optimism on the day of my return, but the fact that the bank's managing director wanted to meet with me—a junior financial advisor—put a spring in my step. I rode the elevator to the executive suite, breezed into a lobby that showcased museum-quality art—*Is that a Van Gogh?*—and announced my arrival to the receptionist.

"I'm here for a meeting with Ms. Decker," I said.

The young woman at the desk smiled pleasantly. "And you are?"

"Patrick Lloyd. I'm an FA here in New York."

"Oh, my. You're in the wrong place. The meeting for financial advisors is in the Paradeplatz conference room."

Paradeplatz was one of Switzerland's famous squares, near the end of the Bahnhofstrasse and Lake Zurich, home to BOS headquarters. BOS/America was filled with such reminders of who we answered to.

"But the message said to meet Ms. Decker in her—"

"You need to hurry," she said. "You don't want to be late."

Apparently, my one-on-one meeting with the managing director was a group session. The message from Decker's assistant had made it sound more personal, and I had spent half the night pondering what it could be about. A promotion? The recognition of "rising stars" in the new world of BOS/America wealth management? It had been silly to let my imagination run wild. I picked my ego up off the carpet and rode the elevator down to the seventeenth floor.

It was straight up on ten o'clock, and the last of the latecomers were filing into the Paradeplatz conference room at the end of the hall. I caught up as the carved mahogany doors were closing. It was packed inside. The room could comfortably seat about fifty, but the headcount was easily double that number. The meeting was about to begin, and all chatter had ceased—which meant that the door closed with an intrusive thud behind me. Like a reflex, heads turned toward me, the only guy still looking for a seat.

A distinct uneasiness gripped me as my gaze swept the room. It was my first time in the Paradeplatz, and under different circumstances I might have been taken with the rich maroon carpeting and burnished walnut paneling. Adorning the longest mahogany table I'd ever seen was the emblazoned gold insignia of BOS: three golden cherubs that symbolized the bank's core principles of discretion, security, and confidentiality. What I noticed most, however, was all the gray hair around that table. A second row of chairs lined the walls, like the back benches of Parliament—less gray hair, but plenty of salt and pepper. The financial advisors in this room were not like me. These were senior advisors, some from New York, and others I recognized only from press coverage of their accomplishments.

"Patrick?"

The voice was little more than a whisper, but I recognized the gravel in my team leader's delivery. Jay Sussman was one of the salt-and-pepper advisors in the second row. I skulked my way over, like a theatergoer arriving halfway through the first act, and took the empty chair beside him.

"What are you doing here?" he asked under his breath.

A door opened on the opposite side of the conference room. In walked the managing director of BOS/America, Angela Decker, with whom I was scheduled to meet. Or so I'd thought. With her—and my quick double take confirmed it—was the chief executive of the International Bank of Switzerland, Gerhardt Klaus.

"Is this the meeting for FAs?" I asked through my teeth.

"Yeah, the *top one-hundred-producing* FAs."

BOS had over eight-thousand financial advisors in the United States. My invitation from Decker's office had obviously come by mistake. "Should I leave?"

"Stay," he said, smiling with his eyes. "Watching you squirm will keep me awake."

The chief executive walked to the head of the table and remained standing as the managing director took a seat at his side. I'd never met Klaus, of course, but it was well known that he never allowed anyone to introduce him at internal bank gatherings. A vice president had sucked up so badly in Zurich last year that Klaus had forever banned all *"welkommen"* speeches.

"Guten morgen," he said. "And thank you for coming, especially those of you who are visiting from out of town."

Klaus had a booming voice that required no microphone. Disciplined living and cross-country skiing kept him fit and looking younger than his years. He'd been born into a family of Zurich bankers at the height of the Second World War, at a time when his country couldn't decide which side it was on. It has been said that certain Swiss banks had suffered no such indecision.

"Each of you was invited to this meeting because we wanted you to be the first to hear a major announcement, one that is vital to the future of the worldwide operations of BOS. Without further ado, I'm pleased to tell you that a final settlement agreement has been reached between the International Bank of Switzerland and the U.S. Department of Justice."

A chorus of murmurs coursed the room like the breeze through a wheat field, followed by sparse and nervous applause. Then silence.

"As you all know," Klaus continued, "both the Swiss government and BOS officials have been engaged in discussions for several months with U.S. authorities. These discussions . . ."

Discussions. Talk about a fudge word. Justice had BOS by the short hairs. The same excesses and mismanagement that had rocked the largest Wall Street investment banks had forced BOS to write down fifty-billion dollars in subprime losses in the fall of 2008. The market was in freefall, the world economy was in shambles, and investors from New York to

Hong Kong were in a state of panic. The oldest and largest Swiss Bank was on the verge of collapse when the government had come to the rescue with a bail out. At that precise moment, the Justice Department swooped in. With the Treasury Secretary and the New York Fed warning that the collapse of institutions "too big to fail" could unleash another Great Depression, someone at Justice had the presence of mind—nay, the stroke of genius—to realize that the time was ripe to make Swiss cheese of the secret Swiss banks. The DOJ officially demanded the names of "serious tax evaders." When BOS balked, they arrested a top financial advisor who was silly enough to state publicly that he'd smuggled a diamond in a tube of toothpaste for a client. When BOS stalled again, they indicted the bank's head of private wealth management. They threatened to indict the chairman, himself. They demanded a "collateral consequences" report from BOS lawyers, which is typically the final step before the indictment of an entire company. Finally, BOS—still in a weakened state, despite the multi-billion-dollar bail out—blinked. It turned over the names of 280 of the most serious tax avoiders. *Poof.* A century of Swiss bank secrecy went up in smoke, just like that. Justice had been hammering away for more names ever since.

Apparently not everyone who worked for the U.S. government was a dumbass. Yet, Abe Cushman had gone unnoticed by law enforcement. Those Ponzi schemes sure are hard to sniff out, especially the ones that last for only two decades and involve a measly sixty-billion dollars.

Hmmm.

"As part of this settlement," the chief executive continued, "we have agreed to release the names of four thousand additional clients over the coming year."

"Four thousand?" my team leader whispered. "This is *good* news?"

I leaned closer. "Actually, the good news is that the bank is offering a free box of *Depend* to each of our clients."

My boss snorted with laughter, a reflex. The chief executive stopped, clearly annoyed. His steely-blue-eyed glare silenced the room—and it nearly sent me running for my own box of adult diapers.

Klaus leaned forward, his palms resting on the polished wood tabletop as he spoke. "I want to underscore that the only names on this list are clients of our cross-border business. This settlement agreement respects the fact that the cross-border business of BOS consists only of wealth management services offered to American residents outside the United States, that it operates entirely out of Switzerland, and that it is completely separate from the BOS/America wealth management business. In other words, this settlement affects less than one percent of the bank's total invested assets. To put an even finer point on it, the settlement does not affect our U.S.-based private wealth management clients."

Yet, I wanted to say.

"Which brings me to even more important news," said Klaus, "and to the real purpose of this meeting. With the DOJ settlement behind us, it's time to look forward. Ladies and gentlemen, I am pleased to introduce the new head of private wealth management for BOS/America, a man who truly needs no introduction, Joe McGriff."

My supervisor and I exchanged glances. His expression matched my unspoken sentiment: *Joe McGriff? You must be joking.*

Advisors and their clients had been walking away from BOS since the fifty-billion-dollar write down of subprime losses. The recent threat of a criminal indictment over bank secrecy had pushed the total loss of assets for the year to over two-hundred billion Swiss francs. BOS was on the fast track to No. 2— not in the world, but in *Switzerland*. The much-anticipated announcement of a new head of private wealth for the U.S. was supposed to restore faith and calm everyone's concerns. The chosen one, however, was from Saxton Silvers.

McGriff entered the room, the picture of Wall Street confidence as a photographer captured him and the chief executive smiling and shaking hands.

It was Bear Stearns, Lehman Brothers, and Saxton Silvers—in that order—on the list of Wall Street investment banks that had gone the way of the T. Rex and the Dodo bird, swept away by the financial tsunami of subprime lending and mortgage-backed securities. McGriff had sewn the seeds of disaster at Saxton Silvers before accepting a presidential appointment as Deputy Secretary of the Treasury, the department's number two post. Government service required him to liquidate his holdings, which meant that he had cashed out at the height of the market. He took twenty-eight million dollars out of Wall Street, and a year later he orchestrated a government bail out that pumped billions of tax-payer dollars back into the disaster that he and others like him had created. It still wasn't clear what indictments might come out of the Saxton Silvers collapse. But there he stood, handpicked by the top executive in the world of bank secrecy: Joe McGriff, our new leader, the power-drunk pilot who had put Wall Street on autopilot, headed straight for the side of a mountain, only to watch the crash from Treasury's ivory tower.

"Gee, I feel better already," my boss muttered.

"Me too," I said, joining in the lukewarm applause.

I left the conference room quickly, as soon as the meeting broke, before anyone could ask what the heck I was doing there.

My palms were sweating as I hurried down the hall to the elevator, but I tried to keep things in perspective. I wasn't the first junior advisor in BOS history to end up in the wrong place at the wrong time. Any number of my predecessors had surely crashed a meeting of top producers. In the hallowed Paradeplatz conference room. With the Chief Executive from Zurich, the managing director of U.S. operations, and the new head of private wealth management in attendance.

Good God, what was I thinking?

The chrome elevator doors parted, and a man wearing a black suit was inside. I entered and pressed a button, but the man froze the control panel with the turn of his passkey.

"Patrick Lloyd?" he said.

"Yes."

He looked like a secret service agent, and my impression wasn't far from the mark. "BOS Corporate Security," he said as he punched the button for the executive suite. "I need you to come with me."

My jaw dropped. I expected some good-natured ribbing from colleagues about the mix up, perhaps even a brief reprimand from a divisional manager. But calling in security was over the top.

"It was a mistake," I started to say, but he wasn't interested. We rode up to the executive suite, and he escorted me into the lobby. I was hoping the receptionist would recount our earlier conversation and clear things up, but she was away from her desk. My escort from corporate security directed me to a leather couch by the window, and he sat in the armchair facing me, as if keeping guard. The expression on his face was deadpan even by Swiss banking standards. Had I still been in Singapore, I would have thought I was in line for a public caning.

I surveyed the lobby. A Jasper Johns original oil painting hung on the wall opposite the Van Gogh. Fresh-cut flowers were placed tastefully around the room in crystal vases. A table by the window displayed a small vase so priceless that there was actually a plaque to identify it as being from the Ming Dynasty. A row of Swiss clocks on the wall caught my attention, each set to the time zone of a different trading market. New York. London. Frankfurt. Tokyo. Hong Kong. Singapore.

Singapore. I thought of Lilly. She worked with

BOS/Asia. Our relationship had been purely business at first, but we ended up dating for six months. Arguably the best six months of my life.

I looked away, then checked the clock again, and a song popped into my head. In Singapore, it was a quarter after one, and I had a sudden vision of Lilly, all alone, and listening to that mega-hit by Lady Antebellum that seemed to be playing nonstop on the radio since our break up.

I'm a little drunk and I need you now.

Yeah, right.

It was four weeks, exactly, since Lilly had texted me and said that I should meet her for a walk on Changi Beach, that she had something important to say to me, and that it couldn't wait. Any dolt could have seen what was coming, but I was so smitten that I'd actually shown up with a blanket and a bottle of wine. This was going to be one of those "talks" that was really just a speech with a few permissible interruptions. It was so over-rehearsed that Lilly had lost all sense that it would hit me like a brick between the eyes. The way she looked on that day would never leave my memory—the sad smile, her chestnut hair blowing in the gentle breeze, those big eyes that sparkled even in the most dismal of circumstances. I was speechless, just like the first time I'd ever laid eyes on her, only this time for far less enchanting reasons. The silence was insufferable once she'd finished, both of us waiting for me to move my lips and say something. Nothing came, and then it started to rain. At least I'd thought it was raining. I felt a drop on my head, and Lilly promptly lost it right before my eyes. She was embarrassed to be laughing, laughing not at me but at the absurdity of the situation, but laughing nonetheless. It was then that I heard the shrill screech in the sky, saw the winged culprit swooping down from above the coconut palms to mock me. A seagull had shit squarely on my head.

This I took as an omen. I put in for an immediate transfer back to New York, and Lilly and I said goodbye for life.

Angela Decker's assistant entered the waiting area. "Ms. Decker will see you now."

Great. More shit to fall from the sky.

I still couldn't believe the big deal this had become. The assistant showed me into the office, and it wasn't just the managing director inside. Joe McGriff, who'd been head of private wealth management for all of one hour, was with her. So was the general counsel. Executives at this level traveled like international diplomats, and it was rare indeed for three of them to actually be in New York at the same time. For the holy trinity of BOS/America to be in a meeting with a junior FA was preposterous.

"There is a perfectly benign explanation for what happened," I said.

"Sit down, Mr. Lloyd," said Decker.

The managing director returned to the leather armchair between McGriff and the general counsel, neither of whom rose to greet me. This had the feel of an inquisition, not a meeting. I took the hot seat opposite them.

"This has nothing to do with this morning's meeting in the Paradeplatz," said Decker. "I told my assistant that I wanted to see you this morning, and she put you on the list of FA's for the ten o'clock meeting. An honest mistake on her part."

I breathed a sigh of relief, but it didn't last. The purpose of *this* meeting clearly wasn't to show me the BOS secret handshake.

"Is there some kind of trouble?" I asked.

The general counsel spoke. "As I'm sure you're aware, Lilly Scanlon's employment at BOS/Singapore has been terminated."

I caught my breath. "No, I was not aware of that. When did that happen?"

"Ten days ago."

"I haven't spoken to Lilly in—I don't know, exactly. Longer than ten days. Can you tell me what happened?"

"To the extent that it pertains to you, yes. Broadly speaking, it has to do with the Abe Cushman Ponzi scheme."

"Cushman?" I said. "I can't believe Lilly would have anything to do with that. I can assure you that I didn't."

McGriff took over. "Mr. Lloyd, why did you go to Singapore?"

His body language made the question anything but innocuous. I tried not to become defensive.

"It seemed like a good career move," I said. "I saw the writing on the wall for Swiss banks. It's no secret that the BOS strategy is to shift to super-high net worth and Asia."

"Why not Hong Kong or Tokyo?" asked McGriff.

I could have recounted my decision-making process; instead, I took the offensive. "Is that what this is about? You think my transfer to BOS/Singapore has something to do with Cushman?"

McGriff ignored my question. "How well did you know Lilly Scanlon?"

"I didn't know her at all before leaving New York. We met in the Singapore office. She was an FA, just like me."

"This is my first official day," said McGriff, "but I've been fully briefed. Don't waste our time trying to pretend that your relationship was purely professional."

Obviously they already knew the answers to most of the questions on their list. This was a test of my truthfulness, not a search for information—so far, at least.

"We dated," I said. "It ended before I left. I've had zero contact since."

"Tell us about her," said McGriff.

I didn't know how to respond. "What do you want to know?"

"We're asking the questions here," said the general counsel.

"I'm just trying to get some color."

"Color" was synonymous with "background" in the BOS lexicon—"*call Goldman for color on the Tesla Motors IPO*"—but from the look on McGriff's face, the operative color here was red. His temper was legendary.

"Listen to me, asshole," McGriff said.

"Joe, please," said the general counsel.

"I'm sorry, but this needs to be said. I spent the last twenty-six years of my career in one of two places—in Washington in public service or on Wall

Street with Saxton Silvers. It pained me to watch that firm go down. I've seen the kind of arrogance that can breed disaster for a bank, and it starts in puppies like you. I'm not going to put up with it. Are we clear on that?"

"Crystal."

"I could have gone anywhere when I decided to leave Treasury. I chose BOS/America. And the first thing on my plate is an internal investigation into a junior FA's possible involvement—*criminal* involvement—with Abe Cushman. If you haven't figured it out yet, let me spell it out for you: I intend to put out this fire immediately. I will not allow it to snowball and sidetrack my plans to make BOS number one in private wealth management. Again, are we clear?"

"All I can say is that I had absolutely nothing to do with Cushman."

"Did you and Ms. Scanlon ever talk about Gerry Collins?" McGriff asked.

Of course I knew the name, especially in the context of Abe Cushman. Collins' gruesome murder had been front-page news everywhere from the *Wall Street Journal* to *People* magazine.

"Talk about him in what way?" I asked.

"Don't be cute," said McGriff.

"I'm trying to understand your question. Are you asking me if we talked about him as a person in the news?"

"No, as one of Ms. Scanlon's biggest clients."

It was the bomb, and all three executives measured my reaction when it dropped. I tried not to squirm, but my voice tightened. "Lilly never told me about that."

"You worked in the same office and slept in the same bed, but she never mentioned Gerry Collins?"

Asking how he knew I'd occasionally spent the night at Lilly's wasn't going to get me anywhere. "If you're telling me that Lilly had a business relationship with one of Cushman's front men, that never came up. Never."

McGriff glanced toward the general counsel. Then his gaze returned to me. "I'd like to believe you, Mr. Lloyd."

"Did you ask Lilly? I'm sure she would tell you the same thing."

"Ms. Scanlon was fired after she was caught red-handed trying to access confidential information about BOS numbered accounts. She refused to discuss it. I suggest you start talking, unless you'd like to join her in the ranks of the unemployed."

I couldn't believe what I was hearing about Lilly, but if it was true, she was in serious trouble. "I have nothing to hide."

"Good," he said. "Tell us about Ms. Scanlon."

Again, I wasn't sure how to respond. "What do you want to know?"

"Everything," said McGriff, his tone deadly serious. "Absolutely everything there is to know about that woman."